A TALE OF TWO LOBSTERS

A Casey Quinby Mystery

A Tale of Two Lobsters
By Judi Ciance
judiciance@gmail.com
Published: October, 2015

ISBN-13:978-1517236175
ISBN-10:1517236177

Also in the Casey Quinby series:

Empty Rocker (November 2012)
Paint Her Dead (October 2013)
Caught With A Quahog (October 2014)

Dedication

To My Husband
Paul Ciance

His encouragement to continue,
his patience to listen and
his help in keeping me in line
are why Casey is back
on the scene.

Acknowledgements

This author wants to thank
Beverly Blackwell and Diana Washburn.
Because of their support, expertise, and
guidance, I was able to bring the
reader yet another suspenseful and absorbing
case in the exploits of Casey Quinby.

A TALE OF TWO LOBSTERS

A Casey Quinby Mystery

by Judi Ciance

To Sue
Enjoy !
Judi Ciance
February 11, 2017

CHAPTER 1

Monday

"Casey Quinby, Private Investigator." I liked the sound of it. Things were moving in the right direction. My life in the commercial world was about to change. I no longer answered to anyone, but myself. I'm now the boss. I looked in the mirror, smiled and repeated, "Casey Quinby, Private Investigator."

Last Friday was my last day as the head investigative reporter for the Cape Cod Tribune. I really had it good there. My boss, Chuck, let me take a lot of liberties knowing I'd end up with stories that would sell newspapers. Were my methods always above board? Hell no—but I got results. I loved my job, but it was time to move on.

I always wanted to be a detective, but when I got hurt at the police academy, I watched my dream crumble and the pieces get swept away with the trash. I moved to Cape Cod to do my rehab at Spaulding, and at the same time I went back to school. I already had a Masters in Criminal Justice, so I enrolled in a two-year journalism program at Cape Cod Community College. While attending school, I worked cold cases for area police departments.

Later, armed with my two degrees, I landed the job at the Tribune. I kept my ties with the PDs, still helping with various cases—cold and current.

I bent down and patted Watson's head. "Know what boy, I may not hold the title of detective, but licensed private investigator is close enough." I looked at the digital clock on the shelf above the toilet. "I've got to get ready for work." I tussled his hair. "You're now my sidekick and keeper of the castle—Sherlock and Watson incorporated."

1

I still had toothpaste in my mouth when my cell rang. I rinsed quickly and answered without looking at the caller ID.

"Is this the famous Casey Quinby, Private Investigator?" It was Marnie. No matter how hard she tried to disguise her voice, that New York accent shadowed every word.

"You'll never pass as a Bostonian. Face it, you'll never *pahk your cah in Hahvurd yahd.*"

"Are you ready for the big day?" she asked.

"As ready as I'm going to be."

"Before you go in, stop over to the DA's office. I walked by your office this morning and noticed an envelope tucked between the door and the jamb. It didn't look too secure, so I took it."

"Did you open it?"

"Of course not. It's your name on the sign hanging over the door—not mine—at least not yet."

"I'm going to swing by Dunkin's. I'll pick up a coffee for you and Annie and a dozen donuts for your office." I smiled to myself. "You never know when I'll need a favor, and a donut or two here and there might help."

"You know Mike and his sweet-tooth. A little sugar and a lot of jelly makes the boss a happy man. I learned that very early in the job. Annie is a good teacher. She even knows what time of the month to tempt him. And, during a big trial, I'm surprised he doesn't gain ten pounds."

"That's the life of a bachelor. He needs a wife or at least a significant other to lead him down the healthy path." I laughed.

"Look who's talking—Miss Junk Food Junkie herself. I've got to get going. Don't forget to stop by my office to pick up your mail." Then, in the usual Marnie fashion, she was gone.

Watson was patient while I got ready for work, but now he paced the kitchen floor.

"Hey, boy, let's go for a short walk." He gave me a yip of encouragement as we walked out the door. "As soon as I get things organized, you'll be able to come to the Village with me. Maybe not every day, but at least a couple times a week."

When I stopped talking, Watson stopped walking and looked up at me. It wouldn't surprise me if one of these days he answered me. We continued on our walk.

My mind wandered to a secret place—so secret that I can't remember where. We were half-way to the beach before I realized how far we'd gone. I pulled on Watson's leash. "Time to go home," I said, and on cue, he turned and headed in the right direction. I shook my head. "I think you understand everything I say. That could be scary."

I fed the boy, gathered up my briefcase and headed out. I was excited about my new adventure, but also a little nervous. I took a deep breath, brushed off my CQ007 license plate and backed my little green Spider out of the driveway.

It was a beautiful day—brisk—but beautiful. The temperature flashed fifty-one degrees on the sign outside the Cape Cod Five. Since I planned on doing some set-up work, jeans and a sweater were the attire of the day. I did, however, make an executive decision to keep a change of clothes at the office. But I didn't think I'd need them today, so I left them at home. In reality, I forgot them—so much for my first executive decision. I shrugged my shoulders, then looked in the rear view mirror. *I'm the boss. I have nobody to answer to. It's going to take a little getting used to, but it's good—everything is good.*

I pulled into Dunkin's, got three coffees, a dozen assorted donuts and an extra bag with my two jellies. I caught myself just as I started to make the right hand turn toward the Tribune. "It's going to take a little time to train the brain," I said. "Brain, listen-up. We now have to turn left. Got it?" God only knows what I would have done if I got an audible response. I'm sure this won't be the last time I'll carry on a conversation with myself, since my office staff consists of me, myself and I.

CHAPTER 2

Instead of trying to park behind the District Attorney's Office, I called Marnie to meet me by the back door. She answered on the first ring. "Were you sitting on the phone?" I asked.

"I just hung up from another call and hadn't taken my hand off the receiver."

"If it's okay with you, I'm going to drop off the coffees and donuts. Can you meet me by the back door?"

"Sure."

"And, don't forget my first official piece of mail as Casey Quinby, Private Investigator. I wonder why someone stuck it in the door instead of mailing it." I tried to make my voice sound mysterious. "Maybe it's a case that's so important they want me to start working on it immediately."

"See you in a few," Marnie said.

If I didn't have to keep my hands on the steering wheel and my eyes on the road, I would have rubbed my hands together in a swirling motion and rolled my eyes back and forth—like the Wicked Witch of the West in The Wizard of Oz when she said, *"I'll get you my pretty and your little dog too!"* It's really good that nobody can get inside my mind. Sometimes when it stores scenes from movies they get shuffled—giving a whole new meaning to the original script. I shook my head. Time for me to lock the vault and get serious.

I pulled into the lot behind the DA's office. Marnie was waiting inside the door. I saw the ten by thirteen manila envelope in her hand. I was expecting a regular business sized number ten. Big envelope … big case? I could only hope.

I got out of my car, brought Marnie the coffees and donuts and took the envelope.

"Annie got in about ten minutes ago. She wants to know if you want to do lunch at Finn's."

"Sounds good, but let me get settled and take a look at my first piece of mail." I examined the front and back. "For all I know, it's an advertisement from somebody selling business machines. I'll give you a call."

I pulled out of the parking lot, crossed Route 6A and turned into the driveway leading to the back of my building. There were three parking spaces—the one closest to the door being mine. The other two were for prospective clients.

I got out of my car, took my goodies, the envelope and my briefcase and proceeded to unlock the back door. Inside, I put everything down and looked around—suddenly overwhelmed by a feeling of accomplishment. My dream of becoming a 'detective' was real. The titles were spelled differently, but in my mind, detective and private investigator were interchangeable.

I settled at my desk and opened the manila envelope that wasn't sealed, only fastened with a clasp. It contained a one-page, hand-written letter, three dated snapshots, a newspaper article about the closing of a Falmouth fish market and a copy of an obituary that appeared in the November 5, 2013, edition of the Tribune. I laid the pictures out beside the newspaper clippings and began to read the letter.

Date: *March 2, 2014*
To:............Casey Quinby
From: *Isabella Deluca*

I wish to talk with you about the death of my uncle, Rocco Deluca. He was the owner of Rocco's Fish Market in Falmouth until Saturday, October 26, 2013, when he closed down the business.

On Friday, November 1, 2013, he was found dead in one of his lobster tanks.

The Medical Examiner ruled the death an accident. The report stated that Rocco was electrocuted when he and an electrical cord he appeared to be holding fell into some water on the bottom of the tank..

That is a brief synopsis of what happened.

On the surface, it does appear to be an accident. It was also rumored to be a suicide. I don't believe it was either.

I'd like to hire you to investigate my uncle's death.

I will be available after two o'clock today.

Thank you

Isabella listed two telephone numbers—her home number and her cell. The area codes and first three digits were from the Falmouth area, so I assumed she was a local.

I put the letter down and picked up the newspaper clipping that had appeared in the Tribune the day before Rocco closed his market. I didn't frequent Falmouth, so I wasn't at all familiar with the area.

I switched to the obituary. Rocco was born in 1936—making him seventy-seven. Isabella Deluca was listed along with a nephew—possibly Isabella's sibling. His wife, Rita, of forty-six years died in 2009. It listed no other living relatives, so I assumed he didn't have children. Isabella would have to fill in the gaps.

There was a picture on the obit, taken when Rocco was much younger. It looked like a person had been cropped from his right side. The other photos were originals. In one, he was on a fishing boat. It was most probably his—a fishmonger and his vessel. Another one was taken with a couple of guys in front of his market. The third was of Rocco standing beside his lobster tanks, smiling and holding two huge lobsters—one in each hand. They had to be at least five pounds.

It was only nine-thirty. Since I couldn't call Isabella Deluca until two o'clock, I had time to get things in my office organized and make a list of stuff I needed to pick up. First, I called Marnie to firm up our luncheon date. Her phone went to voice mail. Before I could leave a message, she clicked in.

"District Attorney Michael Sullivan's office, how can I help you?"

I laughed. "Why are you answering the main line?"

"Tracy had to go to the bathroom and asked if she could transfer incoming calls to me. She's been gone almost fifteen minutes. I think I'll suggest a good laxative." Marnie wasn't her usual sweet self. After a disgusted sigh she added, "This isn't the first time she's done this. Don't get me wrong, I don't mind chipping in—but not when she goes to the bathroom for five minutes, then flirts with the new ADA for the next ten."

"I called about lunch."

"There's another call coming in. I'll buzz you right back." Once again, in the usual Marnie manner, she was gone.

It was quiet—too quiet. I practiced answering the phone. Listening to my own voice was better than nothing.

"Casey Quinby, Private Investigator." *Too boring.*

"Hello, Casey here." *Too Casual*

No sooner had I put the receiver down, the phone rang.

"Good morning, Casey Quinby speaking." I liked the sound of that, it's a keeper.

"Sorry to disappoint you, it's only me." It was Marnie returning my call. "I'm back at my desk, so now I can talk. Are we meeting at Finn's?"

"Yes we are. I'll meet you inside. I'll walk over before twelve so we can get our favorite table by the window."

"See you then."

I got up from my new Eco-Friendly Ergonomic, black leather office chair and straightened the frames that displayed my degrees from UMass and Cape Cod Community College, then stood back to admire them. *You've come a long way, girl.*

I arranged and re-arranged the organizer, the cup to hold my pens and the matching leather frame complete with a picture of Sam and me taken last month on our trip to Disney World. I positioned the two client chairs in front of my desk so I could see out the front window when I was interviewing somebody. Sam taught me a long time ago to keep my back to the wall. That way nobody could sneak up on me, be it in fun or, in his line of work—now mine—an ambush.

CHAPTER 3

"Hello, anybody here?"

I definitely had to install a bell or something to let me know somebody had come through my front door when I'm in the back room.

"Nancy!" I held my arms out to welcome her.

"Before you give me that hug, let me put these goodies on your desk."

I was embarrassed that I hadn't gone to see her before I moved in. She owned the donut shop a few doors down. Ever since the incident with James a couple of years ago, I've stayed clear of places that remind me of him. Nancy's Donut Shop was one of those places. I still go over the whole scenario whenever I ride through the Village. Now that I'm working here, I'll get over it and move on. It's hard to do when a person you thought was a good friend and who had a responsible job as an Officer at the Barnstable Superior Court suddenly let his secret life overpower him. He ended up being convicted of attempted murder and murder. He almost got away with a second murder—and probably would have if Sam hadn't intervened. James was like a son to Nancy. That second murder would have been me. I wondered how those events affected her life.

"I couldn't let you start your first day without a coffee and a sticky bun." She took me up on my still-waiting hug. "I'm so proud of you. When I heard you were going out on your own, I was excited. But, when I heard you bought a building in the Village, I was ecstatic. Barry told me last week."

"Yep, I did it. I made the move. You are now talking to Casey Quinby, Private Investigator." I felt as proud as Mrs. Mallard leading her famous brood of eight across the Boston Public

Gardens. "I know I have to earn my wings, but I hope my business consists of more than following wayward husbands or cheating wives. But, as long as they pay, I won't complain."

"They'll miss you at the Tribune."

"My ex-boss asked me to write feature articles every now and then." I sipped my coffee and, as much as I was full from my jelly donuts, I couldn't resist Nancy's sticky bun. "I don't know what feature he's referring to, but I'm sure I can find something to write about. I'll miss the paper. Chuck told me anytime I wanted to come back, he'd have a job for me."

"He better fill your job, because if I know you—and I do—your new career path is going to keep you real busy."

"Thanks for the vote of confidence and don't forget, I can use the referrals." I nodded.

"That's a given. I've got to get back to the store. I put my paper clock in the window and I'm five minutes past the time I said I'd return." Nancy turned and started toward the door. "Don't be a stranger. I missed you."

"I won't. And thanks for the best coffee break ever." I blew her a kiss as she walked out. "She's a special lady," I said to myself.

I sat down and crossed my arms over my chest. No pun intended, but Nancy gave me food for thought. I didn't want a paper clock for the door, but I need to provide my phone number in a strategic place, either on the door or the window beside it so people can reach me when I'm not in. If I use the office number, I can forward the calls to my cell.

That'll work.

It was time to meet the girls next door at Finn's. I took the letter and pictures with me. Hopefully this was going to be my first case and I wanted to share it with them, even though I had no idea what it was all about. "After all, my friends don't call me Sherlock for nothing. Holmes had to start somewhere and so do I."

CHAPTER 4

Finn's still had their fireplace burning. It wasn't cold, but it eliminated that little nip in the March air. Besides, their patrons enjoyed the charm.

Our usual table was available so the hostess sat me and left three menus. I leaned my elbows on the table, cradled my chin in my palms and observed several other parties coming in for lunch. I opened the menu, and even though I could close my eyes and recite the selections, I pretended I was reading them. I didn't see Barney, the bartender, head in my direction carrying a glass of White Zin.

"Welcome, neighbor." He set the glass down on the placemat in front of me.

"Drinking in the middle of the day on a Monday," I said. "This could spell trouble."

He pulled out a chair and sat down. "I've only got a minute. I'm tending alone today. If you need anything, don't hesitate to come over. You know the Village. It's one big happy family and we're glad you're a part of it."

"Thanks, Barney and vice versa." I toasted him.

"Gotta get back. Later."

Marnie and Annie came through the door just as Barney stepped back behind the bar. They looked at me, then at him, smiled and headed to our table.

"What? It's one of my new neighbors being hospitable. You know—my dynamic personality."

"Gag me." Annie made a motion like she was getting sick.

"Knock it off, you two." I turned to see the server headed toward our table.

"It's the three musketeers. Can I get you, except Casey, something to drink?"

"I'll have a Diet Coke," said Annie.

"Me, too." Marnie laughed. "I'm not my own boss—yet."

"Very funny," I shook my head. "This nice cold White Zin really does tastes good." I swirled the pretty pink liquid around the inside of my glass, then took another sip.

"The special is a cup of lobster bisque and a half sandwich—either crab or shrimp salad—with French fries." The server knew we usually ordered the special, but that was on a Thursday. "Do you want me to give you a minute?" she asked.

"I'll have the special with crab salad," I said.

Annie closed her menu. "I don't want a sandwich, but I'll have a bowl of bisque."

"Now me." Marnie tapped her fingers on the table. "I didn't want a lot, but I can't resist the special. I'll take the crab salad, too."

The server left to put in our order.

I took the envelope from my purse and laid it on the table. "Curious?"

"Marnie told me about the envelope." Annie raised her eyebrows. "Well, are we going to be privy to the contents or are you going to give us clues so we can play a guessing game?"

I opened the envelope and removed the letter and pictures. "I don't want to read it out loud, there are too many people around." I handed it to Annie. "It's short. When you're done, give it to Marnie."

"The niece is brief and to the point." Marnie held out her hand. "Let's take a look at the pictures."

I handed them over one at a time. "The uncle was seventy-seven when he died, so I believe the picture was taken quite a few years ago. He doesn't look that old."

The girls read the obit and studied the picture.

"The next three are beside a boat that I'm assuming is his, in front of his fish market and inside the market by the lobster tanks."

Annie looked up from the pictures. "Wow, take a look at the size of those lobsters. I could go for one of them right now."

"The guy is dead and all you can think about is his lobsters?" Marnie shook her head and handed the pictures back to me.

"Back to the letter. She said she won't be available until two o'clock. I'll give her a call then. She doesn't believe her uncle's death was accidental or a suicide. I'll know more after I talk to her."

Marnie sat back in her chair. "The letter says he closed his business down. Does that mean for the day or does that mean for good?"

"I'm assuming it means for good, but that could be a factor in the case." I saw the server coming with our food, so I put the letter and photos back into the envelope. After our food was served and our server left, we resumed our conversation.

"This is a whole new avenue of investigation for me. When I worked cold cases, I had a murder book that was already assembled to review and dissect. When I helped with current cases, I was involved in gathering information to create a murder book. In each scenario, the case was already determined to be a homicide." I took a bite of my sandwich.

"So, Sherlock, you'll be able to use your acquired skills and conduct your own investigation. I like it," said Marnie. "In this case, the niece feels there is cause for doubt as to the Medical Examiner's findings."

"Yeah. If she hires me, I'll be questioning them. I'm also assuming the Falmouth Police Department never performed a full investigation because it was reported on record as an accident. I may be turning over moss covered stones that have been firmly implanted in the ground for years."

"If you ask me, it's exciting. You're now the 'detective' you always wanted to be." Annie smiled before going back to her lunch.

"I am."

Marnie checked her watch. "We better get going. I'm working on a brief for a drug case and I'm supposed to have a draft ready this afternoon. Are you going to be home tonight?"

"Sam said something about going out to dinner. I'm not sure where or what time he's coming. I'll give you both a call to let you know what I learn about Uncle Rocco after my call to Isabella."

We paid our bill, said our goodbyes and headed to our respective destinations. I couldn't help but stop to admire my new sign—CASEY QUINBY, Private Investigator. I started to hum a line from the song *Forget I Ever Knew You—I'm going to make it on my own somehow.* I had left a lucrative job with the Cape Cod Tribune. Lots of reporters would like the job of head investigative reporter, but me, I wanted more. "I'm the new Casey," I whispered. "I'm going to make it."

CHAPTER 5

It was five after two when I called Isabella Deluca's cell number.

"Hello." She had a quiet, reserved tone to her voice.

"Hi Isabella. This is Casey Quinby. You left an envelope at my office this morning and I'm following up on it." It would have been easier if she was sitting across from me, but she wasn't—at least not at the moment.

"Can I stop by your office tomorrow morning and talk to you about my Uncle Rocco. It's not something I want to discuss on the phone. Is nine o'clock okay with you?"

"I'll be here. You can park in the lot behind my office. I look forward to meeting you." There was nothing else to say.

"Thank you. See you tomorrow."

I hung up and stared at my phone for a few seconds. Before meeting with Isabella, I had to do some homework.

I called Chuck, my old boss. The receptionist answered. "Good afternoon, Cape Cod Tribune. How may I direct your call?"

"Hey, Jamie, it's Casey."

"It's only been one day and I miss you already. How are the new digs?"

"I'm getting settled in," I said. "Let me know when you can come over. I'll stretch the five minute tour to ten, then we'll do lunch."

"It's a date. What can I do for you today?"

"Is Chuck in?"

"He just got back from Subway. Let me put you through to him. Talk to you later."

Chuck picked up on the first ring. "Good morning, Miss Private Investigator. I'm practicing for the day I say, Good Morning, Madam President."

I laughed. "You'll be practicing for a long time."

"I know why you called."

"You do?"

"You missed my melancholy voice." He paused. "By the way, where are the donuts?"

"That's why you miss me."

"I'm assuming you didn't call to shoot the shit. What's up?"

"I need a favor."

"Already?"

"Yep. Can I come over and run a name through the files for past articles in reference to a potential client?"

"Of course," he said. "Your old office is still available. When are you coming?"

"I'll be there in a half-hour. Is it too late for donuts?"

He laughed. "I'll see you then."

I already had a copy of the obituary, but Rocco Deluca was a very popular man in the Falmouth area, so there may have been some human interest stories written about him or his fish market.

I imagined a grin on the front of my little green Mazda Spider. We were both ready for a new adventure. With a fully stocked briefcase and my purse and keys in hand, I headed out the back door.

CHAPTER 6

I tried to surprise Jamie, but without lifting her head, she surprised me. "Good Afternoon, Miss PI."

"You're a physic, or is that a psycho?" I went around her desk and gave her a hug.

"It's good to see you." There was an outside call coming in. "Chuck's waiting for you. I'll talk to you on the way out."

I waved my way down the hallway to his office. His door was ajar, but not fully open. I knocked lightly to get his attention.

He motioned me in. "That was fast. But then, when you were on a mission, you were always fast." He gave me a hug and sat back down.

I took the chair in front of his desk.

"So, you already have your first client?"

"I'm meeting with her at nine o'clock tomorrow morning. It's going to be a different mode of operation for me. My stories for the Tribune were a combination of efforts from a lot of people. I may have overturned key stones in several cases for some of the area police departments, but whether it was a current of cold case, I wasn't the person who did the initial introduction of evidence. That's not to say I won't still work with area PDs, but I'll also work with clients to close cases. Either way, I'm excited."

"Whatever you do Miss PI, you'll do well. And, whenever I can help, don't hesitate to call." He smiled, leaned back in his chair and crossed his arms over his chest. "Besides, somebody has to keep a partial eye out for you."

"Yes, Dad. Between you and Sam, I'm going to have to make sure I close the bathroom door, so I can pee without being watched."

We laughed.

"You've got that right. Now what can I help you with?"

"I'd like to look up any articles that might mention Rocco Deluca. It's his niece who's coming to my office tomorrow morning."

"Casey, did you forget that I live in Falmouth?" He moved his forearms off his chest, leaned forward and rested them on his desk. "I knew Rocco. He was a fixture in town. Not only did he have one of the best fish markets around, he was involved with a lot of organizations and helped a lot of people—a real caring guy."

"I did forget you live in Falmouth."

"He died last November. The funeral was huge."

"That's the same guy." I slid my chair closer to the desk. "I want to get to know him better."

"If I remember correctly, there was no foul play associated with his death. It was a fluke." Chuck lifted his left hand to cradle his chin. "He was doing something to one of his lobster tanks—either cleaning or repairing—leaned over a little too far, accidently caught an electrical cord and fell into the tank."

"You remember it well."

"It was a huge story, and not just in Falmouth, but all surrounding towns. Rocco lost his ambition after his wife died. She was a big part of the business. She always greeted the customers with a warm smile and a 'good morning' or 'good afternoon'. She did a lot of volunteer work in several local organizations. So did he. Great people, dearly missed."

"Thanks for the introduction."

"Why does his niece want you to investigate Rocco's death?"

"I'll be able to answer that after I talk to her tomorrow." I knew a little more than I wanted to share at this moment—even though I knew my conversation with Chuck wouldn't go any further than his office. "I want to know as much as I can before I talk to her. That way I can take what I read today, combine it with what she tells me tomorrow and try to make a complete picture of the life of Rocco Deluca." I looked at Chuck for a reaction. He knew me and I could

18

tell he knew there was more to the story than I was telling him, but he respected my need to stop when I did. "I know I don't have to say this, but please don't tell anyone what I'm working on."

He nodded and that's all I had to see. I had his word. "Next time make the visit before ten and don't forget the donuts."

"You got it, boss." I winked, got up and headed to my old office.

CHAPTER 7

It was four-thirty-five when I finished my research on Rocco Deluca in the Tribune's archives. I straightened the pile of articles I printed and put them into my briefcase. Chuck was gone for the day and Jamie was cleaning off her desk when I walked out to reception.

"Another day, another dollar. Remember what I told you about lunch. Let me know when you can come over." I gave her a wave and walked towards the door.

"I won't forget."

The parking lot was empty, except for my car, Jamie's Jeep and the three vehicles from the night crew. Four-thirty at the Tribune was like the running of the bulls—everybody was out the door and off to wherever as soon as the last number on the digital clock flashed zero.

It was crazy to go back to Barnstable Village. I had all the reading material I needed to introduce myself to Mr. Rocco Deluca. I headed home. I hadn't heard from Sam since last night, but figured he'd be at my house around six o'clock, then we'd head out somewhere for supper—nothing fancy, but I was hungry so I didn't want to dilly-dally.

Watson was pacing inside the front door. "Sorry, buddy." I grabbed the leash, hooked him up and took him outside—and not any too soon. "Thanks for not having an accident." We were coming around the side of the house when I saw Sam's car come down the street. Watson saw it too, and pulled me toward the driveway to greet him.

Sam knelt down, unhooked the leash and wrapped his arms around Watson. "Hi buddy." After they rolled around on the ground for a couple minutes, Sam looked up at me. "Do you want to join us?"

"I'll pass this time."

Sam got to his feet and hooked Watson back up. "Let's take a short walk. I'm sure the boy could use one. I've been at the desk all day, so I could use one too, then we can grab something to eat."

"Sounds like a plan."

"So, how'd it go today, Miss PI?"

"Very good, Mr. Dick."

"I might have my first case. In fact, you know the principal involved."

He stopped walking. Watson sat down beside him.

My guy and my dog waiting for me to reveal the hidden identity. "Does Rocco Deluca ring a bell?"

"Of course it does. If it's the Rocco Deluca I knew—and I emphasize knew—he died last November. I went to his funeral and it didn't look like he was just sleeping when I walked by to pay my respects."

"I didn't say he was my client. I said he was the principal—the main character."

"This should make interesting dinner conversation." Sam tilted his head sideways and looked at me out of the corners of his eyes.

"Speaking of supper. I'm hungry. Where are we going?"

"How about Sam Diego's?"

"I could celebrate my first day on the job with a frozen strawberry daiquiri and some nachos—maybe we could throw in a Mexican pizza for shits and giggles." I grabbed his free arm and started to pull him in the direction of my house. Watson joined in the Sam pull.

"Being led by a woman and a dog. I never thought I'd see the day."

CHAPTER 8

Monday nights, off-season was usually quiet at Sam Diego's. Tonight was no exception. Sam asked to be seated in our favorite spot adjacent to the back bar. Iggy, the bartender, greeted us as we walked by. "Where have you two been?"

"Took a couple side trips, but now we're back in the loop. By the way, I want you to meet Casey Quinby, Private Investigator." Sam handed Iggy one of my business cards. "She officially opened her door today."

Iggy looked at the card. "I'm impressed." He read it again before slipping it into his wallet.

"Any referrals will be much appreciated," I said. "After all, the more clients, the more frozen drinks and nachos—and a better tip."

He nodded and smiled. "You got it. You're my number one go-to PI."

I gave him a two finger salute and followed Sam to our table. The hostess left menus, but we knew what we were having so we pushed them aside.

Before we could order, the server came by carrying two drinks. "These are on Iggy."

We clicked our glasses as we recited our favorite toast,

Here's to it
Those who get to it
And don't do it
May never get to it
To do it again.

I felt like a giddy, impulsive, trying to be mature, young lady on a date, celebrating her twenty-first birthday.

The server returned and we ordered nachos supreme and a Mexican pizza.

I told Marnie and Annie that Sam was coming over tonight, but I'm glad it was only the two of us sharing the table. I wanted to relax, tell him about my day, then go home, cuddle up on the couch with a nightcap and watch an episode of *NCIS Los Angeles* before doing a little muffin buttering under the covers.

I reached across and took his hands. "Sam Summers, I love you."

"Casey Quinby, you're getting mushy on me."

I gave him my best *you're getting nothing tonight* look.

He chuckled. "I love you too, Sherlock."

I took another sip before snapping back to reality. "Let me tell you about my day."

"Good, I've been waiting to hear about Rocco."

"I got a call from Marnie this morning. She was taking her morning power walk before work. When she passed my office, she noticed an envelope tucked into the door jamb. It wasn't a very secure place to leave something, so she took it with her and called me about it when she got to her desk. I met her at the back door of the DA's office to retrieve my first piece of mail."

"Okay, but what's this got to do with Rocco?"

"Just shut up and listen."

"I am."

"The contents consisted of a letter, a newspaper clipping about his fish market, his obituary and several pictures. It was written by an Isabella Deluca. She's Rocco's niece."

"I knew Rocco was well off when he died. I also knew his wife pre-deceased him and they had no children. Is this a probate investigation? Is she questioning the will? Or was there a will?"

"It's got nothing to do with a will or money. At least, at this point, I don't think it does."

"Then what?" Sam was puzzled.

"She has a question as to how he died. The ME ruled the cause of death an accident."

"This should be an open and closed case for you. There was no indication of foul play involved. I know my department wasn't involved, but I'm sure I would have heard something if the Falmouth PD was conducting an investigation—and I didn't. I assume the ME's finding was conclusive."

"Isabella doesn't think so. She's coming to my office tomorrow morning at nine. She didn't want to talk over the phone."

"Interesting." He leaned back and folded his arms.

"After I talked to her, I called Chuck to see if I could use some of the Tribune's resources to look up newspaper articles on Rocco—be it before or after he died." I took a sip of my drink. "That's where I spent my afternoon."

"Did you come up with anything?"

"I found out he was a very popular man. Not only did he have an extremely successful business, he was involved in a variety of organizations and governmental functions in Falmouth. Most of the articles praised his accomplishments and support."

"He was a good man."

I was about to say something else, when our supper came. "Nachos and Mexican pizza—yum! Anymore conversation will have to wait."

"I agree. Now, let's eat."

CHAPTER 9

It was seven-thirty when we pulled into my driveway.

"Why don't you take Watson for a walk and I'll fix some dessert. There isn't much in the line of sweets, but I think I can scrounge up some Oreos and Edy's Moose Tracks."

"Don't make me any of that sissy coffee. I want regular. You can have your French Vanilla." Sam turned to Watson, "Isn't that right boy?"

Watson yelped and shook his rear end.

I patted Watson's head. "I'll have a treat ready for you when you get back." I got up close to his face. "You're going to get something special tonight."

Sam smirked and shook his head. "I get Oreos and he gets something special. Now I know where I stand in this house."

"You better believe it," I motioned them out the door.

Fifteen minutes later they were back. Watson walked in the door and looked around for his treat. When he didn't see anything, he walked over to me, sat down and stared up with the best puppy-dog eyes he could muster.

"I didn't forget you."

Sam was already playing with his Oreos.

I pushed the button on my Keurig to start the big guy's coffee, then went to the freezer to get Watson's special doggy ice cream.

"What's that?"

I pulled the cover off, slid the contents into Watson's bowl and set it on the floor in front of him.

Sam picked up the cover. "You've got to be kidding me—Chilly Wags doggy peanut butter ice cream. What will they think of next?"

While our coffees were brewing, I set the Rocco Deluca file on the table. After we satisfied ourselves with a few bites of ice cream, I opened the file and handed Sam the paperwork and the photos.

He looked at the picture printed in the obit. Without saying anything he picked up the other photos. A warm smile came over his face. "Yep, that's Rocco all right." He shook his head. "He might have been seventy-seven, but he was taken far too young. If I close my eyes, I can imagine him sitting beside me sharing my ice cream."

I didn't say anything—just observed.

"Let me see the letter."

I handed it to him. "Like I said, short and to the point. There are a lot of words missing between the lines. Isabella will have to fill them in for me."

"Let me see the copies of the articles the Tribune ran."

"Of course." I handed him the manila folder. "They're in order. I haven't had a chance to go through them. I printed every article that mentioned him. I can't tell you what I have and what I don't."

"I'll keep them the way you have them. An accurate timeline can be beneficial to any investigation."

"Why don't you give me the bottom half. If I have any questions I'll jot them down, note the date and run them by you when you've finished reading," I said.

"Sounds like a plan."

"I've already finished my coffee. I'm going to make another cup—want one?"

"No, I'm good. I'm saving my liquid intake for later when we watch *NCIS*—a manly show—where a man needs a brew in hand to watch it." Sam smiled.

I swished the empty folder across his face.

The first three articles praised Rocco for his contributions of time and money to benefit several youth organizations in town. Sam's description of the man was right on—ambitious, involved and well loved. The third piece of paper was a copy of an obituary for Maria DeMarco. The name sounded familiar, but my brain was focused on

Rocco Deluca, so I didn't bother reading it. The computer must have hiccupped and kicked out something close to Deluca. I left it in the pile, but moved on to the next editorial. The next one also had the name Maria DeMarco in the title—MARIA DEMARCO, WIFE OF FALMOUTH CONTRACTOR, SID DEMARCO, MISSING. Now I knew why the name was familiar, but I still didn't know why it spit out when I did a computer search for Rocco. This time I didn't put it aside.

There it was about halfway through the article. Maria was Rocco's sister. I was excited with my find. "Sam, stop what you're reading and take a look at what I discovered." I quickly slid the paper I was holding over the one he was reading. He wasn't expecting it. The one page article fell off the table and glided halfway across the kitchen floor.

"What in the world got you this animated?" He got up to retrieve my find.

I didn't say a word. I sat with my hands folded waiting for him to read what I had just read.

"The filing cabinet in my brain needs dusting off. Maria DeMarco was Rocco Deluca's sister." Sam shook his head. "How could I forget that? It's not like we're dealing with a Smith or a Jones."

"I remember reading about it, but since it happened twelve years ago, I wasn't yet employed by the Tribune. If I was, I definitely would have covered it, but that's when I was rehabbing at Spaulding." I don't think Sam heard any of what I said. He was engrossed in re-reading the article.

Finally he looked up. "You know they never found Maria, don't you?"

"I do."

"That case is still very open. I don't think it will ever be solved." He looked into my eyes. "And, don't even think you're going to talk to Chief Mills about revisiting it."

"Don't be an ass. I'm not stupid."

"Maria had no daughters, only three sons. Isabella is Maria's niece."

"In her letter or on the telephone, she never mentioned Maria's name. It was all about Rocco. Tomorrow morning I'll reaffirm that." My adrenaline was flowing, but I kept a cool demeanor so as not to trigger a lecture from Sam.

We thumbed through the rest of the articles. My focus remained on Rocco's sibling. Anything else I read at this point wasn't going to be retained.

"It's almost time for *NCIS*. Why don't you turn the television on and I'll get our libations of choice ready." I wanted to get away from our reading and LL Cool J and crew were the perfect excuse.

"Don't forget my frostie."

"Do I ever? Want some popcorn?"

"Does a snake have hips?"

"What?"

"Never mind—yeah, popcorn will be great."

CHAPTER 10

Tuesday

"*Da, da, da,da,da.... da, da, da,da,da* …. Rise and shine." Sam's attempt to mimic a bugle with an empty paper towel roll failed.

I rolled over and opened my eyes. "You're a total ass. I hope your mother didn't waste her money for music lessons." I pulled the pillow over my head. "You better not be standing there when I move this sack of feathers."

"Just because you're the boss now, doesn't mean you can stay in bed on a work day. Besides, I made you breakfast. Now get up." He turned around and went back to the kitchen.

"Okay, okay. Give me five minutes." I rolled myself off the side of the bed, almost falling on the floor. Once I discovered I could still walk, I shuffled down the hall to the bathroom and held a cold facecloth over my eyes.

Sam had already gotten the paper and was sitting at the table pretending to read.

"Well, where's the breakfast you said you made?"

"If you sit down, I'll get it for you." He pushed the button on the Keurig, turned the oven to broil and poured a glass of Ocean Spray's strawberry kiwi juice for both of us, then walked over and gave me a kiss. "How can you stay mad at this face?"

"Give me my coffee and I'll try to come up with an answer."

"Here's your juice, coffee and Thomas' with cheese."

I looked down at Watson.

"He's already eaten," Sam said.

Breakfast tasted good. "I'm going to be in trouble with the girls today."

"Why's that?"

"I was supposed to call them last night and give them a briefing on the telephone call I made to Isabella."

"I'm glad you didn't."

The look on my face didn't need an explanation.

"You need to keep something in mind. Remember when you were studying for your private investigator's license? One of the fundamental rules was that you shouldn't discuss a case with anyone unless you have permission from the person who hired you. Do you remember that?"

"Now that you mention it, I do." I grimaced. "It's not like I announced it with a bull horn. It was an hour's worth of conversation over lunch. And I haven't been officially hired yet. But I guess that doesn't really make a difference, does it?"

"No. I fall into that category too. Even though I'm a sworn law enforcement officer, I'm not exempt from that rule."

"What do you suggest I do?"

"Talk to Marnie and Annie, explain what we just talked about." Sam took a deep breath. "I know you. I know the three musketeers share everything, and for me to tell you not to is like talking to that wall. What I will say is, not to talk in public." He stood up and got me another coffee. "And, Casey, that also pertains to me."

I took a sip and sat up in my chair—still holding my cup. "Maybe I'm not supposed to confide in you regarding a case, but I'm going to. Nobody has to know."

"Remember, I said it's okay as long as you get permission from your client."

"Got ya. Let me meet with her today, get a feel for her actual knowledge of the facts as she perceives them, then I'll decide if I should approach her with the idea of bringing in you, Marnie and Annie. After all, the three of you are involved with some arm of the law that could be very helpful in the investigation."

Sam looked at his watch. "It's time for me to head out. Give me a call later."

"I noticed you brought the overstuffed duffle bag. Am I to assume you're planning on staying a few nights?"

"You're very observant. As long as my key fits, I'll be back."

"How about pizza, chips and frosties for supper?"

"I can handle that."

"Would you mind if I asked Marnie over? Maloney won't be around until the weekend and I know she doesn't like being alone all the time."

"Fine with me. If you want, you can ask Annie, too."

"She's got some kind of a painting class tonight at the college, so I know she's not available."

"All right, I've got to get going." Sam got up, took his keys off the counter, gave me a kiss, tussled with Watson and headed out the door. "Talk to you later and see you tonight."

I picked up my coffee and watched from the window as he backed out of the driveway.

"Well Watson, I think it's time to get going. What do you think I should wear to meet my first potential client?" I checked out my sweaters. "Here we go—casual." I showered, dried my hair and tied it back in a twisted knot, then slipped on my gray cashmere sweater over a pair of off-white corduroys. I finished it off with my new Navajo cream and black stripe scarf and my LL Bean classic brown boat shoes. "I look good," I said as I admired myself in the mirror.

"Come on, buddy. I'll take you outside, then I've got to get going."

CHAPTER 11

It was eight-thirty-five when I parked behind my building. Even if Isabella showed up early, I had plenty of time to file the articles I'd retrieved from the Tribune's computers. I didn't want them sitting on my desk.

Before I started, I ran over to Nancy's for a coffee. The little bell above the door jingled announcing my arrival. "Hi Nancy," I called out when I didn't see her behind the counter.

I heard her voice from the back room. "Casey, is that you?"

"It is."

"I'll be right there."

I wasn't staying, so rather than sit at a table, I waited at the counter. The smells from the kitchen penetrated the air. It was a good thing I'd had breakfast at home. With Nancy's Donut Shop right next to my office, I could quickly become a candidate for *The Biggest Loser*.

Nancy came from the kitchen carrying a fresh out-of-the-oven tray of sticky buns. "How many do you want?"

"Not today. Sam made me breakfast. But I can't go without my coffee. Why don't you make it a large one." I smiled. "With cream."

"On its way."

"Is that for here or to go?"

"I've got an appointment this morning, so it's to go."

There were a couple copies of the Barnstable Patriot left in the newsstand, so I picked up an unread one, paid for it along with my coffee, and wished Nancy a good day.

32

CHAPTER 12

My filing was done. I had some time to kill before my meeting with Isabella, so I started a list of things I needed for the office. I should have already purchased a Keurig. At least I could have offered her a coffee. Next time.

My cell rang at the same time a person, I presumed to be Isabella, came through the door. I waved her in and motioned for her to sit down. I held up a finger to indicate I'd be right with her.

"Hi Sam. I'll get back to you later." I didn't wait for a reply, just hung up. If Sam checks his watch, he'll know I'm not sitting here alone.

I moved around to the front of my desk where Isabella was sitting. I reached out to shake her hand. "Good morning, I'm Casey Quinby. I presume you're Isabella Deluca."

She returned my handshake. "I am, but please call me Bella."

I studied her, trying not to make her nervous. "Did you come in from Falmouth?" I came back around my desk and sat down.

"From Falmouth Heights. The ride isn't bad this time of the year. It's when the flood gates open and the tourists take over that the ride time doubles."

"You're absolutely correct. But what would I do without them?"

"I agree," she said.

A fresh pad of paper and new gel pen were on the left side of the blotter waiting to be put into action. I took the folder that contained her letter, Rocco's obit and the pictures from my file drawer, opened it and put it beside the pad.

Since Bella didn't mince any words in her letter, I started to highlight the reason she was sitting across from me. "You indicated you wanted to talk to me about the death of your uncle, Rocco Deluca. You said his death, on November 1, 2013, was ruled an accident by the Medical Examiner. I understand he was electrocuted when he fell into some standing water in the bottom of one of his lobster tanks."

Bella didn't respond. She was quiet—petite, with a beautiful olive complexion—dark brown, almost black hair, and warm blue-green eyes. She was dressed casual in a pair of black pants, gray turtleneck and black blazer. I glanced at her purse. It was a Coach—not a knock-off, a real one.

"Before we get started, I have a few questions. Although I've worked investigations for a number of years alongside many of the Cape police departments, are you aware that I just hung my shingle this weekend?"

"I know you did, but you come highly recommended." She leaned back in her chair and crossed her legs. "A friend of a friend of mine works with a friend of yours in the DA's office across the street. My friend's friend's name is Tricia Early. I realize this is a confusing chain of friends, but that's how I ended up coming to you."

It didn't ring a bell. "And who is Tricia's friend?"

"I think her name was Mary or Marcy—something like that."

"How about Marnie?" Tricia obviously didn't say anything to Marnie, otherwise I would never have asked Bella why she was my first client. I wanted to laugh, but restrained myself.

"That's it." Bella nodded and smiled.

"She's one of my best friends." I wondered if this was the time to tell Bella that Marnie has helped me in the past with case research. I decided to go for it. "Marnie assisted me in a couple of my cases."

"Will she be working with you on mine?"

"Only if you give me permission to consult with her." I didn't want to say too much, so I let her make the next move.

"I'm fine with that as long as it doesn't become public knowledge as to your findings. I want to be apprised of them first." She hesitated. "I realize by opening an investigation to determine if the cause of death was something other than an accident, it will cause people to sit up and take notice. Some might even get nervous."

I shook my head in agreement. She made a valid point. "Investigations have a way of bringing out a brigade of nerves—and, in most cases, ready to battle against the truth, even with the innocent."

"Why don't you tell me a little about yourself. But, before we start, would you like a coffee?"

"Yes, I'd like that."

"How do you take it?"

"Cream, no sugar."

I picked up my cell and hit the nine button. "Hi, Nancy, it's Casey. Could you please fix me a couple large coffees, cream only and I'll be right over to pick them up." I clicked the off button.

"You didn't have to do that."

"Yes, I did. Next time you come I'll have my Keurig and we can drink to our heart's content. I don't know about you, but I love my coffee. It's my drug of choice." I laughed.

"I knew we'd be a good match." She nodded.

"Sit tight and I'll be right back." I stood up, smiled and headed out the door to Nancy's. The coffees were waiting for me on the counter along with a small white bag that I presumed were a couple of her pastries. I heard the oven door close, so I called to her. "Can you start me a tab?"

"Of course."

"Catch you later."

Bella was waiting to open the door.

"My friend, Nancy, thinks I need fattening up, so whenever I order coffee she 'attaches' a bag of goodies. I have no idea what she gave us, but I think we should take a look."

"Sounds good to me." Bella watched as I gently tore the side of the bag—careful not to destroy it.

I handed her a napkin and a coffee. "Enjoy my Sunday best china. I haven't unpacked the everyday Fiesta Ware yet."

"I'll be careful not to chip them." She flipped up the tab on the lid and took a sip. "Wow, this is hot."

"Why don't we get started. Our little bag of energy will give us stamina to keep going. Feel free to pick whenever." I reached over and broke off a piece of oatmeal raisin cookie.

Bella did the same. "We should get the business part of this out of the way so we can concentrate on the real reason I'm here." She reached for her purse. "I know you're not doing this out of the goodness of your heart, so let's talk money."

She took me by surprise, but I was glad she was the first to bring it up. "Good point." I smiled. "I require a two thousand dollar retainer up front. After that, I charge fifty dollars an hour, plus expenses to include mileage, any documentation I would have to pay for and lodging, if I had to travel. At this point, I don't anticipate any lodging expenses, but in case there are, I have to let you know about the charges up front."

"I understand. You come recommended, not only for your professional reputation, but for your personal integrity and trust. I have no doubt you'll give me more than I pay for—especially in the category of peace of mind." She took her checkbook out. "Do I make the check to you?"

"To keep everything on the up and up, I drafted a contract for you to look at. It details everything I just told you regarding charges and the services. I'd like to go over it before you write a check."

"Okay. I've never done this before, so you need to tell me what to do."

"Thanks for the vote of confidence." I handed her a copy of the contract. "The first part is pretty standard—name, address, contact information, and anything else most business contracts start off with. It's the next section we need to spend a little time on before we get into the nitty-gritty of why you hired me."

Bella turned to the second page and ran her finger down until she came to services.

I already know what it said, so I sat quietly, drinking my coffee, until she finished reading.

"Sounds fine to me. There is one thing, though."

"What's that?"

"I am assuming you read my uncle's obituary."

"I did."

"Then you know I have a brother, George. He lives on Buttermilk Bay in Buzzards Bay. He's divorced. I never married. Our parents are both deceased. Since we have the same last name as Uncle Rocco, it's obvious he was my father's brother. Uncle Rocco and Aunt Rita didn't have any children. They were like a second set of parents to us. When my brother was in high school, he worked part time at the fish market. He could have taken over the business, but wanted no part of it on a full time basis. I can't say I blame him. He's an accountant. My aunt took care of the books at the market until her death. That's when my brother stepped in to help. Uncle Rocco knew his fish, but when it came to numbers, he didn't have a clue."

"Family helping family—it can't get any better than that. I wish there was more of it in this world." I slid another cookie in front of Bella and put the rest of mine in my mouth. "Did you ever work at the market?"

"No, I love to eat fish, but I don't like to handle them, especially when they're looking at you." She wrinkled her nose and shrugged.

"I get that."

"I didn't work there, but I hung around there. I'd go in sometimes after school, sit in the office and do my homework. My father would pick me up on his way home from work."

I nodded.

"The thing is, I don't want my brother to know what I'm doing. At least not until he has to. Once I sign the contract, I'm the one employing you to investigate my uncle's death. He won't like it. When Uncle Rocco died, George was heartbroken. I tried to talk to him about my suspicions, but he wouldn't hear of it." Bella looked down at the floor, rocking slightly as she spoke.

"You know at some point in time, I'll have to talk to George."

"I know you will, but please let me know before you do."

"Absolutely."

"There's something else I have to tell you. Uncle Rocco had a sister, Maria DeMarco."

I read about her in the articles I printed at the Tribune, but didn't want Bella to know I'd started my homework before our meeting today.

"She was married to Sid DeMarco. He was a big contractor in Falmouth. She was my aunt, but our families were never close. She had three sons. One of them died at five years old from injuries in a car accident. Uncle Rocco was driving the car. Sid and my Aunt Maria never forgave him, even though it wasn't his fault. From that day on, the DeMarcos had nothing to do with the Delucas. That included my family too."

"Living so close and not acknowledging each other. That had to be hard."

"It was. Especially since my brother and I went to the same school as my cousins, Greg and Phil."

"Did they come to Rocco's funeral?"

"No, they didn't. Uncle Sid died a year before Uncle Rocco. We didn't go to Sid's funeral either."

"And all this started with the car accident?"

"Started then, but festered after my Aunt Maria disappeared. One day, she supposedly drove to Boston to visit her cousin in the North End. Uncle Sid said when he hadn't heard from her for a few days, he called Boston. Her cousin said she wasn't there. Aunt Maria was never seen or heard from again."

"Now that you mention it, I remember the story." I wasn't lying. I did remember it, even if I had re-read a copy of it last night. "It happened before I went to work for the Tribune."

"There's more to my story." Bella stood up and walked slowly around the office. She stopped in front of the window, clasped her hands behind her back and stared at the passing cars.

I felt she needed a break. "It's almost twelve o'clock, how about we get some lunch." I continued before she could say anything,

"We could eat at the sandwich shop a few doors down or if you feel like taking a short drive, we could …."

"Actually, that's a good idea. I am a little hungry. The sandwich shop is fine."

I locked the office and we headed down the street.

CHAPTER 13

We finished lunch, paid the bill and went back to my office.

"That was a great Reuben. I haven't had one of those in years. There are a couple of Nancy's cookies left." I got the bag from the back room and set it on my desk. "You know I can't offer you a coffee, but how about a water?"

"Sure. Then I'm ready to get back to my story."

"Uncle Rocco and Aunt Maria might not have spoken for years, but she was his sister. When she went missing, he took it upon himself to find out what happened to her. It was rumored there was trouble between Sid and Maria, but it was never proven. Uncle Rocco even went to Sid to ask him some questions. They had a huge argument—got into a fight. The police were called and Uncle Rocco was escorted off Sid's property and told not to return." Bella paused and took a sip of water.

"Did Rocco get arrested?"

"No, but as he was being led away from the house, he turned and yelled to Sid that he'd find out what happened to Maria and if he had harmed his sister, he was a dead man."

"And the police didn't do anything after he said that?"

"The police all knew Sid and Rocco. They knew there was bad blood between them and figured the threat was made in the heat of the moment." Bella moved to the front of her chair and leaned her forearms on the desk. "From that day forward, Uncle Rocco made it his mission to find Maria."

"Did he ever discuss his findings with his wife or you or your brother?"

"No. I asked a couple times if I could help, but he didn't want me to get involved, for fear I would be hurt. I think he was close to

40

finding out what happened to her." Bella shrugged her shoulders. "Now we'll never know." She got quiet.

"You indicated you aren't convinced your uncle's death was an accident or a possible suicide. Do you think his death might be related to his search to find his sister?"

"Here's the problem. About two years ago, Sid was diagnosed with cancer. Apparently, nobody knew about it until it was too late. It was so far advanced that he opted not to have any treatments. He died three months to the day after he found out." Bella nodded. "To answer your question—Yes, I do think Uncle Rocco's death may be related to his search to find his sister."

"With Sid gone, who would want Rocco dead?" I asked.

"Sid's sons—my cousins."

"Why?"

"Money. If Sid did something to his wife and it was proven, he would have gone to trial for murder. If convicted, his business would 'shit the bed'. Remember, my Uncle Rocco was a very popular, well-respected man in Falmouth and we're talking about his sister. Sid was well-known, but not the most well-liked. Some of his business dealings were questionable."

"What do you mean by questionable?"

"The scuttle-butt around town labeled him as a Whitey Bulger wanna-be, but Sid lacked the qualifications or talent." Bella's eyes opened wide when she realized what she'd said. "I'm not saying Bulger was a good guy. I'm saying that Sid thrived on control, no matter what it took to obtain it. It's public knowledge he was investigated for strong-arming on a number of occasions, but was never prosecuted because nothing could be proven."

"And you think Rocco knew something more than the authorities—something that might lead to the discovery of what happened to his sister?"

"I do believe Uncle Rocco may have stumbled onto something, but wanted to research it more before going to the authorities." Bella hung her head and in a quiet, slightly quivering voice said, "I believe it was that information that got him killed."

I opened my bottom desk drawer and took out a box of tissues. I didn't say anything, just slid them over in front of her. "Let's take a minute."

Bella composed herself, but when she looked up I saw sadness in her eyes. Over the last few hours, she'd laid her cards on the table and, in doing so, re-experienced an unfinished chapter in her life. It was then I realized Bella had hired me as a co-author to complete Uncle Rocco's story.

It was my turn. "Why don't you tell me a little about yourself?"

There was no hesitation. "That would probably be a good idea. I want you to know you're dealing with a sane, rational person and not some crazy." She grinned.

"You're not crazy."

"I'll be thirty-six next month. You already know I have a brother, George. He's thirty-nine. And you know my parents are both deceased. I live in the family home in the Heights. My brother chose to move away from Falmouth, but not far—Buzzards Bay. I think I told you all that before."

"That's okay. We've been talking about a lot of things. A little repeat is a good idea."

"I went to Simmons College in Boston and got my bachelor's and master's degrees in Library Science. I stayed in Boston for six years and worked at the Central Library in Copley Square. It was fun being a city girl, but I missed the Cape. When the Director's position opened at the Falmouth Library, I applied and got the job. I've been there for almost eight years." She smiled.

The change of topic was a good thing.

"Five years ago, I almost got married. Now I'm glad I didn't. I understand he married the girl he was seeing at the same time he was dating me, has two children and is miserable." She chuckled. "Falmouth is a small town when it comes to gossip. You'll find out."

"The only thing I really know about Falmouth, actually two things, are The Quarterdeck Restaurant and the Island Queen."

"The Island Queen is the best, and fastest, way to get to Martha's Vineyard—one of my favorite places. When I want to get away, I jump the ferry and do nothing but eat and shop. Some days I take a book and beach gear. That's one place I would like to live, but could never afford to."

"Have you done anything with your uncle's fish market?

"No, not yet. My brother wanted to get rid of it right away. He didn't like putting out money without getting any in. That's the accountant in him. Since I'm the executor, I decided we were going to wait until this spring or even summer. I'm not in a hurry—he is. He doesn't think we should spend the money to keep the utilities on or pay the taxes. We did have it winterized so we wouldn't have any problems with freezing pipes, but that's all we've done. It's still the same as it was the day Uncle Rocco was found in the tank. That's why I'm coming to you now." She rolled her bottom lip in, held it for a second with her teeth before releasing it and letting out a sigh. "I don't know how much longer I can convince my brother not to do something with the building and property."

"Can I get inside to see it?"

"Of course, I can take you there anytime."

I felt her 'anytime' meant as soon as possible. "What does your schedule look like for tomorrow?"

"I'm the director. It comes with privileges. I don't have any meetings tomorrow, so I'm free whenever." She sat straight up to stretch her back. "How about I meet you at the Main Street Dunkins? It's right up the street from the Library."

A girl after my own heart. "I'll be there at nine o'clock. If something changes, give me a call and visa-versa."

"I think you're forgetting something."

"What?"

"I need to sign the contract and give you a check." She reached for her purse.

"You might think this is my first day on the job, but since you asked, please make the check out to me."

CHAPTER 14

Bella left. I sat back in my chair, clasped my hands behind my neck and stared at the ceiling. I was sure my first case was going to be an adultery, probate or a connect the dots investigation. I was wrong.

My body felt like it was on a merry-go-round—I was firmly seated on a handsomely decorated steed, but my brain was four horses ahead of me. Before I could continue, I had to break down and label Bella's story, then take everything and record it on a timeline.

As I re-read my notes, I grouped similar details together by accentuating them with different colored highlighters. I used yellow for Uncle Sid—green for Uncle Rocco—orange for brother George—and purple for anything else. Instead of using colored three-by-fives, I made a title page for each group and ran a color coded line over it. My organizational methods are my own handiwork. They're my modus operandi.

I jumped when the front door opened and Marnie walked in. "Am I interrupting anything?"

"Nope. I was making space in my mental file cabinet for my new case. I can close the drawer now."

"Before you do that, do you want to fill me in on what you were filing?" Marnie sat down in the chair Bella had vacated an hour before.

"Not now."

"Why?" She had a puzzled look on her face.

"Because, I was going to ask you to come over for supper tonight. We're having pizza and frosties. Of course Sam will be there, too. Instead of going over it twice, I'll fill you both in on my meeting with Bella. How's that sound?"

"The pizza sounds great, but I'm lousy at playing the waiting game." She folded her arms across her chest and pouted.

"I'm not going to change my mind, so wipe that scowl off your face. You'll have to wait." I smiled as I gathered up my paperwork and slipped it into my briefcase.

"What time do you want me there and do you want me to pick up the beer?"

"I'm going to do a couple errands, then swing by Jack's. Why don't you come over around six-ish. If you want to pick up the beer, that would be great."

"I've got to go back to the office for about an hour to wrap up a report, then I'll head out." Marnie got up and started for the door. She stopped, looked around and shook her head. "I'm so proud of you, Casey Quinby—living a dream." She waved as she walked out the door.

I took out the list I'd started earlier. Between the Christmas Tree Shop and Bed, Bath and Beyond, I should be able to pick up everything I needed. Since they were neighboring stores, it wouldn't take me long to get in, get out and get home.

A new Keurig topped the list along with a couple economy boxes of K-cups—one French Vanilla and one regular. I dug in my purse for the coupons I took from the house this morning—two twenty-percenters and one for five dollars. Love those Bed, Bath and Beyond coupons. The rest of the damage I figured I could do at the Tree Shop. They have the best deals on dishes, cups, silverware, napkins—all the extra things I might need to make a client feel relaxed.

I stood up from my desk, walked over to the window and took a couple minutes to take in the view. I felt comfortable being in Barnstable Village—we were a good match—the Village and me.

I glanced at my watch, locked the front door, picked up my briefcase and purse and headed out the back door to my car.

My cell rang. It was Sam. "Where are you? I tried your office and there was no answer."

"That's because I'm sitting in my car."

"Am I picking up the pizza tonight or are you?"

"I am. Marnie's coming over, so I'm getting two—one pepperoni and one mushroom and peppers. I've got a few errands, then I'll call Jack's. I told Marnie to come over around six-ish. She's picking up the beer. What time will you be home?"

"I'm leaving Bourne as we speak. I'll take Watson for a walk and see you when you get there."

"Okay, see you then."

I took a left out of the parking lot onto Route 6A, then turned right onto Phinney's Lane. Bella's story ran around my head like an old-fashioned news reel. I didn't notice the light at Route 132 turn red and I sailed right through. The blast of an air horn from a Town of Barnstable dump truck brought me back to reality. My heart pounded and my hands gripped the wheel. I swerved to avoid an accident. As soon as I cleared the intersection, I slowed down and pulled into the side lot of the Cape Codder. I glanced in my rear view mirror half expecting to see blue lights announcing my violation to the passing traffic. *Thank goodness there was nobody around.* I folded my hands in my lap and rested my head on the steering wheel. I needed a few minutes to compose myself. There was no way I was going to tell Sam or Marnie about what just happened.

CHAPTER 15

Mission accomplished. I purchased almost everything I needed to equip my little office eatery. Now I could be at least be somewhat hospitable when a client walked through the door. And, of course, I had my French Vanilla to comfort me when a client didn't walk through the door.

I checked my watch and called Jack's.

It was five-fifty when I pulled into my driveway. I knew Sam would be there and was glad to see Marnie had arrived. I beeped my horn to get Sam's attention.

He opened the door. Watson was standing beside him. "Hey boy, go and help your mother." Watson bounded across the front yard and jumped up to greet me. He almost knocked me to the ground.

I gave the boy a pat and turned to see Sam and Marnie laughing. "If either of you know what's good for you, you'll come help me."

They both recognized the look and quickly came to my rescue.

Sam tried to give me a hug. "Very funny." I handed Marnie the two pizzas.

"Aw, come on. We were only funnin' you."

Marnie and I went inside while Sam meandered across the yard and eventually made an appearance.

"Will you please hurry up. The pizza will be cold. Want me to put them in the oven for a couple minutes?"

"Good idea. I'll get the beers. Do you girls want a frostie?"

"I do and I'm sure Marnie does too."

She smiled and nodded. "I'll get the table ready."

I turned on the oven, took the boxes from Sam, and slid the pizzas on a couple cookie sheets. I went back outside to my car and got my purse and briefcase.

"I'm dying to hear what happened with your new client." Marnie looked at Sam. "Miss PI wouldn't tell me anything earlier. She said she didn't want to tell the story twice, so I had to wait until tonight. Well, it's tonight, so let's hear it." She picked up her beer, walked over to the table and sat down.

"Hold your horses. Let me get the food on the table, then I'll talk like I was vaccinated with a phonograph needle."

Sam spun around. "Is that why you have the gift of gab?" He smiled and sat down beside Marnie.

I settled myself in with a slice of pepperoni and an ice cold frostie. I turned to Marnie, "First of all, I was recommended by somebody who works in your office. Do you know a Tricia Early?"

"Of course I do. She's one of the new ADAs. I've helped her with some research on a case she's working on. Nice kid. She's from the same neighboorhood Maloney's from, but she doesn't know him."

"She's a friend of a friend of my client. You must have mentioned me to her because she said you were my friend." I smiled. "We've got a lot of friends meeting friends going on here."

"One day last week I had lunch with her and told her about you. Word of mouth is the best way to get business." Marnie put her beer down and rubbed her chin. "Let me see—about that referral fee."

Sam almost choked. "You got her, Miss Marnie." He held up his hand for a high-five.

"If you two have finished, I'll continue. In a nutshell, Bella Deluca's uncle, Rocco Deluca, was found dead in one of his lobster tanks last November. The ME ruled the death an accident. Bella doesn't believe it was. She thinks he was murdered."

"Sam, did you already know this?"

"All I knew is it was something to do with Rocco Deluca. I knew him. He was a great guy. Did a lot for the town of Falmouth."

"Casey, you mentioned his lobster tanks," said Marnie.

"He owned a fish market in Falmouth. He was in the process of closing it down—not for the day, but for good. The police said it appeared he was taking the last two lobsters out of the tank, slipped and grabbed onto a live electrical cord that was wrapped around a pole at the end of the tank. There was still some water in the bottom—about ten inches—and he was electrocuted along with two remaining lobsters."

"I don't see anything out of the ordinary." Marnie wrinkled her face. "Did anybody find evidence to suggest something other than an accident?"

"Apparently not. That's what Bella is trying to do. I'm going to meet her tomorrow morning and we're going to pay the market a visit."

Sam sat quietly. "That happened last November. This is March. Things could have been moved or removed."

"I asked Bella about that. She said nothing has been changed since the day her uncle died. She and her brother are the only ones with access to the property. She said her brother wants to sell, but she won't until she's convinced there was or wasn't foul play involved."

"Casey, I want you to tread very softly with this case." Sam took a deep breath. "As you know, this man was well-known and respected in Falmouth. Part of his family was a piece of crap and the two sides didn't see eye to eye."

"You always tell me to be careful and I respect your concern, but I can take care of myself."

Sam's eyes widened, but he didn't speak.

"I know you want to say something, so go ahead."

"Leave it to you to get a case like this your first day on the job." He smiled and shook his head. "I know you don't want to hear it, but if I can help, I'm here for you."

"Me too," Marnie said quietly.

"Just to let you know, I asked Bella if it was okay to discuss the case with both of you and, of course, Annie. She didn't have a problem with it. The only condition was she didn't want any of my findings getting out to the public without her knowing about them first." I looked at Sam and Marnie. "I'll respect her wishes, as I'm sure you both will too."

"Of course," said Sam.

Marnie agreed.

"Have you thought about your next move after the visit to Rocco's fish market tomorrow?" asked Sam.

"I've thought about it, but haven't made any decisions yet. I need to get any files the Falmouth PD and the ME's office have. Since it was ruled an accident, there are more than likely a minimal number of reports. The ones I'm most interested in are the initial ones."

Sam got up and took the dishes to the sink. "I don't see any problem getting them. Have you ever worked with Falmouth?"

"Not on anything earth-shattering. I had to check with them to confirm some details on a home invasion case for an article I was writing, but I've never worked with them on cold cases."

"Have you had any interaction with Chief Mills?"

"No, not yet, but I'm sure I will."

"He's had his problems within the department, but he's a good man—strict, but fair."

"I'm hoping I won't have trouble getting what I need. When I worked at the Tribune and helped the PDs, I got most anything I wanted without having to divulge the reasoning behind my requests. I hope my rapport with them still holds true now that I'm legally conducting investigations on my own. They used to turn their backs and let me slither under stones. Of course, Falmouth isn't one of the PDs I've worked with."

"You're not a new kid on the block. Believe me, they know you. Why wouldn't they work with you?"

"She's right," said Sam. "Does anyone want another beer while I'm up?"

"No, I'm good," said Marnie.

"Me too. In a little while I'll pull out the Oreos and make us some coffee."

Sam got himself a beer, gave me a kiss on the forehead and sat down between Marnie and me.

"What is it you're looking for in the reports?" Marnie asked.

"When I talked to Bella today, she told me nothing inside of her uncle's fish market had been moved since the police were there. I want to compare pictures taken the day of the so-called accident with the actual scene as it appears today. Remember Bella said the only people with access to the market are her and her brother."

"So you're saying nobody moved or took anything from Uncle Rocco's since they found him dead in the tank." Sam had a baffled look on his face.

"Nothing from the immediate location of the body was …."

Before I could finish, Sam spoke up, "You said the immediate location of the body—what about any other locations in the market?"

"Bella said a couple days later, she and her brother went in. He took all the paperwork from the office. He handled Rocco's books. She told me her brother stepped in after her aunt died because Rocco didn't have a clue as to what to do and George was an accountant."

"Are they going to sell the business?" asked Sam.

"Eventually. That's a sore subject between Bella and her brother. He says there's no money coming in, but there are still bills to pay. He wants to sell and put everything to bed." I took a breath then continued, "Bella wasn't overly concerned because Uncle Rocco was very well-heeled. She believes that his death wasn't accidental and doesn't want to close things out until she proves it—one way or the other."

"You've really got yourself a doozie of a first case," Marnie laughed.

Sam nodded. "I wouldn't have expected anything less for Sherlock."

"It's going to be a challenge, but I'm up for it."

"Marnie, she hasn't told you the half of this case." Sam leaned back in his chair and folded his arms across his chest.

Marnie put her piece of pizza down and turned sideways to face Casey.

"Well?"

"Since you're a newbie to Cape Cod, the DeMarco family name probably means nothing to you." I hesitated, waiting for Marnie or Sam to butt in, but neither did. "The abbreviated version is that the DeMarco family exercises an unwritten control over certain situations in the Falmouth area."

"That's being diplomatic and there's nothing diplomatic about the DeMarco family," said Sam.

"Both of you stop. I'm totally confused. We're into another family. Who are the DeMarcos?" Marnie threw up her hands and looked from me to Sam, then back to me. "I can tell I'm not going to get much more of this story—at least not tonight."

"You're right. I wouldn't want you to have nightmares." I laughed. "Instead of Oreos, I've got all the fixings for a hot fudge sundae. It won't be like Sundae School, but we can pretend. We can watch the rest of *Wheel of Fortune*, then *NCIS* comes on."

"The great and wonderful soda jerk has spoken." Sam took Marnie's hand. "Let's get the theater ready."

"Don't get fresh—my best friend is watching." Marnie winked as they walked toward the living room.

CHAPTER 16

Wednesday

"I don't know where the sleeping time went. I know I need more." I nudged Sam.

He grunted and turned over.

"Don't ignore me or you'll be late for work."

Watson yipped.

"All right you two—I get your message. I think you've formed a conspiracy against me," he yawned. "I hate mornings."

I swung my legs off the side of the bed and slowly sat up.

Sam grabbed my arm and pulled me back down. "Where do you think you're going, my little Sherlock?"

"Off to fight the crime and win the battle."

"I don't think that's how the saying goes, but I get your gist." Sam glanced at the alarm clock on the table by my side of the bed. "It's seven o'clock."

"No kidding—that's why there'll be no fooling around this morning."

"Did you plan it that way?" He laughed, then jumped out of bed and ran down the hall. "First dibs on the bathroom."

I shook my head. "Don't linger. Remember I have to be in Falmouth at nine o'clock to meet Bella."

"I'll have a Mr. Thomas, a glass of OJ and a regular coffee," he yelled, totally ignoring what I just said.

"Be careful or I'll tell you to make it yourself."

"It wouldn't be the first time."

"Shut-up and get out of the bathroom." I set everything up in the kitchen. The juice was poured, the muffins in the toaster and his cup on the Keurig ready to catch the stream of hot java. I passed him mid-hallway, gave him a little peck on the cheek. "Slide the lever on the toaster down and push the brew button on the Keurig. I won't be long. Set mine up and I'll join you shortly."

Sam looked at Watson. "I suppose you want me to fix your breakfast too."

Watson's tail went into a high-powered wag. "Well, boy, you're either real hungry or we're on our way outside for a walk around the house."

I took a quick shower, threw on a pair of dress jeans and a tan turtleneck, then finished it off with a navy, cream and tan scarf. I didn't have time to wash my hair, so I pulled it back in a ponytail. I checked the look out in the mirror. It was good.

Sam's breakfast was already on the table. He was taking my muffins out of the toaster.

"I'd follow that smell anywhere. You don't know what you're missing."

"I'll take my regular over that sissy French Vanilla any day." He snickered.

"Did you get the paper?"

"Yeah, it's on the counter."

"It's strange having the Tribune delivered. I always read it when I got to the office."

"Now you have to pay for one. That's what you get for quitting your job."

I tilted my head and looked at him out of the corner of my eyes. "Aren't we the little cocky one today."

"Just funnin' with you. You know I'm proud and, I might add, very supportive of your new occupation."

"I do. It would be dull if you weren't around. Speaking of being around—are you planning an extended stay in Hyannisport?"

"If the esteemed team of Sherlock and Watson will have me, I'd like to keep my shoes under the bed for a few days—maybe longer."

"I think that can be arranged." I reached over, took his hands, pulled him close and gave him a kiss. "I'll give you a call after I meet with Bella."

"Do you want to go out to eat tonight?"

"Let's see what time I finish. I want to go by my office to drop off the supplies I picked up yesterday and check my answering machine. Who knows, I might be in great demand. Maybe, I'll end up working on three or even five cases at the same time."

"OMG—I don't think I could stand it." Sam looked at his watch. "Hey, Sherlock, we're both going to be late if we don't get a move on."

"I'm ready," I got up from the table and carried our dishes to the sink.

Sam filled Watson's bowls with food and water. "Keep an eye on the place today. We'll see you tonight."

I blew the boy a kiss. "See you later, little buddy." I winked as though Watson knew what I was saying.

CHAPTER 17

At the end of my street, I took a left onto Route 28. Sam went straight toward the Mid-Cape. During tourist season I would have followed him to the highway, but this time of the year Route 28 was a straight shot to Falmouth.

I was anxious to sink my teeth into my new case. Sam dubbed it 'the fish market caper'.

The Dunkin Donut parking lot wasn't even half full. Morning coffee goers on their way to work had already come and gone and the baristas were ready for the next wave of coffee aficionados to come through the door.

Bella was seated at a table in the far corner facing the door. She waved when I walked in.

"I got a coffee, but waited for you before I got a donut."

"I've had breakfast, but there's no way I'm going to ignore the whisper of a soft, sugary jelly donut murmuring my name." I inhaled, trying not to ignore the calling. "What do you want?" I asked.

"Get yours then I'll get mine."

"I repeat—what do you want?" I smiled. "You can tell a lot about a person through their choice of donuts."

"Then I better get a Boston Cream—city wise, but mellow, with a touch of chocolate all in one bite. It brings out the sophisticated kid in me. If I got a boring old-fashioned, you might label me as an old maid librarian." Bella rolled her eyes. "I think, no I know, we're going to get along fine."

I laughed quietly. "I'll be right back." There weren't any customers before me, so I was just that—right back.

We settled in with our morning nourishment.

"How long do we have today?"

"Remember, I told you my job comes with privileges. I booked off for the rest of the day. They can reach me on my cell if something comes up. I figure we can go over to the fish market when we leave here. That way you'll have a visual to go along with my words." She took a bite of her donut and washed it down with a sip of coffee. "Did you bring your camera?"

"Never leave home without it. It's a true reporter's trusty side-kick. Do you ever watch *CSI* or *NCIS*?"

"I do."

"Close your eyes and visualize the white board where they hang the pictures. Then imagine them putting possible clues under the respective picture or pictures—be it a person, place or thing."

Bella's eyes were closed, but I could see movement on the lid as though she was trying to create her own white board.

"You can open them now. That was a simplified version of what I do behind closed doors."

"Keep in mind, any pictures you can't take, I might be able to furnish for you."

"That could be a strong possibility, but for now let's work with new info. Once I get that sorted, and if we need to, we can infuse it with old history." I knew Bella would agree. "There is one thing I want to talk to you about. Of course I'm going to need your help, but I also need you to stay in the background." I waited for her reply.

"I understand. I get excited knowing I'm going to get closure—for me, my brother and, most of all, for the memory of my Uncle Rocco."

"I say this to you because this kind of work can get dangerous. If you scrape too much moss away from the wrong side of the stone, a poisonous spider might crawl out."

Sam would cringe if he heard me now. It's my specialty to dig until I find the hole covered by the slimy moss, uncover it and let the scum crawl out, then kill it with the strongest insecticide available on the market—the law.

"Casey, you're quiet. What are you thinking about?"

I didn't want to share my mission tactics with my new client. "Just labeling the file folders in my head." I hoped my answer would satisfy her—at least for the time being. "I'll keep you informed on everything I'm working on, but you have to promise me you won't do anything on your own unless I've asked you to." I looked over my eyebrows at her and put on my 'I'm not kidding face'.

"I'll behave." She gave me a weak smile.

"It's for your own safety—and for that matter, mine too."

Bella took her last sip of coffee. Mine was already long gone.

"Well, we can't do anything sitting here. Let's go over to the market," I said as I gathered up my trash, stood up and pushed my chair in.

"I'm ready." Bella got up and followed me.

CHAPTER 18

"Do you want to leave your car in the library parking lot and ride with me?" Bella asked.

"Sure."

"Follow me. You can park in the back lot, then we'll head out the side entrance onto Shore Road, then turn left onto Main Street. It's on Davis Straights Road, on the left after Falmouth Heights Road."

I parked my little green Spider, gathered up my stuff, got out of my car and into Bella's cherry-red Jeep Cherokee. "Since I'm not real familiar with Falmouth, I'll let you be the GPS." I chuckled. "That is until you start saying *recalculating, recalculating ... make the next available u-turn*."

We both laughed.

It only took ten minutes to get to the fish market. Bella parked on the side of the building. We sat for a few minutes not saying anything. The sadness I'd seen before returned to Bella's eyes as they traveled back and forth several times across the Rocco's Fish Market sign. I imagined her pain.

"Here we are. Let's go inside."

I didn't answer. She unlocked the door, reached around the corner, flipped on the lights and went inside. I followed her. It didn't look like a closed business. It looked like Bella was coming in to open for the day. The chalk board still had prices written beside the different varieties of fish, lobster, clams and mussels that Uncle Rocco carried at the time of his death.

I didn't realize Bella was watching me read the board."

59

"Check out those lobster prices." She walked over to the counter and set her purse down. "Uncle Rocco hadn't changed them to reflect the change in the lobster shells."

I followed her lead and put my purse and briefcase beside hers, then turned to look at her. "Now I'm confused. The prices change because of their shells?"

She smiled. "I grew up in this business, so I forget the average person wouldn't have any idea what I'm talking about."

"I'm all ears—enlighten me."

"Well, in the summer months, usually July and August, lobsters shed their shells so they can grow. Underneath the old shells are new, soft shells. As the water gets colder, the soft shells will harden. The price per pound of a pound and a quarter lobster last October was $7.95. That was a soft shell price. There is less meat in a soft shell lobster. Once the lobster's shell hardens, there is more meat, therefore the price goes up. Some people say the meat from a soft shell lobster is sweeter and more tender. Maybe they're right. I don't really care; I love lobster any time of the year."

"I'm with you—lobster is lobster—hard or thin skinned or should I say shelled."

Bella smiled and walked over to the lobster tanks located at the end of the glass front display cabinets. "This is where they found Uncle Rocco."

There was obviously no water left in the tank, but there was an electrical cord partially coiled on the bottom. The other end of the cord was still plugged into the wall socket. "Is that the cord they claim electrocuted your uncle?"

"Yes. Don't get me wrong—he was electrocuted, but not by accident." Bella pointed to an electrical face plate about two feet above the tank. "That's where it was plugged in."

I stepped back to take in the big picture. "I can see the plug end of the cord was wrapped around that pole at the end of the tank." I tilted my head and studied the location of the face plate, then tried to determine approximately how long the cord was.

Bella didn't say a word.

"Why would somebody think a medium duty electrical cord, plugged into a regular wall face plate would, be able to break their fall? I realize it was wrapped around a pole several times, but that wouldn't make any difference. And, furthermore, even if Uncle Rocco grabbed onto the cord to catch himself from falling head first into the tank, I can't imagine how the cord would snap in half—exposing live wires."

"Now do you share my concern?"

I didn't give her a direct answer. "I've got a couple questions. I'm going to talk out loud. Stop me when you have answers or want to insert some information."

"Okay."

"Did the police find anything that might indicate Rocco had something in his other hand that would prevent him from grabbing onto the back of the tank?"

"If they did, they didn't mention it to me."

"You never did tell me who found your uncle." I felt stupid that I didn't ask the question earlier.

"We got on a roll, it slipped my mind. My brother, George, had been trying to call Uncle Rocco for a couple days. Rocco told George he was going to start cleaning up the market. He said there were some things he wanted to keep and a lot he wanted to get rid of. He also told him, he wanted to be alone. He knew he had to sell the business, but he wanted to do it when he was ready and not because somebody told him he had to."

"Did George and Rocco have words?"

"I think they may have had a discussion, if you know what I mean."

"I do."

"After a couple days of not talking to Uncle Rocco, George tried to reach him both at his house and at the market, but there was no answer either place. My brother became concerned and called the Falmouth PD. Since Uncle Rocco told George he would be spending time at the market, George asked the PD to send a cruiser to see if my uncle was there. The policeman who responded saw my uncle's pick-up parked behind the market, so he figured Uncle Rocco was inside. He knocked, then banged on the door, but nobody answered. The PD gave the patrolman George's cell number, so the officer called him. George gave him permission to break the lock and go in."

"So the police officer found your uncle in the tank?"

"Yes. He called for the EMT's and radioed the station. They sent out a couple more cruisers, then called my brother. I was the last to know. George called me after he got to the market. By the time I got there, the electricity to the tanks had been shut off and the EMT's had my uncle on a stretcher. He was dead. They conducted several tests and believed he'd been dead for a few days. Needless to say, the smell wasn't pleasant."

"Did you notice anything out of place?"

"I didn't notice anything at all. I saw my uncle on the stretcher and fell apart. George tried to comfort me, but his efforts were wasted. We lost our parents, my Aunt Rita and now my Uncle Rocco. I was a mess."

"What made you think it was anything other than an accident?"

"After a few days went by and I was able to compose myself, I tried to put things together in my mind. My uncle owned his business for almost fifty years. Before that he worked in another fish market in Bourne. I know he was unhappy about closing his business, but I also know he wasn't a careless man. He was very proud of his safety record. He knew what he was doing and the way the *accident* occurred wasn't how Uncle Rocco operated."

"Don't you think his thoughts could have been clouded? Maybe he was reminiscing about earlier, happier years when Rita was there by his side. Or maybe he wanted Rita by his side again and he did take his own life."

Bella snapped around to face me square on. "That's bull shit. He would never, and I repeat, never commit suicide."

"Okay, settle down. You hired me to find the truth. I have to look at the big picture. I have to look at things through your eyes, your brother's eyes, the police department's eyes, the ME's eyes and the eyes of all the people his life touched in the Town of Falmouth." I didn't break the focus she had on me. "You knew this was going to happen. Let me do my job—it's the only way I can get you an answer."

Bella moved away from the tank and sat in one of the chairs along the front wall. She buried her face in her hands and started to cry. In between sobs she said, "You're right. It's hard for me to think there might be the slightest chance he left us on purpose. I know you're doing your job. I'll be okay—bear with me." She swallowed hard, then took a tissue from her pocket and wiped the tears from her eyes.

"Bella, I'll get you answers. It will take some digging, but when I'm done you will know what happened." I walked over and put my arm around her. "You sit while I take pictures."

She put her elbow on the arm of the chair, laid her fingers over her cheek bone and rested her chin in the palm of her hand. "Okay."

I took pictures from one end of the market to the other and everywhere in between. I took more of the tanks from every angle possible—inside and out. I looked around for a surveillance camera, but there wasn't one. That would have made it too easy. My pictures were, of course, after the fact—long after the fact. I needed the pictures Falmouth PD took the day they found Rocco Deluca. Bella said nothing had been removed or changed since that day. I wanted to compare them. My eyes might pick up on something hers didn't. Things are far too familiar to her making it easy to overlook even the slightest change. It's like the *hocus focus* pictures in the Tribune lifestyle section. You can stare at two pictures that are almost exactly alike and not see the smallest change from one to the other.

"Casey," said Bella after about ten minutes of silence, "do you want to see the office and the storage room?"

"I do. Are you up for it?"

"I'm all right now. I want to help—not hinder." She got up and motioned for me to follow her through a door behind the glass display cases.

It was one-thirty when I finished taking pictures and making my preliminary notes. At this time, there wasn't any reason to stay longer.

"I'm hungry. Want to grab some lunch?"

"I could go for something myself. How about the Quarterdeck?" Bella made sure everything was put away and all the locks that were supposed to be locked were, before she followed Casey out of the office.

"I can taste the lobster salad on a Portuguese sweet roll with a cup of clam chowder as we speak." I licked my lips like a little kid who'd just taken a sloppy bite of ice cream.

"They have the best."

"I know. I've been there."

CHAPTER 19

The noontime diners had left, so we had our choice of tables. We moved to the front of the restaurant and took a two-seater by the window. I always like window tables, especially on a main road where someone like myself can enjoy people watching while eating. Some would call that nosey, but me, I call it being observant.

We ordered and made small talk while we waited for our food.

"See those four men sitting across the room from us?"

"I do. Who are they?"

"The guy with the longish blonde hair is the son of the family who own the marina on Falmouth Harbor. I went to high school with him. He was a football and baseball jock—had a girl for every day of the week. The older gentleman to his right is a lawyer in town. I think he's related to some of the town's founding fathers. The person across from him works in the Town Hall. He's the assistant to the Town Administrator. He's relatively new to Falmouth. I see his wife all the time at the library. They have two young children. She brings them into the library for programs and kid's circle readings. I think the oldest one starts first grade next year. I don't know the other guy. I've never seen him around."

The server brought our chowder. I opened the packet of oyster crackers, sprinkled them on top and let them take their warm cream and butter bath before I dug in. "Yum," I said, savoring my first bite. "Just as good as ever."

We were half-way through our chowder, when a thirtyish, well-dressed woman came up behind Bella and tapped her on the shoulder. She turned, got up from her chair and gave the woman a big hug.

"Casey, I want you to meet one of my best friends, Norma Sheridan. And Norma, please meet Casey Quinby. Norma and I have known each other since we came out of our mother's wombs." They laughed.

We reached out at the same time to shake hands.

"A friend of Bella's is a friend of mine," said Norma. "Are you new in town?"

"No, I live in Hyannisport," I didn't add anything else because I didn't know what Bella did or didn't want me to say.

"You're a long way from home."

"Not really. This time of the year it's only a hop, skip and a jump. Now in the summertime, that's a different story. You might never see me up this end."

"Don't blame you," she said.

"Why don't you pull up a chair and sit with us?" Bella slid her chair over to make room.

"I've already eaten, but don't have any place to go. I'll get a coffee." Norma signaled the server.

I wanted this time to talk to Bella about my next move. Obviously, that was going to have to wait.

"So Casey, what do you do?"

I nonchalantly turned to Bella for my answering instructions. Her eyes showed no sign of elevated emotion. I wondered how much Norma knew about Bella's suspicions regarding the death of Uncle Rocco.

"Up until a couple weeks ago, I was the head investigative reporter for the Cape Cod Tribune."

"And now—are you a lady of leisure?"

She might be Bella's best friend, but she was also a nosey busybody. Bella said Falmouth was a small town when it comes to gossip. She was right. The line of questioning didn't seem to bother Bella, so I answered her friend's question.

"No. I left the Tribune and hung my shingle. I'm a licensed private investigator." I waited for a response or another question.

"Is this a friendly lunch or am I interrupting a business conversation?"

"It's both," Bella said and left it at that.

The questions stopped.

Norma looked back towards me. "I can't remember the last time I was in your neck of the woods." Norma fixed her coffee with one Splenda and a dash of cream. "Actually I can. My husband and I went to see Frankie Valli and the Four Seasons at the Melody Tent last August. They were great."

"One of my favorite places to go. Big time entertainment in an inviting Cape Cod atmosphere—how can you go wrong?"

Our lobster rolls came.

We talked for another minute then Norma stood up. "It was nice to meet you. I'll let you girls enjoy your lunch. I've got to get back to the store and I've got a few errands to do first. Hope I see you again." She leaned over and gave Bella a kiss on the cheek. "Ciao."

They both laughed.

"Ciao," said Bella, and Norma was gone.

"What's with the *ciao*?"

"It's her big attempt at speaking Italian. When we were kids she'd come over my house—she'd hear my family talking in Italian. She pretended to understand. That's the operative word—pretended. Sometimes she'd reply with either a positive or negative shake of the head. My family would laugh because they knew she had no idea what they were saying. The word *ciao* became an inside joke between us." Bella smiled. "She's really a good person."

"Does she know your thoughts about your uncle's death?"

"She knows I don't think it was an accident, but she's never asked why and I haven't discussed it with her. As forward and nosey as she seems, I know she doesn't want to get mixed up in it. If she asked and I told her, then she'd feel involved." Bella leaned forward on the table. "Didn't you notice how she changed the subject after you told her you were a private investigator?"

"I did."

67

"She'll be curious, but she won't say anything in front of you. She might ask me later, but I'm not sure I'm going to tell her. She'll find out in due time."

"Speaking of people finding out," I said, "I have to go to the police station and the Medical Examiner's Office to see about getting copies of their respective reports and pictures pertaining to your uncle's death."

"I know you do. I'll probably get a call or two after your visits. Like I said—small town with inquisitive minds." Bella took a deep breath. "I'll deal with it when the time comes. You do what you have to do. And, if they have a problem with it, let me know and I'll see if I can change their minds."

"I'd rather you didn't have to do that. Remember when we talked in my office and I mentioned my friend Marnie—the girl that works at the DA's office? You know she helped me in the past, but I don't think I mentioned my other half, Sam Summers." I hoped this didn't create a cog in the wheel of progress. "He's the lead detective in the Bourne Police Department. He's been instrumental in introducing me to various PDs over the years. Most of the time it helps me break into the circle surrounding the inner sanctum at the various departments. He knows Chief Mills and has offered to give him a call on my behalf." I didn't mention the fact that Sam filled me in a little on the DeMarco family and practically ordered me to stay away from them.

I could envision an imaginary thought bubble forming over Bella's head. I knew she wanted to be involved, but she knew it was the wrong thing to do. That's why she hired me.

"Are you okay with Sam helping?"

"Yes. It always helps to have someone who can cut through red tape. The brotherhood of police officers is pretty tight."

"You've got that right. Chief Mills probably knows who I am only because of cases I've worked in the past. Some I've helped solve gave me an exclusive on the story for the Tribune. This one is different because it's classified as an accident. I'm sure he'll want to know why you think otherwise."

"He may ask you that, but I'm sure he knows why I think otherwise." Bella grew stern. "He hates the other half of my family as much as George and I do—and Uncle Rocco did."

"Before I pay him a visit, I want to get all my ducks in a row. I want to be armed with as much information as possible. I want to compile meaningful questions so he knows I mean business. Today is Wednesday. Give me a couple days to sort things out, then I'll give you a call and we can set up a time to get together." I was already running questions through my head. I wanted to get back to my office and start writing them down. "How does that sound?"

"That'll work. Let me get you back to your car so you can get on your way. I'm going to stop at the library to make sure Dewey is doing his job. Since I didn't get any calls, I'm sure things went smoothly without me." She smiled. "I'll soon find out."

"Am I supposed to know who Dewey is?"

"Librarian talk—the Dewey decimal system—ever heard of it?"

We both laughed.

"Library humor."

Bella pulled up beside my little green Spider that was waiting patiently for me to return and rescue him from the unfamiliar parking lot he'd occupied for the past six hours. I took my cell phone from my purse, then gathered my stuff and slid it into the back seat. Once I started back I'd give Sam a call to let him know I was heading back to Barnstable Village.

I walked over to Bella and gave her a hug. "You take care. If you think of anything you want to tell me write it down. If you need to get ahold of me, call me on my cell. I've always got that strange little beast with me." I laughed. "I feel we accomplished a lot. We've still got a long way to go, but we'll get there." I gave her my best positive look.

"I'm comfortable with you. I haven't felt that way for a very long time. I know you'll help me get the last chapter of Uncle Rocco's life right." She tried to smile, but couldn't stop the tears that formed in her eyes.

"Talk to you in a couple of days." I got into my car and pulled away.

I didn't want to say it, but when I get finished with this case, I'll probably be able to say 'hi' to a lot of residents and, at the same time, hide from others.

CHAPTER 20

I was about to hit number one on my speed dial when my cell rang. I checked the caller ID. It was Sam. "Mental telepathy—you beat me to the punch. I just finished with Bella and I'm on my way back to the Village. I thought I might stop by the house, pick up Watson and take him to my office for about an hour."

"I was calling to tell you I'm leaving in a few minutes, so you wouldn't have to hurry home. I should be there in a little more than a half hour. I can tend to the boy. I figure I'll walk him to the beach and let him run."

"I'm sure he'd like that. I want to check my messages and see if there's any mail I need to look at. I have to remember to have my calls forwarded when I leave during the day."

"Speaking of the day, did you have a productive one?"

"I did. We talked, then went to the fish market. I looked around, took lots of pictures and made notes. I'll print them up when I get to the office. It's going to be an interesting case. I think you'll agree. We finished with lunch at the Quarterdeck. It wasn't busy, so we took our time eating and talking."

"You can fill me in later. Do you still want to go out for supper?"

"Of course. How about Italian? We could go to DiParmas. I haven't had their manicotti in forever."

"I can handle that. Take your time. We'll plan on getting there around six-thirty. Does that sound okay to you?"

"It does."

"I'm going to head out. See you when you get home."

"Later," I said, then pushed the end button.

CHAPTER 21

I pulled into the driveway that led to the lot behind my office. There were two other cars parked there. Since I owned the parking lot, there shouldn't be cars there unless they had business with me or I gave them permission. I looked around before I got out of my car, but didn't see anyone milling about.

Must be some tourists walking around the Village—maybe checking out the gift shop or antique store a couple doors down.

I'll let it slide this time, but on the way home, I'll swing by Lowe's or Home Depot and pick up some private parking signs.

I unlocked the back door, went inside, locked it back up, then went to my office. The light on my answering machine was flashing and the caller ID indicated there were five messages waiting to be heard.

Before I got tied up with calls, I had to do a post office run. I slipped my purse into the bottom desk drawer and put my briefcase on the floor beside my chair. "Be right back," I said to my imaginary colleague. "I'll lock the door so nobody steals you."

There was a sizable amount of paperwork, annoying ads and a few pieces of real mail, stuffed in box number 329. I put it in somewhat of an order, then headed back to 4802 Main Street to sort it out. I unlocked my door and was ready to go inside when I heard my name being called from across the street.

"Casey." It was Marnie. She looked up and down Main Street, then crossed. "I'm on break. Want some company?"

"Come on in, girl. I'll put the coffee on." I grinned. "And, maybe, just maybe, I can find something in the cookie jar to satisfy your sweet tooth."

"I can't come in unless you move." She gave me a little nudge.

I pointed to my PI sign hanging from its bracket over my door. "And who's the boss here?"

"Somebody with the name Casey Quinby." She snickered. "Are you her?"

I shook my head. "By the time we finish with this little bouncing words contest, you won't have time for coffee." I opened the door and we went inside. "Why don't you start brewing while I put this stuff on my desk and get us some cookies."

"Sure enough, boss."

Before I knew it, the aroma of French Vanilla filled the air. I leaned against the counter and closed my eyes. "Ahhh," I said. My drug of choice was beginning to penetrate my inner being.

"Calm down girl. You're having one of your '*When Harry Met Sally*' moments again."

"I bought some sweet cream. Try it. It's good," I grabbed a couple napkins and the plate of Oreos. "I've got the sweets. Meet you at the desk."

One big happy family—those were Barney's words. The Village is one big happy family and I'm beginning to feel right at home.

CHAPTER 22

Marnie came in from my little backroom kitchen carrying our coffees and sat in one of the chairs in front of my desk. "I didn't take a lunch today, so I'm taking an extended break. Annie knows where I am if they need me." She lifted her mug to propose a toast. "To us ... to your new venture ... and to the team."

We both took a sip. "We toast to anything. And I love it."

"So, tell me about your day."

"A great start to a case that I believe is going to be very interesting."

"Interesting how?"

"I really can't answer that right now."

Marnie's face wrinkled up into a scowl. "You can't or you won't?"

"Don't get your dander up. If I could, I would." I took a deep breath, a bite of Oreo, a big mouthful of coffee and leaned back in my chair. "The object, as I see it, is to prove one way or the other that Uncle Rocco did or did not commit suicide. On the road to getting Bella the answer, I think—no, I know—I'm going to encounter a lot of speed bumps and potholes."

"You're dancing, Quinby." Marnie pulled her chair closer, rested her elbows on the desk and cradled her chin in the palms of her hands without ever taking her eyes off mine.

"No, Marnie, I'm not." I returned her stare. "There are a lot of paths leading in different directions, but all are related to Uncle Rocco. I think some of them are easy to follow, but others have red flags strategically placed warning trespassers of impending danger."

"Is it something that you saw today that gives you that impression?"

"Not really. Sam, my ever-valuable walking encyclopedia of danger spots and advice, filled me in a little regarding part of Uncle Rocco's family and Bella confirmed it."

"I'm getting the feeling that Sam isn't thrilled with your first case." Marnie gave me the tilted nod and over the eyebrows look.

I knew I was going to be under the microscope with both Sam and Marnie peering through the ocular lens and maneuvering the adjustment knobs to make sure I was following procedures. "He's okay with it, but did give me his usual pain-in-the-ass flashing of hands warning of danger spots along the way and told me to be careful." I hesitated, then continued, "I'm always careful—we both know that."

"Yeah, right." She stood up and started for the door. "I have to get back to work."

"Let me get my days work organized, my pictures printed and labeled, then I'll go over what I have with you within the next couple of days."

"Okay." Just as she got to the door, she stopped short. "Oh, by the way, one of the reasons I came over was to see what you guys are doing this weekend. Maloney is coming up Friday night and not leaving until Monday morning. He thought maybe we could get together and do some things—eating somewhere being one of them."

"As far as I know, Sam's staying until Monday and we don't have anything planned. So, I'm game for most anything. I'll talk to him tonight and give you a call."

Marnie nodded. "Later," she said as she walked out the door and back across the street to the DA's office.

I thumbed through the mail I had picked up at the post office. There were lots of senseless ads soliciting services to new businesses—most of them a total waste of money. If they did their homework before throwing away postage, they would have known I don't need a landscape service for a parking lot or a pool maintenance company or a free lunch to promote a membership in an all-male athletic club—although the third one could be interesting. The membership one could open up a discrimination suit. I folded it up, put it back into the envelope and filed it in my bottom drawer for future reference.

I glanced quickly at the rest of the mail. Nothing jumped out at me, but I put it in my top drawer. I'll examine it closer when I've got a few extra minutes.

I had plenty of time before I needed to head home, so I took the memory stick out of my camera, slipped it into the appropriate slot in my computer and printed out the pictures I took at the fish market. I also saved them in a cyber-folder entitled Rocco Deluca/pictures. I shuffled them around and numbered them in an order that made the most sense to me. Tonight, when I show them to Sam, I figure I'll label them, then tomorrow when I come in, I'll categorize and identify them on the computer.

I didn't want to forget to stop on the way home to get my no-parking signs. I glanced at my watch. It was four-fifteen—not enough time to enter my notes. Tomorrow morning is turning into a data input session. Somebody has to do it and since I don't have a secretary, looks like it's me.

I gathered my stuff, locked the front door, shut off the lights and started for the back. The flashing light on the telephone caught my eye. "Damn," I said not very quietly. I forgot to listen to my calls. I put my stuff down on one of the chairs by my desk, took a pen and paper from the top drawer and pressed the start message button. The first two were hang-ups. The third one was a wrong number and the fourth one was Marnie. Apparently, she called before she came over and left a message that she'd see me later.

There was a hesitation before the person who made the fifth call spoke. The caller ID read unknown. I almost hung up, then I heard a voice. I couldn't understand what the person was saying. It was garbled. I played it back five times—each time coming up with nothing. I turned the volume up and put it on speaker.

"Casey Quinby," the caller said in a gravelly, gruff voice.

I understood that much. I closed my eyes and tried to concentrate on the voice.

The caller blurted out, "Stay away ….. Falmouth," It was rehearsed. It could have been a male or female talking.

It was muffled and altered, but I was sure I understood the 'stay away' and 'Falmouth'. There were words in between, but I couldn't make them out. I know if I take the tape from my phone and give it to Sam, he could enhance it, then I'd know exactly what message the caller left. I wasn't ready to do that. In my mind, the message wasn't in the words, it was in the manner in which they were delivered.

Here we go.

I hated scare tactics—very amateurish. I wasn't about to let 'mumbles' sway my investigation. It meant I had to watch my back a little better.

I hung up, picked up my stuff and headed out the back door.

CHAPTER 23

Sam and Watson were crossing the front yard when I pulled into the driveway. I beeped and Watson came running.

"How's my boy?" Next thing I knew, I was on the ground trying to protect myself from an attack of sloppy, wet dog kisses. I rolled away and scurried to my feet before Watson had a chance to pin me down again.

Sam crossed his wrists and held them in front of his face to ward off the hazards of having to give me a welcome home kiss. "Yuck, dog germs."

"Go back to your Charlie Brown comics." I laughed and wiggled in under his elbows. "There's nothing more I want to do than share our boy's kisses with you." I rubbed my face against Sam's, then backed away, opened the passenger door and got my stuff.

Sam reached around behind me. "Hand me your briefcase."

I left the no-parking signs in the car, took my purse and followed Sam and Watson inside.

"I don't know about you, but I'm hungry. Let me wash my face, then I'll be ready to go." I looked at Sam. "That okay with you?"

"It is."

CHAPTER 24

The parking lot at DiParmas was about two thirds full—pretty good for an off-season, Wednesday night.

Ben was on the door and greeted us as we came in. "What's the occasion? I haven't seen you guys in forever." He looked at Sam. "I almost thought Casey took up cooking—but then I woke up."

Sam laughed. "I'd volunteer to do the dishes if ...."

"You better not even think about finishing that sentence." I gave them both the evil eye. "But, between friends, he's right. I'm not bad. It's just that I'm not good either. So before this conversation goes any further, I'm getting me a seat at the bar and ordering a glass of White Zin."

"With a side of ice?" asked Ben.

"Of course," I said. "Is there any other way to drink wine—especially the pink stuff?"

By the time we got settled in and before we could order a drink, a Coors in a frostie and a White Zin appeared."

"These are on Ben." The bartender smiled. She reached down and scooped up a glass of ice and sat it down in front of me. "Do you want menus?"

She must be new because we'd never seen her there before. "Yes please. I'll probably get the manicotti and sausage like I always do, but I'll take a look—just for drill."

She handed both of us a menu. "I'll be right back to take your order."

"Take your time. We're not in a hurry." Sam picked up his mug and took a drink.

"Do you want to order an app first?"

"Sure. Since we get salad with dinner, let's get an order of calamari instead of an antipasto."

"I can handle that. Did you catch the bartender's name?"

"Nope, but I'll ask her when she comes back. But, before she does come back, I'd like to propose a toast." Sam held his mug up.

I followed with my wine glass.

"I'd like to toast your third day on the job and the fact that you haven't gotten yourself into any trouble yet."

We clicked glasses.

"Cute—real cute!" I took a sip.

"So, how did your day go?"

Fortunately, there weren't many people at the bar and, better still, there were none to our immediate right or left. That way I could give Sam the rundown of the day's goings-on without having to look over my shoulder after every other word. "It was eventful. I like Bella. I think her concerns regarding her uncle's death may be justified. I don't think she's going in half-cocked. We talked about a lot of things. My initial plan is to get to know her, how she thinks, what she does after the library, her extracurricular activities and her family." Before I could go any further, the bartender came back to our side of the bar.

"What's your name?" Sam asked. "I don't want to yell 'hey you'."

She smiled. "I'm Gabby." She was silent for a minute, then added, "Don't ask. It's a nickname and, yes, I guess I got it for a reason." She motioned to one of the servers that her drinks were waiting at the pick-up station. "You guys want to order now?"

Sam nodded. "We'll start with an order of calamari and a couple more drinks."

"You've got it," she moved to the register to punch in our order.

Sam turned back to face me. "How much did Bella tell you about her family?"

"Her immediate family consists of a brother, George. He lives in Buzzards Bay. Her parents aren't living. She was very close to her Uncle Rocco and his wife, Rita. Now they're both gone. They had no kids. So, it's basically her and George. Didn't I tell you this before?"

"You may have, but I don't remember. Does George have a family?"

"Divorced, but no children." I thought about my own life. My parents—both gone. No brothers or sisters. I was the end of a short line in my family history. That's the tough thing about being an only child whose one parent was an only child and the other parent was the youngest in a very small family. That left me, and with no children, it might stop with me.

Sam rested his hand on mine. "Casey—hello—where are you?"

"I'm right here with my family, minus one," I said. "And until they start serving dog food at restaurants, looks like the minus one is the designated keeper of the house."

"What does Bella do for a living?"

"She's the Director at the Falmouth Library. Before that she worked in Boston. She mentioned which library, but I don't remember. I'd have to check my notes."

"I believe you told me George was an accountant."

"I did." I took another sip of wine. "After Rocco's wife died, he stepped in to help. Bella said when it came to the financial end of the business, her uncle didn't have a clue. She said that George was devastated when their uncle died. Both Bella and George don't believe it was a suicide. Where they differ is that Bella suspects foul play and George believes it was an accident."

"Does brother George know his sister is having a private investigator look into their uncle's death?"

"No, but he will soon enough because once I start asking questions around town, I'm sure he'll get a phone call."

Sam shook his head.

"You talked about the immediate family. What about the *extended* family?"

I knew this was coming and I hadn't had time to figure out what I was or wasn't going to share with Sam. I tried to dance around the question, but it didn't work.

"Well, are you going to answer me?"

"I am—after I figure out what I'm going to say."

Sam's hand came up and his finger came out—pointed in my direction. When he lets his finger help him emphasize his words, I know I'm in trouble. "You remember when you told me you did some research in the Tribune's computer archives and you brought up the DeMarco family?"

"I do."

"What did I tell you."

Out of the corner of my eye I saw Gabby heading in our direction with our order of calamari. "Saved by the squid," I turned to face the bar.

"You're not off the hook. We'll resume this conversation later."

"Here's your starter. I'll be right back with drinks." Gabby set the plate down, took our empty glasses and stepped to the other side of the bar.

"Do you know what you want for dinner? We might as well put in our order when she comes back." Sam dunked a piece of calamari in the marinara sauce and leaned over to give me the first bite. He followed it with a kiss.

"I could get used to this," I winked and kissed him back.

Ben came into the bar from the foyer. "Get a room," he whispered as he walked by.

"The room comes later." Sam smiled.

Gabby came back with our drinks and took our dinner orders. I got baked stuffed manicotti and Sam got lobster ravioli.

CHAPTER 25

We didn't linger at the restaurant.

We pulled into my dark driveway. "You've got to remember to turn the outside light on when you go out."

I pretended I didn't hear him. "I feel like I'm going to burst. Tomorrow night I'm cooking and you'll either eat it or starve."

"Stop trying to ignore me." Sam shook his head. "I'll take Watson for a walk around the house. I don't want anything else to drink."

"I'm having a coffee. You sure you don't want one?"

"Yes, I'm all set." Sam looked at Watson. "Let's go boy. I don't have much energy left in me."

I batted my eyelashes and in a flirty little voice, I whispered, "Save a little of that energy for me."

He didn't even turn around.

Well, so much for that.

I pushed the brew button and headed towards the kitchen table—aka my home office—and my waiting briefcase. I took the folder of notes and the envelope of pictures out and set them on my *desk*. I only printed one set, so until I make a second one, these were earmarked for the story board at my Village office. I had started to lay them out in the order I had them numbered, when Sam walked in.

"Hmmm. Coffee smells good. Can I change my mind? The nip in the air gave me a little boost of energy." He tossed Watson a few treats then sat down and started to study my pictures.

I fixed him a boring black coffee and sat down beside him.

He picked up the pictures one at a time—studying details in each one. He didn't say a word. Every once in a while, he took a sip of coffee. When he finished, he wrapped both hands around his cup and sat back in his chair.

"You did a great job of creating a panoramic scan of the fish market. I've been there many times. If I close my eyes, I'm there again."

"Thanks."

"I'll be interested to see the photos the PD and the ME's office took."

"Bella said that nothing had been moved since November first."

"Maybe she sees nothing moved because she doesn't want to. Comparing the two sets of pictures will confirm that to be true or not." Sam started to rock in his chair. "You've also got pictures of the back room and office area. I wonder if the PD also took shots of these areas?"

"Good question."

"If it were me, and I, along with my guys, were called to the scene, I would insist the whole place be reconstructed in a digital warehouse. Most of the shots might have nothing to do with the case, but, if you've scanned the whole area, you won't miss that one particular shot which might be the clue to solving the whole thing."

I wouldn't admit it, but I liked Sam's detective 101 class. After all, he's the seasoned detective and I'm the amateur sleuth turned PI. Any pointers I get are taken with more than a grain of salt.

"When are you planning on visiting Chief Mills?"

"Before I contact the Chief or the ME, I want to get my notes in order. I don't want to walk in unprepared. Tomorrow I plan on working at the office most of the day. I'm going to make a plan for each department. Some of it will overlap, but I want it to. That way I can compare answers. They should be the same—at least close." I finished my coffee and got up to put my cup in the sink.

Sam handed me his. "Because we're staying home tomorrow night, why don't we wait until then to go over your notes?"

"It's getting late and I want to watch the eleven o'clock news." I picked up my pictures and put them back into the envelope, then slipped it and the folder back into my briefcase. "Oh, before I forget. Marnie said Maloney is coming to Yarmouthport Friday night and not leaving until Monday morning. She wants to know if we want to do something. I told her I thought you were also staying through the weekend." I waited for Sam's reply.

"I planned on it. That is if my tenancy hasn't been terminated by then." He didn't give me time to answer before he jumped up from the table and planted a kiss—one that I didn't want to end—square on my lips.

I wish he answered all my questions that way. "I was supposed to call her tonight, but it's too late now. I'll give her a call in the morning." I shut the kitchen light off.

Sam was already in the living room. He turned the television on in time to hear NBC news anchor, Kim Khazei, open the broadcast with a heartbreaking story of a fatal accident involving a family and a drunk driver. It happened on Route 3, before the McArthur Boulevard exit.

"I wish the news would start with something positive for a change, but I don't think that will ever happen." Sam shook his head. "The public likes sensationalism. It's that sensationalism that captures viewers and boosts ratings."

"All the news teams do it. It affects you more because of your line of work. You live it."

"That's true, but for now I don't care to see any more." He reached over and took my hand. "Want to go to bed?"

"I'm right behind you."

CHAPTER 26

Thursday

Ever since the beginning of the month, when we set the clock ahead and lost an hours sleep due to daylight saving time, I've had a hard time getting up. The sun's rays that used to wake me weren't coming in my bedroom window any more. Now I have to rely solely on the irritating buzz of the digital monster staring at me from the bedside table.

I turned, expecting to find Sam still snoring his way through la-la land. Instead, his side of the bed was empty. I took note of the time. It was six o'clock. I got up and slipped my feet into my slippers. "Am I late for breakfast?" There was no response. I reached the bedroom door just as Sam and Watson came in through the outside kitchen door.

"Good morning, sunshine." Watson scurried across the floor to greet me. Sam stood smiling. "Oh, I forgot, sunshine isn't your favorite word at six in the morning."

"Good morning to you too. Besides, look outside—do you see any sunshine?" I reached down to pat the boy. "Good daddy. He's already taken you for your morning walk."

"You're right about the sun doubling as an alarm clock. In my opinion, they could do away with daylight savings. I'll take the sun any day."

"Give it a couple more weeks and you'll get used to it." I walked over to my Keurig. "Coffee?"

"Yeah and how about that package of cinnamon rolls with the cream cheese frosting you have in the fridge? I'd like to poke the doughboy in the belly a few times this morning."

"As long as you're not poking me," I said as I fixed Sam's coffee then reached down to get my Pyrex baking dish from the cabinet.

"What are your plans for today?"

I sat back in my chair and stared at him. "I told you last night that I was going to spend most of the day at the office working on a plan."

"It slipped my mind. You did say that."

"And you," I said. "What are you doing today?"

"I'm supposed to be setting up an in-service training syllabus for May. I'll probably start working on that. The sooner I get it done, the sooner I can stop listening to the Chief ask me for a copy of it. He knows I hate to deal with paperwork, unless it pertains to a case."

"How come Peggy isn't helping you?"

"She is, but I have to figure out the required classes needed this year, plus schedule time on the shooting range. After that, she puts it in order, types it out and makes the booklets for the attendees." Sam shrugged. "I got up early, showered and walked Watson. I'm going to head out."

"I'll call you later and rescue you from your boredom." I got up and gave him a hug.

"Is that all I get?" He smiled and gave me a kiss.

"Is that all I get?" I sarcastically repeated his question as I pulled him close and planted an *I want sex kiss* on his lips. "Now that's what I call a kiss."

He slapped me on the butt and sailed out the door before I could return the gesture.

CHAPTER 27

The same two cars were again parked in my back lot. Now I knew they weren't tourists, rather somebody who worked in the area and were too lazy to park in the public lot across the street and walk to their place of employment. I brought my newly purchased no-parking signs, my purse and my briefcase into my office. I took the signs out of the bag, then realized I didn't have a hammer or nails to attach them to the fence between the building and the parking spaces. At this point, my only recourse was to walk down to Nancy's to see if she could help me out.

The little bell on the door rang as I went in and, right on cue, Nancy came out from the kitchen and stood behind the counter. "Good morning, Casey," she said stepping from behind the counter to give me a hug. "I just took some sticky buns out of the oven—want one?"

"Nancy, Nancy, Nancy—what are you trying to do to me? Today, I only want a coffee, a hammer and a few nails."

She put her hands on her hips. "My sticky buns taste much better than nails." She laughed. "Wait here, I'll be right back." A minute later she came back carrying a small baggie half full of all size nails and a hammer. She handed them to me and poured a coffee to go.

I reached into my pants pocket to get some money.

The bell jingled and a couple of people came in. "Catch me later."

"Thanks," I said and walked out.

I put up my three no-parking signs—one in front of my car and the other two in front of the cars that were encroaching on my property.

My phone was ringing when I opened the back door. I dashed into the office, but the caller had hung up. I checked the caller ID. It read unknown. The caller left no message. The call on my message machine yesterday also read unknown.

Was this the same person?

I emptied my briefcase, set the photo envelope aside and opened the folder full of notes. I took a red hard-cover binder from my bottom drawer and set it aside. My first order of business was to type my handwritten notes into the computer by date starting from the day I opened Bella's envelope, the initial phone conversation, the first interview here at my office, then the trip to Falmouth. I just finished inputting the preliminary introduction when my phone rang. Again the ID read unknown.

"Good morning, Casey Quinby, Private Investigator."

"Hi, it's me." It was Marnie.

"Did you call me earlier?"

"Yeah, but there was no answer. I didn't leave a message cause I was going to give you another ten minutes and call back. I got tied up and lost track of time."

I took a deep breath.

"You okay?"

"Of course I am. Why wouldn't I be?"

"No reason. Anyway, I'm calling to see if you talked to Sam about doing something this weekend?"

"Yes and no. Yes, I asked him if he wanted to do something, then we got distracted and no we didn't discuss it any further. But, yes, we do want to do something with you guys. We didn't talk about the what. Have you got any ideas?"

Marnie laughed. "I'd love to see you plead a case in front of a judge. The yes, the no, the we, the I, the we did, the we didn't—you'd have him so confused, you'd probably win."

"Actually, last night it was 'the we' drank too much."

"Ah, now I understand."

"Good."

"Do you want to do lunch?"

"How about a salad or sandwich at Finn's?" I didn't want to take a lot of time and I really wasn't very hungry, but Finn's would be okay.

"I already asked Annie, but she has to take her car to have the oil changed. She said next time."

"I'll meet you there at ten minutes of twelve so we get there before the lunch crowd."

I heard Marnie's famous click.

I went back to my computer work. After a half hour, I stopped to take a break. I've never had a job where I had nobody to talk to. I wasn't used this. It was far too quiet. My next purchase was definitely a Bose radio and CD player. If I have time this afternoon, I'll stop at the Cape Cod Mall and run into Best Buy.

It was eleven-thirty when I finished copying my notes. I printed them, punched holes in the pages and put them into their binder. My first official case. If I was investigating a murder, it would be my first murder book, but since Uncle Rocco's death wasn't classified a murder, it's my first investigation book. My day planner was up to date—even had Marnie penciled in for lunch—and my desk was somewhat organized.

I felt pretty good about my life right about now. I owned my own building, just opened my own investigation agency, was working on my first case and things between Sam and me were great. What more could I ask for. My silent applause was interrupted when my phone rang. There it was again—unknown on the caller ID.

"Good afternoon, Casey Quinby speaking."

"It's still morning," said the altered voice from the other end.

I hesitated. "May I help you?"

"Got ya." It was Sam.

"I should hang up on you. Instead, I'll find other ways to make your life miserable."

"How's it going Miss Private Eye?"

"Good. I printed a second set of pictures, finished organizing my notes and started my investigation book. I'm getting ready to meet Marnie for lunch at Finn's."

"I'm jealous. Here I sit broken hearted, spent a dime and only …."

"Don't bother finishing it. I assume my Private Dick is bored."

"Bored, isn't the word for it," he said in a drawly voice. "This is nothing but tedious repetition. I don't know why they can't use the paperwork from last year. The subjects don't change and neither do the laws. But, I'm only half-a-boss and what the big boss wants, the big boss gets. I suppose I shouldn't complain, this is the calm before the storm. In another three months, I'll be bitching about being too busy."

"My man is never satisfied." I chuckled.

"I wouldn't say never." The spark was back in his voice.

"If you do it and get it done, you won't have to dwell on it longer than you need to."

"A logical statement coming from you—hmm, what happened to my Sherlock?"

"Be careful, your Sherlock is cooking dinner tonight—remember?" I laughed.

"Are you staying in the Village today or traveling?"

"I'm going to take a ride to Falmouth to talk to the Medical Examiner."

"Are you calling him first?"

"No, I'm going to appear on his doorstep and hope he'll see me."

"Do you want me to give him a heads-up call? He covers Bourne, so I know him well. It's up to you," said Sam.

"Not right now. If and when I need you to do that, I'll give you a call, but thanks for the offer. Why don't you go to Barney's for lunch. At least it will give you a break away from your desk."

"Not a bad idea," he said. "Talk to you later."

91

CHAPTER 28

Marnie was crossing the street as I came out my door. "Good timing."

"I'd say so." I pulled my office door shut and shook the handle to make sure it was locked.

The table by the window that we liked to sit at was empty, so the hostess motioned us to take it. The front of the dining room was quiet, but the back, nearer to the bar, was inhabited by a group of men mostly in suits. I didn't recognize any of them.

"Is there a big trial going on in Superior Court?" I asked.

Marnie turned to peruse the group of suits. "They resemble a bunch of lawyers—out of their element. They look more like big-city guys." She circled back to me. "If something is going on, I don't know about it. And, I'd say if the DA's office doesn't know, then it isn't happening in Super Court. Maybe it's a big divorce or probate matter?" She shrugged. "Then again, maybe it has nothing to do with the County Court Complex. Let's mind our own business and eat. Remember, curiosity killed the cat and food brought it back."

I laughed. "I like your version better than the real one."

We weren't sitting long before the server came to take our order.

I spoke first. "I'll have a tuna melt with Havarti dill on wheat. I shouldn't have the fries, but I'm going to."

"And to drink?" she asked.

"Oh yeah, a Diet Coke, please."

"I'll also have a Diet Coke, except I want a crab melt on wheat, same kind of cheese.

"Fries?"

"Oh sure, why not." Marnie smiled. "We can get fat together."

The servers smiled. "I'll put this in and be right back with your drinks."

Marnie leaned forward on her elbows. "So what's your morning been like?"

"I was in an organizational mood, now that I've got all my notes and pictures in order, I'm ready to roll." I looked around to make sure we didn't have an audience. "I'm going make a quick trip to Falmouth this afternoon. Hopefully, I can talk to the ME."

"Do you think you should call him first?"

"I debated whether to or not. I don't really know him. I was in his company on a few occasions, but I don't know if he'll remember me. His name is Derek Jenkins. The first time I met him was six years ago at a dinner that had something to do with the Figawi."

"You can stop right there." Marnie wrinkled up her nose. "Explain please—what the hell is the Fugouie—or whatever you called it?"

I laughed. "It's spelled F I G A W I and pronounced FIG-OW-EE."

"Okay, what is this FIG-OW-EE?"

"It's a pursuit style sailing race that goes from Hyannis to Nantucket—the Northeast's first major regatta to kick off the summer sailing season."

"How come I didn't hear about this before?"

"I don't know. When the information comes out, maybe we can get tickets to the Figawi Ball and join in the festivities."

"I'm not going to ask any more. I'll let you take care of it."

Our food came. "Let's eat."

"Getting back to the Upper Cape Medical Examiner, I guess you're going to renew your acquaintance in person."

"I am. Sometimes eye contact works better—sometimes it doesn't, but that's a chance I'm going to take. Sam knows him. He said he'd give Derek a call, but I said not to."

"Why?"

"I want to try it on my own first. Sam knows a lot of people. If I really get stumped and can't get to first base, then I'll ask him." I waited for Marnie to respond.

"I understand. You know if there's anything I can do, I'm right here for you."

"I know that." I finished my Diet Coke. "Do you want to split a dessert?"

"A whole one, no, but a half—I can handle that." She got the server's attention. "What do you want?"

"How about a piece of warm apple pie with vanilla ice cream."

"You're bad—real bad." Marnie ordered.

"Do you ladies want another Diet?"

"Yes, please."

Marnie took the first bite. "This is deliciously evil."

We giggled like school kids.

CHAPTER 29

I felt more like taking a nap than driving to Falmouth, but duty called. I collected my stuff and left out the back door of my office. My little green Spider was the only car in the lot. My no-parking signs worked—at least for now.

The Medical Examiner's office was next door to the Falmouth Hospital, so it was easy to find. There were a couple cars in the lot. I hoped one of them belonged to Derek Jenkins.

The door to the reception area was open, so I went in. Nobody was at the desk. I sat in one of the five chairs in the mini-waiting room expecting to see a person come through the closed inside door. I checked my watch. Ten minutes had passed and nobody showed up. I waited another five, then got up and knocked on the inside door. There was no answer, so I tried the knob. It was locked. I knocked one more time. I knocked so hard, I hurt my knuckles. Nobody answered.

I was about to exit the building, when I heard a quiet, immature voice ask, "Can I help you?"

I turned to see a lady who appeared to be at least in her mid-fifties standing in the open doorway leading to the back of the building. Her outward appearance didn't match her girlish-sounding pipe organs.

I stumbled on my words. "Um, I was wondering if I might be able to talk to Mr. Jenkins?" I felt like a fool. She took me by surprise. My level of professionalism flew out the window.

"Who are you and why do you want to speak to Mr. Jenkins?"

I composed myself. "My name is Casey Quinby." I handed her one of my cards. "I'm a private investigator looking into the death of Rocco Deluca." I had no intentions of telling her any more. My next conversation was with Mr. Jenkins or I was out the door and on the phone to Sam.

"I'll be right back," she said staunchly.

"I'll be right back," I waggled my head and quietly repeated her little grammatical statement. I glanced over to what I presumed to be her desk and mentally jotted down the name engraved on the brass plate—Winnie Parks. The next time I talk to Bella, I'll ask if she knows the delightful Miss Winnie. In fact, I think I'll give Bella a call on my way home to let her know I've made my first Falmouth inquisition regarding the case. I don't want her to get blind-sided. Besides, I told her I'd keep her informed and that's what I intend to do.

A couple minutes passed before Miss Winnie returned. "Mr. Jenkins said he has to leave early today, but can give you a few minutes." Without saying anything else, she turned and started down a small corridor.

I assumed I was supposed to follow, so I did. I recognized Derek Jenkins the minute we walked into his office. He motioned for me to take a seat in the chair in front of his desk. Miss Winnie stood beside the desk. There was no way I was about to talk to the ME with his receptionist, secretary or whatever she was listening to my spiel.

I think he sensed this. "Winnie, I can take it from here."

She looked at me, turned and left without closing the door.

Derek got up from his desk, walked over to the door and closed it, then extended his hand to welcome me. "She can be a little over-protective at times."

He picked up my card. "Casey Quinby. Your name is familiar. How do I know you?"

"The first time I met you was at the Figawi Ball five years ago. At the time, I was the head investigative reporter for the Tribune. The paper bought a table and my boss, Chuck Young, invited me and several other employees to go."

"Good old Chuck. How is he? We went to high school together. Great guy."

"I agree. I left the Tribune a couple months ago, bought a small office building in Barnstable Village across from the DA's office and hung my shingle over the door—Casey Quinby, Private Investigator." I stopped talking and waited for him to respond.

He didn't. He looked back at my card.

I was sure his reading skills were more than that of a first grader, so when he didn't speak, I did. "For the last ten years, along with working at the Tribune, I worked with many of the Cape police departments, helping them with cold cases and some current cases. I've never worked with the Falmouth PD or, obviously, your office, so this is new territory to me. My last case was with the Barnstable PD. It was a ten year old cold case. New evidence was uncovered and with the help of Ernie Mullins, the Mid-Cape ME, we were able to solve it."

"I know Ernie well. Very respected man in the field."

I nodded.

"Winnie told me you wanted to talk about Rocco Deluca's death." He leaned forward on his desk. "That was neither a cold or current case. It was a tragic accident. He was electrocuted while doing some work on his lobster tanks."

"That's what I'm sure I'm going to find on the police reports. I have no reason not to believe electrocution was the cause of death." I leaned forward and looked straight at Jenkins. "I've been retained to retrace the events leading up to and the day of Mr. Deluca's death."

"I'm confused. The police did a complete investigation. What do you think you'll find that they didn't."

"I don't know—maybe nothing—maybe something. That remains to be seen." It was time to ask. "Mr. Jenkins ..."

"Please call me Derek."

"Okay, Derek, I'd like to see your file on Rocco Deluca."

Derek changed his position. He leaned back, folded his arms over his chest and rocked back and forth. "I don't know if that's possible."

97

"Why's that?" I asked. "It's a closed case. I use that word loosely. Maybe I should say a closed file. It wasn't part of a murder investigation, so you wouldn't be divulging anything that was only privy to the police department."

"The family might object."

I debated whether or not to tell him I was retained by Bella. "You've got a point there. So that would be your biggest concern—the family might object to you sharing your medical information with me?"

"Basically, yes."

"Well, then—we don't have a problem. Isabella Deluca is the person who retained me to look into her uncle's death." I kept eye contact and raised my eyebrows to elicit a response.

Derek rolled his eyes and looked at the ceiling. "Can you give me a day to get it together?"

"If you want to check with Isabella, why don't we call her right now? I have her cell phone number and I'm sure she won't mind if we call." I paused to give him a couple minutes to think. "You're my first stop in Falmouth. I was hoping we wouldn't have this problem. If you want to check my credentials we can give a mutual friend a call." I didn't want to do it, but I needed to get that file.

"Who might that be?"

"Sam Summers, the lead detective in Bourne."

"I do know Sam."

"I happen to know he's at the station this afternoon and I'm sure he wouldn't mind if you called him. I understand you've worked lots of cases together. He holds you in high esteem."

"Casey, you have to understand my position. I'm not trying to give you a hard time, but I don't know you. You waltz in and ask for a copy of one of my files. It's not just a random file, but that of Rocco Deluca. He was a pillar of this community and is sadly missed. I do believe you, but I have to cover my butt. Let me give Sam a call." Derek took what appeared to be a directory from his top drawer, flipped it open to the B's and dialed the number for the Bourne Police Department.

"Detective Summers, please."

I forgot Sam was going to go out to lunch. *Please be back, please be back.* I repeated over and over in my mind.

"Hi Sam, this is Derek Jenkins."

I couldn't hear the conversation on the other end, but Sam knew I was planning on paying Mr. Jenkins a visit.

"I have a Casey Quinby sitting in my office." He nodded toward me as he spoke. "She gave you as a reference."

I wish I could hear what Sam was saying.

"Yes, she's asking for a copy of the Rocco Deluca file regarding his accidental death."

Come on, Sam. Convince him to give it to me.

Derek took a deep breath. "If you say so. Yes, I know. Alright, I'll have Winnie make her a copy. Please keep me informed."

I wanted to gloat, but refrained myself.

"You heard me. I'm going to give you a copy. I asked Sam to keep me informed, but I'm also asking you to keep me informed. If you have any questions regarding my reports or if you find anything of interest that I should know about, please contact me."

"I will. Nothing may come of my investigation, but Isabella seems to think it needs to be re-addressed." I thought for a minute. "Derek, I have to ask you a favor."

"What's that?"

"I need you to keep this visit to yourself for the time being. I'd appreciate it if you'd relay that to Winnie too. I'm not going over to the police department today. I know I'll have to make an appointment to see Chief Mills. I'm going to need copies of their reports as well. Again, that shouldn't be a problem because Rocco's death was deemed an accident."

"Let me call Winnie and have her start making copies." He picked up his phone and pushed the number two button. He explained what he needed and hung up. "She said it would take her a few minutes to get them out of archives, then run them through the copy machine."

"I really appreciate this." I felt relieved. Now I could scrutinize the first official report filed in the Rocco Deluca accidental death case.

Less than five minutes later, Winnie knocked on the door. This time she was much more friendly. She handed the folder to Derek.

"Thanks Winnie."

She left and closed the door behind her.

He thumbed through the reports. "They're all here." He handed them to me. "Keep me in the loop."

"I will and remember, mums the word."

We stood up at the same time.

"I'll walk you to the door."

We got to the front office. "Thanks, Derek and thanks, Winnie," I left and quickly walked to my car.

I'm sure Sam's waiting for a phone call, but he'll have to wait a little longer. Dunkin's and my French Vanilla were my first priority, then to Stop and Shop to pick up something for supper. It won't hurt to keep him wondering if I got what I needed from his buddy.

CHAPTER 30

Steak, Kelli potatoes and onions on the grill along with a fresh tossed salad—that should cover the unsaid thank-you to my man. I checked out and headed to Hyannisport. I had forwarded my calls to my cell, so there was no need to make a pit-stop at my office.

Watson was waiting patiently for me, or Sam, whoever got home first to take him out. There was plenty of time for a walk longer than just around the house. I scooped up a handful of treats and off we went. Today went well. I accomplished what I set out to do. I felt good. In fact, I felt so good, I unconsciously broke into a slight jog. Watson followed my lead. Before I knew it, we were at the beach.

"You've got ten minutes to play with your bird friends, then we have to get home so I can start supper." I unhooked his leash and, without hesitation, he was off. I sat on the sea wall and vegged out. I sucked in the salt air and basked in the sun trying to ready my head for my next move in my plan of operation. Once I dissected the Medical Examiner's report, I need copies of the police reports. Hopefully, I'll be able to marry the two and come up with some answers. I leaned forward, rested my forearms on my knees and stared into the sand. The opening lines of an old soap opera popped into my head—*like sands through the hour-glass, so are the days of our lives.*

I whistled and clapped my hands for Watson. He came running. I hooked him up and we walked back home.

CHAPTER 31

The potatoes and onions were already on the grill, sizzling inside their aluminum foil jackets, I was putting the finishing touches on the salad when Sam walked through the kitchen door.

I gave him a little smile and a big kiss. "Hi."

"Is that all—just hi?"

"Oh, did you want to know what happened today at Derek Jenkin's office?"

"Don't be a smart ass, of course I want to know what happened." Sam reached over my shoulder and took a piece of cucumber. "Did he give you a copy of his report?"

"He did and thank-you."

"How come you didn't call me after you left his office?"

"You were busy and I didn't want to disturb you."

"You know if you keep this little charade up, you could be eating alone."

I spun around. "I'm very grateful for your help, but I have to find a way to do these things on my own."

"And you will. Remember, you opened your door on Monday. It takes time. When I first went on the job, I was like you. I was going to do everything on my own. It doesn't happen that way. You have to accept help, then take that help and mold it into your own modus operandi." He gave me a hug. "When you first started working at the paper, I'm sure you relied on advice from a few of the seasoned reporters. You used that advice to become the head honcho." He took another cucumber. "Do you understand what I'm saying to you?"

"I'm sorry." My eyes started to water. "I do understand."

"No need to cry over it."

"I'm not. It's the onion."

We laughed.

"Do you want me to pour you a glass of White Zin?"

"Only if you're drinking with me."

"Of course. There's a frostie calling my name."

"Where's the copy of the ME's file?'

"I figure we'll take a look at it over dessert. I don't expect to find much in the report. I'm hoping we'll find something when we compare Derek's pictures with the ones I took. I used to love to do the picture puzzles in the Tribune. You'd think it would be simple to compare two pictures that on first glance are exactly alike. The more you stare at them the harder it is to see the slightest difference that makes them dissimilar. When I was with Bella yesterday I imagined her looking at the *hocus focus* pictures. That's what they call them. Have you ever tried to do them?"

"You're not going to believe it, but I use picture puzzles like those in the academy when I teach the class about report writing. The new recruits learn the importance of recognizing details and recording them properly. You'd be surprised how many mistakes are made. It's those mistakes that can sometimes make or break a case."

I looked at the clock. "I'll be right back, I'm going to check the potatoes and onions."

Sam got the drinks ready and started to set the table.

"They're ready. If you take care of the steaks, I'll finish the table." I handed him a fork and the plate of meat.

"Chef Sam at your disposal, madam."

"Oh, please. Just do it." I flicked his butt as he walked out the door.

"I'll give you an hour to stop that."

CHAPTER 32

"You outdid yourself. What did you call these potatoes?"

"Kelli potatoes. A friend of mine's daughter makes them. Her name is Kelli. I make a slit, stuff it with butter, sprinkle garlic powder and voila."

"Let's get this cleaned up, then get to work." Sam handed me the dishes.

"You might think this is a case you're working on," I started to fill the dishwasher.

"I'd like to think I'm a contributor."

"A contributor?"

"Maybe a collaborator or a teammate is a better word."

"As long as I don't have to put you on the payroll, you can think what you want."

"I'll let you be creative with however you want to pay me."

"Shut-up and make us some coffee." I wiped the table off and set my briefcase on the spare chair. The ME's report folder was on top, so I took it out first. His envelope of pictures was next, then mine.

Sam brought our coffees over and sat down. "I'd like to look at the pictures first."

I laid Derek's out and mine beside them. Since the ME didn't have any pictures of the back room and office, I put the ones I had of those areas aside. The only pictures we both had were those of the lobster tanks. Surprisingly, we had several taken from the exact same angle. Mine, of course, were minus a body.

He picked up the ME's picture that was taken facing the tank, then picked up mine. The only difference, besides the body, was that mine was taken a little closer. Sam pulled his lips in between his teeth and moved his head in an up and down motion. "Shouldn't there be one like this, only with part of a body showing?" he asked.

I thumbed through the pile. "Got it." I held it up beside the two Sam was holding. "The only thing you can see is a shod foot. Looks like it's caught up on the side like a hook. He must not have fallen all the way in." I set the picture I was holding down on the table and started to look for more showing the entire body. "Here's the full body shot." I handed Sam the picture looking down into the tank showing Rocco in his final position flanked by two lobsters. "Obviously, the two lobsters still residing in the tank met their maker the same way Rocco did. I want to put these in some order so we can compare them."

"The PD should have similar pictures." He went to the cookie cabinet and got us some Oreos while I arranged the working patchwork of stills. "I know accidents happen, but Rocco Deluca wasn't the new kid on the block when it came to working on his tanks. He's cleaned them thousands of times and, I'm assuming had never had a serious accident before."

I made a note to ask Bella about that.

"You may have a point there," he said.

"Also, there's a small ladder in front of the tank—looks like maybe a four footer. If he lost his balance and started to fall, don't you think his leg motion would have moved the ladder enough to knock it over or at least away from the tank?"

"It's possible," said Sam.

"Picture this," I said. "Rocco was standing on the next to last rung—so that would be about three feet up. Judging from where the ladder was, he couldn't reach the back corner of the tank, so he put his left foot into the tank, kept his right foot on the ladder for support, leaned forward and tried to brace himself with his left hand. They said there was a small amount of water in the bottom. He could have slipped and, with his right hand, tried to grab onto something to stop himself from diving head first into the tank. Supposedly, he grabbed the electrical cord that was partially wrapped around a pole at the end of the tank and plugged into a live wall socket." I pointed to a picture that showed the cord in question. "That's how he got electrocuted."

"If all you had to go on was the ME's reports and pictures, then Derek Jenkin's finding for cause of death as accidental was justified. You need to get the police department reports and pictures before you go any further." Sam was quiet.

"Tomorrow morning I'll give Chief Mills' office a call." I looked at Sam. I held my hand up like a school crossing guard stopping traffic. "No, I don't want you to call him first."

"I didn't say a word."

"You didn't have to. I should have stopped at the station today while I was in Falmouth—at least to make an appointment. Hopefully tomorrow I'll get lucky."

"There's no need of going over the ME's reports or looking at the pictures again tonight. If you can clear your head for a couple hours, we can have a good-night drink and watch some television."

"I think I can do that." I knew Sam was right. I neatly tucked the paperwork away, but Uncle Rocco was still very much awake. He tapped an imaginary beat in my head as if to say, *there's no time for sleep—no time for sleep.*

CHAPTER 33

Friday

I wasn't sure how I would be received by Chief Mills, but there was no way around it. I looked up the telephone number for the Falmouth Police Department. "Here goes."

They picked up on the second ring. "Falmouth Police Department—how may I direct your call?"

"Chief Mills' office, please."

"Who's calling?"

"Casey Quinby." I didn't feel the need to say more.

The line went silent for a couple seconds, then a soft spoken female voice answered. "Good morning, Chief Mills' office, Monica speaking."

"Hi, Monica, my name is Casey Quinby. I'm a private investigator from Barnstable Village. I've been retained to look into the death of Rocco Deluca." I hesitated, then continued, "If possible, I'd like to meet with Chief Mills sometime today regarding my client's concerns."

Monica was quiet. I crossed my fingers.

Finally she spoke. "If you'll hold on, I'll check with the Chief."

I took a deep breath. I'm halfway to first base—now, if only, I'm not thrown out. The minute wait felt like an hour.

I heard a connection click. "Miss Quinby, this is Chief Mills. I figured I'd be getting a phone call, but not this quick."

Why did he expect a call? I asked Sam not to call him.

"News travels fast, I guess. I'm going to be in the Falmouth area today and wondered if I could stop by to introduce myself." I didn't want to say too much over the phone.

"I'll be in meetings all afternoon, but I do have some time this morning."

This was too easy. Sam must have called him. I'm sure I'll solve that mystery at our meeting. "I can be there by ten."

"That works. I'll have Monica alert the front desk. They'll have somebody escort you in. See you in about an hour."

"Thank you." The connection ended.

I was ready to leave as soon as I hung up. Watson had been walked, fed and given his instructions to guard the home front. I gave him a playful head tussle and an affectionate hug, then headed out the door.

I'd driven by, but never been inside the Falmouth PD. The parking lot wasn't crowded so it was easy to find a space near the front door. I got out of my car, lifted the strap from my new cross body purse over my head and retrieved my briefcase from the passenger seat. A man leaving the building held the door for me.

The information window was located toward the back of the lobby. I waited for the two people ahead of me to finish their business, then stepped up to the opening in the bullet proof glass. "Hi. My name is Casey Quinby. I have a meeting with Chief Mills this morning."

The officer behind the desk checked his log. He nodded. "Hold on for a minute and I'll get someone to escort you to the Chief's office."

"Thank you." I backed away from the window.

The door leading to the secure reception area opened and a female officer motioned me in. She extended her hand to me. "Hi, I'm Officer Bigelow. Please follow me." A pleasant smile, a friendly voice, but a girl of few words.

I was okay with that. I was afraid that someone might get inquisitive and ask questions. She didn't.

Officer Bigelow delivered me to a waiting Monica. We reached out at the same time to shake hands and collided in mid-motion. "This isn't the first time that's happened." She laughed.

"And, I'm sure won't be the last," I added.

"Have a seat and I'll let the Chief know you're here." She started down the hallway to the right of her desk and disappeared into an open doorway, two down on the left.

I assumed it was Chief Mills' office.

Two minutes later, she reappeared and knocked on a closed door across from the one she had entered earlier. She was only inside long enough to deliver the four word sentence I could hear from where I sat. "Casey Quinby is here."

I was a little puzzled, but shrugged it off.

"The Chief will see you now. He was on the phone before, so I went into the break room and put on a fresh pot of coffee. Chief Mills loves his java. How about you—will you join him?"

A guy after my own heart. "Yes, I'd love it to—cream only. Thanks."

She extended her arm and motioned for me to join the Chief.

I did.

There was a chair strategically placed across from the Chief, in front of a clearing on the desk. I assumed this was my writing space. I had to be straight forward with him. In order for me to have a productive meeting, I needed to know who gave him the heads-up and what information was relayed in that call.

After all the formalities were over, I sat down and got right to the point. "Chief Mills, I appreciate the opportunity to meet with you on such short notice. However, you indicated that you were expecting a call from me. My client fully anticipates that the possibility of her claims could," I hesitated then continued, "open up a can of worms. I've told her I'd keep her informed on everything I investigate. I intend to be honest with her. She may or may not like the outcome."

"I understand." The Chief moved forward and rested his arms on his desk.

"I need to be a recipient of that same trust." I looked straight at him. "I'm sure the Town of Falmouth will be concerned when the nature of my investigation is made public. I probably won't be the most popular girl on the block, but that's the nature of my business, so here I am."

Chief Mills picked up his phone and buzzed Monica. "Could you please bring us a coffee?" He sat back in his chair and casually rubbed his chin. "That was the long way around the question of how did I know you were going to call me." He smiled.

I lifted my arms in the air. "You hit the nail on the head. Okay. Who told you I was going to call?"

Monica brought us coffee and a plate of, what looked like, homemade chocolate-chip cookies. We thanked her and she returned to her post.

He took a sip. "Derek Jenkins's secretary, Winnie."

I put my coffee down, leaned forward and looked at him over my eyebrows. "You've got to be kidding me." I was pissed. I didn't know the relationship between the Chief and Winnie, but at this moment I didn't care. I knew she was a nosey, busy-body, but bit my tongue before I let my true feelings roll out. He knew I was mad.

"Now that we've established the fact that nothing is sacred, let's get to the point of your visit. I heard what Winnie wanted me to hear. Now, I want to hear the real story. The sooner we address it, the sooner we can either put it to bed or work together to examine it. I want you to know, Rocco Deluca was one of my best friends. If his death was anything other than an accident, we will, and I emphasize will, find out and see that justice prevails."

I wanted to get up and hug the Chief. But, most of all I wanted to tell Sam I was sorry, even though he had no idea I blamed him for informing the Chief of my impending call.

"Like I said, I don't have anything on the books for this morning. I'm all yours. Let's start from the beginning. Tell me how you got involved, your ideas and what you need from me."

I noted the concern on his face.

CHAPTER 34

"Last Monday morning, when I arrived at my office, there was an envelope wedged in the front door." I saw no reason to tell him Marnie found the envelope before I got there. "Just a little history—Monday was the first day of business for Casey Quinby, Private Investigator."

"I know that. I did my homework and a little checking. I called the Barnstable PD and talked to Chief Lowe. You got a glowing recommendation. I consider Chief Lowe a mentor and value his opinions." Chief Mills smiled. "Enough of that—let's get back to business."

I felt good. "The envelope contained a letter from Isabella Deluca, a copy of an obituary and pictures. I have it with me." I reached down, opened my briefcase and took out Bella's envelope. "Here's the letter." I slid it across the desk.

He read it to himself, then put it aside. "Can I see the pictures?"

"Sure. Here are the pictures and the copy of the obituary."

"If I close my eyes, I'm back in November, reading the obit for the first time—so sad, so sad."

"I met with Bella on Tuesday morning. She came to my office."

"I haven't seen her since the funeral. I haven't seen her brother, George, either—but then he lives in Buzzards Bay. I know it's not far, but he's got no reason to come back to Falmouth, except to see his sister. I used to see him sometimes on the weekends. He'd help Rocco at the market."

"Bella said that ever since her Aunt Rita died, George helped Rocco with the financial end of the business."

"Rocco and Rita were like Bella and George's second set of parents. When their mother and father died, the uncle and aunt were right there to step in. They were very close."

"I got that feeling when I talked to Bella."

"They did, or should I say do, have other family in town, but they don't speak to them. It's the DeMarco family. Have you ever heard of them?"

This was the subject Sam told me to stay clear of, but since I didn't bring it up I opted to pursue it—just a little. The background information might trigger something later on that could be helpful in my investigation. "I have heard of them." I left it at that, hoping the Chief would continue to fill me in.

"Since I know the confidentiality factor is very important to you, I trust this conversation won't leave my office."

"It will not. I promise you that."

"You'd never know the Delucas and the DeMarcos were related. They were like the Hatfields and McCoys."

Please keep going.

He did. "Rocco's sister, Maria, was married to Sid DeMarco. Maria went missing. She left to visit her cousin in Boston and was never seen or heard from again. Rocco believed Sid had something to do with her disappearance. We investigated, but came up with nothing—all dead ends. And, none of the clues tied anything together. I felt, at the time and still do, most of the clues were fabricated to lead us away from what really happened, but I couldn't prove it." He shook his head. "I believe Sid was involved in Maria's disappearance. And, I'm not the only one."

"Do you still have the case on the books?"

"No, it's been reclassified as a cold case."

"My specialty," I said as I glanced at my shoulder from the corner of my eye. I imagined Sam sitting there, tapping his foot, arms folded and sporting his *I'm not happy with you right now* look.

"I'm going to have another coffee. What about you?" He didn't wait for me to answer and buzzed Monica. "Could we please have two more cups of joe?"

"Thanks. Coffee is my drug of choice. It's how I get through the day."

"I won't get into the DeMarco family any more at this time, but watch your back. They're a nasty bunch—not to be trusted. Besides, Sid died about a year before Rocco, so that would eliminate him as a suspect."

It might eliminate him, but not his sons.

Monica knocked on the door and came in with our coffee. "Chief, remember you've got a one-thirty meeting at town hall."

"I know. Thanks."

"You said you believe that Sid was involved in Maria's disappearance. Could it be that he was the master mind, but not the actual perpetrator? Could it be that Rocco uncovered new information naming one or more accomplices? Maybe he was fixing to go public or gather enough new evidence to ask you to reopen the case."

"That's a possibility." The Chief got up from his desk and walked over to the window. "He was a stubborn man. Maria's disappearance consumed his life, especially after Rita died."

"Before I can go any further, I have to examine everything concerning Rocco's death. For Bella and George's sake, I hope their uncle's death was an accident. But, she hired me as a private investigator to reinvestigate it, so that's what I intend to do." It was time to pop the question. "Since the death was ruled an accident, I'd like to get copies of any reports, pictures or anything else pertaining to the day he was found dead in one of his lobster tanks."

At least two minutes went by before Chief Mills answered. "Chief Lowe said you were good—I told you that. I believe the cause of death was electrocution, but I don't agree one-hundred percent that it was accidental. When it's not deemed a criminal case, we send all reports and pictures to storage. In this circumstance, I personally gave instructions to put everything associated with Rocco's death into an evidence box and kept in our records room. Not many people know I did that. I'm going to call downstairs and have the duty officer get you copies of everything in the box.

Remember, don't share information you feel is confidential without checking with me first. That no-sharing clause includes Bella. I trust her completely, but there's no reason, at this time, to jeopardize her safety. If something concrete comes of this and Rocco's death changes from accidental to criminal, then she'll know what we know."

He was right. I didn't say anything, only nodded.

The Chief looked at his watch, then picked up his phone and called the records room. "Officer Billings, this is Chief Mills. I need you to make copies of everything in the Rocco Deluca evidence box." He stopped to listen to the records room officer, then replied, "Sign it out to me. Do you think you can have it ready in fifteen minutes?"

I sat quiet, listening to the one sided conversation.

"Thanks, I'll be down to pick it up." The Chief hung up. "Okay, that's done. All I ask is you keep me in the loop and if you need anyone to accompany you on an interview or whatever, let me know and I'll have it arranged."

"I really appreciate what you're doing for me. Maybe a fresh set of eyes belonging to somebody disassociated with the case can see something new."

"I hope so." He puckered his lips, then pulled them back in. "I hope so." He folded his arms over his chest and rocked gently in his chair. The rhythmic creak created an eerie undertone to the moment.

My arms danced with goosebumps scrambling to find a warm place to hide.

CHAPTER 35

I waited until I was out of Falmouth and well on my way to the Village before I called Sam. He was either waiting for my call or extremely bored because he answered on the first ring. He must have seen my name come up on the caller ID. "Hi Sherlock."

"Hi yourself."

"So, you've had a good day."

"I have. How do you know?"

"I can hear the smile in your voice."

"You're so full of it Sam Summers." My smile got bigger. "But don't ever change."

"Where are you now."

"I'm on my way to the Village. I came to Falmouth right from the house, so I need to check the mail and all that good stuff. I'm going to grab a sandwich or something light, then stay put behind my desk and go over some paperwork." I wasn't paying attention and almost rear-ended the car in front of me. "Shit," I yelled.

"Hey, what's going on? You okay?"

"Yeah, yeah. I'll blame it on you. You distracted me."

"Good try, but it won't work."

"You didn't ask me if I got in to see Chief Mills."

"Okay. Did you get in to see Chief Mills?"

"This conversation is going to get cut short," I said.

"Naw, don't do that. Gotta keep it light, you know."

"For your information, I did get in to see the Chief. I was there for almost an hour and a half. I left fifteen minutes ago with a folder full of precious cargo."

"He had the information on the Rocco Deluca death at the station?"

115

"He did."

"I'm surprised, since it was ruled an accident."

"I'll explain that to you later," I said. "Speaking of later. What time are you coming home?"

"Today was as exciting as yesterday—not. I'm going to head out around three-thirty unless something earth shattering comes along. What do you want for supper?"

"Let's go to Harry's."

"I'd really like that. I've got the taste sitting on the tip on my tongue and the only thing that can satisfy it is Harry's fried clams."

"I'm good with that. When I get to the office, I'll give Marnie a call. I think Maloney is supposed to be there around four. Maybe they'll meet us."

"Not a bad idea. You said he was going to be around all weekend and they wanted to do something. That'll give us a chance to figure out what."

"I don't really want to talk about the case. I'm sure it will come up, but I'm going to be very vague. I'll explain before we head over to Harry's."

"Whatever you say."

"In time I can fill them in, but right now, I need to be careful what I say and to who—present company excluded."

"Did you mention my name today?"

"No." I thought about it earlier in the day when I mentally accused Sam of being the one who called Chief Mills with a heads-up. "We'll talk. Let me get to the office without distraction, put some stuff in order, then I'll see you when I get home."

"Roger—over and out."

There wasn't much traffic in the Village. Give it another couple months and crossing the street will be like playing a game of dodge ball. The tourists—the right arm of our economy—will have started their seasonal migration over the bridge onto the island for their yearly consumption of chowder, lobster, home-made ice cream and beach sand. I parked in my lot, gathered up my stuff and went inside through the back door just long enough to drop everything off and head out the front—making sure it was secure before I walked away.

There were a couple other late-comers at the post office checking their boxes for the mail. Since I hadn't checked mine for a couple days, it was full of the usual—advertisements, junk and bills. I said my good afternoon to the postmaster, then headed to the sandwich shop next door to get a cup of chowder.

Marnie came in as I was leaving. "Where you been all day?"

"Working."

"I stopped over to the office a couple times earlier, but you weren't there."

"I know. I was working in Falmouth. If you're getting lunch, why don't you get it to go and we'll eat at my office."

"Wait for me. I'm only getting a cup of chowder too."

She ordered. I moved away from the counter to make room for six more people coming in the door.

"I've got water and coffee, unless you want something else."

"I'm good with water."

We started back down the street.

When we got to the door to my office, she turned and made a funny face. "You were supposed to call me last night."

"I know, but I got wrapped up in paperwork and by the time I remembered, it was too late."

"Did you come up with any suggestions of what we could do this weekend?"

"Not really. Why don't we talk about it over chowder? Beside, there's something else I want to ask you."

We put our lunch on the desk, Marnie moved a chair to the front and I went to the kitchen to get a couple of waters.

"Sam suggested the four of us go to Seafood Harry's for supper tonight. You game?" I asked.

"Yeah, Maloney should be here around four o'clock. It's slow at work, so I'm leaving a little early. Do you want us to meet you there?"

"It would be easier. Then we can figure out what trouble we can get into or cause for the next two days. You did say that Annie isn't going to be around didn't you?"

"I forgot what she's doing, but I did tell you that." She smiled. "We've got to find her a boyfriend."

"Careful, I tried that before, it didn't work out and she stayed clear of me for almost a month. We do, however, have to plan a girl's night out. We haven't done one for a while—it's time. She'll feel more comfortable with just the girls. I think she feels like the fifth wheel when Sam and Maloney are around."

"Then a girl's night out it is. Let's change the subject."

I was afraid this was coming.

"You said you went to Falmouth today. Did you come up with anything interesting?"

"Not really." I hated lying to her. "I've got some reports that I have to go over and some pictures of the fish market to compare with the ones I took, but other than that, nothing earth-shattering. I'm trying to take it easy. I don't want to make foolish mistakes or step on the wrong toes."

"Is there anything you want me to research either through the courts or at the DA's office?"

"Not yet, but I'm sure there will be."

"Say the word."

"Thanks. I wish I knew Falmouth better. It's just that far away, making it unfamiliar territory. I've been there several times to things like craft shows and the Falmouth Road Race, but I don't know the 'climate' of the residents. I'm comfortable doing research around here and lower-Cape because I've worked with most of the mid-Cape and lower-Cape PDs. Falmouth is kind of out there by itself. I need time to become familiar with its workings, then I'll be fine." I grabbed the back of my neck and rolled it in my hand. "I did luck out though. I met with Falmouth's Police Chief. He did his homework and checked me out with Chief Lowe."

"I remember Chief Lowe. That must have cut through some red tape."

"It did. I got the recommendation, now I need to earn Chief Mills' trust."

"You won't have any trouble doing that. I'm sure of it."

"Thanks for the vote of confidence."

"You deserve it." She smiled. "I'm going to head back across the street. What time do you want us to meet you at Harry's?"

"Why don't we say six o'clock."

"We'll be there." She waved as she walked out the door.

CHAPTER 36

"Saved by the clock," I whispered.

I put my purse into the bottom desk drawer and laid my briefcase sideways on the front left corner of my desk. Before I started reading the Falmouth PD reports on Rocco Deluca's death, I sorted the mail. Other than a couple of bills, there was nothing worth saving. I slid them into a folder in my top drawer, then turned my attention to my briefcase. I divided its contents into three piles—one with my findings to include pictures and notes, one with the reports and pictures from the ME's office and one with the copies of the contents of the Falmouth PD's evidence box.

I knew what was in the first two piles, so I went directly to the third pile. I walked to my supply closet and took a mini-legal pad from the shelf, then headed to the kitchen for a bottle of water. Once I got going I didn't want to be interrupted. I settled in at my desk, put my cell on mute and took a pen from my drawer. I was about to face the biggest hurdle of my investigation. I had to find an undetermined or unnoticed clue in one of the police reports or pictures that could connect Rocco's death to something other than an accident. It could be one word or the order a sentence was written or the writer's interpretation of the situation.

I started with the pictures. I quickly scanned them and put them in somewhat of an order. I grouped the ones of the outside of the tank together, the inside of the tank showing Rocco, the inside of the tank after Rocco was removed, the back office and the random panoramic images taken of the display cases, the customer waiting area and the freezer displays. Then, I turned the pictures over and numbered them in the upper right hand corner.

I created a murder book, even though Rocco Deluca's death was classified as an accident. Nobody else, at least for the time being, needed to know what I was doing. Marnie and Annie probably wouldn't understand anyway. I doubt if they've ever heard of a murder book. Sam would know exactly what I was up to. But, he'll be on a need-to-know basis and I'll be the one to determine if he needs to know.

I slowly thumbed through the pictures, recording them in number order on my legal pad. I left enough space between them to add notes as I went along in the investigation. I took a clean manila folder from my bottom drawer and labeled it, Falmouth PD pictures. I removed the picture ledger from the pad and, along with the pictures, put them into the folder. Before I started to scrutinize them, I needed to read the police reports.

Whoever took the copies for me did a great job. He even included an inventory of the contents. Multiple page reports were stapled together and, at a quick glance, they appeared to be in the order of the contents listing. I suppose when the Chief asks, one makes his best effort to be efficient. I know I would.

My cell vibrated. I debated whether or not to answer, but I did. "Good Afternoon, Casey Quinby speaking."

"How's Sherlock doing this fine afternoon?" asked Sam.

"Hanging in there. And, what are you up to?"

"Getting ready to leave. Did you talk to Marnie?"

"I did and they're going to meet us at six o'clock at Harry's. If it comes up, I'm going to tell them I don't want to get into my case tonight. First of all, I'm just sorting things out and I don't want to discuss it in a very open place."

"You already told me that. I understand. I know they'll ask because they're interested, but you do have to hold yourself to a level of confidentiality with your clients."

"Thanks, I needed that." I smiled even though Sam couldn't see me.

"I'm leaving in about a half hour. Do you want me to pick anything up at the store?"

"I can't think of anything at the moment. I won't be too far behind you, I'm planning on leaving at four."

"See you in a while."

I felt really good. I liked it when he stayed in Hyannisport, but sometimes I liked my mini-vacations when he spent a few days back at his place in Bourne, too.

As I picked up the first report on the top of the pile, my phone rang again. "Good afternoon, Casey Quinby speaking."

I could hear breathing, but nobody spoke.

"Hello."

Still nothing.

I was ready to hang up when I heard the same muffled, altered voice I heard last Wednesday. "Falmouth," the caller said before he or she hung up.

I listened to the dial tone for a few seconds, then held the receiver out in front of me. I shook my head slowly from side to side. "You bastard. You picked the wrong person to play games with." I hung up the phone, got up from my desk, made sure the doors were locked, then sat back down and started to read.

CHAPTER 37

The first report was dated November 1, 2013.
The time: two-twenty-two p.m.
The investigating officer: Matthew Brady.

I was the first person to arrive on the scene. I reported checking the perimeter and finding a Black Ford 250 pick-up truck parked behind the building next to the rear entrance. I called the station to run the plate number and found it to be registered to a Rocco Deluca, the owner of the fish market. I tried to open the back door of the building. It was locked. I knocked, but noted there was no answer. I knocked several times more—still no answer. I then moved to the front of the building. I tried to open the door leading into the retail part of the market. It was also locked. I also knocked on that door, but like before, there was no answer. I then called the station. Since it was George Deluca, nephew of Rocco Deluca, who called the station to have an officer check out the market, the dispatcher gave me George's telephone number. I called George Deluca and received permission to break the lock and enter the premises. When I opened the door, I noticed a strong foul odor coming from the inside of the store. I found the body of a man who appeared to be deceased, draped over the edge of a lobster tank. I immediately called the station for back-up and the EMTs for medical assistance.

Brady's report went on to say that he was instructed by Officer Tuttle, the senior officer, to check out the electrical box to make sure the breaker was off.

My mind wandered back to my academy days. Report writing 101—just the facts, ma'am, just the facts.

Bella's accounting mirrored Officer Brady's report of the events leading up to the discovery of her uncle's body. I noted that and put an asterisk beside it. I'm curious to know if Bella saw the report, knew Officer Brady or was re-telling what brother George told her. I suppose it didn't make a difference, but I'm still going to ask.

I wonder if Officer Brady took any pictures or if he waited until back-up arrived. Probably waited for back-up.

Before I moved on to the next report, I took the police department pictures back out of their manila folder. The first one should be of Rocco 'draped' over the lobster tank. It was, although I wouldn't call him 'draped' over the tank. All you could see was his foot. It appeared that when he 'fell' into the tank, his foot got caught on the edge. I looked closer at the picture. He had some heavy-duty boots on. I didn't want to get caught up in the pictures, so I tucked them back in the folder and went back to the reports.

A total of three cruisers responded to the call. The first one being, Officer Brady. He was riding single. The other four officers were riding double. All the reports were similar when it came to describing the scene in which Rocco played the main character. The only discrepancy was who checked the electrical box. Judging from a couple of the reports, only two of the officers moved around the market. Both of their reports, except for a few descriptive words, also read the same.

Officer Tuttle, the senior official at the scene, reported that he directed Officer Johnson to find the electrical box and shut off all electrical circuits. Strange, Brady said Tuttle told him to check. He then stated he called the station and asked the lieutenant in charge to send a detective to the market. Officer Tuttle told the lieutenant that nothing seemed out of place and it didn't appear there was a struggle. It looked like an unfortunate accident. Officer Tuttle also told his lieutenant that there was one end of an electrical cord beside Rocco's hand. His take was that Rocco Deluca was electrocuted along with two lobsters that were also found in the tank.

Two detectives arrived on the scene ten minutes after being called. Officer Tuttle gave one of them the number that Officer Brady used earlier to reach George Deluca. A call was made to George to inform him of the situation. The detective's report stated that George's number was a cell phone and he was only five minutes away.

I put the reports down, took a sip of water, sat back in my chair and pondered what I had just read. It sure seemed like Rocco Deluca was the victim of an unfortunate accident, but I still wasn't one hundred percent convinced. As far as the suicide rumor, I didn't see that at all. I agreed with Bella on that one.

I went back to the reports and listed the names of the five police officers and the two detectives associated with Rocco's death investigation—Officers Mathew Brady, James Johnson, Kenneth Brown, Earl Massad, senior Officer Carl Tuttle and the two Detectives, Benjamin Morse and Paul Garrison. Somewhere down the road, I'd need to meet with them. I wanted to run their names by Bella. She might be able to give me a little personal background. One thing that concerned me was that none of these officers appeared to be familiar with Rocco and from all accounts everybody in town knew him. I knew they had to be careful with what they wrote in reports, but something didn't feel right. I made a note of this.

According to Officer Tuttle's report, he was the one who called the Medical Examiner. I would have thought one of the detectives would have called. I jotted that bit of information down on the same page as the report comment.

Then there was George. He wanted Rocco to sell the business. Rocco agreed, but in his own time. George and Rocco had words—a discussion, as Bella put it. A couple days went by. George tried to get ahold of Rocco and was unable to do so. George got nervous and called the police department to see if they'd do a ride by the market. They did and found a dead Uncle Rocco. When they called to notify George, he was only five minutes away. Why was he in Falmouth? I didn't see where George asked them to ride by the house first. It didn't appear he did. Maybe he called a neighbor and asked them to check. "Make a note," I said as I jotted it down so I wouldn't forget.

I looked at my watch. It was four o'clock. I packed up my briefcase, secured my purse on my shoulder, picked up my car keys, flipped off the lights and headed out the back door.

CHAPTER 38

Marnie and Maloney were already at Harry's. Marnie waved as we walked in.

"We got here about ten minutes ago."

I sat in the chair across from her.

"I guess that means I'm getting our drinks and ordering our food," Sam said. "What do you want?"

"A Bud Light and fried clams with onion rings instead of fries." I wrinkled my nose and smiled.

Marnie looked at Maloney. "Ditto for me."

The guys went to the counter.

"Casey, did you find anything of interest in the reports you got from the police department?"

"I found lots of interesting things, but I don't know what to do with some of them until I do some more research. I've got to sit down again with Bella. I'll give her a call sometime this weekend and set something up for Monday morning."

"So you don't have anything of substance to report."

"Nope, but that's good. It means we can have a fun weekend doing what, I don't know. We'll figure it out over supper." I knew Marnie didn't believe me. I didn't give her the chance to ask again. "The guys are here with our beers." I reached over to Sam and took one of the frosted mugs from him.

"How's your first week on the new job been?" asked Maloney.

"It is a change, but it's what I wanted and I'm liking it."

"Marnie told me a little about your first case."

"She did, did she." I took a deep breath. "One of the biggest differences between working at the Tribune and being a private investigator is the level of confidentiality." I took another sip of beer.

"Does that mean you aren't going to share the going ons of Casey Quinby, Private Investigator with us?" Maloney knew the answer, but asked anyway.

I chuckled. "Not right now." I pursed my lips and gave Maloney a slight nod. "I hope you understand." I was afraid of what his reaction would be to my vow of silence.

"Remember, I come from a long line of cops—from patrolmen to detectives to a deputy chief. When you're ready and able to tell us, I'll be the first in line to listen. In the meantime, if you need any help, I'll be there for you."

I felt relieved. "Thanks."

Marnie and I jumped when the little plastic lobster buzzer went off to let us know our order was ready for pick-up.

When Sam and Maloney cleared the area, I looked at Marnie. "That's quite a guy you've got there."

She smiled. "I know."

"There's no place better for fried clams than Harry's." Sam set our tray on the table and slid in beside me.

Maloney sat back in his chair, put a clam in his mouth and made facial gestures like he was a judge in a food tasting contest. "They are very good—sweet and crunchy. We're going to have to do a Boston run. I want you to sample a place in my neck of the woods."

"I can handle that," said Sam. "When are we going?"

"We could do it this weekend." Maloney grinned. "What do you girls think about that idea?"

Marnie looked at me. We both gave a nod of approval.

"Then Boston it is." Maloney was beaming. "We'll figure out the details after we eat. After all, we don't want these juicy little gems of the ocean to get cold."

CHAPTER 39

"Fun night," I said to Sam on the ride back to Hyannisport.

"Yeah, I enjoyed it too. And, we'll continue the fun tomorrow. Did you and Marnie figure out what time we're heading out?"

"They're going to pick us up at ten o'clock. Maloney has more than a clam eating contest in mind, but I'm not sure what. He didn't even tell Marnie."

"We've got nothing else going, so whatever is okay with me." Sam swerved to avoid what appeared to be a bag of trash in the middle of the road.

"I'm glad the Deluca case got shut in the closet—at least for the time being."

"I told you there wouldn't be a problem." Sam reached over and squeezed my knee. "When the time is right, they'll make a good sounding board. And, who knows, as outsiders to the case, they might contribute something that could help you unlock a clue or at least get you thinking about making a left hand turn before coming to the end of the street."

"I like that interpretation."

Sam pulled into my driveway. "I'll take Watson for a short run around the yard. Why don't you make us some coffee. The Deluca case may not have been the subject of conversation at supper, but now I want to make it the subject of conversation while we wind down with coffee and Oreos."

I puffed my cheeks out and got right up close to his face. "Sam Summers, I hope you love me when I'm fat."

He hit me on the butt and unlocked the front door. As usual, Watson was waiting patiently for his mommy and daddy.

"Good boy." I gave him a playful pat as he turned and followed Sam outside.

Once they were out of sight, I went back inside. Not ten minutes later, I heard the door knob turn.

"That was a short run?" I held my hands palm side up in front of me. "Where did you two go?"

"Watson broke away from me and started to run down the street. He was running after something. He finally stopped. When I caught up to him, I hooked the leash to his collar and tried to coax him back in the direction of the house. His attention was still focused on some unspecified thing lurking in the bushes. I figure it was an animal—a squirrel or cat—as long as it wasn't a skunk." Sam shrugged. "We're back now and I'm ready for that coffee."

My briefcase was lying open on the table. "Do you want to look at the reports and pictures I got today?" I pulled them out from the side of the case.

"I've already read the other material you have, so yes, I'd like to see what Falmouth PD gave you." He sat down and picked up the picture folder first.

I let him peruse the pictures taken at Rocco's fish market. He ran through them several times in between sips of coffee and several Oreos.

I didn't say a word, just let him do his thing.

"Will you please get me your pictures and also the ones the ME gave you."

I got both sets out and set them in separate piles in front of him.

He looked at each pile, then started comparing them with the ones from the police department. "They're all almost alike, except in yours there's no foot 'draped' over the front side of the tank." He went back to studying the details. "The cord wrapped around the pole on the right end of the tank doesn't seem above-board to me. Also, if you look at the ME's and the police photos, it would be a hell of a reach for Rocco to grab onto the cord." As he spoke, Sam pointed from the cord to Rocco's foot and back again. "You didn't know Rocco. He wasn't a tall man. I don't think his arm span was long enough to reach the cord. I've got at least six inches on him and I don't know if my instincts would have me diving for an object that couldn't keep me from falling into the tank. If it were me, I'd try to stop myself from falling by lunging forward and trying to grab the back of the tank. He might suffer some type of an injury upon contact with the bottom or edge of the tank, but he wouldn't have gotten electrocuted."

"Interesting."

"Take these pictures to the market. Figure out where that boot was on the tank. Make a chalk mark, then take some measurements. Measure the dimensions of the tank, including the depth, then measure from the boot to the pole where the cord is. Also, since the tank in question is the top tank, ascertain the distance it is off the floor."

"There's a four step utility ladder in the picture from the ME and the PD. When I took my pictures, there was no ladder there. I'll look for it, then I'll stage the original scene minus Rocco."

"Be sure and take those dimensions too."

"I will."

"I'm going to scan the Falmouth reports. Can you make me another cup of joe?"

I went over the notes I'd made earlier in the day while Sam did his reading. I didn't want to interrupt him.

Almost a half-hour passed before he spoke. "I'm not sure whether or not Rocco Deluca's death was an accident." Sam sat forward in his chair and leaned on the table. "Let me clarify that, it may have been an accident, but not in the way it was reported. There were no eye-witnesses or no evidence of foul play."

I shot him a puzzled look. "Are you saying it could have been staged to look like an accident?"

"Something like that. There's lots of pieces—critical pieces—missing. You're going to have to tread softly, but you're good, if there's something to be found, you'll do it."

My brain was on overload. "Let's watch the news, then go to bed."

"I'm going to make a pit stop, then I'll meet you on the couch."

I cleaned up the kitchen, slipped into my P.J.s, turned the TV on and snuggled into my corner of the oversized loveseat. Sam joined me—laying full body—head at one end with feet on my lap at the other.

CHAPTER *40*

Saturday

We were both dead to the world when the alarm went off at eight o'clock. I cuddled up to Sam's back, nuzzled my face into his neck and gave him a couple soft, loving kisses. "Time to get up big guy."

"I heard it. One of these mornings we're going to get to sleep late."

"It's not my fault you wanted to play last night." I giggled.

"If I recall, you didn't object."

"You do have a point there, but now it's time to get up." I pinched his butt, then rolled over and almost fell off the edge of the bed.

He put his pillow over his head and muttered something.

"I can't hear you," I said as I walked by him into the hallway.

All of a sudden, he sprung out of bed and almost knocked me over as he sprinted down the hall. "First in the bathroom." The door shut. I heard the lock click.

"You'll pay for this, Sam Summers." I looked up and shook my head. Watson meandered around the bottom of the bed, slowly walked to where I was standing and plunked down beside me. If I didn't know better, I'd say he smiled. I put my hands on my hips. "You two guys have a conspiracy going on. You can't fool me." I headed for the kitchen to say good morning to my best friend—Mr. Dunkin.

I was sitting at the table reading the Tribune when Sam joined me in the kitchen after his morning fluff and buff. I batted my eyelashes at him. "My don't you look snappy decked out in your new tighty-whities." I laughed.

"Just showing off the abs." He struck a muscle man pose, then went to the Keurig to make a coffee.

"Want some breakfast?"

"Maybe an English muffin, but nothing more. I'm saving it for Boston."

I got up and popped a couple into the toaster.

"Oh, by the way, I forgot to tell you—my boss is sending me to a conference at Quantico in Virginia."

"When?"

"Monday. I'm meeting up with a detective from Worcester and a couple from the Boston area at Logan. Our flight is scheduled to leave at one-twenty."

"What kind of conference and how long will you be gone?" I sounded like a wife.

"I just found out about it yesterday and forgot to tell you last night." He smiled. "Sorry. It's a two day seminar on terrorism. He tried to send me last September, but it was full by the time he called to reserve a spot."

"It must be a popular subject ever since the Boston Marathon bombing last year. It should be very interesting."

"I'm sure it will be. I went to the memorial service for the MIT officer, Sean Collier. The April twenty-fourth service was one I'll never forget it. Such a young guy with so much to offer gunned down by a coward—a no good bastard—performing an act of terrorism on the United States." Sam got quiet. He took a sip of coffee. "April thirteenth will be a somber day, but people will rally and remember why we're Americans—Boston Strong."

I watched Sam's face as he emerged from the frightening memory of a heart wrenching tragedy back to my kitchen table. I stood up and walked beside him. We didn't say anything. I gently cradled his head in my hands and drew it close to my chest.

After a couple minutes, he leaned back, turned and looked up at me. "Sherlock, you're the best."

I smiled. "Times a passing. Let's get ready before the love birds get here."

"Aren't we already here?"

"I guess we are," I laughed. "I guess we are."

CHAPTER 41

Sam brought Watson back into the house after a walk around the yard, gave him a couple treats and filled his food and water dishes. "Hey boy, we're going to the big city. You're in charge." He gave him a ruffled pat on the head.

It was ten o'clock when Marnie and Maloney pulled into the driveway. We were waiting at the bottom of the stairs. Marnie reached over and blew the horn, then waved like an excited little child on her way to *Toys "R" Us* with a hundred dollar gift card, then she got out of the front passenger seat so Sam could sit in the front with Maloney and we could sit in the back and gossip.

"I'm stopping for coffee at the Dunkins by the Sagamore Bridge. Can I interest anyone in a cup?" Maloney asked.

"Of course," said Sam. "And, I'll answer for my side-kick. She'll have one too."

"So now I'm your side-kick?"

"You've got that right partner."

"Knock it off. John Wayne or Clint Eastwood you're not."

Maloney pulled into Dunkin's parking lot. "This one's on me. What does everybody want?"

The guys went inside, while Marnie and I sat in the car and talked.

"Did you and Sam talk about the case last night?" asked Marnie.

I wasn't expecting her question. "We did. Of course he's much more knowledgeable on investigations than I am. I'm using his expertise as a training tool." Without getting into the real nitty-gritty, I tried to satisfy Marnie's desire to know what was happening in the Deluca case. "Up to this point, Sam didn't think Rocco's death was anything more than an accident. After studying pictures taken by two different people and the Falmouth police and reading reports or notes written by the aforementioned group, Sam indicated there may be some logic to Bella's concerns of how her uncle died." I saw the guys exit Dunkin's. "Let's not talk about it today. Let's just enjoy our Boston fun day. I'll catch you up the beginning of next week." I finished just in time.

Marnie nodded in agreement.

"Okay, we're back. You girls can stop talking now." Sam laughed and handed us our coffee.

Maloney got into the driver's seat, got himself ready for take-off, then looked in his rearview mirror. "Have either of you ever been on a magical mystery tour?"

"Nope, but I think we're about to experience one today," Marnie chuckled. "How did I ever get hooked up with this guy?" She glanced at me. "I remember now. Funny thing is, I wouldn't change it for the world." She gave Maloney a little pat on the back of his head.

Sam gave me a look from the corner of his eyes, then smiled.

"Let's get going before we all start chirping," I said.

"What?" asked Marnie.

"Never mind—an inside joke. I'll tell you about it someday."

CHAPTER 42

The ride to Boston isn't bad when you know where you're going and, since it was a Saturday, the traffic was cut in half.

"Where are you going to park?" asked Sam.

"I called Big M this morning about getting us a parking place in Boston. His buddy is at the police lot near Hanover Street in the North End. Big M said he'd give him a call."

"Having a father on the Boston PD is better than trying to call for consideration," said Sam.

"You've got that right," said Maloney. "I figured that would be the best place to park. If we want to go someplace besides the North End or the waterfront, we can hop the MTA."

"It's your call. You're the one who bragged about the fried clams." Sam smirked. "Are you going to tell us where we're going?"

"Nope. I'm the Pied Piper and if you want to eat, you'll follow me."

"Ha," said Marnie. "Just get me my clams."

I was glad Maloney was driving. He knew the area like the back of his hand. "Boston has more one way streets than Carter has pills. I'd get lost or get a ticket for going in the wrong direction on one of the one-ways."

"You get used to it."

We turned down Hanover Street, then took an almost immediate right onto a narrow connecting driveway. There wasn't any parking on either side, in fact, there was barely enough room for two cars to pass each other. In several of the doorways, a couple of old Italian men were standing—smoking cigarettes, talking with their hands and drinking what I presumed to be coffee or maybe expresso. At the end of the alleyway, we made a left, then a couple blocks down another left into a small parking lot. A Boston cruiser was parked at the entrance. As soon as we turned in, the officer in the cruiser got out and came over to our car.

"I'm sorry, this is a private lot." He raised his arm and pointed down the street to what I assumed was a public parking area. "Down there on the right," he said.

Maloney had his police id in his hand. He gave it to the officer. "Officer Russell Maloney, Provincetown Police Department."

"So you must be Big M's son."

"Yes sir."

"He gave me a call. Said you'd be coming to the big city today." He looked around the lot. "Why don't you park beside that black Mercedes over there." He pointed to a spot four in from the road. "I get off at three, but there's always somebody here."

"Thank you, Officer...." Maloney tried to read his name, but the glare from the sun made it impossible.

"Officer McCarthy. Your father and me grew up together in Southie, so you know wees go way back." Another car pulled up behind us. Officer McCarthy stepped away from our car and motioned Maloney to pull into the designated spot.

"Russell Maloney," I said. "I guess I assumed your real name was Rusty."

"That's what everybody calls me. The only time I got called Russell was when my mother wasn't pleased and she wanted me to know it."

Marnie and I waited on the sidewalk while Maloney introduced Sam to Officer McCarthy. The conversation was short.

"Are we ready for the best fried clams around?" asked Maloney as he licked his lips in satisfaction. "If so, follow me."

The three of us shook our heads and laughed.

"The guy has lost it. Maybe we should run for our lives," said Marnie.

"I'll wait till I eat, then I might consider it." Sam smiled.

We walked back to Hanover Street, crossed over the underground tunnel from the big dig and into Quincy Market.

Marnie and I were in our glory. We were surrounded by kiosks and high-end specialty stores. "I want a pink Boston Strong tee shirt." I walked towards one of the vendors.

"Me, too," said Marnie who trailed close behind me.

"I want fried clams, but since she's got her mind made up to get a shirt first, I think I'll get one too," said Sam. "Only not pink."

The three of us picked out and paid for our shirts, then walked back to where Maloney was waiting.

"Now the food?" he asked.

"Now the food," said Sam.

Marnie glanced around. "Where is Faneuil Hall?"

Maloney pointed to a building adjacent to where we were standing. "Faneuil Hall was Boston's first public market. Did you know that? It was built in the seventeen hundreds and Quincy Market was added in the early eighteen hundreds. There's a real interesting history behind it. We'll come up some weekend and I'll show you more of Boston's history."

"I'll hold you to that," Marnie said as she looked around, taking in as much as she could.

"The restaurant is right around the corner." Maloney walked ahead of us then stopped. "Here we are. The Union Oyster House— the oldest restaurant in Boston sporting the best seafood around— including their fried clams."

It was early so we had no trouble getting a seat.

The server came to take our drink order. I ordered a Sam Adams Summer Ale.

"Me too," said Marnie.

Maloney nodded.

"Might as well make it unanimous," Sam said.

"I'll be right back with your drinks and take your food order."

Maloney sat back in his chair. "Well, did I do good so far?"

"So far," I said.

He moved forward and leaned on the table. "Okay, we're not in Kansas anymore, so nobody will know who or what we're talking about." Maloney surveyed the table.

Here we go.

"Casey, can't you fill us in a little on your first official investigation?"

Sam sat quiet with his arms folded over his chest and, without moving a muscle, shifted his eyes from Maloney to me, over to Marnie, then back to me.

"You're right. One of my big concerns was talking in public about Rocco Deluca. He was a very well-known and respected man in Falmouth. Sam taught me a long time ago, that you never know who might be sitting in the booth behind you. That's one way rumors get started and convictions get stalled—when the wrong person becomes privy to your investigation and botches the case."

"We're in Boston. What are the chances Rocco's former neighbor, who moved away fifteen years ago, shows up at Union Oyster House at noon and chooses to sit in any one of the open tables that surround us?" Maloney forced a half smile. "Only saying." He waved his hand sideways and looked around pretending to scan the room for snoops.

"What neighbor?" Marnie asked.

Maloney looked at her. "You should be a blonde. There is no neighbor. That was just a *what-if* story."

I laughed. "Okay, you've made your point. I know you're not going to let up. Let's hold a meeting of the minds."

Our drinks came and we placed our orders.

We toasted to our friendship, we toasted to our day in Boston, we toasted to everything we could think of, finally ending with a toast to the end of my first week as a private investigator.

"Marnie, did you fill Maloney in on the little bit you know about the case?"

"I did."

"Okay, let me brief you on what I've done so far and what I intend to do next week." Since this wasn't supposed to be the topic of conversation while we ate Boston fried clams, I wasn't prepared to lay out the facts to date. "I'm going to use first names only." I nodded until I got a positive response. "You know I met with the niece. She was the one who hired me. We went over her reasons as to why she doesn't believe her uncle's death was accidental. Judging from the obvious, on the surface it appeared to be an accident."

I had just started and already Maloney was engrossed in what I was saying.

"We met a couple of times and talked about her family, her uncle, her aunt, her brother, her uncle's market and her. We talked about Falmouth. We talked about a lot of things."

"Does this girl live in Falmouth?" he asked.

"She does. She went to college in Boston and lived there for a time after she graduated. Now she's the Director of the Falmouth Library."

They had finished their beer. The server came by and everybody, except me, ordered another one.

"We visited the uncle's market where the 'accident' took place. I talked to the Medical Examiner. He was very cooperative and gave me copies of the pictures he took and his official reports. His secretary, on the other hand, is a nosey, busy body—one of the many Falmouth town gossipers. Anyway, then I met with the Falmouth Police Chief. He knew I was in Falmouth asking questions. The ME's secretary made sure of that. Chief Mills checked me out—knew I had worked for the Tribune and was now in business for myself. He checked with the Chief in Barnstable, who fortunately gave me a glowing recommendation. Chief Mills then had the officer in the evidence room make a copy of everything in the uncle's evidence box."

"Wait a minute." Maloney put up his hand like a traffic cop. "Why is there an evidence box if it was considered an accident."

Sam joined the conversation. "I wondered the same thing."

"The Chief wanted one," I said. "Just my opinion, but I think he doesn't buy the accident judgment one hundred percent. He knows

I've been employed by the niece to investigate the uncle's death. He has no evidence to officially re-open the investigation, but I think he's going to take an active interest in mine."

"There's more," said Sam. "Rocco was related, by marriage, to one of Falmouth's rich and influential low-lifes."

"Are you being prejudice because you didn't like the 'low-life' or was it documented this person really was a 'low-life'?" Maloney asked.

"Trust me, it has nothing to do with how I feel. I've said it before and I'll say it again, Rocco's brother-in-law, Sid, went to the James Whitely Bulger school for undercover criminals. And, Rocco and Sid didn't see eye to eye." Sam nodded. "Now do you get a better picture?"

"Bulger came from my neck of the woods. I know exactly what you're saying."

"Right now that's my investigation in a nut shell, but the shell is getting thin. I fully expect the meat to puncture a hole real soon. When that happens, we'll talk again."

Maloney took a deep breath. "Casey, if this brother-in-law dude is as bad as Sam makes him out to be, you need to be real careful—watch your back."

"The brother-in-law is dead." I waited for Maloney to respond.

"What?" asked Maloney.

"Just because the brother-in-law is dead, doesn't mean the rest of his immediate family or confidants attend confession every Saturday." Sam saw the server heading to the table with our food, abruptly stopped talking and nodded in her direction.

Everybody took the hint.

CHAPTER 43

"I have to admit the fried clams at the Union Oyster House were excellent, as good, but not better than Harry's." The ambiance may have helped with my decision. "My favorite part of the food tour was the dessert at Mike's Pastry." I licked my lips pretending to search for the last little bit of cannoli filling.

It was still early, so we walked up State Street, crossed Tremont, then walked through the Commons.

There was some sort of pick-up concert going on. "I spend many weekends listening to musicians trying to be discovered." Maloney started to jive to the music. "Some were good—some could have made more money selling ear plugs."

"This group isn't too bad, but I've heard enough," I said.

"Me, too," echoed Marnie.

We walked a little further past a make-shift art display.

I stopped in front of a wall of water color prints. I recognized some of the scenes. They were popular sites on the Cape. They looked like copies of pictures in the Kennedy Studios. I moved away quickly to avoid a conversation with the artist.

Marnie took Maloney's hand. "The next time we come up, we should stay over. I want more."

Sam smirked.

"I'm talking about more of Boston. Get your mind out of the gutter."

Maloney smiled. "It's still early, we'll take Route 3 out of Boston, then cut over to 3A. There's a place called 42 Degrees N in Manomet. Good place to stop for a drink before we head back on Cape."

"Not only are you a good cop, you're a good tour guide." I patted him on his shoulder.

CHAPTER 44

It was just before seven o'clock when we got back to my house. Marnie and Maloney dropped us off, then headed back to Yarmouthport.

Watson couldn't have been sitting any closer to the door. The minute we opened it, he bolted.

"The weather's nice out now. I think if we're going to be gone for most of the day, we should put him on his run."

Sam agreed. "Since I'm going back to my place sometime tomorrow afternoon and will be gone until Thursday, you'll probably have to bring the boy to work with you."

"I will as long as I'm staying at the office. The other days, I'll try the run." I gave him a look.

"What's that for?" he asked.

"Does that mean you're coming here as soon as you get back?"

"I don't know—could be." He smiled.

We stayed outside for a while and played with Watson. Sometimes I feel guilty not being able to devote more time to the boy, but he knows the routine and it doesn't seem to bother him.

The three of us went back inside.

"Television is crappy tonight—all reruns. I checked HBO and *Saving Mr. Banks* is on at eight-thirty."

"And, you think I want to watch a Mary Poppins' movie?"

"It's not the animated one. Tom Hanks plays the part of Walt Disney. It's supposed to be great."

"What else is on?"

"What about *Captain Phillips*? It's on Starz, same time as the other one. Tom Hanks is in that one too."

"Yeah, I know. So it's Tom Hanks or Tom Hanks?" he smiled and took the paper from me. "Instead of a movie, we could watch

144

Hell's Kitchen or *The Blacklist* or a rerun of *Blue Bloods*, then *48 Hours* followed by the news, then to bed." He put the paper back on my lap and waited for my reply.

"You are so predictable. *Blue Bloods* it is. Hopefully it isn't one we've already seen."

He shrugged. "So what if it is."

I shook my head. "So what if it is? I'm having a glass of wine. How about you?"

"I'll have a frostie, please."

"I like the please." I smiled then headed to the kitchen.

CHAPTER 45

Sunday

It was eight thirty when I opened my eyes and looked at the time. Sam was already up and apparently Watson was with him. Nobody would have cared if I rolled over and went back to sleep, but not knowing what those two were up to would keep me awake, so there was no point to staying in bed.

Watson wasn't in the kitchen. I assumed he was outside on his run. Sam was working on the lap top, so engrossed in his reading that he didn't hear me come in. He was already dressed. There was an empty cup of coffee beside him. He must have been up for a while.

"Hi."

"Hi, yourself, sleeping beauty."

"How long have you been up?"

"About an hour." He never looked up from his reading.

I made myself a cup of French Vanilla. "Want another?"

"I didn't realize I'd finished mine." He handed me his cup. "Sure, thanks."

While his was brewing I moved behind him so I could see what he was so absorbed in. "You're reading about Sid DeMarco."

"Yep."

"Why?" I got his coffee and sat down beside him.

"If Chief Mills has concerns as to Rocco's death not being an accident, then my gut feeling tells me he thinks the DeMarco family had something to do with it."

"Hmm. What do you know about Sid's sons?"

"The apple doesn't fall far from the tree." He sat back and drank some of his coffee. "Do you know what I mean?"

146

"I think so. If this family is so much trouble, how come they've never been put on the chopping block for anything?"

"They have, but nothing major. I remember once they altered a contract the Town of Falmouth awarded them to build an addition onto the public works building. Somebody had the balls to stand up to the family and the DeMarcos paid a healthy fine."

"That's not that bad. It was a money thing, nothing life threatening."

"Well, that's what one might think." Sam sighed. "A month after they got called out, there was a fire in the garage of the person who found and reported the contract discrepancy. The burned-out garage housed a restored Model T Ford. The fire marshal combed every inch trying to find something to indicate the fire was started deliberately. He listed faulty wiring as the cause."

"Was this an isolated incident?"

"Nope. There were lots of things that had DeMarco written all over them, but were always covered up or eliminated."

"Who did the covering and/or the eliminating?"

"It was rumored he had people on his 'payroll', but it could never be proven. Just like Rocco Deluca's death—an accident. But was it? Normally the paperwork would be filed away with all the other dead files and after a number of years destroyed. Obviously, Chief Mills didn't believe it to be an accident. That's why he kept all the reports and pictures in a box locked in the evidence room. I think he's using it for bait."

"Do you think the DeMarco family has 'people' in the police department?" I was sitting on the edge of my chair staring at the computer screen.

"Quite possible."

"Now I have a copy of the contents of the box."

"That concerns me. I think it concerned the Chief too. That's why he's the one who signed it out—not you or one of his officers." Sam logged out of the site he was on and closed the lap top. "How about we go to Stella's for breakfast, then come back and work on the Rocco project."

"That's a unique way of putting it." Give me ten minutes to clean up and throw on a pair of jeans and a jersey.

Sam called down the hallway. "On the way back from Stella's, we'll pick up some steaks at Stop and Shop."

"I might as well do a little shopping too. Since you're not going to be around, I won't be going out to eat as much." I put my thinking face on and rubbed my chin. "Although, it would be a good time for a girls-night-out. I'll run that by Marnie and Annie tomorrow morning."

"Ready?" Sam asked.

"As ready as I'm going to be."

CHAPTER 46

Breakfast at Stella's was scrumptious as usual.

It wasn't busy so Stella got herself a cup of coffee and sat down with us. "Where have you guys been?" She looked at me, then Sam, then back to me. "I wondered if you decided to stay away from Cotuit after your last ordeal with the Mary Kaye Griffin case. You were like an unsung hero in town. Everybody was so grateful that you uncovered the truth about her murder." She smiled. "I still miss her."

"It was tragic. You never think something like that is going to happen in an upscale Cape Cod town. Good thing they didn't have any children. That would have made it much worse."

"So true," she said.

We ordered breakfast and read the paper until our food came.

"By the way, I have some news for you."

"I'll bite, what?" asked Stella.

"I left the newspaper and I'm not working on police department cases anymore, or I should say, not at the moment."

"Then what are you doing?"

I reached into my purse and pulled out my business card holder. I slipped a card out and handed it to her. "Dah, dah—meet Casey Quinby, Private Investigator."

"No kidding—you started your own investigation business."

"I did. In fact, I officially opened the doors last Monday."

Stella leaned over and gave me a big hug and a kiss. "I'm so proud of you." There were a couple people waiting at the counter to pay their bill. "I'll be right back."

"She's a nice lady," Sam said. "And, she makes great pancakes."

"I'm back." She put a plate of Italian cookies in front of us. "Sam, I remember how much you loved these."

"You've got a good memory. Thanks," he said as he took a bite.

"Have you got any extra cards with you? It's not that I know anyone needing your services at the present time, but you never know. I talk to a lot of people here." She smiled. "That's how we became friends, over coffee, pastry and conversation."

I reached into my purse and took out a small plastic zip lock bag. "How many do you want?"

"I can put some out on the counter. I have the right holder for them." She held out her hand.

I gave her about twenty. I glanced across the street at the attorney's offices. "I wonder if the fine attorneys will notice them."

"They still come in, so I wouldn't be surprised."

"Is Attorney Richards still there?" Sam asked.

"From what I understand, he is, but I think he's still trying to get his life back together. Sometimes he comes in for coffee in the morning, but not like he used to. His only crime was being a jerk. His wife will never see the light of day." Stella looked at me. "Will she?"

"No, she's found a new permanent home—one without fancy cars, clothes or status." I shook my head. "Too bad. She did it to herself and tried to bring others down with her. That's what happens when people get greedy—and kill for it."

Sam looked at his watch. "Church must be out, four cars just pulled into your parking lot. We'll be finishing our coffee, then we've got to get going."

"You're right, here they come," said Stella as she took her cup, stood up and headed for the counter.

Sam was in the process of taking a drink of coffee, when his arm froze in mid-air. His eyes focused on four people that had just come in. They sat at the table furthest away from us against the opposite wall.

I didn't see anything out of the ordinary—two couples out for Sunday morning breakfast. "What or who in the world spooked you?"

He put his cup back on the table and leaned in my direction. "See those two couples that just came in?"

"You talking about the ones against the wall?"

"I am."

"I see them. Am I supposed to know who they are?"

"I'll tell you who they are." His voice was so low I had to read his lips to know what he was trying to tell me. "They're Sid DeMarco's two sons and their wives."

"A little far from Falmouth, wouldn't you say?"

"Probably not many people, if any, know them here in Cotuit."

"Do they know you?"

"It's been a number of years, but I'm sure I'll be a familiar face as soon as they peruse the room."

"Are you going to speak to them?"

"I might bid them a good morning—especially if I think it might make them uncomfortable." Sam drank more of his coffee. "Take a good look at them from a distance because I'm not going to introduce you."

"Why?"

"And you have to ask?" Sam gave me his serious look.

I knew better than to question him anymore, but made sure I got clear mental pictures of the two guys facing me. "The two DeMarco boys like having their backs to the wall just like you and Maloney." I smiled, but didn't look at Sam.

"Trust me, it's for the same reasons, only different players. They don't want the element of surprise any more than we do. The only difference is in our case it's police officers watching out for assholes like the DeMarco brothers. In their case, it's asshole vs. asshole and who could be the biggest one. Do you understand?"

"Sounds like something from the movies."

"Unfortunately, it's all too real."

151

Stella came over with the coffee pot. I put my hand over my cup. "I've had enough—anymore and I'll float home."

"Me, too."

"When you get some time, come in for lunch and tell me all about your new eye-spy business."

"I will."

I could see Sam's eyes move in the direction of the DeMarco's table.

The restaurant was starting to fill up with the church crowd. Stella's daughter was at the register when we walked up to pay. Without being obvious, I stood where I could get a closer full-face image of each of the DeMarcos. I committed the visual photograph to my mind.

Sam nudged me, put his hand on my back and, without saying a word, guided me towards the door.

Greg and Phil DeMarco spotted him.

"Good morning, Detective Summers. What brings you to this neck of the woods?" Phil asked.

"Funny, I was going to ask you the same question." Without hesitation Sam said, "Best blueberry pancakes around—that's why I'm here."

Sam didn't wait for Phil to reply. He joined me at the door.

We waved to Stella and headed out to his car.

"Well, now you know what Bella's cousins look like. If you ever see one of them anywhere close to you, I want you to call Chief Mills or me immediately."

"Were the women with them their wives?"

"Yep." He shook his head. "I've met Greg's wife. Her name is Alice. The other one I've only seen walking with her husband. I've never been formally introduced and, frankly, don't care. Just want to remind you—they're a dangerous bunch. The bad-girl lawyer's wife in the cold case you worked for Barnstable PD is an angel compared to Phil and Greg. Someday all their lies will be exposed and the truth will bite them in the ass."

"Point taken." I left it at that. Sam was agitated and to keep him talking about the DeMarcos would only make it worse. "Do you want to take a ride to Falmouth?"

"Sure. It's early. I figure I'll head back to Bourne around six o'clock. That'll give me plenty of time to pack and straighten out my briefcase."

"Maybe you can familiarize me with the town I'll be spending a lot of time in for the next few weeks," I said. "I've never been to Falmouth Heights where Bella lives or to Falmouth District Court. Those are two places I'd like my tour director to point out to me." I reached over and rested my hand on his knee. "I've got a pad of paper in my purse, so I can note any other places of interest you think might pertain to Uncle Rocco's last few weeks or months."

"Do you have Bella's address?"

"Not with me. Give me a minute and I'll Google it."

"I'm impressed. When did you get a smart phone?"

"A couple weeks ago. I didn't tell you cause I didn't want to bear the brunt of dumb phone jokes." I hit the Google app and typed Isabella Deluca. Since she was involved in town meetings and belonged to several public organizations, several stories of interest came up, but not her address. "Hmm."

"Did you get it?"

"Not yet."

"You might have to go on the internet, then through White Pages."

I should have practiced before I tried to be the big shot, but I wasn't ready to let Sam know I didn't have a clue what I was doing. "For some reason my email app isn't responding. We must be in a dead zone—no pun intended." I didn't look in his direction. A smirk could definitely make for an uncomfortable afternoon and I didn't want that to happen.

"Let me call dispatch at my office and ask them to look it up."

I didn't object.

Sam repeated the address he got from the desk officer. "I know approximately where it is. Years ago, when I was a kid, a bunch of us used to go to the Heights on the Fourth of July. They've got a great fireworks display."

"Maybe we can go this summer."

"It's a date." He smiled. "Not to change the subject, but pretty soon Route 28 curves to the left. Just after the curve on the right are three beautiful Cape style houses, manicured to perfection. You can't miss them. You might want to make them number one on your points-of-interest list. They belong to ….."

My excitement overtook me and I cut Sam off. "Why?" I asked.

"If you let me finish, I'll tell you."

"Sorry." I took my camera from my purse and readied it to snap a picture of whatever it was Sam was about to show me.

"Why aren't you using your new smart phone?" He laughed.

"I forgot to put a new roll of film in it, smart ass."

"Okay, there's nobody behind me, so I'll slow down as best I can. We're coming to the curve so get ready." He practically came to a stop as we reached the three houses he'd described to me.

I must have taken at least six or seven rapid succession pictures as we crept by. "Now tell me who owns the houses I'm going to submit to house beautiful on HGTV."

"The biggest of the three belonged to Sid DeMarco. The other two belong to his sons."

"Who lives in Sid's house now?"

"His second wife."

"Do they all get along?"

Sam shrugged. "From what I've heard, they do not."

"That's got to be hard."

"According to my buddies at the Falmouth PD, it's not a marriage made in heaven. To add fuel to the fire, she owns the controlling interest in the family business."

"How did that happen?"

"Sid signed it over to her before he died."

"Did the boys know about it before the fact?"

"Rumor has it, they didn't."

"Has it affected the business?"

"I don't think so. I have to admit, the actual construction business is one of the best in the area. Why, is a mystery in itself. But from what I understand, both boys followed in Sid's footsteps. That includes keeping a little group of controlled-confidants. It appears the sons graduated with high honors from their father's alma mater—the college of scum and corruption."

Whether Sam wanted me to or not, I intended to do more checking into Phil and Greg DeMarco and the family business. He won't approve, but I need the background information to rule them in or out of my case. I'm sure Bella can and will help me.

"Why so quiet? You haven't written anything except the location of the DeMarco houses." He gave me a quick glance. "I can read you like a book."

"If that's true, then I suggest you stop reading cause I don't think you'll like the story."

Sam shook his head. "Out of sight—out of mind. I'm going away for a few days and you're determined to get into trouble."

"No trouble—just research. Let's ride by Bella's."

"Good idea."

Bella told me she lives in her family's house in the Heights. The address Sam got from the desk officer was 43 Cobble Creek Road.

"Casey, I'm not sure where to turn, so you need to put the address in my GPS."

I took it out of the glove compartment and punched in the address. It came up immediately. "Says we should be there in eleven minutes."

"Let me know where to turn before we get to the street so I don't overshoot the runway."

"Roger, my captain." I gave Sam a two finger salute. "Here we go. Take the next left, then the second right."

Cobble Creek Road ran through a neighborhood of well-established, well-maintained, typical Cape style homes. Bella's was about halfway down the street on the left.

"I can't imagine living alone in a house that big," I said. Her car wasn't in the driveway and both the doors on a detached two car garage were closed. I didn't intend to stop anyway. I just wanted to know where she lived. Even though I had her address back at the office, I wrote it beside number two on my points of interest list.

"Do you want me to turn around and ride by again?"

"No, I'm fine."

"Okay. Enjoy the scenery. Next stop, the Falmouth District Court."

Since it was Sunday, there weren't any cars in the parking lot.

Sam pulled up to the front entrance. "Do you want to take a picture?"

"I don't see a need to, but since we're here, I suppose I'll snap a couple." I listed the Courthouse beside number three.

"Is there any place else you'd like to see while we're here? If not, I'd like to ride by Rocco's Fish Market."

"Why?"

"I haven't seen that place for a long time and I'd like to re-familiarize myself with the set-up."

"We can't get inside."

"I know, but I can look in the windows. I just feel like it. Okay?"

"Actually, I didn't take any pictures of the outside, so while we're there I think I will."

CHAPTER 47

Sam pulled into the side lot of Rocco's market. "If I was new in town or a tourist, I'd stop here to buy fish. It doesn't look closed."

"You're right," I said.

"Every once in a while, Rocco would offer lobster rolls. It was when Rita was alive. She'd make them and he'd sell them. He wasn't a restaurant, but, oh man, those soft squishy rolls mounded with fresh lobster meat." Sam closed his eyes. "I can taste them as we speak."

I looked around to make sure nobody was watching. "I know there are businesses all around but it's Sunday, most of them are closed. I'd like to get my pictures taken and your window peeping done so we can get the hell out of here."

"I don't want somebody calling Bella to tell her two people are at her uncle's fish market taking pictures and being nosey. She wouldn't know it was us and might get upset." I waited for Sam to respond.

"I suppose you've got a point. You do your thing, I'll take a quick look, then we'll high-tail it out of here."

I took eight pictures—some of the back door, a back window, the front and back parking lots, the front door and a couple of the front of the store. I was standing by the road taking the last picture, when a car drove by, slowed down, then turned around and drove by again going in the opposite direction. I hurried back to the car to jot down the description of the vehicle. It was a navy blue BMW SUV with a Cape and Islands vanity plate, so the person most probably was a Cape resident. Unfortunately, I didn't get the letters or numbers.

Sam saw me dash back to the car. "What's the matter?" he asked as he walked over to me.

"I think we'd better leave. Our little role play as tourists hasn't gone unnoticed. While you were looking in the windows, a car went by, slowed down, turned around and came by again."

"I think you're paranoid."

"I may be. I hope it was a friend of Bella's and, as we speak, they're trying to reach her to ask her what's going on." I took a deep breath. "If she figures out it was me, I hope she'll give me a call."

"I've done all the looking I can do from the outside. The shades are down in the front windows, so I couldn't see inside. Let's head back to Hyannisport."

"You don't have to say that twice. It's such a nice day, why don't we get Watson and go to the beach for a while before you have to leave."

"You do have good ideas—sometimes." He smiled. "What are your plans since I'm not going to be around to bug you for a few days?"

"I'm going to concentrate on the reports. Maybe I can find an *i* that's not dotted or a *t* that's not crossed. I also need to set up a meeting with Bella to let her know I'm going to be doing some digging. She already told me there's a huge gossip train in town. I'm sure the minute I start asking questions, I'll be given a ticket to ride."

"Just remember, at this point, Rocco's death was ruled an accident. He was struggling with stuff from his past—the disappearance of his sister and the death of his wife. It could be assumed he wasn't thinking straight and got careless. The argument in favor of an accident is pretty compelling. Until you uncover concrete evidence, that won't change."

"It would have been so much easier if there were surveillance cameras." I looked at Sam.

"If there were, you wouldn't be working the case."

"True."

"Jot these few things down. They can be food for thought."

I got out my pad of paper and pen. "Shoot."

"Motive, vandalism, paperwork—either from the market or Rocco's house—an appointment calendar or book—if he has one—possible outstanding bills and check out his will. You need to get inside his house. I'm sure Bella can arrange that. Once you start, George will probably scrutinize your every step. From what you've said, he wants no part of an investigation."

"You can't blame him. He's an accountant. He thinks different than us. His world is cut and dry. Our world, for the most part, never is. He was told accident. He can't or won't see beyond that."

"Then you have the DeMarco brothers. They don't have minds—at least normal ones. They don't think. They just act. They're dangerous." He glanced at me. "Do you hear me? Dangerous. You're going to have to do some digging. Just don't dig a hole big enough for somebody to bury you in. There's a saying I heard a long time ago—anger is only one letter short of danger. Don't get the brothers angry."

"I'll watch my back. If it makes you feel any better, I'll check in with Marnie for the next couple nights."

"I'm going into the Stop and Shop by the lights and get us a couple of Italian subs, two sodas and some chips. I feel like having a picnic on the beach. Do you want anything else?" he asked as he made a right turn into the parking lot.

"That's one reason I love you. You can turn it on or off at the drop of a hat." I chuckled. "A picnic with subs sounds fine. I'll wait here."

CHAPTER 48

Because we were taking a cooler and a blanket and were also on a time constraint, we drove to the beach rather than walk. I was surprised when we pulled into the parking lot. There were more cars than I thought there would be. "Summer's right around the corner. The weekend warriors are already making an appearance."

Sam parked near the furthest opening onto the beach. "Did you bring Watson's leash?"

"I did." I handed it to him.

"Once we get settled, I might let him loose. It all depends on how many people are near us."

"Now I know why you went so far down," I said.

Sam looked around. "Here, you take the boy and I'll grab the cooler and beach bag. You know Watson's been spoiled. Dogs aren't supposed to run free on the beach. Actually, I don't think they're supposed to be on the beach at all."

"I'm pretty sure it's only during certain hours and it doesn't start until the beach officially opens for the season." I smiled. "We have a little time before that happens." Watson didn't seem to care. He was happy just being outside. "He appears very comfortable curled up on the blanket between us." I reached over and patted his head.

"I'm sure he knows there's food in the cooler and if we're going to eat, so is he." Sam lay down beside Watson and whispered in his ear, "Aren't you boy?"

I took Watson's water dish and food bowl, a couple plastic plates and a few napkins from my beach bag and set them on the blanket. "There's still a ball, one of his tug toys, a chew bone and a bag of doggie snacks in the bag. This must be what it's like to pack to bring a child for a beach outing."

Sam looked at me. "Not even close."

"How do you know?"

"Strictly observation—strictly observation."

I gave Watson his chew bone, to keep him occupied while I questioned Sam. "Can I change the subject?"

"Of course."

"Do you know what Mrs. DeMarco the second's maiden name was?"

"I don't. Why do you ask?"

"Obviously, she came into the picture after Maria DeMarco went missing."

"Don't jump to conclusions. It seems as though the second was in the picture before, but not as a girlfriend or a mistress."

"Explain."

"I think she worked at the business. If this had happened in Bourne, I could tell you a lot more. Then again, if this happened in Bourne, you wouldn't be looking into it."

"Why?"

"Do you have to ask? Let's put it this way, the investigation would have been conducted a lot different."

"Are you saying that the Falmouth Police Department turned the other way when it came to their probe into the case"?

"No. I hold the Falmouth Police Department in the highest esteem. Between you and me, what I'm saying is that several individuals within the department might not have been as diligent as they should have been." Sam's serious side was fully exposed.

"When we first talked about Chief Mills, you said he had his problems within the department. Is this what you were referring to?"

"This could be part of it. Again, it's been kept under wraps. It's an internal matter and he wants to keep it that way."

"It's like the kids game of pass-the-secret. It starts with a fact and, by the time it reaches the end of the line, it doesn't even resemble what was originally said."

"That's what I'm saying." Sam nodded. "Remember I told you I thought the Rocco Deluca evidence box was being used as bait—that accident cases aren't kept in records lockdown where criminal cases are?"

"Okay. So my digging into Rocco's 'accidental' death could cause some individuals a renewed concern of not only my case, but older related cases."

"Do I need to say more?" Sam sat up. "Enough talk—I'm hungry."

"Here's Watson's stuff." I handed him the bowls, a bag of food and a bottle of water. "If you do that, I'll get ours ready."

"Sounds good to me."

Watson yipped.

"He is our dog." I laughed. "I don't want to talk about me anymore. Tell me about the terrorism seminar you're going to."

"Since it all happened so fast, I won't get my packet until I get there. It would have been much nicer if I could have reviewed it beforehand. The other three guys I'm going with are in the same boat." Sam shrugged. "My Chief wants me to teach a class on terrorism in the next academy. We've never done one before."

"Haven't you got a new class starting in a couple weeks?"

"Yep. So it will be a busy time when I get home. Usually I have to write a synopsis and submit it for approval, then write a syllabus and put together related handouts. This time the Chief told me he didn't need to approve it."

"He has a lot of confidence in you."

Sam took in a deep breath and slowly let it out. "That he does."

"So do I." I leaned over and gave him a kiss. I looked at my watch.

Watson was starting to get a little restless. The seagulls knew he was on a leash, so they teased him more than usual—knowing he couldn't chase after them.

I looked at Sam. "Are you up for a run on the beach?"

"You want to run?"

"I'll probably end up walking, but I'll give it a try."

"Let's go."

That's all Watson had to hear and he was off with Sam in tow. I tried to keep up, but after a couple minutes, my leg let me know I couldn't continue so I walked back to the blanket and waited for my guys to return.

CHAPTER 49

We spent more time at the beach than we intended to, so Sam had to hustle to get his stuff together to head back to Bourne.

"Time to get a move on." He moved his duffle bag and a hang-up by the front door.

I put my arms around his neck and pulled him close. "It sure is going to be quiet around here for a couple of days." I gave him a kiss.

"Casey Quinby, nothing is quiet when you're involved."

"Isn't that what keeps it interesting?"

"I'm not sure if that's what I'd call it." Sam cradled me in his arms. "I'm going to miss this."

"Me, too."

"Promise me you'll behave."

"I'm not a child."

He looked me straight in my eyes. "You know what I mean."

"I promise." I held my hands up with my fingers crossed.

Sam shook his head. "I'll call you when I get to Quantico."

"Learn a lot and have some fun, if you can."

"I will. Now I'm out of here." He got down on his knees and tussled a little with Watson. "Take good care of our girl while I'm gone."

"Love you Sam Summers."

"Don't go getting mushy on me," he said. "But I love you too, Casey Quinby."

I watched and waved as he pulled out of the driveway.

CHAPTER 50

It only took a half-hour to put the beach stuff away. I looked around the kitchen. I wasn't hungry, but my Keurig was calling. While my coffee was brewing, I took out my briefcase. The temperature on my deck thermometer read an unseasonably high seventy degrees. I took advantage of the lingering sunlight and brought Watson outside. I hooked him to his run, then went back inside for my coffee and reading material.

It was quiet, no breeze—nothing to disturb my concentration. The only papers I took from my briefcase were the reports from the police department. Sam had looked at them more than me, so now it was my turn to examine them.

I wasn't through the first page of the first report when my cell rang. It was still inside on the kitchen table, so I had to scramble to answer it before the caller hung up. "Hello."

It was Marnie. "Just checking in. Is Sam still there?"

"No, he left about an hour ago. I was just relaxing on the deck with a coffee, looking over some of the paperwork on Uncle Rocco."

"Maloney's still here and we're going out to dinner. Do you want to come?"

"No, not tonight. You guys have fun—eat something for me. I have too much homework."

"Are you going to your office tomorrow?"

"I'm not sure what time, but I'll give you a call when I do. When we hang up I'm going to call Bella. Sometime early next week I need to meet with her."

"Okay. If you need me, call." And with that she was gone.

I held my cell out in front of me. "I will."

Marnie's call reminded me I had to call Bella. Her number was programed into my contact list, so I pulled it up and hit the connect button. I was getting ready to leave a message when she answered.

"Hi Casey. What's up?"

"I called to see if we could meet sometime next week?"

"You tell me when and I'll arrange for coverage at work."

"Actually, is it possible to meet tomorrow?"

"I have an early morning meeting, but I can be free around ten o'clock. Does that work for you?"

"It does. Why don't I meet you at the Dunkin's near the library? I want to go over some things and ask you some questions."

"Is there anything I can answer for you now?"

"No, it's better we do it tomorrow."

"Okay, I'll see you then."

"Tomorrow," I said and punched the end button.

I went back to my reading. It appeared that because the death was immediately deemed an accident, there wasn't a full investigation conducted. It was self-contained, as evident by contents in the evidence box. I assumed the rumors of a suicide obviously weren't shared by the Falmouth PD. I started a list of things I wanted to go over with Bella.

First, I want to bring her up-to-date on what I've been doing. She needed to know I've seen the Medical Examiner and have had a meeting with Chief Mills. I want to ask her about Winnie. I'm sure if Miss Winnie called the Chief about my visit, she didn't hesitate using her self-proclaimed position as the town crier to tell her cronies.

Second, I want to do a walk-through at Rocco's house. I want to feel the man's spirit. I want to get to know him. I want to observe his daily surroundings. How he lived at home could carry over to his life in the community or, for that matter, in how he conducted his business.

Third, it's time to meet brother George. Bella may not agree, but it has to be done. Even though she hired me, he should know what's happening. Of course, I don't have to report to him, Bella can let him know what she wants to share. I just don't like the element of surprise when it involves me. I want to be introduced by somebody I know and trust, rather than being approached from behind and tapped on the shoulder.

And fourth, even though Sam is dead against it, I need to know more about the DeMarcos—not just the brothers, but the second wife and even the dead Sid. There are too many unanswered questions. I promised Sam I'd be careful and I intend to keep that promise, but the DeMarco questions have to be answered. At the moment, I intend to keep this part of my investigation between Bella and myself. I see no benefit to involve George—maybe at a later date, but not now.

I put the reports away, made myself a bag of popcorn, poured a glass of White Zin with ice and was on my way to the living room when my cell rang. I set everything down, picked up my phone and checked the caller ID. It was Marnie.

"Hi."

"Hi yourself. Are you and Watson holding up the fort?"

"Yeah. I've been doing my homework and coming up with a plan of action to follow while he's gone." I sighed. "He needs to give me some space. Don't get me wrong, I appreciate his help, but he's got to realize I am very capable of flying solo. For the next three days, I'm going to bust my butt to cover all the ground I can. After all, if I'm going to make it as a PI, I've got to prove it. Otherwise, the only cases I'll get are nasty probates, cheating spouses or insurance surveillance. Those aren't the types of things I left a very lucrative job for."

Marnie didn't say anything—at least not to me. She had her hand over the phone saying something to Maloney.

"Forget what I said. It's just Sherlock feeling sorry for herself," I said.

"I have all the confidence in the world in you. Pull that chin up off the floor, get yourself a glass of wine and curl up on the couch. I think the *Amazing Race* is on."

167

"You know me like a book. My White Zin and a humongous bowl of popcorn are already sitting on the table alongside the couch and as soon as I get off the phone, I'll turn the boob tube on."

"Maloney's going back to P-town tomorrow, so I'll catch up with you sometime during the day."

"Sounds good." Before she could say anymore, I pulled a Marnie and hit the end button.

CHAPTER 51

Monday

Morning came far too quickly. The empty bed syndrome messed with my head all night. I just couldn't sleep. Images of the DeMarco brothers popped in and out, the car outside of the fish market drove by, Miss Winnie's 'pleasant' face grinned at me and the thought of working with a police department that was having internal problems was the frosting on the cake. The last thing I remembered, before the alarm clock went off, was thinking I made a mistake.

Why did I ever leave the Tribune?

Watson slept soundly beside me. "My little body guard," I whispered softly.

He must have heard me. Slowly, his head turned in my direction and his eyes opened. If I didn't know any better, I'd say he had a smile on his face.

"Ready to get up?"

He jumped down off the bed and headed for the front door. Usually Sam took him outside for a walk around the house, but for the next few days, it was my first chore of the morning. "How about I put you on your run while I get ready for work?"

He quickly changed his position and moved to the back door. My back yard is enclosed with a stockade fence, so luckily my neighbors didn't have to undergo the charm of my Red Sox Joe Boxers and Patriot's tee shirt.

The boy was outside and I wasn't vying for the bathroom, so I took my time. Watson's food and water were waiting when I brought him in. I knelt down beside him. "I'd take you with me, but I'm not going to be in the office most of the day. It's supposed to be nice out though, so I thought you might like to stay on your run." I gave him some treats. "I'll stop by later and check up on you."

I decided to forgo my coffee until I met up with Bella at Dunkins. Then, I'd have to make my first decision of the day. Do I want to be fairly good and get a number two or do I want to indulge myself and get a number one? I rocked my hands up and down. It wasn't a hard decision, a number one—two jelly donuts and a medium coffee. Case closed—decisions should all be that easy.

I didn't see Bella's car in the parking lot. I went inside and looked around. I didn't see her, but then I was ten minutes early. The little two-seater in the corner was empty, so I picked up a newspaper and went over and sat down. There was nothing earth shattering on the front page. I supposed that's a good thing. I was just about to turn to the sports section to read up on the beginning of Red Sox season when Bella came over to the table.

"What, no coffee?"

"Not yet, I waited for you. But, I'm ready now. You get yours and I'll be right behind you." It wasn't busy, but I didn't want to lose our table. It's kind of tucked away in the corner, out of ear shot.

I got my number one and Bella got an ice coffee and an egg and cheese croissant.

"I was going over my notes last night and I have a question. Yesterday, Sam and I took a ride around Falmouth. We stopped at Uncle Rocco's market. I took some pictures of the outside while Sam tried to peek inside. We were just about ready to leave when I noticed a car drive by, slow down, turn around and ride back in the direction it just came from. It could be my imagination, but I'd bet whoever it was wondered who we were. I was hoping you'd get a call about it."

"I'm surprised I didn't. Lots of people in town are wondering why we haven't put the building or the business up for sale. They know we're not going to open it."

"I tried to get the license plate number, but except for the fact that it was a Cape and Island issue, I wasn't able to get any of the letters or numbers."

"What kind of car was it?"

"A relatively new navy blue BMW SUV." I took a bite of donut. "It was probably nothing."

Bella set her coffee down. "You don't have to look any further. That was my brother, George."

I sat back in my chair. "You've got to be kidding me. Why didn't he stop or why didn't he call you?"

"That's a good question."

The look on Bella's face was neither sad nor mad—it was somewhere in between. "If that was me riding by and I saw people poking around, I'd stop. I would have thought you were agents from a real estate office or even prospective buyers." She appeared puzzled. "At the least, he should have called me."

"Maybe the good Miss Winnie's gossip train made a stop at the wrong station and the conductor said a little too much to one or more passengers." I shook my head. "Is your brother friendly with any of the Falmouth police?"

"Of course, we grew up with almost half of them."

"Then I'd say our leak could be one of Falmouth's finest." I continued, "It may or may not have been done intentionally, but I'm going to find out. I'm sure if you call George, he'll know who I am and why I was snooping around the market."

"Well, let's find out right now." Bella took her phone from her pocket and speed dialed George. She was about to hang up when he answered."We need to talk."

I couldn't hear George's side of the conversation. I hoped Bella would put him on speaker, but she didn't.

"Are you working from home? Good, then we'll be there in about a half hour."

I took a deep breath.

"Yes, we'll. Don't be an asshole. I'm sure you know who I'm talking about."

I felt like a third party, but sooner or later I knew this was going to happen.

"I'll properly introduce you to her." She held her phone away from her ear.

I could hear her brother yelling, but couldn't make out what he was saying.

"Shut-up. For once in your miserable life, you're going to listen to me. I said we'll be at your house in a half-hour and I expect you to be there—understand." She hit the end button. "I'm sorry. George and I never fought—we were always very close. Since Uncle Rocco died, things have changed."

"Bella, I don't want to tell you what to do, but maybe you should cut him a little slack. From what you told me, he was very close to Rocco. Sometimes guys have a harder time dealing with tragedy than we do. That's probably why he can't even entertain the idea that your uncle could have been murdered." I reached across the table and took her hand. "Let's talk to him. Let me tell him what I've done. I think it will be better if he knows what's happening, rather than us doing things behind his back. I know it will be better if he hears things from us and not after it's been passed from person to person." I took the last sip of my coffee. "Does this make any sense to you?"

She nodded. "It does. I should have told him from the start what I was doing. We've never had an issue with trust. I hope I didn't ruin that."

"We'll work it out." I stood up. "I'll drive, you be my GPS."

We threw away our trash and headed out to my car in the parking lot.

CHAPTER 52

Nothing was said between us for the first twenty minutes of the ride to Buzzards Bay.

I knew we were getting close, so it was time to strike up a conversation. "I've ridden by the road to Buttermilk Bay many times, but never driven down it. Friends of my parents had a summer place there. They visited several times, but I never went with them."

Bella nodded. "It is a beautiful place. The beach is really nice. It's too shallow for large boats and since the Cohasset Narrows bridge is fixed and low, no masted vessels can pass."

"I've heard that."

"In a couple miles, at the next set of lights, you're going to take a right on Jefferson Road, then go past Woodside Avenue and Hill Street. George's house is just after the Jefferson Road curve on right."

I turned off Route 6, then followed Bella's directions. She didn't give me a street number, so I slowed down to a crawl until she told me which driveway to pull into. The house was beautiful—a typical Cape Cod style with weathered shingles, white trim and a periwinkle blue door. The front lawn was manicured and the landscaping appeared to be professionally done. I couldn't help but remark on the hydrangeas. "Those are my favorite flowers. The color matches the door." I felt foolish after I said it. It was obvious I was just trying to make conversation.

"Casey, it's going to be okay." She took a deep breath. "Things will be said, but in the long run, I'm sure we'll work it out. We have to. We're the only family we've got."

"You're right. You do what you have to do. I'm here for you to lean on."

"I appreciate that. Let's get going."

We both got out of the car. Bella led—I followed. He must have seen us pull in. Just before we reached the door, it opened and a person, I assumed to be George, was standing there to greet us. He stepped forward and put his arms around Bella. No words were exchanged. I moved away trying to give them space.

A minute passed before Bella turned to me. "Casey, I want you to meet my brother, George."

I held out my hand. He took it.

You could tell Bella and George were siblings. Except for the fact that Bella was petite and George was probably six feet, they both had the olive complexion, dark brown hair and blue-green eyes.

"I'm glad to meet you. Why don't we go inside?"

Bella smiled and followed her brother.

I followed Bella to a glass enclosed porch that showcased gorgeous views of his private beach and Buttermilk Bay.

"I put a pot of coffee on. I know Bella and I will have a cup. Casey will you join us?"

Bella smiled and spoke for me, "She's a java junkie too."

"I like her already," said George as he headed in the direction of the fresh coffee-brewing aroma.

I tried to look around without being obvious, but it didn't work.

"It's beautiful, isn't it. When he bought this house it needed lots of work. He didn't care. He said he bought it for the view. It took several years to finish the remodel, but I have to admit, it was worth it." Bella looked toward the kitchen. "George is the aggressive one—the one with imagination. He can envision what can be, whereas I exist in the moment. He should have been an architect. He's so creative. Instead, he became an accountant, where his mind revolves around numbers and everything is cut and dry." She rolled her eyes. "But, he has done well in his chosen profession. Actually, if you think about it, he has the best of both worlds."

174

"I'm back. You two can stop talking about me now." He laughed and set a tray of coffee and cookies on the table in front of Bella and me. "Sorry for the store bought cookies. Next time my sister needs to give me fair warning that she's coming to visit."

"Don't believe him. Numbers and creativity, yes—cooking, no." Bella picked up one of the store bought chocolate chip cookies and examined it as though it had been entered into a bake-off contest. "I'm the one who inherited the baking skills."

"I know you two didn't come here to check up on me." George tilted his head from one side then to the other.

"You're right. First and foremost, I wanted to meet you." I looked straight at him. "I understand I almost did that yesterday." I didn't let him respond. "Why didn't you stop when you rode by your uncle's market?"

"How did you know it was me?"

"I happened to see a car go by, slow down, turn around and ride by again. It's my job to be observant. I noted the color and make of the car." I didn't want to give him Bella's name, but I also didn't want to dance around the facts. "I mentioned it to your sister and, voila, you got caught."

"Since Uncle Rocco died, I often ride by the market. Most times I don't stop and I don't go inside unless I'm with Bella. It's been five months since the accident that took his life, but no amount of time will erase the memory of the last time I saw him." George's voice cracked. "About a week before he died, we had a discussion about selling the business. I have to admit, it got rather heated. I walked out. When I tried to reach him to apologize, it was too late." George didn't look at us as he spoke.

"Casey, as I told you, my brother and I don't agree on how our uncle died. That's why you're sitting here with us now." Bella looked at George who was still studying the floor. "I can't one-hundred percent agree it was an accident, but my brother is adamant that it was. If you can convince me it was, then I'll accept it, but until that time, I won't."

175

George glanced at me then turned his attention to Bella. Tears formed in his eyes. "My sister is stubborn. She takes after our mother. That scares me. Our mother would insist our father was wrong, especially when it came to family and, in most cases, she was right." George leaned back in his chair and closed his eyes.

I knew he was reflecting on past memories.

"I don't know how much Bella told you about some of our relatives, but we have several that I don't admit exist anymore."

"I'm sure you're talking about the DeMarco family."

"Yes."

"Bella did tell me, but unbeknownst to her, I had already done some research on them. They are, let's say, a shady bunch."

"That's putting it mildly," said Bella.

"I know I'll have questions regarding them. When I get that part of the investigation organized, we'll talk. There's no sense in making the DeMarcos a topic of discussion right now. The main reason for our meeting today was to introduce myself and let you know why I'm hanging around."

Bella smiled. "George, if Uncle Rocco's death was anything but an accident, I feel confident Casey will be able to tell us. Please give me the time she needs to do her job. As soon, she's done, I promise I won't hold you back from settling uncle's legal matters and let his memory rest in peace."

George turned to look out over the water. "Beautiful isn't it. I don't need a couch with a person jotting down notes in a mini-spiral journal charging me over a hundred dollars a session to keep me sane. It's just me and the Bay."

I was a little set back with the sudden change in George's psyche. I glanced at Bella. It didn't seem to concern her and, since I had just met her brother, I figured it was normal behavior to exhibit a displaced change of mindset. I wanted to leave, so rather than prolong the exit, I stood up to indicate I was ready to travel.

Bella followed my lead. George stayed seated.

I again extended my hand. "George, it was nice to meet you."

It was as though he bounced back from a land beyond. He stood and shook my hand. "I appreciate your efforts on behalf of my sister and me. I'll look forward to meeting with you again."

It was the appropriate cut-and-dry response to a first-time meeting with a stranger.

Bella gave her brother a hug. They exchanged a quick kiss, then we left George on the porch looking back out over the water. Our meeting was over. I followed Bella to the front door.

"Bye," she called to George.

There was no reply.

We let ourselves out and in minutes were on Route 6 headed back towards Falmouth.

I checked my watch. It was almost one o'clock. "I'm hungry. Want to stop and get something?"

"Sounds good to me, but let's go someplace other than Falmouth."

"If I turn around, we can go to Barney's. Their foods pretty good and they've got Keno. Maybe we can get lucky."

"I've been by there umpteen times, but never stopped."

"In the summer you have to know what times to come, otherwise you end up waiting for sometimes an hour. We should be okay today."

We pulled into Barney's parking lot and, just as I suspected, we missed the lunch crowd. I wanted to sit at the bar, but figured if we were going to talk about our visit with George and what our next stop should be, our conversation could be picked up by inquisitive ears. The sign by the door read SEAT YOURSELF. We took a table by the front window.

As soon as we sat down, the server appeared. "Can I get you something to drink?"

We both ordered Diet Coke.

"I hate it when they pounce."

I nodded in agreement.

"What's good?"

"I usually get fried clams, but I think I'll get a cup of chowder and an order of onion rings."

"Healthy choice," she laughed.

"That's me—an article right out of *Prevention* Magazine."

"I'm going to get your fried clams, so if you need a fix, feel free to take some."

"Don't tempt me."

The server brought our drinks, then took our food order.

"What did you think of my brother?"

"I liked him. There's no denying you're brother and sister—at least physically. But, I think you reside on opposite sides of the spectrum of life. He's 'Mr. Show Me the Facts', whereas you're "Ms. I have a Dream"—hence the accountant versus the librarian."

"We've been accused of that before."

"Since there's nobody sitting real close to us, I want to go over a few things with you. Meeting George was on my list for today, but he was number three." I reached inside my purse and took out my mini-legal pad. "One more thing before we move on—George never told me why he didn't stop when he saw me checking out your uncle's market."

I knew by the puzzled expression on Bella's face she shared the same concern. "We moved on to another subject, so maybe it slipped his mind."

I didn't buy her explanation, but right now I had other things I wanted to discuss. "I've already been to Falmouth and talked to a few people. I paid an unannounced visit to the Medical Examiner, Derek Jenkins. I met his secretary, Winnie Parks. Do you know her?"

"Winnie Parks," repeated Bella. "She's probably the first link in Falmouth's major gossip chain. I wouldn't be surprised if she's the one that somehow alerted my brother you were looking into Uncle Rocco's death. She thrives on stuff like that."

"It practically took an act of Congress to get past her. And, even when I did, she wanted to stay in Mr. Jenkins office to listen to my spiel. Fortunately, he dismissed her. Apparently, she has a reputation of eavesdropping because he got up and closed his door."

"She's got one of those public jobs—once you've got it, you've got it for life. And she knows it, so she takes full advantage of her position. She's been called on the carpet before, but short of stealing there's nothing anybody can do."

"She knew I was there about Rocco. I had to tell her or she wouldn't even consider giving me the opportunity to talk to Mr. Jenkins. And, after he told her to give me a copy of his findings on the accident, her mind shifted into first gear. I knew the ME had a one o'clock meeting, so I figure she used the rest of the afternoon to practice her Lily Tomlin switchboard impersonation—one ringy-dingy...two ringy-dingys."

"What makes you think she made some phone calls?"

"I know she made at least one—to Chief Mills."

"You've got to be kidding?"

"I'm not. Miss Winnie is one of those people you want to wash right out of your hair." I took a drink of soda. "Know what I mean?"

"I called the Falmouth PD to make an appointment to see the Chief. He was expecting my call. He's the one who told me he'd received a call from Winnie Parks. Before I got there, he had me checked out from head to toe. He knew why I was there. He even called the Chief in Barnstable. Fortunately I've worked on many cases with the Barnstable PD, so Chief Lowe gave me a great recommendation."

"I'm impressed, but not surprised."

Now I had to be careful what I said. "The Chief gave me a copy of the contents of the Rocco Deluca evidence box." Hopefully, Bella didn't fully understand the concept of an evidence box. "At this point I'm reviewing everything. It takes time, so you'll have to bear with me."

"I understand. All I ask is that you don't hang me out to dry."

"I told you I'd keep you informed. Let me work the pieces and get them in some kind of order, then we'll go over them together. That's why you hired me."

Our food came. We put our conversation regarding the case on hold. The next half hour consisted of small talk, food and a few games of Keno.

The last winning number of the final Keno game we played popped up on the overhead screen. Bella checked her printout. Her eyes lit up like floodlights. "Casey, you're not going to believe this. I'm buying lunch. My four numbers came out. I won a hundred dollars."

"You've got to be kidding," I checked her ticket, then laughed. "I must be your lucky charm."

Bella paid the bill and we left.

CHAPTER 53

She was still talking about her win when we pulled out of the parking lot and headed in the direction of the Bourne Bridge. "When I lived in Boston I used to play the Lottery every once in a while. I'd make lists of what I'd do with the money if I won. I had a list if I won five million, one for two million, one for five-hundred thousand and even one for five thousand. Seriously, I had lots of time on my hands."

I nodded. "I think the last time I played the Lottery was four years ago. I was working a case in Bourne and stopped to have lunch at Barney's. I didn't win though—never have."

"After we do whatever is next on your list, we can stop for an ice cream."

"Okay with me."

We were approaching the base of the bridge when Bella asked, "What's next on the agenda?"

"I'd like to go over to your uncle's house."

Bella got quiet. "Let me check to make sure I have the key." She shuffled through her purse and came up with a ring holding three keys. "I've got them—a key for the market, and two for the house."

"Are you okay with going there today?"

"I know it has to be done, so we might as well do it now. You need to know the houses in Uncle Rocco's neighborhood are close together. Most all his neighbors know my car, but nobody knows yours. We're liable to have gawkers. And, trust me, they might come over to see what's going on, but once they see it's me, they should go back into hibernation."

"I'm sure they mean well. If I were you, I'd be glad they're watching out for the house. If they turn their backs, it could be an easy mark for vandals."

"You're right. I should look at it positively."

"Let's go meet the neighbors." I smiled. "Remember, I don't know where we're going, so you've got to be the obnoxious GPS lady again."

"It's not far from here. We should be there in ten minutes."

I followed her directions. It was ten minutes to the second when we pulled into Rocco's driveway. We got out of the car and started towards his house.

"Hold up for just a minute. I want to give my office a call." She moved a few feet away, took her cell from her purse and, I assume, dialed the number to the library.

I took my camera from my purse and snapped a few pictures of the front of the house. As I turned, I noticed the curtain in the front window of the house across the street move. The snoops were already in place watching our every move. I felt like I was under a microscope.

Bella finished her call and joined me on the porch. "They're doing just fine without me."

"We're being watched by the person or persons across the street. I was tempted to spin around and give them a big wave, but I behaved myself."

"That would have been the one to do it to. Old lady Martin flirted with my uncle for as long as I can remember. We used to make a joke of it. After Aunt Rita died, Miss Martin took it upon herself to be Rocco's personal body guard."

"Miss Martin?"

"Yeah, she never married. She grew up in that house and will probably die in that house." Bella realized what she'd said. "That was a morbid statement." She looked across the street and whispered, "Sorry Miss Martin."

It wasn't funny, but it was. I started to laugh. "She must think I'm here from some real estate company and you're getting ready to put the house on the market. I wonder how long it will take her to let the rest of the neighborhood know."

Bella smiled. "I'll bet you the rest of the money from my Keno win, she'll walk over here before we leave."

"That's a sucker's bet."

"We could toy with her or just have a neighborly conversation and say nothing. I'm sure that would ruffle her feathers." Bella moved forward and unlocked the door.

"Let's have the neighborly conversation."

Bella and I went inside. I followed her listening and taking pictures as she moved from room to room giving me a complete tour of the house.

"Did your uncle keep any paperwork related to the business here or did he keep it all at the market?"

"As far as I know, he kept it all at the market and now George has it at his house."

"What about his personal paperwork?"

"He used one of the bedrooms as an office. Since Uncle Rocco gave my brother complete control of anything that involved numbers, I'm sure all his personal financial and related stuff is also with George."

"Can we take a look at what might still be here?"

"Sure, I don't have a problem with that."

We walked to the end of the hallway and turned left into the office. It was so sterile, it appeared staged. I stood in the doorway and looked around.

"Casey, what are you thinking?"

"This room doesn't match the rest of the house. There's nothing out of place. It doesn't look like it was ever used."

"My brother might be able to explain." Bella walked behind the desk and opened several of the drawers. "Both of these are empty." She closed them, then checked the remaining two. The top one had several pens, a pencil, some elastics, a container of paper clips and an old wooden school ruler. The last one had a hanging file full of empty manila folders.

"Can I see if there's anything in those drawers?" I pointed to a three drawer file cabinet on the opposite wall."

"Sure," she said.

The top and bottom drawers were empty, but the second one had three photo albums and two boxes of pictures. At a quick glance, some were very old.

Bella picked up the albums and brought them over to the desk. She started to flip through the pages stopping occasionally to take a closer look.

I finished with the file cabinet, so I walked over beside her and watched as she reminisced. "This is one of my parents, George and me. I must be about five. That was thirty-one years ago." She leaned her elbows on the desk and cradled her face in her hands.

I rested my hand on her shoulder. "Why don't you take these home with you. I always get comfort when I take out old family photos. It brings back good memories."

I helped her gather everything up. We made sure all the drawers were closed and left the room. "Do you want me to close the door?"

"Yeah, I think so."

We hadn't reached the living room, when the doorbell rang.

"Miss Martin?" I smiled.

Bella set her stuff down on the couch and answered the door. "Hi Miss Martin. What can I do for you?"

I put my hand over my mouth to hide an uncontrollable grin.

"I'm just checking to make sure everything is all right. Your brother was here the other day, but you haven't been here for a while." Miss Martin tried to look around Bella into the house where I was standing.

"Everything is fine, Miss Martin. A friend of mine wanted to see Uncle Rocco's house."

"Is she interested in buying it?"

"Miss Martin, I think you should go back to your house. We have some things we have to check out, then we'll be leaving. You'll be the first to know when we're ready to sell." Bella took a step back. "Good-bye," she said and closed the door.

184

"I'll help you with those albums and photo boxes." I bent down and took them off the couch. "You lock up and I'll meet you at the car." I wanted to give her some space to gather her thoughts before we left.

"I'll just be a minute.

"Take your time." I looked at Miss Martin's house. One of the curtain panels was pulled to the side. I couldn't see her standing there, but I'm sure she was. "Maybe I'll go into my song and dance routine for the neighbors."

I was checking for phone messages when Bella opened the car door and got in. "I don't know about you, but there's a cone of chocolate peanut butter ice cream at Smitty's calling my name."

"Show me the way."

CHAPTER 54

Bella ordered her chocolate peanut butter cone and I got a dish of amaretto cherry chip. "Cute place," I scooped up a bite. "Hmmm. This is really good."

"Been here for years. I love it." She licked around the top of the cone to catch a couple drips. "Let's sit." Before I could answer, she was already halfway across the room. "Is there anything else you want to go over today?"

"There is one more thing, but we have covered a lot, so if you want to take a break, we can wait."

Bella didn't hesitate, she replied immediately, "Go for it." She pulled a couple napkins from the holder on the table and wrapped them around her cone.

I took another bite, savoring it until it was gone. "I want to talk to you about the DeMarco family."

She stopped eating.

I kept talking. "I met them Sunday. Actually, I didn't really meet them. Sam and I went to breakfast in Cotuit and your two cousins came in with their wives."

She went back to her chocolate peanut butter. "How did you know who they were?"

"I didn't—Sam did. He pointed them out to me. I wanted him to introduce me, but he flat out refused. As we were leaving, Phil spoke to Sam. It was strictly a brief exchange of words between two people that didn't particularly like each other." My ice cream was starting to melt so I took a break from our conversation and caught up with my eating.

"Has Sam had dealings with them in the past?"

"Indirectly, yes. He told me to take a good look and if I ever saw either one of them in an uncomfortable radius of myself to call him or Chief Mills. He said they're dangerous and not to be trusted."

"He's right. I'm family and I'm afraid of them."

"What about George. Does he associate with them?"

"No, neither one of us has for years."

"Do you think they could have had anything to do with your Uncle Rocco's death?"

Bella took a deep breath and let it out slowly. "The thought crossed my mind, but that's where it stayed. I never mentioned it to anybody, not even George."

"You told me the first day we met that you thought Rocco might have some information that could help find out what happened to Maria."

"I did say that."

"I'm concerned about that information. When we went into your uncle's office, it was stripped clean. The desk drawers and file drawers were empty except for a few supplies. There were no storage boxes in the closet or anywhere around the room, for that matter. It was the same way at the market." I leaned back in my chair. "I can't imagine if there was evidence regarding his sister's disappearance, he would have destroyed it."

"Neither can I. But, like I told you he never shared it with me or my brother." She rubbed her eyes and sighed. "So, I don't know what he had."

"Do you know if he had a safety deposit box somewhere? It's a possibility he kept what evidence he thought he had in one. If he did, there has to be a key."

"He never mentioned one to me."

I knew the next question was going to get a reaction—which way, I wasn't sure. "Bella, do you think George might have taken all the paperwork from Rocco's house to his?"

She didn't say anything.

"We know he took everything from the market. Actually, he probably had most of it anyway, since he did the books. Maybe he took the stuff from the house for safe keeping. Maybe Rocco did confide in George about the Maria information he was working on. Maybe George thought your cousins also had wind of his findings. All these maybes could have something to do with your uncle's death."

"Are you saying my brother knows more than he's telling us?"

"No, not necessarily. I'm saying there's a paperwork trail somewhere." I watched Bella's face. Her eyes were darting back and forth like she was trying to find something. "I need time to work on this," I said.

"Okay. Is there anything you want me to do?"

"Not right now." I thought for a minute. "I do, however, have a favor to ask."

"Anything."

"I don't want you to talk to George about any of this." I didn't break eye contact with her until she answered.

"You know he's going to ask me, don't you."

"I'm sure you'll get a call tonight."

"Keep it light. Just tell him I'm reviewing reports that I got from the Medical Examiner. Since George knows it was ruled an accident, he shouldn't prod you for more information. I know that's pretty generic, but I hope it will satisfy him."

"Whatever you think is best is what I'll do."

"I appreciate that. It will make it much easier to get the answers I need."

Bella nodded.

"We've covered enough for today. Sam's away, so I don't have any distractions to keep me from going over what we accomplished. If you're not doing anything tomorrow night, why don't we do dinner somewhere and I'll let you know what I've come up with."

"I'm free."

"I'll give you a call tomorrow morning and we'll decide where to meet." I pulled into the library parking lot.

"I'm going to check on Dewey before I head home." She got out of the car and leaned back in before she shut the door. "Thanks Casey, talk to you tomorrow."

I waited until she got to the side door of the library, then waved and drove away.

CHAPTER 55

Things were getting interesting. I was beginning to formulate theories, but knew I had to tread softly. It's always touchy when family was involved and this case is no exception. I visualized a puzzle. The pieces on the left side portrayed the DeMarco family. The pieces on the right fit together to reveal the Deluca family. There was an empty space dividing the two sides and there were no pieces left in the box to join them together.

I was stopped for a red light at the corner of Route 28 and Strawberry Hill Road when my cell rang. I fumbled to get it out of my pocket. "Hello."

"Where are you?" It was Marnie.

"Oops, I forgot to check in." I waited a minute. "I'm on my way home. I've been in Falmouth all day."

"Do you want to do supper tonight?"

"No. I'm going to stay in and do some work. It was a busy day and I want to get my notes organized. "

"I can get subs."

"Not tonight. I'll be at my office part of the day tomorrow. I'll give you a call when I get there. Later."

"Later."

I didn't mean to be so abrupt with Marnie. I needed to be alone tonight. I didn't notice the traffic light turn green, but the car behind me did and leaned on the horn. I wanted to exercise my middle finger, instead I vented to my dashboard. "Okay asshole, okay—I'm moving."

I turned the radio to 99.9. John Legend's *All of Me* was playing. I remembered watching him on television when he performed his song at the Grammys last January. In an interview he said he was inspired by his then girlfriend, now wife, to write it. *I wonder what delightful parts of my dazzling personality would motivate Sam if he was to compose a song for me.* I snickered.

I pulled into my driveway. It felt strange to be home this early on a weekday. I checked my watch. It was a little after three. Watson must have heard me. I left my stuff in the car and walked around to the back of the house. His leash was stretched as far as it would go. I ran over to give him a hug, but when I bent down he literally pushed me backwards.

"So you want to wrestle," I moved closer so he wouldn't choke himself. After a few minutes of tussling back and forth, I rolled away and stood up. "How about a walk to the beach?"

I unhooked his leash from the run. We walked to my car. "Let me take my paraphernalia inside and I'll be good to go."

It was perfect weather for a walk—high sixties with a gentle breeze. I tried to jog, but my leg wouldn't cooperate. One good leg and one bad leg don't figure into the equation for a run. I shrugged it off—at least I can walk. Watson didn't care whether we walked or ran, he just liked the idea of the change of scenery.

There were only a few people at the beach. Most of them were doing the same thing we were. A little further down from where I was I saw a young couple playing in the sand with their children. They were showing them how to make a sand castle. I smiled. The mom and dad were laughing—probably having more fun than the kids.

Watson saw his seagull friends, so I let him free run. As soon as I unhooked him, off he went. I wasn't worried. I knew he wouldn't go far. Every few feet, he'd stop and turn to make sure I was still behind him. *What would I ever do without him?*

I walked up to the wooden wall that separated the parking lot from the beach and sat down. I looked at my watch. It was too early to call Sam. I sat for another half-hour, then called to Watson. He looked at his seagull friends, then to me, then again to his friends. I won out. He bounded back to where I was sitting.

"Good boy." I reached in my pocket and took out some treats for him. His butt and tail were going a mile-a-minute. "Time to start home." I hooked him up to his leash and off we went.

When we got in the house Watson walked to the pantry, then turned and gave me the 'I'm hungry' look.

"Okay, buddy, we might as well have some supper before I get engrossed in the life and times of Uncle Rocco." I took out the bag of Kibbles 'n Bits and filled his dish. "There, you should be set for the night." But, if you're good and let mommy work, maybe there'll be some doggie ice cream in your future." I gave him a head pat.

I wasn't very hungry, so I made myself a Fluffernutter, opened a bag of sour cream and onion kettle chips and poured a glass of White Zin over ice. How can you go wrong mixing peanut butter, marshmallow crème and squishy white bread? I set myself up at the table, then took my notes and a red pen from my briefcase and started the task of eating, drinking and reading.

The notes I took at George's house were on top, so that's where I began. I was impressed with his house, both outside and in. I guess accountants make good money. I wonder if Uncle Rocco paid him. I went to my closet and got a new mini-legal pad and started to make a list of questions. I'm sure Bella said he works for himself, but I'll check that out. If so, maybe she can furnish me with some of his client's names. But, before I contacted any of them, I'd talk to Sam to see if I can legally do that—at least at this point in time in my investigation.

Since George was Rocco's moneyman, I wonder if Bella knew anything about how much Rocco or the fish market was worth. I know one relates to the other, but usually there's some kind of separation. That brings me to the question, was Rocco's fish market a sole proprietorship or was it incorporated? I should be able to check it out on the internet. I wrote that down and starred it. Bella did say that the main reason George wanted to sell the business was because it wasn't bringing in any money to pay bills, such as electricity, water, taxes. But, Bella said Uncle Rocco was well healed, so she wasn't worried. If push comes to shove, I might ask to see the books. My degrees are in criminal justice and journalism, but when I was at UMass I minored in accounting.

I took a couple bites of sandwich and downed them with White Zin—great combination—then sat back in my chair. It's so much easier for me to mentally sort things out when I'm the one asking, pondering and answering the questions.

I was on my second re-read of what I had written, when a bell went off in my head. "This should have been number one," I said out loud. I spoke as I wrote, "Why was George in Falmouth and only five minutes away from the fish market when the police, who discovered the body, called him?" I three-stared the question. I flipped back through some notes I made when I first took the case. This was one of them. That shouldn't have slipped my mind. Too many things happening too fast. This is why I needed to get organized without anyone sitting beside me or looking over my shoulder.

On my next meeting with Chief Mills, I'd ask him about George. I know the Chief is anxious to see what my investigation uncovers. I know he's known George for a long time. I need him to share George's personality traits and whatever background information he thinks I should have to establish a profile of Rocco's nephew.

I finished my supper, put my dishes in the sink and poured myself another glass of wine. I had just settled in when my cell rang. "Hello."

It was Sam. "Has my Sherlock broke any nails yet trying to crawl under a rock?"

I missed his sarcasm. Almost. "How's it going down there in Virginia?"

"It's intense, but interesting. I'm glad I came." He sighed. "We just got out of class."

"Then you haven't had supper?"

"Nope. There's not much around here, so we decided to grab something at Subway."

"I'm sorry. You could have had a gourmet fluffernutter with me."

"The guys are calling. I'll talk to you tomorrow."

"Bye." He was already gone. I went back to my reading.

Rocco's house was next in my pile of notes. It was nice, but nothing out of the ordinary. It was apparent that it had been well maintained over the years. Rocco's wife, Rita, died five years ago in 2009 and he never remarried. I was impressed at Rocco's housekeeping skills. Everything was neat. Nothing seemed out of place. Of course, I'd never been in the house before, but from first observations, I'd hire him as my housekeeper.

The one room I was overly concerned about was his office. Even though the rest of the house was very neat with everything in place, it wasn't sterile. There were things all around that made Rocco's house his home. He, or Rita, must have been readers. There were two, five shelf bookcases completely filled. I didn't check out the titles, but figured they were pleasure books. The couch and loveseat in the living room had decorative throw pillows on each end. There were vases, knick-knacks, framed family pictures, a mantle clock displaying the correct time, a couple neat piles of magazines and a pair of, what I assumed to be, Rocco's slippers under the coffee table. I find it hard to believe Rocco would move everything related to his personal life or business out of his home. I made a note to ask Bella about this. Something didn't set right with me, so I gave it two red stars.

Then there was Miss Martin. This little old lady didn't miss a thing. She could be the key into who took out enough boxes to empty a complete room. If Rocco did it himself, it would answer lots of questions, but I don't think he did. And, if it was anybody but George, it would open up a whole new chapter in my investigation.

I'd had enough White Zin, but wasn't ready to hit the sack, so I got up from the table and headed towards my Keurig to make a cup of French Vanilla. I had just loaded a K-cup and pulled the lever down to start the brewing process, when Watson jumped up from his corner, started barking and ran to the back door.

"Whoa, there buddy." I walked over beside him. "What's the matter?" I kneeled down and tried to calm him. "Did you have a bad dream?" He stopped barking, but still seemed anxious. This wasn't like him at all. I turned on the outside light, but didn't see anything. I checked to make sure the door was locked. It was. Even still, I left the light on. I moved across the kitchen to the front door and repeated the process. With Watson by my side, I held onto his collar and opened the door. Sam had changed the dim little light I'd had for years to a much brighter one that lite the entire front yard. I didn't see anything, but left both lights on. "You're little squirrel friends must have had a late night party." I managed a smile, but was a concerned. Watson didn't go back to his corner. Instead, he curled up next to my chair.

I had forgotten to take my coffee off the counter after I checked out the front yard. It had cooled down, so I popped it into the microwave. There were still a few things I wanted to go over before watching the news and going to bed.

I hadn't talked much to Bella about her cousins. Their names came up, but we didn't get into particulars. I wasn't quite sure what to ask. Sam didn't want me to get involved with the DeMarco family at all, but I had to. I'd tell her Sam pointed out their houses last Sunday when we took our ride through Falmouth. Then I'd ask her what she knew about their business. I also wanted to know more about the step-mother and her role in the DeMarco family now that Sid was gone. I'm sure I'd come up with more questions, but those were a start.

It was ten minutes of eleven when I finished getting ready for bed. That gave me just enough time to take Watson out to the back yard before the news came on. I hooked his leash to his collar, unlocked the door and went out onto the deck. Before I walked down the steps, I scanned the yard. Everything appeared to be normal. I felt brave walking around in the daylight, but never did like the dark. We did a little circle walk, Watson did his business and we headed back to the house. We had just started up the stairs, when I thought I heard a rustle in the bushes behind my car. Watson didn't flinch. He didn't seem concerned. I shrugged my shoulders and we went inside.

Must have been my imagination.

I turned the TV on, flipped to NBC, then curled up at the end of the couch. With Sam not here, Watson claimed the other end. I watched the news and the weather, then woke the boy and we both went to bed.

CHAPTER 56

Tuesday

I didn't want to get up when the alarm clock went off. I reached over and hit the snooze button. The additional eight minutes felt like one. Watson nudged me with his nose. "If you're going to play Sam, you better get up and make me coffee," I laughed. "Hey, how would you like to come to my office today?"

Watson yelped and wagged his tail. Either he knew what I just said or it was a signal that he needed to go outside. It didn't take much to know he was ready to go out.

I lazed around trying to get my brain in order. First thing was to call Marnie. It was time to bring her on board. It was time to meet the DeMarcos. Everything I've heard up to this point about the DeMarco family, past and present, is trouble. I want to know if any of that trouble was documented—if any one of them ever went to court and did time for whatever reason or reasons. Sam said Sid was a participant in several confrontations, but he was never found guilty. As far as Sid's sons, the only discussion was a directive to stay away from them. That wasn't going to happen. Since Sam wasn't going to be back on the Cape until Thursday, I had two full days to get some answers.

I was on my second cup of coffee when my phone rang. The caller ID read unknown.

Here we go.

"Hello."

"Good morning." It was Sam.

"What's with the unknown on my ID?"

"I borrowed my buddy's phone. I forgot to plug mine in last night and it didn't even register one bar this morning."

"What time is class?"

"In a half-hour, so I thought I'd give you a call now because I don't know what the day's schedule will be. They've got a lot of information they want to cram into this three-day seminar, but I'm liking it."

"Will you be teaching it at the next academy?"

"That's what the chief has in mind. It's intense, but interesting and the instructor is very good. I hope I'm half as good as him. "Enough of the business stuff. How are my girl and the boy holding up?"

"We're doing just fine. I was in the process of planning my day when you called. Watson's coming to the office with me—at least for the morning." There was no way I was about to tell Sam that I was having Marnie look into the DeMarcos. "I'm going to call Chief Mills to see if he's free around one o'clock. I want to ask him some questions about brother, George."

"What kind of questions?"

"How well the Chief knows him—his involvement in the community—his personality traits—his friends, if he knows who they are—is he friendly with any of the Falmouth cops? Stuff like that." I stopped to catch my breath.

"Nice run-on sentence." He laughed.

"I haven't finished. Then, I want to ask him if I can interview the police officers who found Rocco's body at his fish market."

"Will you be doing that before Thursday?"

"Probably not. I need a little time to get the questions together. I have some, but I'm sure I'm only going to get one shot at these interviews, so I want to get them right."

"If you wait till I get home, I'll help you with the questions."

"I'd like that. I'll run what I've got by you, then you can help me refine them and probably add additional ones." I smiled, but he couldn't see me. "That means Thursday, I better put clean sheets on the bed."

"You're on." Sam hesitated. "I've got to get going. Talk to you later. Love you," he said softly.

"You too." I held the phone against my chest and closed my eyes. "Miss you Sam Summers," I whispered.

Okay, Casey Quinby, time to get back to the business at hand.

First I have to make the call to Marnie, then the Chief, then Bella to make plans for dinner.

Marnie answered on the first ring. "Sitting on the phone or expecting an exciting call?"

"Neither—slow morning—just plain bored. Are you about to make it more interesting—I hope?"

"I think so. I should be at my office by nine-thirty. Want to come over for coffee?"

"I'll take my coffee break at nine-forty-five. See you then—gotta go, my other line is beeping."

Okay Marnie's in place, now to call Monica in Chief Mills' office. Per the Chief, she had given me her direct line so I didn't have to go through the main switchboard. I dialed, but my call went to voice mail. "Hi Monica, it's Casey Quinby. I was wondering if I could meet with the Chief sometime this afternoon. Please call me on my cell to let me know." She had one of my business cards, but I gave her my number anyway.

Next, was to call Bella. I punched in her number.

"Morning Casey."

"Love how the phones announce the caller—at least most of the time." I smiled. "Are we still on for dinner?"

"We are. Where do you want to go?"

"There's an Italian Restaurant in Mashpee I've wanted to try. It's called Soprano's," I waited for her reply.

"Good choice. My friends go there all the time, but I've never been. What time do you want me to meet you?"

"How does six o'clock sound?"

"Hold on for a minute."

I heard her desk phone ring.

"Dewey's calling. I'll see you at six."

I put my phone away, hooked Watson to his leash, picked up my briefcase and purse and headed out the front door. I opened the passenger side—Watson jumped in. I closed the door, went around the front of the car, opened the back door, put my stuff in and got into the driver's seat ready to head to the Village. I had just put the car in reverse when my cell rang. My cell switchboard was busy this morning. That famous person, unavailable, showed up on the caller ID.

"Hello."

"Hi Casey, it's Monica. I spoke to Chief Mills and he said he'd see you at one-thirty this afternoon. I'll be downstairs to meet you."

"Thanks, I appreciate it. I'll see you then."

Watson sat patiently, not barking a word. I patted his head, reached in my pocket and gave him a treat. I swear he smiled.

So far my day was moving just as I'd hoped it would. Everything was in place. I backed out of the driveway and we were off to the office to meet Marnie.

CHAPTER 57

The coffee was brewing and a couple Danish pastries from Nancy's were waiting to tempt the palate when Marnie walked through the door at nine-forty-five.

"Right on time."

She walked over and gave Watson a hug. "You told me there'd be coffee waiting. I hope it's strong. I need something to keep me going today." She looked at the pastries. "I'd have come sooner if I knew I was getting fed too." She snickered. "Or am I being bribed?" She didn't give me time to answer. "And if so, I accept."

"Well, my little gumshoe, you wanted to get involved, so now I'm going to involve you." I broke off a piece of cheese Danish and stuck it in my mouth as I got up to get us a coffee. "I don't have any flavored cream because it doesn't go good with my French Vanilla."

"That's a matter of opinion."

I returned to the front office carrying our drug of choice. "Here, hot and strong."

I took a sip. "Hmmm," I rolled my eyes and took another sip, then looked at Marnie. "Wash that bite down and we'll get this show on the road."

"Okay, boss, what's happening?"

"Miss Levine, your mission, should you choose to accept it, is to research the DeMarco family of Falmouth." I laughed. "Wasn't that the famous line from *Mission Impossible*?"

"Close enough." She shook her head.

"How much time do you have?"

"It's real slow. I asked Mike if it was okay for me to spend some time with you this morning and he said sure."

"Good. I can explain the aforementioned mission."

"Have you got an extra pad of paper and a pen?"

I reached into my bottom desk drawer, pulled out one of my mini-legal pads and handed it to her along with a pen.

"Here's the brief version. My client, Bella Deluca, is related to the DeMarco family. There's bad blood between the two families and, as I understand it, has been for years. I guess the DeMarco's aren't the most upstanding citizens of Falmouth, but are one of the wealthy ones. They own a construction company—a big one. The father's name was Sid. He has two sons—Phil and Greg. He was on his second wife when he died. His first wife went missing years ago. I have it written down, but you'll see it once you start looking at their history. She was never found. It was rumored that Sid had something to do with it."

"What does the DeMarco family have to do with Bella's uncle's death?"

"Maybe nothing, but I'm not so sure of that. Sam emphatically told me to stay away from the DeMarco's. He said they're trouble. I guess the father taught his sons how to skate on the edge of the law without breaking the line—or at least without getting caught. There've been lots of incidents tied to both the father and the sons, but either witnesses can't remember or they just disappear. Since I'm not from Falmouth and haven't been involved with much in that neck of the woods, I need to know more."

Marnie got up from her chair and walked to the window.

"Take a minute to think about what I just said. I'm going to get us another cup of coffee." I stood up, took our cups and headed to the kitchen. Watson followed me. "Hey boy, want some water?" I assumed the wag of the tail was a yes. I filled his bowl, set it on the floor, then took our cups and headed back to my desk.

"I can do lots of leg work over the computer. If I need to physically check something out at either District or Superior Courts, I can do that without anybody asking questions." She smiled. "The beauty of being an ADA."

"I have to ask you to be real discreet. I don't want Mike to ask Sam what's going on. I'm not investigating the DeMarco family, but I think it's important enough to know some background since it could be one of those *on the line* incidents. And, if the sons broke the line, I want to know." I raised my eyebrows and nodded. "Do you get my point?"

"I do. Are you in the office the rest of the afternoon?"

"No. I've got a one-thirty appointment with Chief Mills. Within the next couple days, I'd like to talk to the police officers who answered the call for Rocco's fish market, so I need to run that by the Chief. I'm sure there will be no problem." I didn't want to go into a long discussion about George so I didn't tell Marnie I'd be asking about him too. If something came out of my meeting then I'd run it by her, but right now I was just drawing straws. "Tonight I'm meeting Bella for dinner at a place in Mashpee."

Marnie tilted her head and looked in my direction.

I caught her disapproval of her not being asked to join us. "I'm still getting to know Bella. I want her to feel comfortable tonight. I want her to talk about her family and the DeMarco family. I want her to talk about her brother. And, I want her to talk about her."

"You have a lot of wants."

"If they all go well, then I'm going to ask her about the police officers of record. I'm sure she must know them."

Marnie looked at her watch. "I know Mike said I could meet with you this morning, but I don't want to push it. I've been here a little over an hour." She stood up. "Why don't you call me when you get home. I don't care what time it is."

"I will. I'm going to leave before noon, take Watson home and head to Falmouth."

"Do you want me to check in on Watson after I get out of work?" she asked.

"I plan on coming home in between the meeting with the Chief and dinner with Bella, so thanks for asking, but he should be okay." I smiled.

"Okay. I'll talk to you later." Marnie waved as she walked out the door.

CHAPTER 58

It was almost eleven o'clock when I left the office and headed to Hyannisport to drop Watson off. I figured I would be home between three and four so I hooked the boy to his run and let him enjoy the outside. I filled his bowls, gave him a couple treats, made sure I looked presentable, then started for Falmouth. I made one stop for gas, then checked my watch. I was still too early to go to the station. I didn't want to go to the Dunkins in Falmouth because I didn't want to bump into anyone—namely Bella—so I opted to stop at the one in Mashpee.

I brought my briefcase in with me to go over a couple of my notes before my meeting. The place was so empty, I could hear a French Vanilla ice coffee calling my name. I settled in at a table for two in the furthest corner of the room. I was so engrossed in my reading I didn't realize I wasn't alone.

"Hi."

I looked up to see a man standing in front of me. I recognized him right away. It was Greg DeMarco.

"May I sit down."

"If you're making a formal request, you forgot to wear your tuxedo. If you want a friendly conversation, I'm not in the market for making new friends. If you want to engage in a bull-shit session, I can go with the best of them. If you understand that, then sit down, otherwise that seat is taken." My heart was beating a mile a minute. I didn't go to Falmouth because I didn't want to bump into anyone. Here I am in Mashpee and of all people to bump into, Greg DeMarco. This was awkward, to say the least. There was so much I wanted to ask him, but couldn't.

"I was in the area to price a job. When I pulled in to get a coffee, I saw your car in the parking lot."

"You saw my car? How do you know what my car looks like?"

"It was parked in the library parking lot the other day. I saw you standing beside it talking to my cousin, Bella, then you got into it and drove away, so I assumed it was yours."

"Besides, the lime green color and the CQ007 license plate is a dead give-away."

"Okay, now that the formalities are out of the way, what do you want?"

"I understand you've been hired by Bella to investigate the death of our Uncle Rocco."

"Maybe I was or maybe I wasn't. Either way I'm not going to acknowledge your statement with a positive or negative response." I took a drink of my coffee trying to stall for time before deciding what to say next. He beat me to the punch.

"Look, I'm not trying to cause problems or trouble. A couple people in town asked my brother and me what was going on. We told them we had no idea."

I looked him straight in the eyes and asked, "I don't suppose you'd care to tell me who those people were?"

"Falmouth, or at least parts of Falmouth, is a tight knit community. Even though my family and the Deluca families haven't seen eye-to-eye for a number of years, it doesn't mean we don't share mutual acquaintances. My father and Rocco were both businessmen. They both did a lot for the community. Even though the scale is tipped in Rocco's favor, believe it or not, my father wasn't as bad as he was made out to be. Pope Sidney, he wasn't, but neither was he Jack the Ripper."

"Why are you telling me this?" All I could remember was Sam's rendition of the DeMarco's and the Deluca's—and how dangerous Sid was and the sons are. "You didn't answer my question. Do you care to tell me who told you about me?"

"I will tell you one. She's the Falmouth Town Crier—Winnie Parks."

That came as no surprise to me.

"She told my step-mother. They hang in the same circle. If those two know something, the whole town knows." Greg looked around before continuing. "My step-mother is hell bent on finding out what's going on. I'm sure you'll find out she's not one of Phil or my favorite people. We tolerate her because she's a principal in the family business."

This conversation was concerning. I wanted to know more, but I didn't want to say too much. For all I knew, I was being set up and I didn't like it one bit.

"My father had his problems. In some shape or form, we all do. But, my father was dead when Uncle Rocco died and my brother and I, even though we're no angels, aren't murderers."

I thought back to when we bumped into the DeMarco brothers last Sunday morning at Stella's. Phil did all the talking—Greg didn't say a word. I wondered if Phil sent Greg to talk to me—but then, Greg said he stumbled on me by chance.

"Who said anything about you and your brother being involved? It wasn't me."

Greg was quiet for a minute. He shifted in his seat. "My step-mother said I should be concerned."

"What's your step-mother's name?"

"Candace, but they call her Candy. Her name fits her to a tee— she's sweet, but sticky. Once she sucks you in, you can't get rid of her. It took my father lots of years to figure it out. By the time he did, it was too late."

I took a deep breath. My Rocco investigation was taking on a new twist. I wasn't sure where it was going, but knew it wasn't dead-ended. I checked my watch. It was almost one o'clock. I had plenty of time to get to my meeting with Chief Mills, but not enough time to get into the step-mother subject with Greg DeMarco. He opened the door and I wanted to hear more. "I have to leave, but would like to meet with you again."

"That can be arranged."

I didn't like the use of the word *arranged*. I felt Sam sitting on my shoulder, hitting me up side of my head trying to get me to shut-up. I ignored him. "Are you available tomorrow morning?"

"I can be."

Now the tables were turned. When he sat down, he wanted to talk to me—now I want to talk to him. "How about I meet you at Stella's at nine?"

"I'll be there." He stood up to leave. This time he checked his watch. "You better get going. You don't want to be late for your meeting with Chief Mills."

I didn't say anything about having an appointment with the Chief. I waited until I saw his truck leave the parking lot. He headed north on Route 28 towards Falmouth. I jotted down a description of his vehicle. It was a shiny black, unlettered Ford 250 with an extended cab—probably his personal truck. I tried to grab the plate number, but could only get the first two numbers. It will be easier to get it tomorrow at Stella's.

CHAPTER 59

I was a few minutes early when I walked up to the front desk cage, but Monica was waiting for me. She signaled the duty officer to open the door. I signed in and followed her to the elevator.

Once inside and the door closed she said, "I didn't want to say anything downstairs, but the Chief is anxious to talk to you."

"Why?"

"I don't know. He's kept his association with you pretty quiet."

I figured that lack of communication included her, so I didn't feed into the conversation. I was glad when the door opened and I saw the Chief standing by Monica's desk.

He held his hand out to greet me. "Good afternoon, Casey."

I returned the gesture and the greeting.

"Why don't we head down to my office? I could go for a coffee. How about you?" he asked.

I was all coffeed out, but didn't want to refuse his offer. "Sure," I said. "A good cup of coffee always stimulates the brain."

"I already made a pot in anticipation of your request." Monica turned and walked towards the break room.

"Come in and sit down."

The same chair I sat in last time was waiting for me.

"It's good to see you again. Did you have a chance to review the reports I gave you?"

"I did. On the surface they seemed in perfect order." That was my key phrase, perfect order, but my on purpose use of the word *seemed* denoted I may have detected a glitch in one or more of them.

The Chief picked up on it immediately. "I don't like the use of the word *seemed*—please explain."

Just as I started, the door opened and Monica came in carrying our coffees. "If I remember correctly, Casey, you use cream."

"You're right. Thanks." I reached out to take my mug.

"Thanks, Monica. Please hold my calls—that is, unless it's an emergency."

"Sure thing, Chief." She left closing the door behind her.

"Let's get back to the reports." The Chief leaned forward on his elbows and folded his hands as if in prayer.

"The reports were pretty much all identical. In the past, most police reports written about the same incident were identical regarding the facts, but the actual writing reflected the officer's personality. I should add—reports that I've been privy to. Also, all the facts were reflected in all of the reports. I question if all five of the officers went into the back room or the office and if so, did they all observe the exact same things." I stopped to take a sip of coffee. I wanted the Chief to have time to think about what I just said.

"Are you saying that one person wrote the report and the others, for the most part, copied it?

"It appears that way to me."

He opened his bottom drawer and took out a manila folder. When he laid it on the desk in front of him I could see *Rocco Deluca* written on the tab. He opened it and took out a piece of paper that listed the names of the investigating officers. Chief Mills took the pose of *The Thinker* using his desk instead of his knee to rest his elbow and brace his chin. Either he read the list of names a hundred times or after each name he paused to reflect on each officer. Whatever the case, it felt like an eternity before he spoke. "When do you want to conduct the interviews?"

"As soon as we can get them set up."

He picked up the phone and buzzed Monica. "Please come to my office. I need you to look up something for me."

She appeared within second with pen and paper in hand.

"You won't need to take notes." He handed her the list of names he wanted her to research. "I want to know the schedules of those five officers."

"Yes sir," she said and began to leave.

"Monica, wait a minute. You might as well get the schedules of the detectives also. I know I don't have to tell you, but I'm going to anyway—I don't want you discussing this with anyone." He nodded.

She, in turn, also nodded to acknowledge his directive.

"I don't know whether or not you are aware that I've had some problems within the department. I'm not saying these officers are part of the problem, but I don't take anything for granted. Sometimes I'm too close to the problem and a new set of eyes helps me open mine wider. Hopefully, nothing will come of this, but I need to know my officers are doing their jobs."

Sam always told me police reports are written on facts and not works of fiction—that an accurate report can make a case and an inaccurate one can break a case.

"Do you have anything else you want to discuss while we're waiting for Monica to get back to me?"

"I do have a few issues. How well do you know George Deluca?"

"I've known him for years. I haven't seen much of him since he got divorced and moved to Buttermilk Bay. He's a smart kid—keeps a pretty low profile. He worked for one of the accounting firms in town before he went out on his own. I understand he's doing quite well. I used to see him at the fish market every once in a while, usually on weekends. As far as I know, he's never been in trouble—maybe a traffic violation or two, but nothing else."

"Did you know he had words with Rocco days before he died?"

"No."

"I supposed there'd be no reason for you to know unless a disturbance was called in."

"I will tell you, he's nothing like his cousins—Phil and Greg DeMarco."

"How so?" I pretended I knew next to nothing about the DeMarco brothers.

"I don't know how much Bella has told you about the DeMarco family, but trouble is their middle name—the whole bunch of them. When their father, Sid, died things quieted down, but when he was around there were lots of unanswered questions regarding incidents that happened in town. He was a thorn in my side when he was alive and only half of it has been extracted. But, that's another story we won't get into now."

There was one more DeMarco question I had to ask and that was about Candy—according to Greg, the not so sweet mother-in-law. "There is one person in the DeMarco family I'd like to know a little about."

"Who's that?"

"Candy."

"Candy DeMarco—the molded pawn in Sid's game of chess." He smiled and shook his head. "Sid thought his little piece of eye candy could be customized to his specifications—to share his desires, yet cower to his authority. Didn't happen. She had her own agenda which included Sid's money, but not Sid."

"Interesting. Does she get along with his sons?"

"Nope. They tolerate each other only because of the business."

This was not the time to tell Chief Mills about my unplanned meeting earlier today and my planned meeting for tomorrow with Greg DeMarco.

There was a knock on the door.

"Come in."

"I have the information you requested." Monica handed him the list he had given her earlier. He looked it over. "Thanks. Casey, do you want another coffee?" he asked.

"I'm good," I said.

He handed Monica his mug. "Is there any left?"

"There is. I'll get one for you."

"She's a good kid. Every once in a while, I have to remind her that anything she hears here has to stay here. Her dad is an attorney in town and I know, on occasion, he's asked her to look something

211

up for him. She almost lost her job because of it. It was a lesson learned and I haven't had a problem since."

"That's youth." I smiled. "I was there once myself."

There was the knock again and Monica came in with the Chief's coffee.

"Thanks. Have there been any calls?"

"Nothing I couldn't handle. Oh, one though—the town manager asked if you were going to be at the budget meeting tomorrow. He wants me to call him back to confirm with a yes or no."

The Chief checked his calendar. "You can tell him I'll be there—ten o'clock, right?"

"Yes sir, ten o'clock at town hall. I'll let him know." She smiled and left the office.

I didn't ask any more DeMarco questions. Since he opened it up and if I needed to, I could revisit that subject later.

"Three of the five officers are working tomorrow. Do you want me to set up interviews with them? Also, the two detectives are on the schedule. The other two officers are off until Friday."

"That'll work." I really didn't want to conduct the interviews until after Sam got home. His expertise in formulating questions far exceeds mine, but I didn't want to give up the opportunity to keep the investigation moving forward. It might work to my advantage. I'll ask my questions tomorrow, then take the answers and run them by Sam. He can hone my questions and I'll finish the remaining two interviews on Friday. It actually could prove interesting because, for the most part, it will be a new set of questions and the last two officers won't be able to collaborate their answers with the first three interviewees. The detectives will be my biggest challenge. Sam will definitely have to give me some pointers.

"You can conduct the interviews in my conference room at the end of the hall. That way there will be no distractions. I won't attend. You can fill me in afterwards."

"I'm free whenever, so whatever time is best for you works for me."

"They change shifts at three o'clock. How long do you think each one will take?"

"Probably no more than a half hour. If somebody sends up a red flag, then I might have to do a re-interview."

"I'll schedule them beginning at one-thirty." He checked the list. "Since Brady was the first officer on the scene and he's working tomorrow, why don't you start with him—then Johnson and finally Tuttle. Detectives Morse and Garrison get through at four-thirty, so I'll have them come in at three-thirty and four o'clock respectively. If something changes, I'll give you a call. If not, I'll see you tomorrow after you're done."

"I really appreciate this."

"The feeling is mutual."

I stood up and reached out to shake the Chief's hand. "I've got to get back to Barnstable and work on my questions. I'll see you tomorrow afternoon."

"That you will," he said and walked me to the elevator.

I waved to Monica on the way by. "See you tomorrow."

She was on the phone, but nodded to acknowledge that she had heard me.

CHAPTER 60

I had to be careful because my mind was running in fifty different directions and I was behind the wheel. There was no reason for me to go back to my office. I had everything I needed to make up my set of questions. I did, however, want to check in with Marnie to see if she found anything of interest regarding the DeMarco family, but that could wait until I got home.

It was only three-fifteen and I wasn't meeting Bella until six-thirty. I had plenty of time to walk Watson, set up my home office, talk to Marnie and get ready to go out to dinner. Traffic was light, so it took no time to get home. When I got out of the car I could hear Watson barking. He must have heard my car pull in the driveway. Either that or the squirrels were teasing him and he was yelling for them to go away.

I peeked around the back corner of the house. Watson saw me and immediately came running. When he jumped up, I fell to the ground and was literally showered with dog kisses. "Okay, okay," I jokingly yelled as we wrestled around on the grass. Leaving him out on his run for a few hours worked.

"Hungry," I said as I got up.

His tail was wagging a mile a minute.

"Then, let's go get you something to eat."

I picked up my stuff, unhooked Watson, walked around to the front of the house and headed to the front door. I lost my back door key a couple years ago and haven't had a new one made so the front door was my only means of entry.

No sooner had I set my briefcase and purse on the table, my cell rang. It was one of my unavailable friends calling. "Hello."

"It's me," said Marnie.

"I just walked in the door. Let me get Watson settled and I'll call you right back."

"Call my cell."

"Will do."

I got the boy taken care of and sat down with a bottle of water, a pen and my mini legal pad and proceeded to call Marnie back. Before I finished making the connection with her, my phone clicked notifying me a call was coming in. I switched over to get it, but the person must have hung up. I checked my voice mail, but there was no message.

Oh well. Whoever it was will call back.

I punched in Marnie's number—this time finishing it.

"Hi Casey. How did you day with the Chief go?"

"Actually, it went very well. I'm going back tomorrow to interview three of the responding officers and the two detectives."

"That's great. I guess the Chief really has concerns about Rocco Deluca's untimely death."

"I think you're right. I appreciate his haste in setting up the interviews, but I wanted to run my questions by Sam before I asked them. Since he's not going to be home until Thursday, that's out of the question. I'm going to try to reach him tonight and tell him what's going on. He knows I'm going to meet Bella, so I won't be home until sometime around nine."

"I don't think you have to worry about your questions. You've done this hundreds of times before. It's no different just because you're out on your own."

"I know. I guess the only difference now is that now I'm getting paid to ask." I smiled and gave myself a little pat on the back.

"Back to business," said Marnie. "I couldn't spend as much time as I wanted to with the research. We got a little busy this afternoon and two of the other ADAs were out of the office. I didn't find much, but I'll continue tomorrow. Are you coming to the Village in the morning?"

"I am. I'll be there around ninish. Should I wait and have coffee with you?"

"That's a date."

"I'll fill you in on my meeting with Bella tonight."

"Have a good dinner and I'll see you in the morning." And in true Marnie style she was gone.

Oh shit—I remembered I have to meet Greg DeMarco at nine tomorrow morning. I punched in Marnie's number.

She answered on the first ring. "Long time no talk to. What's up?"

"I forgot. I have a meeting tomorrow morning at Stella's with Greg DeMarco."

"You what?" she asked trying to restrain from yelling. "And you forgot."

"I don't want Sam to know. I'm sure he'll find out in due time, but right now you're the only one who knows." I stopped for a minute then continued, "Do you understand what I'm saying to you?"

"I understand, but I don't like it one bit. Why are you meeting him?"

I felt a lecture coming on so I cautioned her to sit tight. "Because I am and that's all you have to know at this time. I trust you to keep that to yourself."

"You're such a difficult person, Casey Quinby. I don't like it when you make me promise to do things I don't want to do."

"Get used to it girl. If you want to help me, that's one of the prerequisites. Now, enough said, I've got some work to do, then I'm getting ready to go out. I'll talk to you tomorrow after my meeting with Greg."

The phone went dead.

I held my phone out in front of my face. "At least you know who I was with if I go missing." I was glad she didn't hear me say that, even though it was the truth. I still had some time before I had to get ready to meet Bella. There were lots of questions I wanted to ask her. I took out my mini-legal and started to write. When I finished my list I sat forward in my chair, rested my elbows on the table, folded my hands together like a closed door church and read and re-

216

read what I had written several times. If I took a list of questions out of my purse while we were in the restaurant, it would be tacky. It would be far more professional if I committed them to memory, so with that in mind, I reviewed them again.

I didn't feel like having my usual afternoon cup of French Vanilla. I was too anxious. I didn't want to be calmed down. I was on a roll. I wanted to get the show on the road, so I tore the page of questions from my pad and slipped it into the side pocket of my purse. I didn't intend to use the written word, but just in case my mind went blank, I had a back-up.

I was halfway down the hall when my cell rang. I scurried back to the kitchen. "Hello."

There was no answer.

I repeated my greeting, "hello."

Again, there was no reply.

I punched the end button.

Must have been a wrong number.

I headed back to the bathroom.

The shower felt so good that I stayed in a little longer than usual. Since I forgot to put the bath mat down, I was careful not to slip on the tile as I reached for one of my favorite soft Egyptian salmon colored bath towels. Sam never appreciated them. Said 'a towel is a towel and I paid way too much money to be wrapped like an Egyptian'. I think he just used that as an excuse to unwrap me. I crossed my arms over my chest, embraced my shoulders, looked into the mirror and gave myself a hug. "I miss you Sam Summers— hurry home."

I perused my closet for something to wear. I figured I'd get a little spiffed up for my dinner with Bella, so I took out a navy tank top, a navy and white polka-dot sweater and a pair of navy slacks. I needed a splash of color, so I pulled my new lime green and navy scarf from my dresser drawer and got my lime green sandals from the closet. I checked myself out in the mirror. "I'm likin' the look girl," I nodded to confirm my self-admiration.

If I didn't know better I'd say Watson, who was lying beside the bed watching me admire myself, smiled. I gave him a pat. "Want to take a walk around the house before I go?"

The words walk and food were the top two on his vocabulary list. He was in the kitchen and I'm sure was sitting in front of the door before I even left the bedroom.

I hooked his leash to his collar and we headed outside. The thermometer read sixty-six degrees. The sun let us know spring was on the way and summer was following close behind. One good thing about Daylight Savings, it stayed lighter later. I liked that. We walked around the house a couple times, then went back inside. I put his food in his dish, gave him a hug, grabbed my purse and headed out the door.

CHAPTER 61

Bella was waiting in her car when I got to Soprano's. I checked my watch. I wasn't late, in fact, I was ten minutes early. I pulled into an empty space beside her and got out of my car.

"You must be hungry. I know I am."

"I was ready and didn't feel like sitting around the house and yes, I am hungry." She smiled.

We gave each other a friendly hug and went inside.

It was pretty crowded. We waited at the podium for the hostess. "I have a table on the bar side or, if you'd like to wait, I'll have a table opening up shortly in the main room," she said hand gesturing the location of both areas as she spoke.

I looked at Bella. "Your choice, it doesn't matter to me."

"The bar is fine."

The hostess picked up two menus and motioned for us to follow her. "Your server, Tina, will be right with you." She handed us each a menu, then stood a wine list on the table between us.

I looked at Bella. "Let's have a drink and an appetizer before we order dinner."

She didn't answer. She sat staring at her menu.

Maybe she didn't hear me.

I repeated what I just said only a hair louder. "Do you want to get a drink and an app first, then order dinner?"

It was as though somebody flipped a switch in her brain. She appeared startled. She stopped looking at the menu and sat up straight. "Sure, that sounds fine to me."

Something wasn't right. She appeared distant.

Before I had a chance to say something to her, our server appeared at our table. "Hi, I'm Tina. I'll be your server tonight. Can I get you a drink and perhaps some appetizers?"

I started. "I'll have a glass of White Zin with a glass of ice on the side, please."

Tina looked at Bella. "I'll have the same."

"How about an order of fried calamari?" I asked.

Bella nodded.

I tried not to show my concern with her withdrawn behavior, but I had to know what was bothering her. If it was something she didn't want me to know, I'm sure she would have made up some excuse and cancelled our dinner date. But, she didn't, so I was determined to find out what was wrong.

I started to make small talk. "So, how did your day go?" I asked. "Did Dewey behave himself?"

She tried to smile, but it was strained. "Thank goodness I have Dewey. He's the only norm in my life right now." She played with her fingers—moving them in and out between each other, then rubbing them as though they hurt.

"Do you care to share whatever is bothering you?"

"Casey, right now you're the only one I can confide in. I know we just met, but I feel we have a connection over and above your capacity as a private investigator. I hired you to help me with my Uncle Rocco's death, not to be my sounding block or baby sitter. I hope you know that." Her eyes shifted from mine, to the table, back to mine.

"Bella, understand I wouldn't be here with you if I thought of you as just a client. I believe we've started a friendship that will continue long after my contract with you is over." I detected a smile of relief before I continued. "I know something is bothering you tonight. I'd like to help you if you'll let me."

"I do want to talk about it. It's like a double edged sword—one side represents the case and the other side represents my life and when it gets to the point, they come together. Does that make any sense to you?" She gently bit her top lip.

220

"You better watch that lip thing or you'll need to put on more lipstick." I tried to get her to relax. "I think I do, but why don't you run it by me and we'll talk about it."

"Remember my friend, Norma Sheridan. You met her the day we had lunch at the Quarterdeck."

"I do."

"I hadn't talked to her since the day you met her. She came by to see me this morning. Apparently, she finally decided to ask me why I was in your company."

"And you told her."

"Yes I did."

"And she offered you some advice."

"She certainly did."

"Well?"

"I was surprised. Instead of trying to understand, she told me I should leave well enough alone. Norma said there are lots of people talking about me and what I'm trying to do." Bella took a deep breath then continued, "I told her that I wasn't trying to cause any problems, I was just trying to get the truth regarding Uncle Rocco's death."

"Do you think she was being the spokesperson for somebody or was she talking for herself?"

"I'm not really sure. I know she's friendly with Phil DeMarco's wife and that she talks to George every once-in-a-while."

Tina came with our drinks. "Two White Zins with ice on the side." She set them down in front of us. "Your calamari will be right out."

"Thanks." I picked up my glass to offer a toast to Bella.

Bella followed my lead.

"You'll like this one."

> *"Here's to it*
> *Those who get to it and don't do it*
> *May never get to it*
> *To do it again."*

We clicked glasses and laughed.

Our calamari came. Since we weren't in a hurry, we opted to wait to place our order. "Now that we've got some wine and food in us, do you want to talk?"

"Yes, I'm okay now. I just felt like I got blindsided by Norma. I didn't expect it from her. I thought she might call me to ask what was going on, but I didn't think she'd confront me like she did."

"My concern is why. Why would she be so adamant for you to back off?" A lot of scenarios began to run through my head and some of them I didn't like at all. "Has anybody else said anything to you?"

"No, nobody."

"Okay, let's put Norma on the back burner for now. There will be plenty of time to discuss her later." I wanted to move on. Besides, I needed to look into this Norma thing on my own. I ran through my mental list of questions. "What about your cousins?" I asked. I didn't think the time was right to tell her I talked to Greg DeMarco earlier in the day. I will, but not right now.

"What do you want to know?" she asked as she ate a couple pieces of squid and took another sip of wine.

"They seem to be a thorn in Falmouth's side. Do you know if they've been in serious trouble or just mischievous stuff?"

"I know they've had their share of problems. I don't think they've ever been arrested or spent any time in jail." Her puzzle face re-appeared. "Wait, I think they did a couple overnights in the House of Correction, but were released the next morning."

"Why?"

"I think one time was when they, along with a few of their friends, were involved in a fight. I believe they had been drinking and one thing led to another and, bingo, the cops were called."

"So no charges were filed."

"No, or if there was, they were dismissed. My Uncle Sid probably had something to do with that."

Tina came by to check on us. Our calamari plate was empty. "I guess you didn't like it." She smiled. "Have you decided what you want for dinner?"

"I'd like chicken parm with penne, please," I said.

"And, I'll have the Saltimbocca, but I'd like angel hair for my pasta."

"Good choices," said Tina. "Can I get you both another glass of wine and a basket of garlic knots?"

"A girl after my own heart. We'd like both." I handed her my empty glass.

Tina left and we resumed our conversation.

"What kind of a relationship did Sid have with his sons?"

"He was tough. They did whatever he told them to do. He was a nasty man."

"You're saying he, Sid, was a nasty man, but you haven't painted your cousins as being real bad—I'm talking dangerously bad."

"That's because they aren't. At least deep down inside I don't think they are. They play the tough guy roll because that's all they know. That's how they grew up. My Aunt Maria had no say in how her boys were raised. She was a nice person. I don't think Sid was very nice to her—just like he wasn't very nice to the boys. I think he treated her the same way—with no respect. I totally agreed with my Uncle Rocco about her disappearance. I wouldn't be surprised if he did have some information linking Sid to Maria's death."

"Since they didn't find her, I don't know if the records actually say death. After a certain number of years, the courts can pronounce a person dead, but that's for legal purposes only." I thought for a minute. "For our information, I'll ask Marnie to check that out for me and I'll let you know."

Tina brought our wine. "Your dinners will be out shortly," she said then turned to wait on a new set of customers three tables down from us.

"Back to my cousins. You do know they aren't the sole owners of DeMarco Construction Company." She leaned forward. "Their step-mother Candy has the controlling interest, but I think there was a stipulation in the will that said she couldn't do anything with the business without providing for the boys. And, there was also something about not being able to sell. I don't know all the particulars and I don't care, but it's something I thought you might want to know. "

I could see the wheels turning in Bella's head.

"So she's a black cloud hanging over their heads?"

"She sure is and she knows it. You think Sid wasn't liked, well Candy is liked even less."

I filed that information in my head. It could come in handy.

We both took a break in the conversation to enjoy a couple sips of the nectar of the Gods.

I eyed my glass and smiled. "You know, my friends try to get me to drink red wine. They say this is sissy stuff." I swirled the pink colored liquid around trying to coat the inside of the glass. "It doesn't leave a film on the surface like theirs does. I tell them red wine clouds the brain, while my pink stuff lets me see things clearly." I laughed and set my glass down.

"And the great philosopher has spoken." Bella raised her glass. "I think we should toast to that."

We did.

"Before we go any further, I have a question to ask you."

"Anything."

"Are you happy with the way the investigation is going?"

Bella got serious. "I am. Sometimes I react to something I don't want to hear, but that's me. I hope you understand. I want you to continue." Then Bella asked, "Why do you ask?"

"I don't know. I want to make sure you're satisfied with how I'm handling things."

"I have the utmost confidence in you. If I do have a problem, I'll let you know. Meanwhile, let's get back on track. Are we all set with my cousins for now?"

"One more question—do you know if Candy's dating anyone?"

Bella gave me a strange look. "I don't know. Do you want me to ask around?"

224

"No, I don't. Remember, you hired me to do the snooping. Let me stick my neck out. If I need to run something by you, I will. But, don't you go getting curious on me."

"Let's put the DeMarcos to bed," she said.

"I'm fine with that."

"Has anyone, other than Norma, confronted you regarding your ideas related to Uncle Rocco's death?"

"No, she's the only one."

Our food came. We both still had a half full glass of wine, so Tina didn't ask if we were ready for another. "Enjoy, I'll be back to check on you."

I didn't want to destroy the ambiance surrounding our dinner, but I had a few questions still needing to be answered. "Bella, this may be a difficult question, but it needs to be asked."

"I'm okay."

"Have you and George made any decisions about selling the business yet?"

Bella became subdued. "George and I had coffee this morning. He briefly went over some of the financials with me. I was confused because I'm not a money person, so he had to explain most everything at least twice. I know he's handled the money for my uncle, both business and personal, since my aunt died, but I was surprised at the balances he showed me."

I put my fork down and leaned forward to hear more. "Was there more than you expected?"

"No. There was much less." Bella shook her head. "When I told him the numbers couldn't be right, he got quiet and said we should talk someplace other than a coffee shop. I knew if I pushed the issue the result wouldn't be pretty, so I agreed."

"Did you make plans to meet?"

"We did. He's coming to my house Thursday evening. He said he'd bring the books and try to explain them to me."

"Will you give me a call after you talk to him?"

"I will. I'm afraid I'm not going to like what he has to say."

We both went back to our dinners.

"Did he ask you how the investigation was going?"

"Nope. He didn't bring it up at all."

"I find that strange. But, let's get through the money issues, then we'll confront him with a whole new set of questions."

"That works for me," she said. "How's your dinner?"

The change of subject was just what the doctor ordered. I felt there was something else that Bella hadn't told me, but for now I wanted her to try to relax and get her thoughts back together.

There wasn't much conversation during the rest of the meal until out of nowhere Bella asked, "When am I going to meet Marnie?

I lied, just a little. "She wanted to come tonight, but had already made plans. That means we have to do this again soon." I grinned.

"I'd like that. Casey, I …." Bella started to say more, then stopped.

"Bella, what's wrong?"

"Casey, I haven't told you the whole George story." She stopped for a minute, looked around the restaurant, then looked back at me. "He did tell me something else. I know it sounds bad, but please listen and think about it before you respond."

I was stunned. I had no idea what she was about to say.

"My brother is in trouble—financially." She picked up her wine and, after staring at it for a minute, took a drink. "It seems that he's got a gambling problem. I guess it's nothing new, but this was the first time I heard about it. He said that's why his wife left him."

I could see the discussion between her and her brother thrust a dagger into her heart. He was all she had left. "Do you think the words exchanged between your uncle and George had something to do with this?"

"I asked him and he said no. He said Uncle Rocco didn't know about his problem."

Then it dawned on me George was stealing from the business. "So your brother was skimming and because your uncle didn't have anything to do with the books, he had no idea what was happening."

"That's about it."

George needed money and without money coming in, he couldn't hide what was going out. If Rocco sold the business, George could play with the numbers, take what he needed and nobody would ever know what happened. But, if Rocco lingered on, things would surface and George would be toast.

He wouldn't.

I looked at Bella.

She studied my face. "Remember, think about what you're going to say."

"Right now I'm not going to say anything except I want dessert and an after-dinner drink. How about you?"

"I like you Casey Quinby." She smiled. "Thanks."

Tina walked by with dinners for another table. "Be right back," she said.

"I'm having a tiramisu and a Bailey's on the rocks," I licked my lips.

She smiled. "I'll have a Bailey's, but I want a cannoli."

Tina took our order.

"Your friends were right. This place is amazing. As Arnold Schwarzenegger said, 'I'll be back'. And next time I'll bring Sam."

"I don't remember him saying anything about Sam." She laughed. "That's my English classes talking."

Our desserts and drinks came. We finished the evening with small talk, paid our bill and headed out to our cars.

"I'll be back on the job early, boss." I snickered.

"You're crazy."

"Believe me that's a compliment," I said as I reached over and gave her a hug.

"Take it easy going home and I'll talk to you sometime tomorrow."

I watched as she pulled away. I felt sorry for her. I was sure the rest of the story wasn't going to be pretty.

CHAPTER 62

It was almost eight-thirty when I left Soprano's parking lot. We'd been there for two and a half hours. I enjoyed it and I think Bella did too. We got a lot accomplished. She gave me food for thought—some of which I'm not sure how to handle.

I was stopped at the lights by the Dunkin Donuts where I bumped into Greg DeMarco earlier in the day when my cell rang. This phone was going to drive me crazy. I didn't bother to check the ID, I just answered it.

"Hey Sherlock." It was Sam.

"What a day I've had."

"I've got some time, do you feel like filling me in?"

"I'll do my best. I'm on my way home from having dinner with Bella. I don't remember if I told you I was meeting her. Anyway, we went to a place in Mashpee called Soprano's. It was excellent. When you get home we'll go."

"You implied you had a trying day. Dinner at an Italian restaurant doesn't sound very trying to me."

"It was dinner and conversation."

"Am I going to have to play fifty questions or are you going to tell me what you talked about."

"Well, let's see." I teased. "Bella talked about her cousins, Phil and Greg DeMarco, her Uncle Sid, Aunt Maria and Candy, the step-mother."

"I told you not to get involved with that family." There was silence from Sam's end of the phone.

"I know what you told me. I'm not involved with that family. I have a client that felt she needed to tell me some things about them.

228

Tough shit if you can't accept that. They might very well end up having something to do with the case I'm investigating."

"I didn't mean to get you upset. I know you're doing what you have to do. All I ask is that you be careful."

I didn't feel like getting into the George scenario. "I didn't write anything down while I was with Bella, so when I get home I'm going to do just that while it's fresh in my mind. You'll have lots of reading material when you get back."

"What else did you do today?"

"I had a meeting with Chief Mills. I asked him about the interviews with the responding officers. He jumped on it—had his secretary check the roster to see if they were on duty tomorrow. Three of the POs and the two detectives are, so he set up times for them to meet with me. The last two are scheduled for Friday."

"Are you okay with the questions or do you want to call me when you get home?"

"I think I'll be okay," I said as I made the turn leading to my house. "It might work out better. The questions for the Friday interviews will reflect your input. That way if the guys I see tomorrow tell the other two the questions I asked, they'll be totally surprised when they find out the questions aren't the same. They'll be out of luck if they've rehearsed their answers."

"You've got a point there. Good thinking."

"That's about it."

"Okay, if everything's on time, I'll be home Thursday around three o'clock."

"I feel a pizza, beer and stay-at-home night on the horizon."

"You got it. See you Thursday—sweet dreams."

I missed him so much. Good thing I had Watson to keep me company. I pulled into my driveway. "Damn, that front light." It was pitch dark. I thought Sam had fixed the sensor so the light would go on around dusk. Obviously the light burned out again or the sensor went bad. I shook my head and got out of the car. I had piled my stuff on the passenger seat and some of it slipped onto the floor, so instead of trying to reach across to pick it up, I walked around to the passenger side to retrieve my paperwork. As I walked to the front door, I glanced around in the darkness. I never did, and still don't, like being alone in the dark. I knew everything was okay when I heard Watson bark.

No sooner did I get inside, my cell rang. "Here we go again." This time I checked the ID. It was Bella. "Hi. Is everything okay?"

"Yeah, I'm home. I enjoyed our dinner very much. On the way I thought about the things I told you regarding George. There is one thing I forgot and I wanted to tell you before you did your interviews tomorrow."

I couldn't imagine what she was about to say. "This time I had paper and pen ready. Go ahead."

"He wasn't totally honest when he said he called the police because he couldn't reach our uncle. George told me he was near the fish market the day Uncle Rocco was found. My brother said he got an anonymous phone call telling him to check the market out, then the caller hung up. He said he had no idea what the caller meant. He tried calling Uncle Rocco, but couldn't get ahold of him. He had a feeling something was wrong. That's when he called the police station and that's why he was so close."

"I'm glad you called tonight. I just got home, so I haven't written anything down yet. This information could help me decide what I want or don't want to ask. Thanks, I'll talk to you tomorrow." I disconnected the call. Now I was confused. Do I believe George's story or is he trying to fabricate something to cover his tracks. He had motive, there's no question about that, but I can't imagine George harming, let alone killing, his uncle.

I grabbed the flashlight under the kitchen sink, hooked Watson to his leash and headed out the door to take him for a short walk around the house. When we got back inside, I gave him some treats, then settled in at the kitchen table to work on the questions for my interviews.

I rested my elbows on the table, cupped my hands around my face and stared at the blank pad of paper and pen in front of me. The words just wouldn't come. It was a game I had to play and, frankly,

I wasn't sure if I was experienced enough to win. I had a better feeling about meeting with Greg DeMarco than I did interviewing the police officers.

Something wasn't right—something didn't fit. Who made that call to George? Somebody wanted him to be a suspect or at least a diversion. I took a deep breath and let it out as quickly as I took it in. "George didn't do it. My gut tells me he's being set up." I picked up my cell. It was nine-forty—too late to call Sam and I didn't want to repeat everything to Marnie, so I had to shit or get off the pot. I couldn't go into those interviews half-cocked, so it was now or never. I put my cell away.

I knew I was in for a late night, so I got up and made myself a French Vanilla.

Since the police officers' reports were all so much alike, I was anxious to see how similar their answers were going to be. It's been five months since Rocco's death, so the first thing I'm going to ask is for each one to retell his story from the time he got the call to go to the fish market to the time he returned to the station. Whatever they tell me should match the reports on file.

Once the opening questions are out of the way, I'll ask how well each one knew Rocco—how long, in what capacity, did they frequent the market, were they involved in any of the organizations he was? That will give me follow-up information if I need it.

Then, I want to know if any one of them knows George or Bella, and if so, how—did they grow up together, live near each other, go to school together, from their personal lives or through the police department? I have a half-hour with each of the officers, so I should be able to make these questions work.

As far as the detectives go, I'll use the same questions, but with much more caution. These two guys have been on the department for years—before Mills became Chief. I'm sure their association with Rocco goes back a ways. They're experts in interrogation or they wouldn't be in the position they're in. This is really when I need Sam.

I sat back in my chair and drank my coffee. Watson was curled up in the corner not paying one bit of attention to what I was doing. He was very content just gnawing on his chewy bone. I wasn't used to the quiet. Usually the TV is on—even if I'm not watching it. It's the voices, they keep me company. But tonight I had to think. I had to be serious—tomorrow was going to be a big day.

I read my notes over a couple more times. There was nothing else I could do tonight. I put away my paperwork, put my cup in the sink and moved to the living room to watch the eleven o'clock news.

CHAPTER 63

Wednesday

Morning came quickly. It was six o'clock. "They don't give you enough time to sleep," I said to Watson who was lying beside me keeping Sam's spot warm.

He turned his head and gave me a sloppy cheek kiss.

I wasn't ready for a face washing, so I held his head to give me enough time to kick the covers off my feet and jump out of bed.

I had plenty of time before my meeting with Greg DeMarco at Stella's. He said he'd be there at ten. That meeting should last less than an hour, then give me time to come home and walk Watson, before I have to head to Falmouth for my one-thirty interview.

It was still too early to call Marnie, besides I told her I'd call after I met with Greg and I don't feel like getting a pre-meeting lecture. I popped a K-cup into my Keurig, fed Watson and walked out to the driveway to get my Tribune. I held the folded paper to my chest. "I miss you guys," I whispered.

CHAPTER 64

The morning rush was over. Stella had her back towards the door re-stocking the pastry shelves when I walked in. "Morning, Miss Stella."

She snapped her head around. "Casey, good morning. What brings you to this neck of the woods?" She asked as she came around to give me a hug.

"I have a little business meeting and thought this would be the perfect place to conduct it." I smiled.

"The conference table in the corner is available," she laughed quietly.

"That works." Before I could say anything else, Greg DeMarco walked in. I shifted my eyes from Stella to Greg.

Stella got the message. My meeting was about to start.

I walked over to Greg. "Good morning. I just got here myself and haven't ordered coffee yet."

"My treat," he said. "And how about a pastry to go along with it."

I looked at Stella. "I'll have my usual, French Vanilla and how about one of your famous sticky buns."

"And you sir?"

"Sir." Greg looked in my direction. "That's a first." He tilted his head and glanced in my direction for a response. Seeing none, he continued, "I'll have the sticky bun too, but regular coffee—black."

"Why don't you two take a seat and I'll bring them over," Stella said as she walked behind the counter to fill the order.

"Follow me to the conference table." I pointed to the one in the corner.

"Why do I feel like you've done this before."

"You're very observant." I didn't want him to think I'd let down my guard and this was a friendly, casual meeting, so I took my mini-legal and a pen from my briefcase and set them on the table. From the look on his face, I'd say he took the hint.

Greg looked around. There was a suit reading the newspaper sitting alone four tables away from us and a couple on the other side of the room trying to control their three or four year old child. "Looks like we're good to go."

The tough guy was nervous. I wondered if his brother knew where he was and with who.

I doubt it.

Stella brought our coffee and buns to our table. "Let me know if you need anything else."

Greg went to get his wallet from his back pocket.

"Eat—we'll take care of that later," she said as she headed to the kitchen.

"Our last conversation ended on the subject of your step-mother, Candy." I wasn't going to beat around the bush. Greg DeMarco wasn't stupid. "Why did she think you should be concerned about Bella re-opening the investigation into Rocco's death?"

"I don't know." He looked me straight in the eyes as he took a drink of coffee and without putting the cup down he repeated his answer more emphatically, "I don't know."

"Tell me more about Candy. Where is she from? How did she originally come into the picture? Is she actively involved in the business or just a name on paper? Since your father's death is she involved with anyone?"

"You ask a lot of questions, but I guess that's what an investigator does."

His face was expressionless. I wasn't sure if that should bother me or not. All I knew is that I had to proceed with caution. "Since you know I'm being paid to do this, I have no qualms about what I ask." I was running this show and I wanted him to know it.

"Fair enough," he said. "Let's begin with where she came from. I don't think her family had deep roots anywhere. I know at one point she lived in Rhode Island—not sure what town, but Rhode Island—then Fall River and New Bedford. She did her senior year at Falmouth High, but I don't think she graduated. We're not exactly sure. There was no need to know, but I can find out if you want me to."

"No, if I need to know I'll get it myself."

"She didn't enjoy an upright reputation. In fact, she was known as a wild and promiscuous girl." Greg shook his head. "How my father got involved with her I'll never know. I have my opinion of how it happened, but no facts to substantiate it."

"Why don't you share it with me?" I asked.

He shrugged. "Remember, it's only my opinion."

"I will."

"My parent's marriage was not one made in heaven. Maybe at one point it was, but I think it started to go downhill when my youngest brother was killed in an automobile accident. They didn't try to hide the fact they weren't getting along. After my brother died, we didn't do much as a family anymore. We never went out on the boat. It sat moored at the marina for a couple years, then my father sold it. They fought constantly—mostly at home in front of us. In public, they played the role of Howard and Marion Cunningham from *Happy Days*."

"So, Miss Candy showed up, dangled her booty in your father's face and he bit."

"That's what I think. I think he got involved with her while still married to my mother and Candy played her trump card."

"Do I smell blackmail?"

"Both Phil and I have always felt that way, but were never able to prove it. Then, my mother went missing. Five years later, almost to the day, my father married the virtuous Miss Candy." Greg took a minute to compose his thoughts. It was obvious that the lack of family ties bothered him.

At this point, I felt like a psychologist rather than an investigator.

"And now, she has control over part of our lives. It stinks." He took a deep breath and let it out slowly.

"You said she has control over your lives?" I asked. I remembered what Bella told me regarding Candy having controlling interest in the business, but I wanted to see if Greg would verify it.

"The business is our lives. It's what we know and know well. I'm sure you looked us up. We operate a very successful operation. In turn, we live very well—so does Candy. She holds the controlling interest. We're her puppets and she pulls the strings." His voice elevated. "I hate her."

I looked around. The suit and the young couple had left. Apparently, during our conversation two ladies came in and were sitting next to the table that had been occupied by the young couple. They were involved in a conversation and didn't react to Greg's voice.

"You know your Uncle Rocco was researching the disappearance of your mother."

"I did and deep down inside I wanted him to find something. The rumor about town was that he had some leads." Greg hung his head. "Now we'll never know what they were."

"Do you think your father had anything to do with the disappearance?"

"I truthfully don't know," he said then stood up.

I wasn't ready for him to leave.

"I want another cup—how about you?" He reached for my cup.

I knew Stella didn't come over to our table to ask about a refill because she didn't want to interrupt our conversation. "Yes I would, thanks." I didn't want to get into the Maria story at this time, so when Greg returned with our coffees, I changed the subject.

"Let's get back to Candy. Do you know if she got involved with anyone since your father's death?"

"My brother and I were sure she was involved with someone long before my father's death. He was a sick man, especially the last year of his life. The once spirited, high strung person he was, died long before his body quit working. She's cagy. We tried to find out who the other person was, but couldn't. We had our ideas, but

237

none of them panned out. Now our hands are tied—legally. It sucks."

"Maybe we can explore your ideas further. Let me think about it."

"Okay." Greg checked his watch.

"Do you have to leave?"

"No, just checking. It's a habit I guess." He smiled. "My father always said that time was money."

"I've ridden by the DeMarco compound, how in the world do the three households live together on the same piece of property?"

"It's not easy," he shook his head. "Believe me, it's not easy."

"Let's move to another subject."

"Fine with me."

"What can you tell me about your cousin, George Deluca?"

"We used to be close. He's an accountant and from what I understand a good one. When he got divorced he moved out of Falmouth to Buttermilk Bay. I've never been to his house, but from what I hear, it's beautiful." Greg shifted his eyes away from mine.

"I know all that. Tell me something I don't know." I leaned forward on the table closer to Greg.

"I know he helped Uncle Rocco out in the business when Aunt Rita died."

"Keep going," I said without moving my position.

"What do you want me to say?"

"I want you to tell me about George and the business."

Greg fidgeted in his chair. "Promise that you won't tell anyone what I'm about to tell you came from me. My brother doesn't even know."

"You have my word." I knew what he was about to tell me, but wanted to hear it from him.

"George was having a financial problem and I think he was skimming money from the books."

"What makes you think that?"

"Last November, right after Rocco died, George came to me to borrow some money. He told me about his gambling problem and that he was in debt—big debt. He never said with who. He figured I had inherited a sizable amount when my father died. You know the story—Candy was the executor. I didn't want to go into details with him, but tried to explain that I didn't have it to lend. He didn't believe me, yelled some familiar expletives, got in his car and drove away." Greg rolled his eyes. "I haven't seen or heard from him since."

"If he was skimming, maybe he wanted to put the money back into the business so when it got sold, the books would show clean. Speaking of selling the business, Bella wants to do it now and George is stalling. Now I think the missing money is the reason."

"You could be right," he said.

"I need one more answer." I didn't give him a chance to say anything before I asked the question. "Yesterday when I saw you at Dunkins, you knew I was on my way to meet with Chief Mills. I want to know who told you." My face turned to stone. He knew I was serious. He knew I meant business.

It was the longest two minutes I'd experienced in a long time. If I spoke first, I might never know, but if he broke the silence I'd have my answer—an old sales tactic that worked just as well in an investigation.

"I overheard one end of a telephone conversation between Candy and I don't know who." He stopped and looked around again. "Her office door was open. When she saw me walk by, she stopped talking, got up and closed her door." He cupped his hands around his face and rubbed his eyes. "You've got to believe me. I assumed she reacted to what the caller had just told her. Whoever she was talking to must have mentioned your name, Uncle Rocco's name and a meeting with the Chief. I heard her ask when the Casey Quinby meeting with Mills was supposed to take place?" He sat high in his chair as though a weight had been lifted from his shoulders. "That's all I know."

I stared at him for a second. "Greg, I believe you."

Stella held up the coffee pot and nodded.

I shook my head to denote a negative response, then turned towards Greg. "I appreciate you meeting with me. "I handed him one of my cards. "If you think of anything else, please give me a call."

"I will. Also, I have a favor to ask. Phil doesn't know I met with you today. In due time I'll tell him, but for the time being could we keep this our little secret."

"That's a reasonable request. I don't see a problem with it." I extended my hand to shake his. "Thank you," I said. "I'm going to talk to Stella for a few."

Greg pulled his business card from his pocket. "This is my personal cell. If you need me I'm the only one who will answer this number." He smiled. "I'm sure we'll talk soon."

"Probably so," I said. "Have a good one."

He nodded and left me standing in front of the pastry case.

My meeting with Greg went longer than expected, so I didn't have time to go back to Hyannisport before heading to Falmouth. Watson should be fine, but if I needed her to, I'm sure Marnie would go over after she got out of work and check on him.

Stella came out from the kitchen. "Is your friend gone?"

"He's not a friend, but yes he's gone and now I have to get going." I gave her a hug.

"See you soon?"

"When Sam gets home, we'll be over." I picked up my briefcase, gave Stella a wave and headed towards my car.

CHAPTER 65

The PD parking lot was crowded—more than any other time I'd been there—must be a class going on. Like before, Monica was waiting for me.

"I'm glad you're early. The Chief wants to talk to you a few minutes before you start the interviews."

I followed her to the elevator. There were a couple other people that got in with us, so we didn't say anything until we got off and the door closed.

"We've got a class going on today."

"I thought something like that was happening, parking spaces were at a premium."

I looked down the hall from Monica's desk. The Chief must have heard us talking. He was out of his office and headed down to meet me. "Are you ready?"

"As ready as I'm going to be."

"The conference room is all yours. The three officers coming in today are Mathew Brady at 1:30, James Johnson at 2:00 and Carl Tuttle at 2:30. Detectives Morse and Garrison will be here at 3:30 and 4:00. Why don't you go ahead and get set up. Let Monica know when you're ready and she'll send Brady in when he gets here." The Chief patted me on the back. "I'll talk to you after you finish with Tuttle."

"Thanks Chief." I left him standing with Monica and headed down to my waiting make-shift office. I positioned my paperwork in front of a chair at the end of the table and pulled out the chair directly across from me to indicate that's where I want the interviewees to sit. I was ready. I stuck my head out of the door, waved to Monica, then moved back inside.

Five minutes went by before Mathew Brady entered the room.

I reached across the table and held out my hand to greet him. "Good afternoon Officer Brady. My name is Casey Quinby." I pointed to the chair I'd pulled out from the table. "Please have a seat and we'll get started."

He nodded.

"Do you know why you've been called here today?"

"No, I'm sorry I don't. I was just told I was going to be interviewed and to be here at 1:30." He folded his hands and rested them on the table.

"I'm a private investigator. I've been hired to look into the death of Rocco Deluca."

A puzzled look came over Brady's face. "Rocco Deluca's death was ruled an accident."

"Yes it was, but certain questions have been raised that need to be answered." I positioned my mini-legal and picked up my pen ready to write. "I've read your report. I understand you were the first officer to answer the call to check out Rocco's fish market."

"I was."

"You stated the building was secure, meaning the doors were all locked and there was no broken glass to indicate a break-in. Is that correct?"

"It is."

"Did you call the station to inform them of your observations?"

"I did."

"And what happened next?"

"The dispatcher told me the original call came from Rocco Deluca's nephew, George. The nephew asked that the responding officer call and let him know what they found. The dispatcher gave me the nephew's cell phone number and I called."

"You told the nephew nothing seemed out of place—that there didn't appear to be a problem?"

"I did." He stopped for a minute, then continued, "There was one other thing. A black Ford 250 pick-up truck registered to Rocco Deluca was parked behind the building."

"Then what happened?"

"He gave me permission to break the lock and go inside to check things out. He appeared anxious."

"When you went inside did you find anything unusual or out of place?"

"First the smell was awful, so right away I knew something was wrong. Then, I observed a body draped over one of the lobster tanks."

"Aren't there windows in the front of the market? Couldn't you see this from the outside?" I asked.

"There are windows, but they were covered by closed blinds, making it impossible to see inside without going in."

"Okay. What did you do then?"

"I called the station for back-up and the EMTs for medical assistance."

"At some point in time, the nephew showed up. Do you remember how long it was after you called him to when he showed up?"

"No, it became pretty hectic. I knew Rocco was dead, but I wasn't about to touch anything until my back-up came. At that point I didn't know what happened. I could have been standing in the middle of a homicide scene and, if that be the case, I didn't want to contaminate anything."

"Did you visually observe anything out of the ordinary?"

"Everything looked normal. It didn't look any different than any other time I'd been there and I'd been there many times. It was always very neat and clean." He shook his head. "The only thing that seemed odd was an electrical cord plugged into a wall socket, then wrapped around a pole at the end of the tank. The female end was in the water on the bottom of the tank"

"An electrical cord?"

"At the time I thought it was a strange place for an electrical cord to be—because of the water and all. You know what I mean—water and electricity don't mix."

"Yes I know."

"Apparently that's what killed him. The ME said he was electrocuted. The ME ruled it an accident."

"There's no doubt he was electrocuted. The ruling of an accident is what's being questioned."

Brady got quiet, kept his hands folded on the table, but leaned back in his chair. He didn't look at me. He stared at his hands.

I glanced at my watch. I still had ten minutes left. "After the other officers got there, did you check out the rest of the building? Or did you stay in the room with the tanks?"

He thought for a minute before answering. "I was instructed by Officer Tuttle to check the electrical box and make sure the circuit breakers were shut off. Officer Tuttle was the senior officer on the scene."

"Were they off?"

"Yes."

"All of them were off?" Something wasn't right. I couldn't put my finger on it, but I needed to look at the inside the electrical box. I made a note to call Bella when my interviews were over to see if she could meet me at the market.

"I believe so."

"Did you make the second call to tell him his uncle was dead?"

"No, I gave his cell number to Officer Tuttle and I believe he gave it to one of the detectives, who, in turn, called George."

"How long would you say it was before George arrived at the market?"

"Not long at all—maybe five or ten minutes."

"So it appeared he was close by."

"It does."

There was a knock on the door. It was Monica. "Officer Johnson is here."

"Thanks."

She closed the door.

"Officer Brady, thank you for coming in today. If I have any more questions, I'll be in touch." I reached into my pocket, pulled out one of my business cards and handed it to him. I held out my hand to shake his, then stepped back and opened the door. My next interview was with Officer Johnson. I stayed standing to greet him as he came into the conference room.

"Good afternoon, Officer Johnson. Have a seat. My name is Casey Quinby. I'm a private investigator. I've been hired to look into the death of Rocco Deluca."

"That was sad. A man who'd worked so hard all his life and for what?"

"How well did you know him?"

"He was a fixture in town. I've lived in Falmouth all my life, so I know him well.

Johnson was far more relaxed than Brady. It didn't seem to faze him that a case he'd worked on was being investigated even though it was ruled an accident.

"Did you know his nephew, George?"

"I knew him, but didn't really know him—if you know what I mean. He was older than me, so we didn't run in the same circles."

"Did you know his niece, Bella?"

"Only from the library. My wife takes my daughter there for story hour. I did it a couple times on a day off. She loves her books."

I didn't feed into his light hearted conversation. "Let's get back to the fish market location. I understand you were riding double the day you got the call to go to Rocco's Fish Market?"

"Yes, I was with Officer Tuttle. He was the senior officer on the scene. He's the one who took charge and gave us our marching orders. Brady was the first responding officer and we were next. Brady's the one who made the initial call to the station for back-up. That's when we responded."

I hadn't quite figured out if Johnson was cocky, over-confident or nervous, but I intended to find out. I continued with the interview, asking him the same questions I'd already asked Brady. When I asked about checking the electrical box, Johnson said that Officer Tuttle asked him to do it. Brady said he did it. That was my first red flag.

"So, let's see, you said you were the first person who checked the electrical box to see if the circuits were off." Is that right?"

"Yes, it is."

"Were they off?"

"Not all of them—only the one labeled 'lobster tank and wall plates' was in the off position."

"I assume that it tripped when the electrical cord that Rocco appeared to be holding fell into the water in the bottom of the tank?"

"I'm no electrician, but I think that's what happened."

I locked eyes with Johnson. "In a case like this, or any case that involves a death, facts are facts—there's no room to think something happened—it either did or it didn't."

Johnson sat up straight and folded his hands on the table. "Yes, ma'am."

I'd been ma'amed. Either I'd been labeled the old lady or he finally decided to take this interview serious. I opted for the latter.

"Do you know how long it took George Deluca to get to the market after he was called?"

"I don't, because I don't know exactly what time he was called."

His answer was direct and to the point. This time he didn't add an 'I think'. If nothing else, he learned how to conduct himself in a job related interview—maybe.

Just as I had done with Brady, I reached into my pocket, pulled out one of my business cards and handed it to him. "Thank you for your help. If you want to add anything else, don't hesitate to give me a call."

We shook hands, he nodded and headed down the hall to where Monica was standing.

I waited to see if Johnson stopped to talk to the uniform leaning against the far wall in Monica's office. The uniform, who I assumed to be Tuttle, acknowledged Johnson, but didn't engage him in conversation.

I heard Monica's telephone ring, then watched as she motioned for the uniform to walk down to where I was standing. I greeted the third interviewee, then asked him to have a seat.

I started the same way as I did with the other two. "Good afternoon Officer Tuttle, my name is Casey Quinby, I'm a private investigator who's been hired to look into the death of Rocco DeLuca." I moved to the other side of the table. "Please have a seat."

"I was unaware there was a problem with that case." He stopped, then continued, "It was determined by the ME, that Rocco's death was accidental. His hand was next to an electrical cord in the bottom of the tank. I couldn't imagine why he was using a live, open ended cord near water. It appeared he was electrocuted when he fell into one of his tanks."

"That was the speculation, but some things have surfaced that have created questions as to whether or not it was an accident."

"What things?" Tuttle asked.

It was time to nip his attitude in the bud before it tried to take over. "At this time, I'm not at liberty to discuss that with you. As I said, I'm conducting an investigation and would appreciate it if you'd answer some questions for me. If, and when, my findings indicate concern, you'll be one of the first to know."

"Who are you working for?"

"You'll know when it's time for you to be privy to that information. Right now, your cooperation would be much appreciated." I leaned back in my chair, folded my hands over my chest and smiled.

He did the same.

What a jerk.

"I've read your report, along with those of the other responding officers and the two detectives who were called to the market the day Rocco was discovered."

Before I could say anything else, Tuttle piped in, "If you've read the reports, then you know what happened."

I snapped forward, this time resting my arms on the table—my smile gone. "I'm not sure what your problem is but, I'm here to conduct this interview and you're going to be an active participant. If this bothers you, then I can have Chief Mills sit in as an observer. It's your choice." The ball was in his court. His glare was piercing, but I wasn't about to give in.

I started to get up from the table.

"I don't need the Chief to be here," he finally said. "I'll answer what I can."

The shift in attitude concerned me, but he spoke first—I won this battle.

"Rocco Deluca was a good friend. A piece of me died with him. A better man you couldn't find."

"I'm truly sorry for your loss. I didn't know him, but have heard the same thing from others."

"It infuriates me to think that he died from anything other than an accident." Tuttle's head dropped close to his chest. "I heard the rumors of suicide. Rocco would never do that. He did miss Rita, but not enough to end his life—she wouldn't have wanted that."

"Actually, the suicide theory was mentioned, but has been put on the back burner."

Tuttle suddenly looked up. His face wrinkled in unease. "Then what?"

"It's being investigated as a possible homicide."

Tuttle was speechless.

"Who'd want to harm Rocco?" He shook his head as he spoke. "I don't understand." He reached up with both hands, rubbed his face and mumbled, "I just don't understand."

I took a deep breath and sat quiet while Officer Tuttle composed himself.

"I'm sorry for my earlier actions. I was rude and I do apologize." He extended his hand to shake mine. "Can we start over?"

I shook his hand and smiled. "Of course."

"I want you to know if there's anything I can do, please let me. If, in fact, it was a homicide, I want to help take down the bastard who did it."

"I appreciate that. I have no authority to say who is or isn't going to be involved, but since you were part of the initial case, I'm sure the Chief will rely on your input. My suggestion is to keep everything we talked about today to yourself. That includes not sharing stories with any of the other officers being interviewed."

"I understand."

I checked the time. Because of our rocky introduction, I was going to have to cut Tuttle's interview short. In a roundabout way, his actions gave me insight into his person. "There's a couple questions I'd like to ask. Do you remember if it was Officer Brady or Officer Johnson you sent to the back room to check the electrical box?"

His eyes narrowed, then closed. He scratched his left palm, then clasped his hands together. Then all actions stopped. He slowly opened his eyes. "As I recall, Officer Brady was standing beside the tank when we arrived. I looked over the top of the tank and saw the cord and the water. I assumed Rocco had been electrocuted. I asked him if he'd checked the electrical box. He said no. I turned to Officer Johnson and asked him to go do it. Since Brady was the first responder, I wanted him to stay beside the body."

"So at that time, it was the three of you in the market."

"Yes, Officers Brown and Massad came about fifteen minutes after we got there and Detectives Morse and Garrison about ten minutes after they were called."

I thought back to Brady's answer. He said he checked the electrical box, but Tuttle confirmed Johnson's story that Johnson did the checking.

"Did Officer Johnson say the circuit breaker to the tank area was on or off?"

"I distinctly remember him saying it was off. The rest were on, but that one was off. If Rocco was, in fact, electrocuted and the current was still live, we didn't need a second casualty, so I wouldn't let anyone touch the body until I knew that to be true."

"Did you call George Deluca from the market?"

"No, I gave the number to one of the detectives and he made the call."

"Do you remember which one it was?"

"I don't."

"I understand that George showed up at the market about five minutes after he was called."

"I can't say if it was five minutes, but it was very soon after he was notified. I thought that a little odd because George lives at Buttermilk Bay and that's more than a five-minute ride. Then, since he's in business for himself, I figured he may have been meeting with a client. I should have asked, but it didn't enter my mind. I'll admit, that was bad police work, since I'm not a rookie." He lifted his arms and shook them in disgust. "All I could think of was that my friend died as a result of a terrible accident. The idea of homicide never crossed my mind."

"You weren't the only one. And, I didn't say it was a homicide. I said I was investigating it further than an accident because some things didn't fit. At this point, it's still classified as an accident. Do you recall what happened when the ME arrived?"

"Nothing out of the ordinary. Derek came in, looked the situation over and, after viewing the scene asked if the electricity to that section was turned off. I assured him it was. He asked if we had taken all the pictures we needed at that time. I told him we did. He proceeded to take pictures of his own. When he was done, he instructed the EMTs to get Rocco's body away from the tank and onto a stretcher. We all knew Rocco was dead and had been for probably several days. The stench wasn't good. The ME then performed further tests. I'm sure there are certain things he had to do for the record."

"What was George's reaction when he saw his uncle?"

"Not good. He was a mess. George and his sister, Bella were very close to their aunt and uncle. Since their Aunt Rita died five years ago, Rocco was the only family they had left."

"What about the DeMarcos?"

"They're family by blood only. There's lots of animosity between them. Has been for years. So, I stand behind my statement, Rocco was the only family they had left."

I didn't want to get into the DeMarco family so I changed the conversation.

"Did you know that Rocco was getting ready to sell the market?"

"I did. I'd have coffee with him several times a week. He told me he was getting ready to put it up for sale, but he wasn't in any hurry." Tuttle smiled. "Rocco never did anything in a hurry."

I wanted Officer Tuttle to be gone before Detective Morse showed up, so it was time to wrap it up. As before, I stood up, reached into my pants pocket and pulled out a business card. "Here's my card. If you think of anything else, please give me a call." I held out my hand to shake his. "Thank you for your time and your help."

"And, if you need me for anything, you know where to find me." He smiled. I walked with him down to Monica's desk, then went back to the conference room.

My two biggest challenges were coming up—interviews with Detectives Morse and Garrison. I was nervous. They'll be trying to get inside my head at the same time I'm trying to get inside theirs. Questioning these guys will be like questioning Sam.

That might not be a bad way to conduct these two interviews. Just pretend I'm questioning Sam.

I was ready.

I was re-reading the detective's reports when Monica knocked on the door and came in. "Chief Mills buzzed me. He wanted to know if you were done with your first three interviews."

Oh shit.

"I was supposed to meet with him when I was done." It was two-forty-five. "I've still got time before Detective Morse gets here. If it's okay, I'll go talk to him now."

"He's waiting," she smiled and went back to her desk.

The Chief's door was cracked open. I knocked and went in. "Sorry, Chief. I got so wrapped up in the interviews, I forgot I was going to meet with you when I finished with Officer Tuttle."

"That's okay. I was buried with paperwork and lost track of the time myself." He shuffled some papers around to form a neat pile, then slid it aside. "How did they go?"

"Question—how long has Brady been on the job?"

"Not long." The Chief went into thinking mode. "Two, maybe three, years at the most."

"Is he a wash-a-shore?"

"He is. He started the police academy in Quincy, but finished it here. He originally was from Marshfield. The Chief in Marshfield is one of my closest friends. Officer Brady is his nephew."

"What happened in Quincy?"

"No problems—he just didn't want to be that close to Boston. His academy record to date was great. He was tops in his class. His uncle asked if we had any openings. We had a class only one week into the program, so I offered him the opportunity to transfer. He took it." Chief Mills rubbed his chin. "Why do you ask?"

"In my opinion, he's still operating like a rookie—but, that's strictly my opinion. Officer Johnson and, of course, Officer Tuttle are far more into the wearing of the blue. I assume they've been on the job much longer and take liberties not yet available to Brady."

The Chief looked puzzled. "You need to explain."

"I'm not positive, but I think I'm right when I say that Brady wrote the reports for himself and his fellow officers. I haven't talked to the two remaining officers yet, but their reports are much the same as the three I've already interviewed. They all reflect an assignment from a Reports 101 class." I hesitated, then continued, "I would say that if you check Brady's file, he's never been involved in something like the death of Rocco Deluca. And, since it was ruled an accident, the other officers didn't figure anyone would be scrutinizing reports so they had Brady write one for all with just a slight tweak in each."

There was a knock on the door. "Come in."

It was Monica. "Chief, I just got a call from Detective Morse. He and Detective Garrison have been called to investigate a break on Jetty Lane."

"Thanks."

Monica turned and headed back to her desk.

"Casey, I know you're not familiar with most of Falmouth. Jetty Lane goes off of Quaker Road and dead ends at the Ocean. The property values are all in the millions, especially the ones right on the water. Morse and Garrison are my two top guys. We'll reschedule with them, probably next week."

"Since we've got some time, can we talk about Officers Johnson and Tuttle?" I asked.

"That works for me."

"Let's start with Johnson."

"He's a Falmouth boy—been on the job for about ten years. He can be a little over confident, but he does a good job. I haven't had any complaints from residents or fellow officers. Sometimes he talks too much, but that doesn't make him a bad cop." He laughed. "Good family man."

"And Officer Tuttle?"

"One of my best. His family has deep roots in Falmouth. He loves this town. He was crushed when Rocco died." The Chief stopped, took a deep breath. "Do you think Tuttle filed a tweaked Brady report too?"

"I do. But, my interview with him clarified questions I had. I'll write up my report and get it to you within a couple days after I conduct the last two officer interviews. Next week will be fine to re-schedule my meeting with the detectives. I'll work that out with Monica when I'm here Friday."

I stood up. "Time to get back to my office and get to work." Just as I picked up my briefcase and purse, his phone rang.

"Good morning." He gave me a one finger salute, took out one of his cards with his cell number on it, pointed to the number and mouthed that he'd see me on Friday.

I returned the gesture and left his office. Monica was busy with paperwork. I slid Chief Mills' card into my purse for safe keeping. "See you Friday," I said and headed for the elevator.

CHAPTER 66

It was early to stop to see Bella, but I wasn't about to go to Barnstable, stay for an hour, then drive back to Falmouth. I pulled into the Library parking lot. Her car was parked in the directors spot. The most she can say is that she can't leave right now. Although, she did say she enjoyed certain perks being the boss.

I didn't want to walk behind the desk without checking with the receptionist first so I waited in line to ask if Bella was available. "Good afternoon. Is Bella Deluca in?"

"She is, but she has somebody in her office at the moment. Are you here to interview for the programs director job?"

I wanted to laugh, but didn't want to appear rude. "No, I'm a friend. I was passing by so I thought I'd stop to say hello. Do you think she'll be free soon?"

The receptionist looked up behind me at the wall clock. "Probably no more than five minutes."

"Thanks. I'll wait over by the magazines." I nodded, went to the magazine section, picked up a *Travel and Leisure* and situated myself so I could see Bella when she walked out of her office.

It was exactly five minutes when Bella emerged with a relatively young girl in tow. I stood up so she could see me. I quietly waved, then waited for her to acknowledge me.

She nodded. I put my magazine back where I found it and walked towards the reception desk where Bella was standing.

"Good afternoon," she said in her professional voice. "Let's go to my office." Once inside and the door closed, she asked me about the interviews. "How did everything go today?"

"Well, I interviewed the first three officers, Brady, Johnson and Tuttle. They were the first three to respond—Brady being number

255

one. I think I told you all the officers' reports were very similar. A few words were changed, but the guts were the same. I'm pretty sure I've straightened that problem out and it's really no big deal. I was happy with today's results. Instead of going over everything with you now, I'll give you a copy of the report I'm going to write up for the Chief. I was supposed to meet with the two detectives, but they got called out to investigate a break-in at a house on Jetty Lane."

"Jetty Lane—you should see those houses. They're huge. And a location to dream about." She shook her head as she spoke.

"That's what the Chief said."

"So, if you're not going to go over the interview info, how come you stopped by to see me?"

"I was wondering if we could go over to the market. There's something I want to check out."

"Sure. Let me clean up my desk and we'll head on over."

"I'll wait for you in the magazine section. I started to read an article on Boston and I'd like to finish it."

"I won't be long."

I was on the last sentence when Bella tapped me on my shoulder. "I'm ready."

"Okay, I'll follow you. There's no sense in leaving a car here and having to come back to get it."

"Come with me. We might as well go out the side door. My car is parked right beside it."

I was a few parking spaces away, so Bella backed out, then waited for me to get settled and pull up behind her. It took less than ten minutes to get to the market. We parked in the back.

She had the market key in hand when she got out of her car. "I don't want to linger in the parking lot. Some do-gooder might see me and decide to stop to chat." She smirked. "Remember, chat in Falmouth is another word for gossip."

"Ah, I get your drift." I shadowed her as she walked inside.

"What is it you want to look at?"

"The electrical box."

"Why?"

"Let me look first, then I'll explain it to you."

"Fair enough."

Since we came in through the back door, we were already in the back room where the electrical box was located. I pulled a flashlight and a pair of latex gloves from my purse, set the light on a table beside the box, slipped the gloves on then opened the box. I turned on the flashlight and visually examined the circuit breaker that controlled the flow of electricity to the lobster tank area. I check the other breakers to see if anything looked different from the one in question. I went back and forth several times.

"You're killing me. What are you looking at? "

"Be patient. I'm not quite sure myself." I went back to studying the entire box. "Will you please go into my purse and get my camera for me?"

"Sure." She handed me my camera.

"Now I need you to hold the flashlight so that it's focused on the number four breaker." I pointed to the breaker I wanted to be the center of attention. Before I took any pictures I studied the breaker. With Bella holding the light, I was able to move my head to view the area around the breaker from several different angles. "You're doing a good job. I'm going to snap some pictures."

Bella didn't say a word. She knew I'd found something important to the case.

"Okay. I got what I wanted."

"Now are you going to tell me?"

"Yes. First of all, I put gloves on because I want the PD to dust for prints. The only ones they should find are Rocco's, maybe George's and Officer Johnson's. Second, I looked up different ways people get electrocuted. We all know electricity and water don't mix. And, yes the marriage of the two can be deadly, but not every time. Also, some articles I read said that the circuit breaker should trip when the source of the active electric current hits the water. After reading that, I got an idea and wanted to check it out."

"Now that I'm confused, can you explain that in layman's terms."

I took the flashlight from Bella and shined it on the lobster tank breaker. Without touching the panel, I pointed to a spot that looked like something had been wedged between the breaker and the side of the box. "My theory is that something prevented the breaker from doing its job. If the breaker didn't trip, then the electricity didn't stop flowing. If that be the case, we are definitely looking at a homicide."

Bella stepped back, walked to her uncle's desk and half sat on the corner. She folded her arms over her chest and stared at the floor. "I told you it wasn't an accident."

"There's lots more work to do, but I think this is enough to create reasonable doubt with the accident ruling." I took my gloves off and put them back in my purse. I didn't want to leave any signs of my investigation behind. "Bella, you need to keep this information to yourself. We don't want anyone tampering with evidence. You can't even tell George." I kept my eyes focused on hers.

"I won't discuss it with anyone except you."

"Let's get out of here, before anyone wonders why we're snooping around." I shut the door to the electrical box, made sure everything was the same as when we came in and motioned for Bella to head to the back door. "I'm going to say good-bye now. I don't want to hang around the parking lot. I'll give you a call sometime tomorrow."

"If you need me tonight, I'll be home."

"Okay—ready."

Bella opened the door and we went to our cars.

I couldn't wait to talk to Sam. There was so much I wanted to go over with him.

CHAPTER 67

I was glad to be home. Watson was waiting not so patiently for me right inside the door. He didn't wait for me to get his leash. I let him run. Fortunately, this time he stayed close because I was in no mood to chase him.

"Hungry, boy? I'm sorry I'm so late. Let's get you some food."

As fast as he ran out of the house, he ran back in.

"I guess you are hungry." I reached down and tussled with him for a few minutes, then went to the pantry to get him something to eat.

"Yum—Kibbles and Bits." I laughed.

I got myself a glass of White Zin over ice, turned the TV on to the six o'clock news and sat down on the couch to relax before I started writing my report. I remember watching the first half of the news and part of the weather, but that was all. Watson nudged me. My cell was ringing. I jumped off the couch to answer, but it went to voice mail before I could reach it. I checked the caller ID. It was Marnie.

I looked at the clock. It was seven-thirty. I pulled her number up and hit the call button.

"Where are you? You were supposed to call me after your meeting with Greg DeMarco."

"I know I was. I planned on coming home between the meeting I had with him and the interviews at the Falmouth PD, but it didn't work out that way. I got home just before six, sat down with a glass of wine to relax before I got started with my reading and fell asleep. If you hadn't called I'd probably still be curled up on the couch lounging in la-la land." I snickered. "Actually, I'm glad you did call. I've got things to do before I really go to bed."

"I'm not letting you off the hook. Tell me what happened with Greg DeMarco."

"My meeting with Greg went very well. We talked about his immediate family, about his business and about his association with his cousins."

"Is that all you're going to say?"

I knew Marnie was irritated, but I didn't want to go into the details.

"Do you think he and/or his brother has anything to do with Rocco's death?"

"That much I will tell you. No, I don't."

"If you're not going to talk about Greg DeMarco, how about filling me in on the interviews with the cops."

"I only interviewed the first three responding officers. The detectives got called to investigate a break-in at a multi-million dollar property. The Chief is going to reschedule them for sometime next week."

"Did anything come out of the three officer interviews?"

"Yeah, I don't remember if I told you I thought the reports they filed were too similar—like one person wrote them."

"You did tell me that."

"One of the officers is a rookie. They were too much like an assignment from a Reports Writing 101 class. It's my guess he's our author. It was poor police practice, but in all fairness, the death was ruled an accident. In most accident cases, the reports are filed away never to be read again."

"That doesn't make it right."

"No it doesn't, but it happens. I haven't started to write my report for the Chief yet. I intended to do that tonight, but the sandman had other ideas. I may start it when I get off the phone, then finish it tomorrow morning. I plan on coming into the office early. Do you want me to stop at Dunkins?"

"A chocolate glazed would make a great peace offering."

"Would two buy me some future favors?"

"Depends on what they are?" She laughed. "See you in the morning."

"Yes you will." I punched the end button.

My little half-hour snooze was enough to get the juices flowing again. I took the paperwork out of my briefcase, set it on the kitchen table and started sorting through the piles. I had to decipher the notes I'd scribbled on my mini-legal pad during the interviews. I re-read the reports Brady, Johnson and Tuttle submitted back in November. There was no doubt there was one author and three tweekers. First thing tomorrow morning, when I got to the office, I'm going scan them into my computer. On each report I'm going to insert things I heard in the respective officer's interview, then put my additions in red.

There wasn't much more I could do tonight, so I filled my glass with more ice and wine and headed back to the couch. This time I took my cell with me in case Sam called.

I checked the TV Guide, *Survivor* was on CBS at eight o'clock. I'd missed ten minutes, but nothing earth shattering usually happens within the first ten minutes of any show. I used to faithfully watch every episode, but for some reason, this season I didn't. I blamed Sam. He doesn't like the show—thinks it's all a put on. Put on or not, I liked it. It ended with two new tribes being formed.

I looked at my phone. "Well, Sam Summers, guess you're enjoying your last night with the guys," I said out loud. Watson lifted his head to make sure I wasn't talking to him, then resumed his curled up position on Sam's end of the couch. I read the blurb for *Law & Order:Special Victims Unit.* It involved a columnist who was working with the police department on a story regarding a hate crime case. I wasn't a columnist, but we were 'newspaper sisters'. Enter Olivia Benson—love that lady. I was deeply involved with the story when they broke for commercial and my phone rang. I sighed. "Bad timing Sam." Why didn't he call an hour ago. I didn't care much about what happened in *Survivor*, but Olivia and I were about to solve a crime and I didn't want to let her down.

I answered without checking the ID. "Bad timing."

"Casey, it's George Deluca." He was frantic. "Please, you've got to come fast! I'm at Falmouth Hospital."

I sat straight up on the edge of the couch. I held my cell with one hand and motioned to George as though he could see me. "Whoa, whoa, whoa George. What's wrong?"

"It's my sister! She's been in a terrible car accident. She's in a coma. I didn't know who else to call. Can you come—come to the hospital?" George didn't wait for a reply. "Please."

"Calm down. I'm on my way.

"They're operating on her now. I've got to go. I'll meet you in the lobby."

I grabbed my purse and my car keys and flew out the door, only stopping for a second to make sure it was locked.

I wasn't exactly sure where Falmouth Hospital was, so I quickly entered it into my GPS. The directions came up. The fastest way was Route 6. I backed out of my driveway and headed in that direction. Bella said she wasn't going out tonight. Said she was staying home if I needed to get ahold of her.

It took me thirty-five minutes to get to the hospital. Since visiting hours were over, there were lots of empty spaces. I got one opposite the front door. I grabbed my purse and ran across the sidewalk into the building.

George was pacing the floor and ran towards me when the sliding doors opened. His face distressed and his eyes puffed from crying. "Casey, come with me. She still hasn't come out of surgery, but we can wait upstairs in the waiting room. They said the doctor would be out to talk to me as soon as he's finished operating." He grabbed my hand and dragged me behind him as though I was a little child trying to escape.

I scurried up beside him, not pulling my hand from his. "George, what happened?"

"She was in a terrible accident." His voice crackled. "I'll tell you when we get upstairs."

The operating room where Bella was being operated on was on the third floor. The elevator seemed to move at a snail's pace. We probably could have walked it faster. The door finally opened. George ran out and I followed. Halfway down the corridor we made a right, went through a set of automatic doors, then took a left into a waiting room. We were the only ones there.

George buzzed the nurse's station. "This is George Deluca. I'm back. Has anybody been looking for me?"

I could hear the person on the other end. "No. The doctor is still in with your sister."

Apparently, there wasn't anything to report and, besides, it's not the nurse's position to say anything unless the doctor has instructed her to do so.

I was already sitting, waiting for George to finish and join me.

His breathing was labored. "Casey, thank you for coming. I didn't know who else to call." He rested his elbows on his knees and cupped his hands around his face. But his tell-tale body movement couldn't disguise his fear of losing his sister—his best friend—his only family.

I put my arm around him. "I'm here. When you're ready, tell me what happened."

The next move was his. I let him compose himself. He looked up at the intercom a couple times, then at the door leading to the nurse's station, then back down to the floor in front of him. I sat silent.

Finally he spoke. "Apparently she went out to get a pizza. She has a thing about pizza delivery. She always told me she didn't trust the insulated bags they put them in to keep them warm. She thought they bred germs." He tried to smile at the memory, but it didn't last.

"How did you know this?"

"The police said there was a full pizza on the seat beside her."

"Where did the accident happen?" I asked still watching George's facial expressions.

"Not even a mile from her house." His voice dropped to a whisper. "The same spot where my cousin died. I'm sure she told you about that accident involving Uncle Rocco."

I didn't want to get into anything to do with the DeMarco family, but had to respond. "Yes, she did."

"They, the police, said her cell phone was on the floor near the gas pedal. They figured she was making a call, lost control and hit the tree. I have her cell and her purse." He reached beside him and lifted a plastic bag containing both items. "I have a problem with the police's theory. Bella never, and I repeat, never used her cell phone while driving. She'd pull over to make a call, but never while she was behind the wheel."

"Have you looked at her cell?"

"No, why?"

"Can I see it?"

George took it out of the bag and handed it to me.

It hadn't been damaged in the accident, so I was able to turn it on. The problem was it needed a password to get into it. "Do you know her password?"

George shook his head.

I thought for a minute. I punched in Boston, nothing—then tried library, nothing—then Dewey. It opened. I should have tried that first since he was her main squeeze.

George tilted his head sideways to watch what I was doing. We both sat straight up when we read the name that appeared as the last person she was attempting to call. It was me.

"Did you talk to her?"

"No. I didn't. I saw her earlier in the day. She told me she was going to be home all night if I wanted to talk to her. I had a busy day and was tired, so I worked a little on my reports, briefly talked to a friend of mine, then vegged out on the couch."

"There had to be a reason she was trying to reach you." George took a deep breath. "Can you think of any? Maybe something to do with what you talked about during the day."

"No. Nothing we talked about would spark an impromptu call."

George flexed his back and rolled his neck. "There's something I have to talk to you about."

I couldn't imagine what he was about to say.

"I don't want to talk about Uncle Rocco's investigation, except to say, whatever happens with my sister, I want you to continue with your work."

"We'll talk about that later, but for your piece of mind, I will." I was surprised, but glad he brought it up. I had a bad feeling about Bella's 'accident'. Somehow, I felt the two Deluca 'accidents' were related. "Right now our first concern is Bella." I took his hands in mine.

He nodded.

"I'm getting a water." I pointed to the vending machine in the corner. "Do you want one?"

"Sure," he said and started to reach into his pocket.

"I've got it."

We sat quiet, waiting for someone to come through the door to update us on Bella's condition. Ten minutes passed. The quiet was deafening. My leg was starting to ache, so I got up to stretch it. I was on my second circle around the room, when the doctor came through the nurse's station door. I stepped aside so he would know to address his comments to George.

"Are you Bella's brother?" He reached forward to shake George's hand. "I'm Doctor Michaels. Your sister is one lucky lady. She has a couple broken ribs, there's a bad fracture on her left arm between her wrist and elbow and she suffered a concussion. It's the concussion that put her into the coma."

"Does that mean she's still in a coma?" George set his bottle of water down and started to fidget with his fingers.

"She is, but I feel confident her head injuries are not life-threatening. We're not going to move her to a room tonight. I want to keep eyes on her just in case she needs immediate attention." The doctor hesitated then continued, "Which I don't anticipate."

"Are we able to see her now?"

"I'll authorize it, but only for a short time." Doctor Michaels looked at me. "Are you a relative?"

Before I could say anything, George answered. "Not a blood relative, but as close as you can get."

"Does this almost relative have a name?"

I moved forward and stood beside George. "Casey Quinby." I held my hand out.

"I'll put both your names on the approved visitor list. If she responds to treatment tonight, then I anticipate moving her tomorrow. I'd prefer she gets moved to a private room. Right now, she doesn't need the company of a room-mate, but she's going to need the encouragement of her family." He gave us both the over-the-eyebrow nod.

We acknowledged him with a positive gesture.

"Let's go in." Dr. Michaels pushed the call button on the intercom and instructed the nurse to open the door.

We followed him to the cubicle they'd assigned to Bella for the night.

He looked at George. "I'll contact you tomorrow, probably sometime around noon. Make sure you leave your number at the desk."

"I will, but I plan on being here."

"Okay then I'll see you around that time." He turned to leave, then stopped. "Remember, don't stay long. She needs her rest—and so do you."

George gazed at Bella, then me, then back to Bella. He had tears in his eyes. I put my hand on his back. "She's going to be fine. She's a little broken right now, but she's strong. She'll bounce back. Just remember, she's going to need your help."

"Casey, will you be there to help her too?" Not only did he sound like a scared child, he looked like one.

"Of course I will."

We were careful what we said just in case Bella could subconsciously hear us. We spoke very little and in a whisper. It was almost midnight when I started back to Hyannisport. I stood up from the chair I had slid up beside Bella's bed. "Now that we know she came out of the operation okay and there's nothing else we can do tonight, I'm going to head back to Hyannisport."

George didn't say anything, just nodded.

"You know, you should think about going home and trying to get some sleep. If you want, I'll meet you here around eleven-thirty tomorrow morning."

George started to get up.

I motioned him to stay seated. "Unless I hear from you, I'll see you tomorrow." I kissed my finger tips and touched Bella's forehead. "Rest," I said before I turned and headed to the nurses station to sign out.

CHAPTER 68

My heart was broken. Bella looked so helpless, so frail and there was nothing I could do—at least nothing in the hospital room.

As I drove home, I mentally filled in my schedule for tomorrow. The first thing I needed to do was make arrangements for Watson. I could bring him to the office in the morning, then back home before I went to the hospital, but it was after that. Barring any problems, Sam was supposed to be back to the house around three o'clock. I couldn't take the chance. If Sam was late maybe Marnie could check on the boy.

The timing and place of Bella's accident didn't sit well with me. Since George wanted me to continue with the original investigation, it was time to explore the idea of a connection between the two 'accidents'. Things were moving fast and furious. I still had interviews left to conduct and reports to compare. Then there's the examination of the electrical box. I want Sam to give me his opinion on my findings. I'm going to have to ask George for a key to the market. I'll dance around the reason, but since he's on board with the investigation into Uncle Rocco's death, I don't think it'll be a problem. If Sam's on time tomorrow, maybe we can check it out. I don't want to wait. If it is evidence that proves the breakers were tampered with, then I don't want to take any chance of somebody finding out and eliminating it.

I was almost to the Route 149, West Barnstable exit off Route 6 when a dark blue or black fancy pick-up truck passed me. The person driving must have been doing at least eighty—maybe more. He or she sped by me swerving dangerously close to the driver's side of my car. If I wasn't paying attention, the wind tunnel might have sent my little Spider sailing out of control.

"You asshole," I screamed. There was no way I could have gotten the plate number or read what appeared to be a bumper sticker on the bottom of the tail gate. I got my breath back, flipped on my right blinker and made my turn off the Mid-Cape. Once back on track, I got to thinking. *Was that little episode on purpose—maybe to scare me—or warning me to back off? Then again, it could have been nothing—just me being paranoid.*

I was never so glad to see my driveway and a working front door light. Actually, I left so fast I must have left a light on inside. Watson was waiting for me. I took him out for a quick walk around the house. I was exhausted. I slipped on a pair of joe boxers and a tee shirt, brushed my teeth, set the alarm and the boy and I got into bed. I rolled over and gave him a pat. "Daddy will be home tomorrow."

CHAPTER 69

Thursday

The alarm was an unwelcomed sound. I pulled the pillow over my head until the snooze alarm went off for the second time. Watson just ignored it.

Since Watson was coming to the office with me, I fixed his breakfast before I got ready. It was seven o'clock when we pulled out of the yard. I stopped at Dunkin's and got donuts for Marnie, Annie and me. I felt so bad that I hadn't seen Annie, but she seemed to be going one way and I was going the other. When this case is done, it's definitely time for a girl's night out.

There was a car parked behind my building. Before I got out, I looked around. I didn't see anyone, so Watson and I got out, I unlocked the back door and we went inside. My Keurig was sitting on the counter calling my name. It was coffee time. Before my cup was full I had already eaten half of one of my jelly donuts. I was just about to pour cream into my coffee when there was a knock on the door behind me. I jumped and turned at the same time. My eyes automatically focused on the knob. I hadn't locked the door when I came in. There was a man standing outside. I picked up my hot coffee and headed for the door. Watson sensed something was wrong. He walked beside me. I opened the door a crack. "Can I help you?"

"I got here early and didn't notice your sign. I wanted to tell you I was leaving."

"I did wonder who was parked there. I've had problems before, that's why the signs." I didn't want to engage in any further conversation. "Thank you. Time to get to work."

He walked to his car and I closed and locked the door.

At eight o'clock I called Chief Mills on his personal cell number. He answered immediately. "Hello."

"Hi Chief Mills, it's Casey Quinby."

"I figured I'd hear from you this morning. I'm glad you called on this number and not through the switchboard."

"George Deluca called me from the hospital. He was frantic. He told me about Bella and wanted me to come to the hospital. He said he needed to talk to me, so I met him there. I waited with him until Dr. Michaels finished operating on Bella and came out to talk to George. It was late."

"How is she?"

"The doctor said she was very lucky. She's pretty broken up and has a concussion, but he said she'd be all right."

"Do you know where the accident was?"

"George told me. I'm meeting him at eleven-thirty at the hospital. I thought I'd take a ride by the place where it happened first. He also told me that's the same spot where Rocco had an accident and the youngest DeMarco boy died."

"That's right." He was silent, then spoke. "It's too much of a coincidence. I'd like to meet with you, but not here at the station and probably better if it wasn't in Falmouth."

"Are you in uniform today?"

"No, why?"

"I could meet you at a place called Stella's in Cotuit Village. It's out of the way enough that unless you know somebody from the area, you probably won't be recognized. I can be there by nine-thirty. That would give us about an hour to talk, time for me to ride by the accident scene and take some pictures, then meet George."

"I'll be there. If something comes up, I'll give you a call."

"See you then," I said and hung up.

No sooner did I set my cell down on the desk, it rang. "Hello."

"Good morning." It was Marnie.

"I'm running a little late. I walked to my car to leave and noticed I had a flat tire. I called AAA and they're on the way. I don't know

271

how long it's going to take. If they get here soon, I should be there by nine."

"I won't be here."

"Why, what's happening?"

"It's a long story, but I'll sum it up. Bella was in an accident last night. I was at the hospital with George until midnight. She's got some broken bones and a concussion. She's in a coma or at least she was when I left. I think George would have called me if she came out of it during the night."

"Was it an accident or an 'accident'."

"My thinking exactly."

"What's your next move?"

"I just got off the phone with Chief Mills. I'm meeting with him at nine-thirty at Stella's in Cotuit. It should be interesting. When I leave there I'm going to take some pictures of the accident scene, then be at the hospital to meet George at eleven-thirty."

"Will you give me a call?"

"I will, but I don't know when. I've got Watson with me. I'm going to swing by the house and put him on his run. Do you think you can get away, go check on him and put him inside? When I talked to Sam Wednesday night, he figured he should be at my house around three, but you know how that goes. Oh, by the way, your chocolate glazed peace offering and eleven more are in a box sitting on the counter in the back room. You've got a key."

"Yes I do. I'll pick them up and I'm sure I can go check on Watson, probably around noon."

"Thanks. I'll get back to you soon."

"Promise me you'll be careful."

"I promise."

We both clicked off at the same time.

There was no sense starting to write my report, I'd just get started and have to put it aside. "Hey, boy, something's come up and I have to take you home." I hooked him to his leash, picked up my briefcase and purse and headed out the back door.

CHAPTER 70

There were several cars in Stella's parking lot, but since I didn't know what kind of car the Chief drove, I had no idea if he was there or not.

Instead of bringing my briefcase in, I took my mini-legal and stuck it inside my purse, then headed for the door.

Stella looked up as I came through. She waved.

I glanced around the room before I walked up to the counter. Chief Mills hadn't arrived. He wasn't late—I was early. I gave Stella a hug. "We've got to stop meeting like this." I laughed.

"Twice this week."

"I'm going to have to start paying you for office space."

"Another meeting?"

I started to answer, when the door opened and Chief Mills walked in. If I was a patron I wouldn't figure him for a Chief of Police.

"Going undercover," he whispered as he joined me at the counter.

We both smiled.

"It's not often I can do a dress down during the week. I keep a pair of jeans and a couple tee shirts in my office. This is a welcome change along with the change of scenery." He looked around the restaurant. "I don't remember the last time I was in Cotuit. If the pastry is as good as it smells, it won't be the last."

I patted Stella's back. "Trust me, it is."

Stella pointed to the corner table where I usually sit. "Your office just became available. Let me wipe down your 'desk' so you can get started." She grinned, grabbed a wet cloth and got us set up. "Coffee for both of you?"

"Of course. And, I'll let you decide what calories we should consume this morning." I glanced at Chief Mills. "Is that okay with you?"

"You're running the show."

"I'll be right back," said Stella.

"I like the place already," the Chief said as he took a quick look around to make sure he didn't recognize anyone.

"Let's get started." I got my pad ready. "I told you I got a call from George, met him at the hospital and stayed until midnight."

"You did."

"I'm concerned that Bella's 'accident' wasn't really an accident. At this time, I can't prove it, but it's my gut feeling. When she hired me, she told me that Falmouth has a gossip mill. She said she didn't discuss her decision to have me investigate her uncle's death with anyone—not even her brother. She also said that once I started to look into it, the rumor would travel like kids with tin cans and string. The facts, or what a person would perceive to be the facts, would get a little more distorted each time the can was passed on."

I stopped talking when Stella brought our coffee and crumpets. She set them down and without saying anything, turned and left.

"Bella hit the nail on the head. I've had problems with the rumor mill before. They've actually almost botched several of my department investigations." The Chief picked up a blueberry scone and took a bite. "Wow, these are great."

"Told you," I said and took a bite of mine.

"Yesterday, after I left the station, I swung by the library to talk to Bella. I asked her if we could go over to Rocco's market after she got off work. She was getting ready to leave anyway, so I waited until she closed up her office, then followed her to the market. We parked in the back so as not to draw any unwanted attention. We were inside for less than a half-hour."

"What were you checking out?"

"The electrical box."

A puzzled look came over the Chief's face. "You're going to have to explain."

"When I did the first three interviews, Brady said Tuttle instructed him to check the breakers. He said he did and when I asked if they were off, he said yes. From his answer, I assumed he meant they were all off since he didn't single out the one for the tanks." I stopped to see if I'd get a comment or at least a reaction.

The Chief only nodded for me to continue.

"When I interviewed Johnson, he said Tuttle told him to check the electrical box. Johnson reported back to Tuttle that the breakers were all on, except the one for the tanks." I took a break to sip my coffee and gather my thoughts so I got them right. "Officer Tuttle confirmed the information Johnson gave me."

"I don't like where this is going." The Chief firmly placed his elbow on the table and balanced his chin on his fist.

"The first time I went to the market with Bella, I didn't look inside the electrical box. The detectives probably didn't look either since it was ruled an accident. When I looked inside the box, I discovered markings beside the tank breaker. In my opinion, something was lodged against the breaker to keep it from tripping, therefore allowing electricity to keep flowing into the water. Somebody wanted to make sure there was no way Rocco could survive. Then after the person made sure he was dead, the instrument used was removed and the breaker was shut off."

"Do you think you and Bella were spotted at the market yesterday?"

"It could be a strong possibility. If somebody doesn't want Rocco's 'accident' to be investigated and knows Bella paid a private investigator to do exactly that—and thinks that this private investigator might have stumbled onto something—then I do believe we were."

The Chief sat back in his chair and folded his arms over his chest.

Stella motioned from behind the counter. I nodded and she came over with a pot of coffee to refill our cups.

"Thanks," we both said in unison.

"Chief, I believe Bella's 'accident' last night was not an accident. If the person involved in Rocco's death has become paranoid and thinks I've come up with evidence that could change the cause of death ruling from accident to homicide, then he or she is desperate. Since Bella is my employer, with her out of the picture, I'm out of a job."

"But since Bella didn't die last night and if your theory is correct, then she's still in danger." He shook his head. "What about George? Have you shared any of this with him?"

"No. But I will tell you one thing. Last night, before we knew what was happening with Bella's condition, he told me if something should happen to her, he wanted me to continue with my investigation."

"That indicates to me that George didn't have anything to do with Rocco's death. Do you agree?"

"I do. Whoever is behind this whole thing did a good job of casting guilt on George. If that person finds out George was willing to continue the investigation, then he could have a bull's eye on the back of his shirt too." I took a deep breath. "Another thing I haven't mentioned. Last night, on my way home, I was almost to Exit 5 off the Mid-Cape when a pick-up truck sped by me, nearly running me off the road. I couldn't get the plate number because I was too busy trying to prevent myself from hitting the guard rail." I didn't mention the bumper sticker because I wasn't sure that's what it was. "Maybe I'm just being paranoid, but it was awfully close."

"I don't like the sound of that one bit."

I checked my watch. "I've got to get going. I want to take some pictures of the accident scene before I head on over to the hospital."

"I'm going to go to the scene with you. I personally want to look around. Then I plan on going back to the station and have Detectives Morse and Garrison start an investigation."

I sat straight up in my chair.

The Chief noticed. "Don't worry. They're my best guys, trust me. Before I confided in you, I did some checking. I know you're Sam Summer's other half. I'm sure he told you I've had problems within the department. But let me assure you, Morse and Garrison share the same upright caliber as Sam. I trust them with my life."

"Thank you," I said. I gave Stella a hug. "The rent checks in the mail."

She laughed.

"I'll be back. Those scones were the best." The Chief extended his hand to her.

She wiped the flour off hers and took his hand. "Thanks," she said. "And, watch that girl for me."

"I'll try," said Chief Mills.

"Why don't you follow me since I know the exact location."

"Sounds like a plan."

The Chief pulled out of the parking lot and I followed.

CHAPTER 71

The Chief parked about fifteen feet away from the accident scene. I pulled up behind him.

"We didn't mention the other accident that happened here almost twenty-six years ago. I'd only been on the job for a couple years." The Chief pointed to a tree off the road just before the bend. "That's the same tree Rocco hit. The youngest DeMarco boy was killed instantly. He didn't have a seat belt on. Rocco swerved to avoid a dog that had run out of the woods, but lost control. He hit the tree and the dog. His nephew hit the windshield and was rushed to the hospital with brain injuries. He died a week later. It was tragic."

"Why would somebody pick this exact spot to recreate an accident?"

"Earlier today, you said you thought George might be the person being set up to take the fall. This could indicate the one or both of the DeMarco brothers are being set up. It's public knowledge Rocco may have discovered something significant in the disappearance of his sister, Maria. Most people in town think Sid, the father, had something to do with it, but with Sid dead why would Rocco continue—unless he came up with new evidence that could implicate someone else."

"Whoever is behind Rocco's death and Bella's near death 'accident' must now be walking on nails trying to figure out what to do next." I took out my camera and started to take pictures of the entire area. "Chief, take a look at this." I pointed to a set of tire tracks that stopped before the place where Bella's car went off the road into the tree. I snapped another series of pictures. "I worked a case that happened in Bourne a few years ago. I wasn't working with any of the PDs. I was there as the investigative reporter for the

Tribune. It was a hit and run death of a sixteen-year-old girl." I stopped to catch my breath. I felt Becky's presence looking down on me. "Because it was a hit and run, the Bourne PD initiated an investigation immediately. One of the key pieces of evidence was the sets of tire tracks." I looked at the tracks around where we stood.

"The problem with that is these tracks have been compromised. The scene was deemed an accident and from my observation many cars have stopped to check it out. I'm assuming that's where the car came to rest."

We walked to the side of the tree. There was a giant gash in the front and glass, probably from the headlights and windshield, created a three foot blanket around the base. Footprints in all sizes and shapes had broken the patterns that would have allowed any specific tire recognition.

"Like I said, I'll talk to Morse and Garrison. If there's something to be found, they'll find it."

"Will you keep me in the loop?"

"I will and I expect you to keep me updated on anything you uncover—no matter how insignificant you think it is."

I wanted to say yes Dad, but knew better, so I kept my mouth shut.

"Give me a call after you leave the hospital. Also, don't tell George about our conversation. He'll know when I feel the time is right." He walked me back to my car. "Be careful. If you need me for anything, call. And, use my cell. I don't want anything running through the switch board." He waited until I got into my car and started down the street.

CHAPTER 72

I half expected George to be waiting for me in the lobby. He wasn't. I walked to the information desk. "Could you please tell me if Bella Deluca has been moved from the third floor?"

"No, but she's only allowed to have family visits."

"I know. I was here last night. Thank you." I headed for the elevator.

It was just eleven-thirty. George was waiting for me. He put the magazine he was reading down and stood up as soon as he saw me come through the door. "Morning." He appeared more upbeat.

"How's Bella doing this morning? Is she out of the coma?"

"She fades in and out. Dr. Michaels hasn't been by yet, but he hasn't called either so the nurse said he's probably on his way."

"Has she been able to talk to you?"

"Not really. She tried, but nothing. I think they have her sedated. I don't even know if she knows what happened and where she is."

"Did you call the library to let them know she won't be in?"

"I did. I didn't know how much I should say, so I told them she wasn't feeling good and she'd be out at least until Monday. I didn't want to get into particulars. They'll know more this morning as soon as somebody sees the Tribune. I'm sure I'll get phone calls. I'll deal with that later."

"George, you know as well as I do news travels fast. You're going to get calls. Just tell them she was in an accident—that she's okay, but sore. If they want to visit, tell them the doctor suggested no visitors for at least a week."

"This sucks," he said and sat back down.

"Yeah it does, but we want to keep your sister safe. If I have to sit here with her, I will. We can take shifts. Our main concern is Bella."

The door from the nurse's station opened. "Good morning, George. Good morning, Casey," said Dr. Michaels. He directed his comments to George. "I just left your sister's room. She's more alert than I expected. She told me you were in to see her."

"She talked?"

"Not in full sentences, but enough for me to understand what she was trying to say. She also asked for you Casey."

"Thank you," I said.

"I'm going to do my rounds. I'll be back in a couple hours to check on her. In the meantime, it's okay to visit. Talk to her, hold her hand, if she's thirsty she can have a little water, but be careful she doesn't take too much at one time. She seems to be afraid of something, so make sure she knows you're there and she's not alone."

We both agreed. The doctor left and we went to sit with Bella.

I had to be very careful what I said about Bella's accident. And I definitely wasn't going to talk to George about my conversation with Chief Mills.

"What's your next game plan?" he asked.

"I don't want to talk about anything here," I whispered. I motioned with my head in Bella's direction. I ignored the look George gave me and leaned down to talk to Bella. "Good morning," I said softly. "Bella, can you hear me?" She didn't open her eyes or speak, but she squeezed my hand slightly. I knew she could hear me.

There were only a few ice cubes floating in the glass beside her bed. I took it from the table and handed it to George. "This looks pretty stale, why don't you get her some fresh water and a new straw." I knew he didn't want to leave, but sitting beside a sick person in a hospital wasn't his bag—especially when it was his sister.

As soon as George left the room, Bella opened her eyes enough to make out a shadow of a person sitting beside her. "Casey?"

I could barely hear her. I leaned in close to her face. "Yes Bella, it's me."

"I ….." She tried to speak. "I called you."

It was so faint, but I knew what she said. "You tried to call me didn't you?"

"Yes."

"A black truck …." She seemed to drift off.

I looked up to see if George was on his way back. I didn't see him so I leaned back close to Bella. "Can you hear me?"

"Yes."

"Did you say a black truck?"

"Yes. Hit me." She drifted back out.

"Rest." I rubbed the back of her hand to let her know I was still there. She didn't have to say anymore. A black truck—it was a black or dark blue truck that tried to run me off the road or scare me. What that person doesn't know is that after the initial shock, scare tactics infuriate me.

A few minutes went by before George returned with a fresh glass of ice water. He handed it to me and I set it on her bedside table.

"Did she wake up at all?"

"She did. She knows we're here. Now she can rest." I smiled.

I glanced at the wall clock behind Bella's bed. "I have to make a phone call. The reception stinks here, so I'll probably have to go down to the lobby. I won't be gone long." I stood up to leave. "Do you want a coffee or a cold drink?"

"A Diet Coke would be great."

"Be right back."

I walked through the lobby, out the front door and stood off to the side in front of the windows. I didn't want to take any chances that someone might hear my conversation. I dialed Marnie's cell.

She answered on the first ring. "Hi, I've been waiting for your call. You're not going to believe my day. Remember I told you I

282

had a flat tire? There was nothing wrong with it. Apparently, somebody decided to be a jerk and let the air out of it."

"Who told you that?"

"The guy from AAA. He couldn't find anything wrong—except that it was flat as a pancake. He put the spare on and told me to get the flat one checked. Said I should have it checked out at a tire place. I told him I would. That's the first thing."

"And, pray tell, what else made your day eventful."

"You're not going to like the next one. I went to your house to tend to Watson. He wasn't there."

I started to panic. "What do you mean he wasn't there?"

"Calm down, calm down. When I went into the back yard, his leash was still hooked to the run, but he wasn't hooked to the leash."

My heart pounded out of my chest. "What happened?"

"Apparently he got loose and decided to explore. I ran around the neighborhood clapping and yelling his name. I was halfway down the street when a lady came running out her front door with Watson at her heels. She said he was wondering around her yard, knew he wasn't supposed to be, so took him in figuring she'd see you when you got home."

"Do you know her name?"

"Said her name was Alice Reynolds."

"I know Mrs. Reynolds. Sometimes she gives Watson treats when we walk by."

"Are you okay?" Marnie asked. "You sound stressed."

"I don't like to admit it, but I am. I met with the Chief and now I'm at the hospital. I'm going to try to leave here by one-thirty or so. I really hope Sam gets home on time. I'll call you later. Thank you. And don't forget to get that tire checked." I got it all out in one fell swoop without missing a beat, then hit the end button. I didn't want to talk anymore. I just wanted to be alone with my thoughts.

"Could you please tell me where to find the soda vending machine?" I asked the lady at the information desk.

She directed me to go down the hall and take the second left. I got George's Diet Coke and a bottle of water for me. The elevator door opened as soon as I pushed the button. I wasn't in a waiting mood, so that suited me just fine.

George was holding Bella's hand when I got back to her room. "She opened her eyes and mouthed a few words. I couldn't understand her, but she tried to talk." He was encouraged.

"That's a good thing. It will take time, but she'll be back. After all, she has to check up on Dewey to make sure he's keeping the library running up to snuff."

George smiled.

I walked around the other side of the bed and sat down.

We'll get the bastard who did this to you.

My mind shifted from Bella's 'accident' to my encounter with a speeding truck, to Marnie's flat tire, to Watson being unattached from his leash. I knew I couldn't do anything more about these incidents while I was sitting in a hospital room. Bella knew I had been there. I knew I'd be back, but I had to get going.

"George, I'm going to take off. There are a few things I have to check on. Don't hesitate to call if you need me. And, be sure to let me know what Dr. Michaels has to say. She appears to be stable, he might move her to a private room this afternoon." I got up, leaned over and gave Bella a kiss on her forehead, then walked to the other side of the bed and gave George a hug. "I'll talk to you later."

George sat back down and took Bella's hand again.

Before I pulled out of the hospital parking lot I called Chief Mills. "Hi Chief. Got a minute?"

"Wait a second, I want to close the door." There was a slight pause. "Okay, what's up?"

"I've been with Bella and her brother since I left you this morning. She opened her eyes briefly and acknowledged the fact that I was there . She even managed a slight smile. She tried to talk, but only a few words came out. It's the few words that concern me."

"What did she say?"

284

"I asked her if she tried to call me just before the 'accident'. She said 'yes'. Then she said 'black truck'. I repeated it to her. She said 'yes'. Then she said 'hit me'. After that she drifted back out of it. Chief, it was a dark blue or black truck that I encountered on the Mid-Cape. I don't believe it's a coincidence. It was the same truck."

"I'm going to assign an officer to the hospital. He'll be in plain clothes so as not to draw attention. She'll be okay as long as she's in the surgical ICU. But, I don't want her to be alone in the general part of the hospital where anybody can go."

"I'm leaving now. I may swing by my office, but I'm going to work most of the day from home." I didn't say anything about the Marnie or Watson incidents. There was nothing to tie them to Bella's case, so until I could prove a connection I had to keep the information between Marnie and me—and, of course, Sam when he gets home.

"Later," he said and he was gone.

Before I got into my car I did a sweep around the parking lot—at least in the area where I was parked. There were a couple of black pick-ups, but small ones. Nothing like the one that almost kissed me. I slowly rode up and down the other aisles checking out any trucks parked in the lot. I was satisfied none of the ones I saw were the black hearse of death.

CHAPTER 73

Instead of going to the Village, I called the Tribune to talk to Chuck. "Glad I caught you in."

"What's up?" he asked.

"Could I come by and use the computer again?"

"Sure, come on over—your office awaits."

"I really appreciate it. Can't let you know what's happening, but maybe when it's all over and if it's newsworthy, I'll give you an exclusive."

"Did I hear the word maybe? The other day you said you would give us an exclusive."

"Did I say that?" I missed those guys. "A mere slip of the tongue. Of course, I will give you an exclusive."

"I'll see you when you get here."

One of the girls from the back office was sitting at Jamie's desk. "Hi, is Jamie around?"

"She took a half day today, so I'm sitting in for her. You're Casey right?"

"Yes."

"Mr. Young said you'd be coming by and to tell you he's in his office."

"Thanks," I said and walked down the hall. Chuck's office door was open. I stuck my head in. "Hi, boss."

He didn't look up. "I'd know that voice anywhere. Come on in." He snickered, got up from his desk and gave me a hug. "Things are far too quiet without you here."

"I wish I could say the same."

Chuck pointed to my office. The door was shut but there wasn't anybody at the desk.

"Are you still holding it for me?"

"I wish you'd reconsider, but I know you're living your dream and I wouldn't want it any other way. Go ahead and do what you have to do. Come see me before you leave."

"Thanks, I will."

I went across the hall to my old office. It was quite obvious nobody had used it since I left. It needed a good dusting. The only clean spot was the one I used last Monday. But, I wasn't there for that. I needed access to the Tribune's data base and the connection to the Registry of Motor Vehicles. My old password worked for both.

It was time to check the archives for stories that mentioned the five Falmouth Police Officers and the two Detectives that were involved in the Rocco Deluca story. I didn't care about traffic stops or insignificant incidents. I was looking for something with some meat. I knew the detective's names would pop up more than the officers only because it's the detectives that do the investigating.

I ran Brady's name first. The Chief said he'd only been on the job a few years so I didn't expect to see much. I set the timeline to start four years instead of three just in case the Chief's numbers were off. I pushed the button to start the search. Within seconds Officer Brady's name appeared in big, bold letters. I read the article. It was three and a half years ago—he was a real rookie. Good thing I went further back. He was involved in a giant drug bust that seized cocaine with a street value of over a million dollars. A huge feather in his cap. Apparently he was at the right place at the right time. Detectives Morse and Garrison were also mentioned in the article, but then I'd expect that. I closed that story and moved on.

The next article was small, but interesting. Apparently Brady was engaged in an altercation at one of the local bars in Falmouth. He wasn't on duty, but because of his position, the local reporter felt it necessary to expound on the incident. I read further. There it was. The fight involved Brady, the DeMarco brothers and a couple other local boys. It seems as though Brady, Greg and Phil did a number on the other two—landing one in the hospital with a broken nose. No charges were filed, but Brady was suspended for two weeks. So Brady and the DeMarco's were friends. Funny he didn't mention that. He only said he'd been in the fish market lots of times. I wonder if he knew George. I made a note to ask about both things.

Everything else in the file was trivial.

I typed in Johnson's name. Lots of small articles came up. Most of them didn't have anything to do with the police department. Apparently he volunteered his time on programs involving kids. I jotted that down. There were no articles indicating Johnson had any problems in or out of the department.

Officer Tuttle was the senior officer that answered the call. He'd been on the job for almost twenty years and had been a resident of Falmouth his entire life. He was good friends with Rocco. I started the search on Tuttle. He didn't lack for press time. I scanned the stories. Some were human interest ones. He was a hands on type of guy, knew the area and was involved in lots of civic groups, but most of the articles were related to the department. He saved several cats from trees, was mentioned in many automobile accident incidents, helped capture a bank robber, went undercover to expose a drug ring—*That was risky. Too many people knew him*—and even delivered a baby in the back of an SUV. He appeared squeaky clean. A genuine good cop—more should take after him.

I hadn't conducted interviews with the two remaining officers yet, but since I was here I looked them up anyway.

I checked my notes to make sure I got the names right—Officers Kenneth Brown and Earl Massad.

I started with Brown. I wasn't sure how long he'd been with the department, so I asked for a fifteen year search. Judging by the articles that came up, he'd been with the Falmouth PD for about ten years. His name was listed in an obituary as the son of William Brown who died as the result of a boating accident in Falmouth Harbor. It named three siblings—one brother and two sisters. I read the names again. One of the sister's names sounded familiar. I couldn't put my finger on it, but I wrote it down so I could check it

288

out later. Like Johnson, there wasn't anything that would make me stand up and take notice.

Before I sent Brown's files back to archives, I noticed there were several articles of interest that happened before he became a cop. Fourteen years ago, he was involved in an accident. According to the write-up, it wasn't his fault and it wasn't his truck. It belonged to the company where he was employed at the time. "You've got to be kidding me," I said out loud, forgetting where I was. I looked up to see if anybody heard me. Thank goodness I'd closed the door. Officer Brown was previously employed by DeMarco Construction Company.

Oh, the webs we weave.

I read it over and over again. I made notes. Brown's interview was tomorrow. I'll run this by Sam tonight and have him help me formulate questions. I printed out the obit on his father and the accident story. I closed my eyes and tried to pull up an image to match the sister's name. The sister, I knew that name—why? It didn't work, I drew a blank.

The last responding officer was Earl Massad. Nothing came up under his name. Any information on him would have to come from the Chief.

The Chief gave Detectives Morse and Garrison glowing recommendations. He said they were his go to guys—that he had complete trust in them. I'd spent more time than I expected to on the five officers, so I held off on the background checks on the detectives. I closed out the Tribune data base and opened the one connected to the Registry of Motor Vehicles.

I didn't have plate numbers or the types of vehicles driven by Brady, Johnson, Tuttle, Brown and Massad, but I figured I could get them by searching their names in the RMV files. I was right. Brady, Brown and Massad drove pick-up trucks. Tuttle had two vehicles registered in his name—a Burgundy colored Ford Explorer and a Misty Green Honda Accord. Johnson was the family man with the white Toyota Sienna. I printed the information for my files.

I switched the search to their driving records. Brady and Brown had numerous traffic violations, mostly for speeding. Most were old, but a couple were recent issued by off Cape departments. Brown's old accident was listed, but there weren't any other problems.

I closed out the RMV site and signed off the computer. I was in the process of gathering up my stuff and getting ready to leave when Chuck knocked on the door. I waved him in. "What's up?"

"You're not going to like it. One of the late-shift guys from the newsroom cut across the parking lot to pick up a sandwich. On the way back, he recognized your car and noticed two flat tires."

"What!" I yelled, then sighed in disgust.

"Come on, I'll go outside with you to see what's going on."

I left my stuff inside and we walked to my car. I folded my arms. I was pissed.

Chuck bent down to check them out. "Casey, they've been punctured."

I shook my head. "You remember my friend, Marnie? Well, when she started to leave for work this morning, one of her tires was flat. I talked to her before I came here. She said it wasn't punctured, but it was flatter than a pancake. The AAA driver said he had no idea what could have happened, but that the tire appeared to be okay."

"Do you think somebody is trying to send you a message?"

"I do. And, I intend to find out who." I glanced up above the employee entrance. "Chuck is that camera hooked up?"

"As far as I know it is."

"Can we check out the footage from the last two hours?"

"Of course. I'm sure Marty from IT is still here. He works until five and most times stays later. Let's go inside."

I followed Chuck to the IT department. Marty got up when he saw us come in. "Casey, good to see you," he said as he looked toward Chuck. "To what do I owe this visit?"

"I think we've got a problem. It appears that Casey's car was vandalized while she was here doing some research. Somebody punctured her tires while she was parked in the lot. Apparently, the person didn't see the camera. Do you think you can pull the footage for the last two hours. Hopefully, we'll see something we can use to figure out who did this."

"Yeah, that shouldn't be a problem." Marty went back to his computer and started to play with the keys."

I can work a basic computer, but I can't make them sing, dance and talk back. I stood behind Marty and stared at the screen. Chuck moved in beside me. We didn't say a word.

After five minutes Marty announced, "It's showtime. I hope you were parked in a spot the camera scans."

"She was—two spaces from the employee entrance."

"Then there should be no problem."

Footage of the parking lot appeared on Marty's screen. My car, along with several others, were in clear view of the roving eye. Everything seemed normal. Marty fast forwarded the footage, still scrutinizing every frame. "Whoops," he said. "I think I saw something. Let me slow it down and back it up a little."

The three of us stood with our eyes now glued to the picture show in front of us.

"Sorry, it was a dog. Marty started to run the footage again this time not quite as fast. Nothing seemed out of the norm. About twenty minutes into the airing, something appeared to move across the screen. "Okay, this is not an animal." The three of us focused on what looked like a person nervously checking out the lot. At this point we couldn't tell if it was a male or female. The image was small to medium in height, but since it wore baggy sweat pants and an oversized sweatshirt with a hood, it was almost impossible to determine body structure.

The sneakers, however, could hold the clue. They weren't run of the mill Niki's or Converse. I'd seen them before, but I didn't know where. They were definitely designer. "Can you freeze one of those frames?"

"Which one or ones do you want?"

"I want a couple good shots of the sneakers and I want some shots of the hands."

Marty slowed the frames down to a snail's pace.

"There I want that one," I said abruptly.

My voice broke the intense level of concentration. Chuck and Marty jumped.

"You lookin' to give me heart failure?" Marty laughed. "I feel like I'm in a scene from *CSI* or one of those shows."

"Can you zoom in on the hands?"

Marty played with the buttons and voila, there it was, a perfectly clear picture.

"Can you print that for me?"

"You can get most anything from this program if you know what buttons to push." Marty smiled. "The Tribune spared no expense. They installed the best. The cameras are weatherproof and the images are in color."

I took the picture from the printer next to his desk. There was no question, the hands belonged to a female. They were small, manicured and there was a diamond wedding band on the ring finger of the left hand. "This is great."

"Now, how about one of the sneakers."

"You've got it," said Marty as he moved back and forth examining each frame to get the best shot. "Here, how about this one?"

It was perfect. "Great. Can you enlarge it like you did the hand?"

"Coming right up."

Again Marty produced a perfect image.

"Just one more. I know this person's wardrobe leaves something to be desired, but if I could have a couple close-ups to study, maybe I'll see something we missed."

Three more pictures from different angles rolled off the printer.

I looked at Chuck. "I'm going to have Sam take a look at these later today. Can he get a copy of the tape if he needs one?"

There was no hesitation. "Absolutely, just give me a call and we'll have it ready." He gave Marty a nod. "If I'm not here, you have my permission to release it to Casey."

"Thanks boss and thank you, thank you, thank you Marty. You've helped more than you know."

"It's my job, ma'am." He laughed. "This is the most excitement this department has seen since I've been here."

Chuck and I left and went back to his office. "Casey, will you keep me informed as to what's happening?"

"I will. And, if it pans out, your exclusive will be front page news." I gathered up my stuff, gave him a hug and started for the door.

"Aren't you forgetting something?"

"I don't think so."

He stood with his hands on his hips shaking his head. "You have two flat tires."

"Oh, yeah." I let out a sigh.

"Sit tight, I'll call my buddy, Pete, at Cape Tire and ask him if he can come over with his flatbed and take your car to his shop. He's good. " Chuck made the call. It was short and to the point.

"He said no problem. He'll meet you in the parking lot. And, he's not going to charge you for the tow."

"I appreciate it. I'll keep in touch. Thanks for everything."

I waited in the lobby until I saw the Cape Tire truck pull up, then headed out to my car.

The driver examined the tires. "I take it somebody doesn't like you."

"I think that's an understatement."

I got into the cab and rode back to Cape Tire with my little green Spider secured to the flatbed of the truck.

Pete greeted me at the door to the waiting room. "I'll check the tires out, but my guy says they can't be fixed. The good news is they're a standard size and I have plenty in stock. One way or the other I'll have you on your way in less than a half hour."

"I can't thank you enough," I said as I shook his hand.

"You're welcome. See you in a bit."

It was three-twenty. I still hadn't heard from Sam. I figured this was a good time to call Marnie. Her cell phone went to voice mail. She must be either away from her desk or busy. Probably better if I call her when I get home. That way I can talk without looking over my shoulder. I took a break from my case and picked up a *People Magazine* that was sitting on the table next to me. It was the best spring fashion issue, plus a special shape section to tell you how you can look a size smaller. I should go out and buy a copy. Since Sam's been spending time in Hyannisport, my eating habits have gone from bad to worse. I don't even want to know how much I've gained. I was halfway into an article on hair and makeup trends when Pete came in from the shop to tell me my car was ready.

"We put two new tires on the front, checked the other two and put them on the back. You're good to go." He handed me a bill.

The only charge was for the tires. "I really appreciate this."

He smiled.

I paid the cashier, got into my car and headed home.

CHAPTER 74

I was exhausted and concerned. Somebody wanted the investigation into Rocco's death stopped—I was sure of that. They figured if Bella wasn't around, then there'd be nobody pushing the issue. They were wrong. Marnie's flat tire wasn't a natural occurrence, although it was made to look like one. And, puncturing my tires was definitely a deliberate act to scare me off. It didn't work. Thinking back on what Marnie told me about Watson being loose doesn't resonate well with me either. The more I thought about the day, the more my blood started to boil. Puncturing my tires was bad enough, but hurting Bella and screwing with Marnie and my boy didn't cut it.

I was hoping to see Sam's car in my yard when I drove up the street. It wasn't and I hadn't received a call, so I assumed he was still flying around over Boston. Watson wasn't waiting for me behind the door, instead he was curled up in his corner by the refrigerator. His eyes were sad.

I knelt down beside him. He whimpered, but didn't move. "Watson, it's okay I'm home." I cuddled him to my chest. He nuzzled his face under my chin. He was shaking. He didn't appear hurt, but he sure was scared. "Don't worry boy, I'll find the bastard. Then he'll be the one shaking and scared. We'll both deal with him." I got up and got some treats from the pantry. I think he finally realized he was safe—mommy was home. Sam will be livid.

I poured myself a glass of White Zin, took a couple sips and started to take my notes and pictures from my briefcase. It's a good thing Sam wanted to stay home and have pizza tonight because I'm not going anywhere. I picked up the picture Marty took of the sweatsuit clad figure combing the Tribune parking lot. I wondered what direction it came from. I made a note to ask Marty to go back further in the video and check it out. If the person came from the front of the building, several of the businesses on Main Street have surveillance cameras and a check of their videos could produce a vehicle he or she arrived in. The digital clock on the stove flashed four. I remember Chuck said that Marty doesn't leave before five o'clock and sometimes stays later.

I used my cell and hit the number six—the direct line to the Tribune. I asked to be put through to Marty. I took a couple rings before he answered. "Hi Marty, it's Casey."

"What's wrong?" He must have thought I encountered a problem after I left him.

"Nothing that you can't solve for me."

"Thanks for the vote of confidence. What do you need?" I could hear him put me on speaker.

"Is there anyone there with you?"

"No. Don't worry I wouldn't have put you on speaker if there was."

"Sorry, I knew that. Anyway, could you check the video again and find the footage that showed where our mystery person came from."

"You mean where the mystery ninja entered our lot?"

"I do." I liked the name Marty assigned to our interloper.

"Give me a minute." It was just that—a minute. "It appears that he or she came through the gate in the front, off Main Street. What do you have in mind?"

"I know there are some surveillance cameras on several of the Main Street businesses. If they were up and running, they might have caught our tire slasher getting out of a vehicle or being dropped off. Either way, a description of that would be helpful and, maybe, if we got lucky we'd be able to get a plate number."

"Are you home?"

"I am."

"I helped a couple of the businesses put their systems in. The only difference is their images aren't colored like ours. Give me

296

your number. I'll go scouting and give you a call back. It might take me a few minutes, but I'll get back to you."

I gave Marty my number. The line went silent. There were no good-byes.

I figured I had some time, so I gave Marnie a call. She must have been sitting on her phone.

"I've been waiting to hear from you. Is everything alright?"

"I tried to get you earlier, but you didn't answer. I presumed you were busy, so I went about my business and now, here I am."

"Fill me in. What was your day like since I last talked to you?"

I started to recount my story, then stopped. "Know what, I'm going to have to go over everything with Sam when he gets home. Why don't you come over and have pizza and beer with us, then I'll present the events of the day to an audience of two."

"I'll be there. Oops, gotta go—my bosses phone is ringing."

I said good-bye to a dial tone, then hung up—but I was used to it.

I still hadn't heard from Sam. I looked at Watson. He had moved from his corner to beside my chair. "Want to go outside?" He looked at the door, then back to me. I stood up. "Come on, I'll be with you." I hooked his leash to his collar, picked up my cell and the two of us went outside. He stopped on the top step and looked around, then continued down the remaining two. Whatever happened to him earlier started in the back yard, so I didn't go in that direction. We walked up and down the short street in front of my house a couple times. We were on our way back when my cell rang.

The caller ID said unknown. I hesitated, then answered on the third ring.

"Stay away from Falmouth," said the caller in a barely audible voice.

I'd had enough. "Well, if it isn't 'mumbles'." I waited to see if they hung up.

They didn't. "Stay away." This time it was much clearer.

I tried to figure out the gender, but couldn't. "No. You stay away." I cut the call short. My hand was shaking—not because I was scared—I was mad. Watson hugged the side of my leg. He sensed something was wrong.

"Let's go home and wait for daddy."

Just as we walked in the door, my cell rang again. "What do you want!" I screamed.

"Casey, it's me."

"Sam, where are you?"

"What's wrong?"

"I'm just a little stressed. I'll tell you when you get home." I didn't want him to be upset, so I tried to lighten the conversation. "Marnie's coming over. We're going to have pizza and beer." I didn't want to tell him I had a rough day. He'd find out soon enough.

"I've left the airport, heading south on Route 3. I just passed the Boston gas tank in Dorchester. Right now the traffic doesn't seem too bad. I should be there no later than six."

"We'll be waiting. I missed you Sam Summers."

"I missed you too, Casey Quinby. Let's not get mushy. We'll save that for later." He laughed.

"I've got another call coming in. See you soon." The caller ID read Tribune. It was Marty. "Is this my go to IT man?"

"Reporting for duty." He snickered.

"Did you find anything out?"

"Yes and no. There are a few businesses with cameras, but the entrance to our lot is out of range. The church across the street put one in last summer when they had some problems with vandalism."

"I remember that. Not only did an intruder steal stuff, they vandalized the sanctuary," I said.

"You're right. I helped them with the install. Their system is just like ours. I think they're our best bet, but the person I have to talk to won't be in until tomorrow morning. I told the secretary I needed to see him as soon as he comes in. She said she'd have him give me a call."

"I appreciate your help."

"If I think of anything else, I'll be in touch."

"Okay, talk to you in the morning." The church footage could be the big break I needed.

Watson let out a couple subdued barks to get my attention. He was standing in front of the pantry.

"Want something to eat? If only you could talk and tell me who unhooked you from your run." I picked up his dishes and filled one with Kibbles and the other with fresh water, then sat back down to study the mystery ninja pictures.

I was sure it was a female. I've never punctured a tire, but I'm sure it would take some strength to do so. That means we're dealing with a strong female—small, but strong. I thumbed through the pictures until I came to the one of the sneakers. I slid it out and resumed my thinker position. They were navy blue. I looked closer. There were small red spots on them, but I couldn't make out what they were. I went to my bedroom to get my magnifying glass from the top drawer of my nightstand. The somethings were tiny red lobsters. These were custom sneakers—big bucks. The puncture-for-hire ninja must have gotten paid well for her services. I had clues, but nothing was coming together.

It was time to take a bathroom break before Marnie and Sam showed up. Watson didn't even look up when I walked by him.

My break got cut short by a loud knocking on my front door. "Be right there," I yelled through a mouthful of toothpaste. I did a quick rinse, wiped off the white ring around my mouth off and ran down the hall to see who was doing the pounding.

It was Marnie. She waved when she saw me. "Let me in she mouthed."

I stood on the inside of the locked door and tried to give her my best scowl. "Go away." I mouthed back.

She laughed.

I unlocked the door. Watson greeted her before I could.

"Where's your key?"

"In my purse."

"Why didn't you use it?"

"Because you were home and I didn't want to barge in unannounced," she said as she struck a hands-on-hips pose.

"Yeah, yeah, yeah."

"Where's Sam?"

"On his way." I glanced at the clock on the stove. "He called about an hour ago. As soon as he gets here we'll get a couple pizzas from Jack's. I don't want to go out, we'll have them here."

She agreed.

My half-filled wine glass was sitting on the table.

She headed towards the refrigerator. "In the meantime, I'll have a beer. I've got a question for you—don't take offense—okay?"

"I won't. What's your question?"

"Do you think there's any possibility Watson's leash wasn't totally hooked to the run when you left him earlier?"

"I know it was secure. I pulled on it to make sure. There is no way he could have come loose, short of the mechanism on the run breaking."

"Then somebody released him."

"No question about it," I said.

"Do you have any idea why?" she asked.

"I do, but I'll get into that later after Sam gets here." The ice in my White Zin had melted so the pink stuff I was drinking looked like Chardonnay. I must have made a face when I took a sip.

Marnie laughed. "Why don't you pour yourself a fresh glass?"

I shrugged. "I will when we get the pizza."

We went outside to sit on the deck. I didn't bother to put Watson on his leash. I figured he'd had enough adventure for the day and would stay put. No sooner did we sit down, he got up and started to run for the side of the house.

I flew down the stairs to follow him and literally collided with Sam as he came around the corner.

"I knew you'd be happy to see me, but I've only been gone three days. Did you miss me that much?" He wrapped his arms around me, gave me a big kiss and pulled me close like he was never going to let me go.

Watson jumped up and ran around uncontrollably.

"Marnie did you keep Sherlock out of trouble while I was gone or did she hoodwink you the same way she does me?"

"I refuse to answer on the grounds it may tend to incriminate me."

"You need not say more. The second I'm gone she locks Sherlock in the closet and slips into her sneaky sleuth skin."

"My what?" I shook my head and repeated Sam's description. "Sneaky sleuth is hungry and you've got the pizza run." I folded my arms over my chest and smiled. "I'll call Jack's. By the time you get there they should be ready."

"Aye, aye captain. I'm on my way."

I called Jack's and ordered our favorites—one pepperoni and one mushroom and peppers. "Let's eat outside."

Marnie gathered up the plates, napkins and silverware I'd laid out on the counter earlier. "If you open the door, I'll get it set up. I didn't have enough hands to grab the cheese."

We were waiting and ready to get this show on the road. I knew it might be a long night, so I didn't want to lollygag. We were the perfect picture of friends getting together to eat and shoot the shit. Only this shit was about to hit the fan.

Sam woofed down his first piece, then chugged half a bottle of beer. "There, now I'm ready."

"Ready for what?" I asked knowing darn right well what he was talking about.

Marnie slid in closer to the table.

"I guess it's my story you're talking about." I sat back in my chair. "I don't want any comments unless they're constructive." I looked over my eyebrows at both of them.

They sat like statues and didn't say a word.

"I'll start this by saying Uncle Rocco's death was not an accident. It was made to look like an accident. It was very carefully planned. If Bella hadn't stepped forward with her suspicions the person or persons responsible for the 'accident' would go to their grave knowing they got away with murder."

"You've got enough evidence to prove that?" Sam asked.

"I believe I do."

"Then apparently I don't know half the story because the evidence I was aware of is circumstantial and it's very hard to convict somebody using circumstantial evidence. Direct evidence proves a fact without the need to draw an inference of another fact. Eyewitness testimony and confessions are examples of direct testimony."

"I know that. You're not going to like some of the things I'm going to tell you, but I don't want you to fly off the handle until I'm finished. And even then, I might or might not want to hear what you have to say."

Marnie knew what I was talking about—my Wednesday morning meeting with Greg DeMarco at Stella's.

"Tuesday, on the way to a meeting with Chief Mills, I bumped into Greg DeMarco at the Mashpee Dunkin's. He told me he knew I'd been hired by Bella to investigate Rocco's death. I wouldn't confirm or deny, but wanted to know his source of information. Apparently, it came from the ME's secretary. She's best friends with the step-mother." I could see the frustration building on Sam's face. "He said his step-mother told him, he and his brother should be concerned. That didn't sit too well with Phil and Greg."

"How did he know where to find you?"

"Said the meeting was purely coincidental. Said he saw my car in the parking lot."

"How did he know it was your car?" asked Marnie.

"He told me the CQ007 was a dead giveaway."

Sam shook his head. "I don't believe it, but we'll leave it at that for the time being."

I hesitated knowing my next statement wasn't going to sit well with Sam. "Since I had more questions for Greg, I suggested a meeting Wednesday morning at Stella's."

Sam's face wrinkled up. He took in a deep breath and let it out slowly, but didn't say a word. He didn't have to.

"Then I left for Falmouth. The Chief and I talked about what I'd done to date and my interpretation of the situation thusfar. I asked about interviews and he was more than happy to accommodate me. He told me that he'd had some problems within the department, so he wanted any information I uncovered to come directly from me to him. And if I needed him for any reason, to call. He gave me his personal cell phone number."

"You didn't let on that you knew there were problems within the department did you?"

"No, I did not."

Sam was on the edge of his chair. "What else did you talk about?"

"I asked about Candy DeMarco. He gave me an ear full. The Chief said Sid thought of her as his little piece of eye candy and could mold her to his liking. Apparently, it didn't happen. Chief said she had her own agenda that only included Sid's money, not him." I looked at Sam. "Do you know who she is?"

"By reputation only. The Chief hit the nail on the head," Sam said.

"I need another piece of pizza and some more wine. Let's put this on hold for a bit."

Marnie stood up. "I'll help. Sam, want another beer?"

"I do. I need something to keep me mellow." He looked at me and shook his head.

I knew he didn't like what he was hearing, but he wanted in and I wanted him in too.

Armed with pizza and drinks, we started up our fish market conversation right where we left off.

"Wednesday night I went to dinner with Bella. We went to a place in Mashpee called Sopranos. It was really good." I looked at Marnie, "We'll have to go there some night when Maloney's in town. Anyway, Bella talked about her uncle and her cousins. She said he was a real bastard. She also said he was terrible to her aunt."

"He was a bastard to everyone he couldn't control and Candy was worse," said Sam. "That was a well-known fact."

"Bella brought up Candy's name. She said when Sid died she got the controlling interest in DeMarco Construction. Phil and Greg were pissed. As Bella put it, Candy's a black cloud hanging over their heads. Somewhere in the will there's a clause that Candy has to provide for Phil and Greg and she can't sell the business without taking care of them. Bella wasn't sure of the exact wording, but that was essentially what the stipulation said."

"I can't imagine that whole crew living together at the family compound without killing each other." Marnie shrugged.

"Greg said it isn't pretty."

"I'm sure it's not," said Sam.

"There was one other interesting thing Bella brought up." I took another sip of my wine. "She wanted to talked about George. Apparently, he has a gambling problem and is or was into somebody for a lot of money. Remember he was doing the books for Rocco since his wife died last year. Well, he was skimming from Rocco's business. Rocco trusted George. When Rocco died, George wanted to settle the estate, which included selling the business immediately. Bella wasn't in a hurry. But, she thought there was ready money to keep the bills paid. George knew differently."

Sam's detective mind was in full throttle. "I don't like to say it, but if somebody from the outside looked at this whole scenario, George had motive to kill his uncle."

"I thought of that and I think after Bella heard his story she had her doubts too, but she wouldn't admit it. He's her only family and she's scared. She said he was going to go over to her house Thursday, tonight, to go over the books with her."

"So are you going to talk to her tomorrow to see how the meeting went?"

"No. There's a problem."

"I'm confused," said Sam.

"It gets worse." I cleared my throat. "Wednesday I met Greg. It was interesting, but we'll table that for now. Then I went to Falmouth PD to do the interviews. Again, we'll talk about them later. I only met with three of the officers, the two detectives got called out on a case. There were a couple of discrepancies in the reports of the officers I interviewed. It had to do with the electrical box and the breakers being on or off and who did the actual checking to see if they were."

Sam had a puzzled look on his face and Marnie just sat and listened, taking everything I said in.

"What could you possibly find in the electrical box?" Sam raised his eyebrows questioning my statement.

"Listen and I'll tell you. I had a feeling and I wanted to check it out. Since this death was never investigated because it was deemed an accident, nobody looked inside the box at the breakers. I stopped at the library and waited for Bella to get off work, then we went over the fish market. I found something very interesting. It appeared that the circuit breaker for the tanks had been jammed. When the live electrical cord by the tanks hit the water, the breaker didn't shut off."

"You could see this?"

"Yes, I have pictures." It was starting to get dark and the temperature had dropped. "Let's resume this meeting inside."

Marnie went over to the counter. "I'm going to make coffee. Anybody want to join me?"

"I'll have one. I have a package of Oreos in the pantry. Could you plate some for me?"

Sam gave Marnie a nod. "Sounds good to me."

I continued with the events of the last few days. I slid the folder of pictures out of my briefcase and set it on the table. The ones of the electrical box were on top. I handed them to Sam. "Look closely at the one marked tanks." I waited a minute for him to study the image. "Tell me what you see."

"You're right. It appears that something was jammed behind the breaker." He smiled. "I want you on my team."

"Anyway, after Bella and I left the market, she went her way and I came home and started on my paperwork. I'd done as much as I was going to, got me a glass of wine and went into the living room to watch some TV. I was just getting into *CSI* when my cell rang. It was George. He was at the Falmouth Hospital. Bella had been in a bad car accident and he wanted me to come as fast as I could."

"You didn't tell me that," said Marnie.

"No I didn't. By the time I talked to you, I figured I'd tell you and Sam at the same time."

"Continue," Sam said.

"It seems she had gone out late to get a pizza and was run off the road not far from her house." I looked at Sam. "It was the same spot as the accident Rocco was involved in that killed Sid's youngest boy."

"You don't have to go any further. Somebody figured if Bella was out of the picture the investigation would go away." Sam took an Oreo and popped it into his mouth.

"Bingo. That's what I thought. But, what that somebody doesn't know is that George wants me to continue."

Sam was quiet. I could tell by the look on his face he was in his thinking mode. "Is there anything else you should be telling me?"

Marnie piped up. "Do you think the flat tire I had and Watson being loose in the neighborhood is related somehow?"

Sam looked from Marnie to me. "Well?"

"Yes I do, but there's more."

The two of them leaned forward on the table waiting for me to continue.

"Wednesday night on my way home from the hospital I was almost run off the Mid-Cape just before Exit 5. This morning after I had a meeting with the Chief and made another stop at the hospital to check on Bella, I went to the Tribune to access their computer data base. When I came out I had two flat tires. They were punctured to the point that I had to buy two new ones."

"So somebody was trying to scare you?" The expression on Sam's face went from concerned to angry.

"That's what I figure. The problem is it didn't scare me, it infuriated me."

"You're dealing with a dangerous person," he said.

"I know that, but I have something else. Take a look at these. Marty, the IT guy at the Tribune, printed them for me." I slid them across the table between Sam and Marnie. "They're of our tire-puncturing ninja."

Sam looked up. "It's a girl," he said.

"Yep. Now we have to figure out who. I had Marty blow up her hands and her feet. Notice the diamond wedding band in this one." I handed Sam the picture I was describing. "Then take a look at the sneakers. They aren't your run-of-the-mill, buy me at Macy's kind. They're the designer, big-bucks kind. And, fortunately, the Tribune's cameras take colored images, so they're navy blue with little red lobsters."

"Sherlock, you've just earned a seat next to your name sake."

"Coming from Bourne's highest private dick, I'll take that as a compliment."

"This is mind boggling," said Marnie. "Should I be concerned about going home to an empty house?"

"You should be just fine. If you're uncomfortable though, you can stay here."

"No, I'll go home. And, speaking of that, it's getting late and it is a work night, so I'm going to take off and leave you love-birds alone. One more thing, are you coming to your office in the morning?"

"I am. I'll call you when I get in."

"Don't forget. I'll be waiting." She got up and gave Watson a head pat. "Take care of her. After all, that's what the other Watson does."

We laughed. We waited in the doorway until Marnie was out of the driveway and part way down the street before we went back inside.

"Tomorrow I've got the last two officer interviews along with the two detective ones. The officer interviews will be pretty much the same as the ones I already did. It's the interviews with Detectives Morse and Garrison I'm concerned with."

"Do you have copies of their reports here?"

"I do." I started to thumb through the pile of papers. "Here they are." I pulled them out and handed them to Sam.

"They're cut and dry and to the point. They say the same things, but aren't identical like the officer's reports. That's why they're detectives and not still POs. They do their job."

"It will be a little different interviewing Officers Brown and Massad. I know I'm interviewing them for their roles in the discovery of Rocco's body. Now, I feel Bella's accident is related to the investigation into Rocco's death, but I don't know if I'm at liberty to talk with them about it."

"That could be touchy. I'd check with Chief Mills. He might give you the go ahead. But, it'll be a moot point if neither Brown or Massad are involved in the investigation of Bella's accident. I know you can ask the Chief, but ask them for their addresses. Another thing—throw in a few more questions about how well the officers knew Rocco and his family. By family, I also mean his extended family—the DeMarcos."

"Now you want me to talk about the DeMarcos?"

"As it pertains to your case with Bella, yes. Other than that, my first statement concerning them still stands."

I didn't want to get into a pissing match with him. I was too tired and had more important things to concentrate on.

Sam flipped through the papers still piled on the table. He stopped when he came to the RMV files. "Why did you run the names of the five officers through the Registry of Motor Vehicle data base?"

"On a whim. I wanted to see what they drove."

Sam reviewed each file. "Now that I know you have these, you really don't have to ask for their addresses." He hesitated for a minute. "Ask them anyway and jot down their reaction to your question.

"Okay."

"I see an Explorer, an Accord, three pick-up trucks and a Toyota mini-van."

"That's what it says. Oh, I forgot to tell you something Bella said this morning when I went to see her. It was very faint, but I know she said 'black pick-up' and a couple minutes later finished her thought with 'hit me'."

"Find out if any one of these guys who own the pick-ups was working Wednesday night. And, if so did they have anything to do with investigating the accident."

I walked around to the back of the chair Sam was sitting in and started to massage his neck. I leaned down and kissed his cheek. "I missed you. It's time to put this stuff away for now—tomorrow is another day."

"You don't need to tell me twice. I'll take the boy outside, you clean this up and I'll meet you in the boudoir." He spun me around and pulled me close to him. "It's good to be home." Watson started to whimper. "Don't worry boy, I didn't forget about you."

I scurried around while Sam was outside, then quickly changed into the special nightgown I put on when I want to tempt Sam. It hasn't failed me yet, no matter how tired he is. I ran down the hall to brush my teeth, then made it back to the bedroom just as the front door opened.

"Ready or not, here I come."

CHAPTER 75

Friday

There was a welcoming smell of coffee coming from the kitchen. Sam was standing at the counter slicing English muffins for the toaster. I tip-toed up behind him and slid my arms around his waist. "Now I know you're really back and last night wasn't a figment of my imagination." I kissed his neck.

"Trust me I'm back."

"What time do you have to be to work?"

"I have today off. I might stop in later just to make sure there's nothing pressing, but other than that I'm free."

"My interviews with Officers Brown and Massad are this afternoon—one-thirty and two respectively. I have to give the Chief a call to see if the detectives are still available. Since I have the addresses for all the officers I want to ride by their houses before the interviews."

"Why?"

"Because I want to. Why don't you come with me? I'll show you where Bella's accident was. I also want to stop at the hospital to see her. We can make a day of it."

"How exciting."

I punched his arm. "You're the seasoned detective, you might even think of something else I should be looking into, or say or ask."

"Since you put it that way, how can I refuse?" He smiled.

"If you haven't put those muffins in the toaster yet, why don't we go to Stella's."

"I can handle that."

"It's still early, why don't we take the boy for a short walk first, then head out."

"I'll get ready."

We walked halfway to the beach and back—just long enough.

"I'll fill his bowl. We shouldn't be late, so he'll be okay."

Before we headed out the door, I checked the outside light. It came on just fine.

"What's with the light check? I fixed it before I went to Virginia."

"I thought you did. When I came home the other night, though, it wasn't working and it was really dark."

"Well, it seems to be working now. I don't know why it wasn't working then." We headed towards the cars. "Why don't we take my car? Yours kind of stands out in a crowd. Since we're going to be playing super sleuth, my boring sedan is the better one to be in."

"Fine with me," I said as I got into the passenger side.

"Did you bring your camera?"

I checked my briefcase. "Yep, it's here." I took it out to show him.

He backed out of the driveway. "And we're off. Stella, here we come."

There were more cars in the parking lot than I had ever seen before. "Looks like she's busy today."

There were a couple spots left in the back. Sam pulled into one of them.

I thought Sam was going to burst out laughing when we walked through the door. Half the restaurant was filled with Red Hatters. The rainbow of purple and red killed the normal ambiance.

"Why are all those ladies dressed that way?" He raised his eyebrows as he looked around.

"Haven't you ever heard of the Red Hatters?"

"No, I can't say that I have."

"Stella waved and pointed to the back corner. There must be an empty table." I walked over and sat down.

311

Sam followed but not without doing another scan of the room. "What are they all about?"

"I know they have chapters and a Queen Mother and get together to go out to eat. Some even go on trips. But other than their obsessions with red and purple, I don't know anything else about them. I will say one thing, it always looks like they're having fun." I smiled. "Stella's on her way over. What do you want to eat?"

"Casey, again this week." She leaned over, gave Sam a hug and came around the table and gave me a kiss. "What can I get you guys?"

"Coffee for both of us and I'd like a cheese Danish." He looked at me. "What do you want?"

"I'll have a couple of those blueberry scones I had the other day."

"Coming right up."

"She's amazing—never stops. I guess she won't be able to visit today. That's okay, we got lots to do."

"You mean you've got lots to do. I'm just the chauffeur."

"Whatever."

Stella brought over our food and coffee. "It's a meeting of the girls. They come in once a month." She chuckled. "Sam, I saw you giving them the once over. You have to admit, they do make a fashion statement."

"That they do," he said.

"Looks like they want refills. Talk to you before you leave."

"I'm glad she's part of our lives now."

Sam nodded in agreement.

We sat another twenty minutes, then Sam went up to the counter to pay our bill.

I stood by the door, waved when she looked over and mouthed that I'd see her later.

CHAPTER 76

The first place we went was to the sight of Bella's accident. There was still yellow tape cordoning off the area. He went past it and pulled over into a clearing.

"I've got my camera in case you see something I should take a picture of. I took some the other day when I was here. Did you see them?"

"I only glanced at them. Since I've seen the actual site, they'll mean more to me when I study them tonight." Sam walked around by the tree Bella hit, careful not to walk over something that could be important.

"Remember the Becky Morgan hit-and-run you investigated in Bourne a few years back?"

"Yeah, I do. How could I forget? You almost got yourself killed because of your renegade investigating."

"Clamp it. That's not why I mentioned it. See those tire tracks." I pointed to several sets of tire tracks embedded in the dirt next to where Bella's car was. "Do you think you could take impressions of those and have them analyzed like you did with the ones from Becky's case?"

Sam got close, then bent down to inspect them. "They're not clean tracks. They've been compromised by other vehicles and shoe treads, probably from the officers at the scene. It would be a waste of time. What I can say is that these tracks were made from both cars and trucks, but that's all." He shook his head. "In my opinion, not good police work."

"I tried."

"Was there any rear end damage to Bella's car?"

"The Chief didn't mention any."

"When you talk to him today, ask him."

I jotted Sam's question down on my mini-legal.

"Look over there." He pointed to a spot about ten feet from where he figured Bella hit the tree. "There's a group of bushes and some small scrub pines that are smashed down or have broken branches. That damage could have been a make by the pick-up truck she said was following her or the emergency vehicles that answered the accident call. There's nothing definite to go by here. Sorry."

I took a couple pictures of the area Sam was talking about. "If there was something concrete, I know you would have found it. Now we're back to square one."

"This is a police investigation not a CQ007 probe. I'm sure Chief Mills will share information with you, but it's up to his detectives to do the investigating." He folded his arms and tilted his head to one side. "Do you understand me."

"I understand, but I don't agree." I took one more look around. "Well, it doesn't appear we can do any more here. I'll get the list of addresses for the POs who responded to the fish market call." I walked back to Sam's car and used the back seat as my portable desk. I fished through the paperwork and pulled out the piece of paper I'd written them on.

"Do you have an idea where any of these are?"

"No, but if we put them into the GPS, it will show us how far away they are. Then we can go back and start with the closest one."

"That will work, I guess."

I read the address off to Sam for each officer and he read me the distance showing on the screen. Tuttle's house was the closest—he lived in the Heights only five miles away. Sam put in the address and we left the accident scene.

"What are you going to do when we ride by?"

"I'm not sure. I just want to see where each one lives. If something jumps out at me, I'll write it down."

"Tuttle's house is going to be a half mile up on the right."

"Good it's on my side of the street. Please slow down as we go by."

The Honda Accord was parked in the driveway. Tuttle was probably at work. There was nothing that looked out of the ordinary. Everything was neat. The lawn was freshly mowed, the early spring flowers were starting to bloom and the trees were showing their fine crop of leaves.

"I'm done here." I looked at my paper and gave Sam the next address. It was Brady's house.

"I think that address is in an apartment building. We'll know soon. It's seven miles from here."

Sam was right. Brady lived in a small apartment complex. It was neat, for the most part. We rode around the parking lot. It was a work day so there were lots of empty spaces. Judging from the cars that were there, most of the occupants were members of the younger set. More than half of them were pick-ups. I looked at the plate number I had for Brady. It didn't match any in the lot.

"This one was a big nothing. The next address is Brown's. I haven't met him yet, so I can't put the man to the house."

"Is that what you're doing?"

"Just humor me. I know what I'm looking for. Call it woman's intuition."

Brown's house was in a well maintained family style, middle class neighborhood. The lots appeared to be quarter acre. "I'd say these houses are no more than fifteen or twenty years old. Nice area." I checked the house number I'd written down.

"Should be right around the next corner," said Sam.

I knew Brown was working today, so I didn't expect to see his truck in the yard. The house was nice, but nothing like the two on either side of it. As we rode by, something caught my eye. "Sam, could you please turn around and go by again?"

"Did you see something?"

"I'm not sure. Go slow and I'll let you know."

Sam turned around and moved at a snail's pace as he rode by Brown's.

"Stop for one second. I need to get the plate number for that BMW SUV at the house next door." I wrote it down next to Brown's name. "Can you call your office and run this plate?"

"I can, but do you want to check out the other addresses first?"

"No, I think we're done. Let's go to the Dunkin's on Main Street and I'll show you why I want to know who that BMW belongs to."

I slid my notes and paperwork back into my briefcase and sat back in my seat trying to decide what to do next.

When we got to Dunkin's, I took my briefcase and went to a table for four in the back. I wanted room to lay my stuff out. Sam got us coffee.

"So tell me what's running around inside your head."

"First I need you to run that plate."

Sam called his office and gave them the information. "No, I'll wait." He put his hand over his phone. "That should take them less than two minutes."

I shuffled through my stack of papers. "Ah, here it is. I've seen that SUV before. Remember when we were at the fish market taking pictures, a navy blue SUV rode by, then turned around and rode by again. When I told Bella about it, she said I didn't need to check it out because it was her brother's. That sounded logical so I didn't pursue it. When we met with George, I asked him about it. He acknowledged it was him."

Sam held up his hand for me to be quiet. "Okay, I'm ready," he said. He repeated the information his office retrieved from the Registry and punched the off button. "It's not registered to George. It's registered to a Jeffrey Sheridan and the address was the same one as where the vehicle was parked."

"Sheridan, Sheridan—why do I know that name?" My mind was overcrowded and needed a good cleaning. "Two navy blue BMW's—registered to two different people—what are the odds?" I shrugged my shoulders. "We might as well make the hospital stop now. If Bella is up to talking, I'll run that name by her."

Sam agreed.

316

We got to the hospital. Sam bumped into a friend of his. I left him talking while I asked the lady at the information desk if Bella had been moved to a room. "She's in a private room on the second floor of the east wing." She wrote the room number down and handed it to me.

"Thank you."

Sam saw me start to walk towards the east wing, said good-bye to his friend and joined me at the elevators. "That was Mark Warren—good guy—he retired from Bourne PD and now he's second in command of security here. He deserves it." Sam smiled. "Has Bella been moved?"

"She's in a private room on the second floor." I showed him the room number.

"Did I tell you Chief Mills was going to have a guy in plain clothes watching her?"

"No. That tells me he thinks her accident was an attempted homicide."

"That's putting it strongly."

"It is what it is." He gave me the 'I'm-not-kidding' look. "With that new bit of information, I'll tell you again to be careful and watch your back. Don't take any unnecessary risks."

"Yes, sir."

Our conversation stopped when the elevator door opened into the main corridor of the east wing third floor. The room routing sign directed us to the left. Bella's room was three doors down. When we walked in she was elevated to almost a sitting position. I was glad to see George wasn't there.

"Bella, this is Sam Summers. Remember I told you about him?"

Very slowly and quietly she responded, "I do. I'm sorry I can't shake your hand, but it's a little weighed down at the moment." Between her arm cast and the intravenous lines she was pretty much grounded.

I leaned down and gave her a kiss on her forehead, then sat down beside her and took her hand. "Has George been here today?"

"No, he hasn't, but Norma Sheridan has."

My heart stopped.

Sam's head snapped around. I got the 'don't-say-anything' look. Sam has a face vocabulary I understand completely.

"Do you remember her?" Bella asked.

"I do. Your friend I met at the Quarterdeck."

"Yes, that's her. Her brother, Ken Brown, was one of the responding officers when they found Uncle Rocco."

My mind was spinning in umptinine directions. I wanted to cut our visit short, but knew that wasn't an option.

Dr. Michaels came into the room. Sam stood up, moved closer to the door, but stayed within earshot in case the doctor said something that could be used to help Bella. I stepped back away from the bed.

"Casey, don't leave yet."

"I'm afraid she's going to have to," said Dr. Michaels. "You're scheduled for x-rays. They should be coming to get you momentarily. You'll be tired and probably sore when they're done, so I want you to rest. I'm leaving instructions for no visitors until after two o'clock." He folded his arms and rested his chin on his chest. "Do you hear me?"

"I don't want to hear you, but if it gets me out of here sooner, I'll listen," Bella said slowly, trying to smile in between her words..

"Do what the good doctor says. I'll check in with you later." I gave her a comforting kiss, saluted the doctor, then Sam and I left.

There were several other people in the elevator, so we didn't say anything until we got inside the car.

"My interview with Officer Brown is going to be interesting."

"I'd like to be a fly on the wall."

"I'm afraid I'd have to swat you if you were." I laughed—only kidding. "I want to get to Falmouth PD early so I can go over my notes and the new information we got this morning. Some of my questions are going to change and I want to add a few additional ones. If we go to lunch now, I'll have forty-five minutes to myself."

"I could go for a hot dog. There's a DQ on Main Street."

"Let's go."

318

CHAPTER 77

Sam dropped me off at the PD. "I've got a few errands to do and if there's time I want to stop by my office. Call me when you're done."

I had just finished my notes when Monica knocked on the conference room door. "Officer Massad is here for his interview."

"I'm ready for him."

A burly, neat-as-a-pin poster boy appeared in the doorway. I was impressed. He knew he was scheduled for an interview in the Chief's office today, I wondered if that prompted the picture-perfect office look.

"Good afternoon, Officer Massad."

I motioned for him to take a seat across from me.

I introduced myself the same way I did with the other three officers. "The reason you're here today is to talk about Rocco Deluca's death."

His facial expression didn't change.

"You were one of the responding officers. Is that correct?"

"Yes, it is."

"Did you know Rocco?"

"Most people in town knew Rocco."

His answers were short. He paid attention in Interview 101. "Did you notice anything out of place at the market?"

"No."

"I should preface that with—were you familiar with the market?"

"I'd been there many times."

"How well did you know Rocco?"

"He used to go fishing with my father."

Now I was getting somewhere. "I assume you grew up in Falmouth. Do you know the DeMarco family?"

"I went to school with Phil and Greg. I graduated a year before Phil."

"Were you friends?"

"More like acquaintances—not close friends."

I asked Officer Massad the same questions I had asked Brady, Johnson and Tuttle. Nothing sent up a red flag. He appeared to be a good officer and a good person.

"Thanks for coming in today," I shook his hand and got ready for my last officer interview.

I was anxious to talk to Officer Brown. I neatened up my space and readied myself. I hadn't closed the door, so Monica stuck her head in. "Ready for the next one?"

I nodded. "Officer Brown, please come in and have a seat. Do you know why you're here today?"

"I believe it's to talk about the death of Rocco Deluca."

"Did you talk to any of the other officers I've already interviewed?"

"No."

My question was the bait and he got caught. Somebody gave him a heads-up. "It's my understanding you're friends with the DeMarco family. Is that true?"

"I know them."

"It's also my understanding you more than know them. You worked for them before you came on the police department."

"I worked for them, but you don't have to be friends to work for somebody." His eyes pulled away from mine and wandered around the room.

"How about the Deluca family, namely George and Bella?"

"Um, I know them. Bella is a friend of my sister. I know her more than I know her brother."

"So, I assume you knew their Uncle Rocco?"

"I did."

320

"Were you familiar with the fish market before the day you answered a call to assist?"

"Yes."

"Do you recall which officer was told to check the electrical box to see if the breaker to the tanks was off?"

"I can't recall."

"Your report is very similar to the one Officer Brady wrote. Did you use his to write yours?"

"No."

"I'd like to get back to the DeMarco family. Since you worked for them, you must have known Sid DeMarco?"

"He was my boss."

"Did you know his wife?"

"If you mean Maria, I knew of her."

"How about his second wife, Candy?" I detected an air of uneasiness. "I understand she worked for the business before the first Mrs. DeMarco went missing."

He thought for a minute. "She was the secretary."

"So you did know her?"

He didn't answer.

"I'll take that as a yes." I took a deep breath. "Are you still friendly with her?"

"I never said I was ever friendly with her."

I pretended to read my notes. "You're right, you never did say you were friendly with her." I sat quiet and didn't say a word, still pretending to read my notes.

"Just a couple more questions. You know that last Wednesday night Bella was in an accident about a mile from her house. You weren't one of the investigation officers were you?"

"I work days."

"That's right. So the answer is no. It was terrible, she almost died." I looked him straight in the eyes. "Frankly, I don't think Rocco Deluca and Bella Deluca's 'accidents' were accidents. I think they were carefully planned murders and in the eyes of the murderer, one was successful and one wasn't. I think that the murderer figured with Bella out of the way, the investigation into Rocco's death would be over and life could go back the way he or she knew it."

Again he said nothing—just sat and stared at the table.

I stood up and extended my hand to him.

He got up and reluctantly shook it, then left without saying another word.

Mission accomplished.

I left my stuff on the conference table and walked out to Monica's desk. "Is Chief Mills available?"

"He is. He's been waiting for you to finish. Go on down to his office. I'll buzz him to let him know you're on your way."

I took a deep breath and headed towards the Chief's office.

"Come in," he said as I approached the door. "Have a seat. How did the last two interviews go?"

"I changed it up a bit. You and I both know most people can't keep their mouths shut. I was a lowly investigator, and a female at that, questioning their job in a police matter. I don't think Johnson and Tuttle said anything, but I do think Brady talked to Brown. I told each of the officers not to talk to anyone about why they were here. When I asked Brown if he knew why he was called in for an interview, he said he believed it was something to do with Rocco Deluca's death. I asked him if he talked to any of the other responding officers and he said no. I'm sure he did—in my eyes, he lied."

"What about Massad?"

"I think he's in the same category with Johnson and Tuttle. I didn't find anything that would cause me to dig further. But, Brown, on the other hand, he definitely has a problem. I may have gone overboard on my questioning, but he fed right into what I was asking and not in a good way."

"Explain."

"I'd done some research on each of the officers before I did the interviews. It appears that Officer Brown worked for DeMarco Construction before he became a police officer. I asked him if he

322

was friends with the DeMarcos. He said he knew them. Then I said I knew he'd worked for them. It was after that he couldn't look me straight in the eyes. I asked if he knew Maria DeMarco. He said he did. When I asked about Candy, he got fidgety. He was very careful how he answered questions pertaining to her. I asked him about Bella's accident. I probably went too far when I told him I didn't think Rocco and Bella's 'accidents' were accidents. I told him I thought they were carefully planned murders."

The Chief rocked back and forth in his chair.

"That's what I ended my interview on."

"You do have a big set." He shook his head. "You know that if you're right and Officer Brown has stepped over the line, he'll be gunning for you. Not to say that you've involved the DeMarco's."

"No Chief, not the DeMarco's, only one, Candy DeMarco. I'm working on evidence that will implicate her in my investigation and will probably tie her into an investigation of Bella's accident. I'm not sure how she and Brown are connected, but they are."

"Do you need help getting that information?"

"I'm sure I will. I've got a couple more things to check out, then I'll get back to you with what I've got."

"You've got my cell number. If you need me, call."

"I will." I checked my watch. "Is there any way you can get ahold of Detectives Morse and Garrison to cancel for this afternoon?"

"No problem. I'll call them personally."

"Thanks. Sam's picking me up in five minutes. I'm going to check on Bella, then head home. I'll give you a call within the next couple days."

He walked me to the elevator. Monica wasn't at her desk. "Take care of yourself."

"I will." The door opened, I walked in and pushed the down button.

CHAPTER 78

I waited in front of the set of double doors for Sam to pull up. I opened the passenger door and got in. "How were things at your office?"

"Same as they were when I left. I went through some mail and talked to my boss. Nothing exciting happening. I filled him in on the conference. I guess I am going to teach a class on terrorism. What about you, how did the interviews go?"

"The first one was fine. Ken Brown was second. During Brown's interview I kind of accused him of knowing more about the death of Rocco Deluca and the accident that Bella was involved in."

"What did you say?"

"I said I thought Rocco was murdered and somebody tried to do the same thing to Bella."

Sam eyes opened as wide as quarters. "Did you tell Chief Mills that?"

"Yep."

"We need to talk."

"First I want to go to the hospital. I didn't get much time with Bella this morning, so I want to go back."

"I'm going to drop you off. I didn't have time to go to my house before I came to get you, so you do your thing and I'll be back in a couple hours. Figure out where you want to go for dinner."

"Can we do one more thing before we leave the station?"

"What's that?"

"Ride through the parking lot. I want to check the dark colored pick-ups and see if the plate numbers I have for Brady and Brown match any of them. They should both still be here. I just want to look at their trucks."

"We can do that, but you're not getting out of this car. Take a picture if you want, but that's it."

"I'll accept that."

Sam rode up and down between the parked cars and trucks. "You got those two numbers ready. We're coming up on two dark colored pick-ups parked next to each other." He slowed down.

I checked the numbers for a match. One belonged to Brady and one to Brown. I quickly snapped a few pictures and Sam drove off.

"Back on track—we're headed to the hospital."

"Yes, boss."

Sam drove up to the main entrance and I got out. "See you in two."

He nodded and drove away.

I was glad he didn't come with me because I had a few things I had to do before I went inside. I walked away from the doors and sat on a bench usually used by smokers. I fished my cell from the bottom of my purse, looked up Greg DeMarco's number and punched it in.

"Hello," came a voice on the other end.

"Hi, is this Greg DeMarco?"

"It is. Who's this?"

"Greg, it's Casey Quinby."

"Casey, good to hear from you. Is everything okay?"

"Actually, I need to ask for a favor. Are you someplace you can talk?"

"Yeah, I'm in my truck on my way home."

"Okay, is there some place you can pull over?"

"There's a convenience store just up the street, I'll pull in there." A couple seconds later he said, "All right, I'm off the road. What's up?"

"Remember you said you'd help me if you could? Well, I think you can. But, you have to promise me that you won't discuss it with anybody—that includes your wife."

"Not a problem. I told you I'd help and, if I can, I will."

"Do you know a Ken Brown? He's with Falmouth PD now, but he used to work for DeMarco Construction?"

"Of course I know him. We used to be the best of friends."

"Used to be?"

"That's right. What do you want to know about him?"

"How well does he know Candy?"

Greg laughed. "Everybody knows Candy, some more than others. Ken is one of the more. They thought they were being cute. They thought nobody knew what was going on. They've been an item for years. I wouldn't trust him as far as I could throw him."

That confirmed my opinion of Brown. "Do you think she could have manipulated him enough to kill Rocco?"

"Wow, you're kidding. I hadn't thought about it."

"You know that for years, Rocco had been doing research on the disappearance of your mother. Bella and George seem to think he'd found something. If he did and it panned out, Candy, instead of your father, could have been the one who made her disappear. I believe Brown was either part of it or at least knew about it. The two of them couldn't take the chance, so they killed Rocco."

"If Candy did murder my mother and she was convicted, then she'd probably spend the rest of her life at MCI Framingham. And, the business would come back to my brother and me." Greg hesitated, then continued. "What do you want me to do?"

"Brown's shift is over at three o'clock. I rattled him enough that he's going to want to talk to Candy as soon as he leaves the station. Does he usually come over to her house or does she go somewhere to meet him?"

"A little of both."

"I need you to be home to see which way it goes. If she leaves, can you follow her?"

"I can."

"If you follow her, just make sure she doesn't see you. By the way, what does she drive?" I asked.

"A black Ford 250. It belongs to the business, but it isn't lettered."

I made a mental note.

"What if he comes over?"

"Note what time he gets there and what time he leaves and if she does or doesn't leave with him."

"I can do that."

"I don't think you should follow Brown. He might pick up on you faster than she would." I stopped to consider what I just said. "I'm outside the hospital now, but I'm going in to check on Bella. Call me either way." I was just about to hang up when I thought of something else. "Wait a minute," I said. "I'm going to give you Sam's cell phone number just in case you need to reach him."

"Why would I need to call him?"

"You'll know. Later," I said and hung up.

I went back inside and headed towards Bella's room. I stopped abruptly when I rounded the corner and saw Norma Sheridan sitting beside Bella's bed. She saw me before I had a chance to backup and hide until she left.

Bella's eyes were closed. Norma held her finger to her lips. "Shhhh. She just fell asleep," she whispered. Norma got up from where she was keeping vigil over Bella and walked towards the doorway where I was standing. She motioned for me to follow. I did.

Once away from Bella's room she stopped. "I've been here for a couple hours. Apparently she had a bad night. She told me she didn't get much sleep and was very tired, so I could leave because she wouldn't be much company." Norma looked around at a young couple who'd sat down in the seats two away from us. "Let's move over to the corner." She didn't wait for a reply. She got up and I followed.

"Did she seem like something was bothering her?"

"Of course something's bothering her." Norma snapped. "Somebody tried to kill her."

Wonder where that came from.

"I'm sure you know about the accident."

"I do, but it was just that—an accident." I kept my sentence short. I felt she was prying into what I might know. What she didn't realize is I wasn't about to tell her anything. In fact, I was picking her brain for what she might know.

In between conversations two young girls with a couple screaming kids planted themselves across from us. I could sense Norma's frustration.

"I used to do volunteer work here. There's a room downstairs where we can go to talk."

I really didn't want to talk to her anymore, but figured if I appeased her, then she might go away.

"Follow me."

Once in the elevator, she pushed the button marked B.

"Where is this room we're going to?"

"In the basement. It's the old break room."

I shrugged my shoulders. "Whatever."

The sign on the wall opposite the elevator read MAINTENANCE followed by an arrow pointing left. We went right. About halfway down the corridor Norma stopped and knocked on a door that looked like it hadn't been used in years. She tried the knob. It wasn't locked. I detected a look of relief on her face.

She pushed the door open, reached around the corner to flip on the light and walked in. As soon as she realized I was following her lead, she spun around, slammed the door, grabbed my arm, flipped the lock and threw me to the floor.

Pain shot through my head as it hit the cement. I tried to move, but Norma's foot was firmly imbedded on my back.

"Who's in charge now bitch?" The hostility in her voice was frightening. She walked to the door to make sure she'd locked it. She had.

When I attempted to lift my hands up to examine my head, I felt a sharp blow to my ribs. "Oh shit." Now my whole body was screaming with pain. "What are ….."

"Shut up. I don't want to hear you whimper." She didn't move.

I tried to determine if she was standing close enough for me to grab her ankle and pull her down. She wasn't.

"What's the matter? Don't like being helpless?"

She had me right where she wanted me. I was at her mercy. I had to think.

"I'm going to tell you a little bedtime story and you're going to listen. When I'm done I'll give you a little something to help you sleep."

Her threat didn't land on deaf ears.

She moved back a few steps, pulled up a chair and began her sick rendition of a fractured fairy tale. "Once upon a time there was a girl who couldn't mind her own business. She interfered in the execution of the perfect murder. This girl, we'll call Bella, engaged the services of a PI, we'll call Casey, to aid her in destroying lives of innocent people." She hesitated.

I piped up, "Innocent people?"

"I'm telling the story—you're listening."

A sound came from the hallway outside the door to hell. I wanted to scream, but when Norma moved her eyes in the direction of the noise, she lifted her hand to reveal a thirty-eight snub nose with her finger firmly affixed on the trigger.

"Don't move," she whispered as she waggled the pointer finger of her free hand liked a teacher scolding a child. She looked at her thirty-eight and smiled. "Don't test me, I will shoot you," she mouthed.

I understood her perfectly.

Satisfied the outside intruder was gone, she resumed her vigil over my limp, motionless body.

"Story time is over."

"Why don't you tell me the continuing version starring Norma Sheridan?"

"I suppose I could since you won't be in any condition to re-tell it when you leave here."

My heart was pounding out of my chest. I was scared. None of the scenarios running through my head were good. Maybe if she got engrossed in her story, I'd be able to make a move. It was a chance I had to take. *Stay calm,* I told myself. *Be patient, don't rush.*

"I don't intend on spending the night with you so let me give you the abbreviated version." She remained seated with the thirty-eight still manned, ready to be put into use if she deemed it necessary. "Let's start with a little background. Phil DeMarco's wife, Elaine, is my friend. Through her I became acquainted with Candy, her step-mother-in-law. Unbeknownst to me, Candy and my brother were, and had been for many years, strange bed-fellows. I found it hard to believe because my brother lives next door to me and I never saw Candy there. Eventually, the two of them confided in me about their relationship. At the time her husband, Sid DeMarco, was still alive. She never got caught. Probably because he was so sick or maybe didn't care. Who knows?" She stopped to take a breath.

"I haven't got all day, so enough of the background." She fidgeted a little in her chair, but didn't loosen her grip on the thirty-eight. "You know Sid's first wife went missing. Candy had a hand in that. Sid was investigated in the disappearance, but they couldn't pin anything on him. Hell, they couldn't find a body."

My bad leg started to ache. I tried to move it slightly without causing her to take notice. It didn't work.

She stood up. "Are you getting bored with my story?"

"No."

"Then stay quiet and let me finish." She sat back down, still with gun in hand waiting for me to make a wrong move. "Candy confided in my brother. When Rocco Deluca made it known that he'd found new evidence in the disappearance of his sister, Candy panicked. She convinced my brother to talk to Rocco. He went to the fish market on the day Rocco died just to speak to him."

"How did you know he talked to Rocco?"

"You ask too many questions."

"I only asked one."

"One too many." Two minutes that seemed like two hours passed before she started to talk again. "Ken told me what he was going to do. I told him not to get involved, but he wouldn't listen to me. I waited until he left his house, then rode by the market. His truck was parked in the back lot next to Rocco's. I drove down the street and pulled into the parking lot at the convenience store, then walked up behind the market. The back door was unlocked. I went in and hid in the back room. I could hear the conversation between the two of them. It got heated, but Rocco said he had no intension of getting rid of the new evidence. He told him to get out and take his sorry ass back to Candy. Ken left without knowing I heard every word spoken between the two of them."

"So Ken didn't murder Rocco?"

"Ken—he won't even step on a spider. He was just trying to appease Candy. All he was doing was keeping his little piece of tail happy."

I didn't know whether to ask her to continue. Fortunately, I didn't have to.

"Rocco followed Ken, locked the door behind him, then went back to the front of the market. He didn't see me. Rocco was standing beside the tanks when I walked in. I startled him. He jumped when he saw me. He wanted to know how I got in. I told him. He talked but didn't give me his undivided attention. Instead, he pulled up a ladder and started to work on his tanks. He held onto the pipe at the end of the tank and turned slightly to see if I was still there. I was. Said I could stay and talk as long as I wanted to, but he had wasn't going to listening. He turned back, still holding onto the pipe. There was an electrical cord plugged into a wall socket and wrapped loosely around the same pipe. I started to leave. That's when I saw the electrical box. I figured there was still water in the tank and I knew that water and electricity didn't mix. So I looked around, found a piece of metal lodged in the office door to keep it from closing and jammed it behind the breaker marked tank, then walked back to the front of the store. I told him I wasn't ready to leave. He told me to suit myself, then turned back and leaned way into the tank. I pulled the ladder out from under him. He was helpless. I grabbed the dangling cord, pulled it tight and dropped the loose end into the tank. He let out some awful noises, then lay lifeless draped over the tank. I put the ladder back so it looked like he'd slipped off it, told him to rest in peace, took the metal from behind the breaker and left, locking the door behind me."

"What about Bella. Who tried to kill her?"

Norma laughed quietly. "It wasn't me. Candy can take credit for that one. And, by the way, she did a good job on your tires—didn't she?"

"She didn't do that alone. Somebody dropped her off and waited the couple minutes for her to sprint into the Tribune parking lot, work her magic with the ice pick and run back onto Main Street."

"My first vehicle was a Ford 250—just like Candy's."

I didn't say anything. After hearing her 'bed-time' story, the Rocco story and the Bella story, I was all storied out. I wasn't looking forward to her next move.

"Too bad you won't be able to share the makings of a New York best seller with anyone."

She got up and hovered over me. Her eyes were dark and cold. I wanted to thrust myself sideways to try and knock her off balance, but the gun, still clutched tight in her right hand, dangled at her side. I may have been able to take Norma, but I didn't stand a chance against her thirty-eight. I took a deep breath and slowly let it out.

"I hope you enjoyed that because it will be your last." She backed away from me. She quickly glanced in the direction of the door, then back to me. Nothing was said.

Sam, where are you?

"We've played this little game long enough. It's time for me to compose myself and resume my bedside manner—Bella should be about ready to wake up."

"Norma, don't do anything foolish."

"I don't intend to do anything foolish. I intend to do something creative." She reached into her jacket pocket and pulled out what appeared to be a syringe.

My heart began to race. I had to make my move. I rolled my body like a human log in her direction, but could only muster enough strength to make one complete roll. She kicked me in my side—the same one she'd kicked before. I was helpless.

"Bitch, you shouldn't have done that."

CHAPTER 79

"Hello."

"Sam, this is Greg DeMarco."

"How did you get my number?"

"Casey Quinby gave it to me. We talked earlier today."

"About what?"

"She asked me to check out some things for her."

"Things?"

"Yeah, things. I did what she told me to do. I'm supposed to call her to let her know what happened."

"Okay, Greg, this is all shit. I'm just pulling into the Falmouth Hospital parking lot. Where are you now?"

"About six miles away."

"I'll wait for you in the lobby." Sam ended the call without waiting for a response. He parked, ran across the lot and hesitated just long enough for the automatic doors to open. From the window he could see the entrance to the parking lot. A black extended cab pick-up drove in and parked four spaces away from him. It was Greg DeMarco.

Sam walked to the door to meet him. "I dropped Casey off a little over an hour ago. I assume she's upstairs with your cousin." His comments were sharp and to the point. "Before I, or we, go upstairs I think we should sit over there and have a little conversation." Sam pointed to a cluster of chairs in the far corner and motioned for Greg to go in front of him. "Have a seat."

"Look, Sam, I'm not trying to cause any problems. Casey asked me to do her a favor and I did."

Sam sat on the edge of the chair with his hands pressed against his knees. "I'm afraid to ask what the favor was."

"It involved my step-mother and Ken Brown. Apparently, Casey had a talk with Brown earlier today and she thought he might try to contact Candy after his shift was over. She asked me to watch to see if Candy took off sometime after three-thirty or if Brown showed up at Candy's."

"Did she leave or did he show?"

"He showed, but they left about fifteen minutes after he got there. Casey told me if Candy left, to follow her, but if Brown did come over and they left together, not to follow him. She felt, because of his training, he might realize he was being tailed whereas she wouldn't. So, I followed Casey's instructions."

"Why did you have my cell number?"

"When she gave it to me, I asked her why." Greg looked straight at Sam. "She said in case I needed to reach you. I asked her why I'd need to call you. She said I'd know, then she hung up." Greg shook his head. "After I got the information regarding Candy and Brown, I was supposed to call Casey."

"What did she say when you told her?"

"She didn't say anything. I can't get ahold of her. She's not answering her cell. That's why I called you." Greg appeared frustrated.

"She's probably upstairs with Bella. Sometimes cell service doesn't work in hospitals." Sam stood up and moved away from his chair. "I'm going upstairs. Why don't you come with me and we can both talk to her at the same time."

Greg followed Sam to the elevator. "I know we've had our differences in the past, but trust me, I want to help get to the bottom of Rocco's untimely death. And, I assure you that neither my brother nor I had anything to do with it."

"Casey already told me that."

When the elevator door opened, Sam and Greg made the left in the direction of Bella's room. The door was open and Norma Sheridan was sitting beside the bed holding Bella's hand.

Sam looked around the room for any signs of Casey.

Norma ignored it. "Hi Greg," she said without standing to greet them. "Who's your friend and what brings you here?" She was curt and short with her words.

"My friend is Sam Summers. We're here to meet up with Casey Quinby."

"I dropped her off at the main entrance about an hour and a half ago. Now I'm back to pick her up." Sam again perused the room.

Norma's face wrinkled in a puzzling disguise. "I'm sorry, but I don't know a Casey Quinby."

Before anyone else could speak, Bella woke up and slowly opened her eyes.

"Bella." Norma patted her friend's hand. "It's okay, these gentlemen were just leaving."

Bella pulled her hand away from Norma. Her eyes blinked in slow motion as she studied Sam and Greg. "Greg, what are you doing here?"

"I'm with Sam."

"Who?"

"Sam Summers—Casey's detective friend." Greg looked at Norma, who said nothing.

She had moved her chair back from the bed so she could get up and make a direct line to the door when the time was right.

"I haven't seen Casey at all today." The whisper was labored, but everyone understood what she said.

"What about you Norma—have you seen her?"

Norma was quiet.

Bella turned to face Norma. "You met her at the Quarterdeck last week."

"Oh yes, I know who you're talking about now." She smiled. "I've been here for at least two and a half hours and I haven't seen her."

"That's Casey. She probably remembered something she had to ask the Chief and took a cab to the station. When she gets talking and involved in something she loses all track of time. I'm a little early so I'm going down to the cafeteria to grab a coffee. I'll wait about a half hour and if she's not back, I'll give her a call." Sam started towards the door, then turned towards Norma. "Nice to meet you."

Greg gave him a strange look. "I can talk to her later," he said. "Bella, you get yourself better. If there's anything you need don't hesitate to call."

"Tell Phil and Elaine I said 'hi'." Norma smiled and turned back to face Bella.

"Will do," said Greg as he followed Sam out and down the hallway.

They got into the elevator without saying a word to each other.

Once the door closed, Greg looked at Sam. "What the hell was that all about?"

"I need to call the second floor nurse's station."

Sam walked over to the information desk. He took his badge from his pocket and showed it to the volunteer on the desk. "I need you to call the east wing, second floor nurse's station then hand me the phone."

"Sir, I can't do that."

"You can and you will, otherwise I need to talk to your supervisor."

The volunteer let out a sigh. "Okay, but please step over to the other end of the desk. We'll use that phone."

Greg walked behind Sam, but kept his distance.

The volunteer dialed the number. She handed Sam the phone when the nurse answered.

"This is Detective Sam Summers from the Bourne Police Department. I need you to make sure nobody can hear your conversation."

"That's good." He turned to face the wall so his voice wouldn't carry any further than where he was standing. "There is a woman visiting in Bella Deluca's room. I need to know approximately what time she arrived and if she's been there all day." It didn't take long to get an answer.

"You're sure she left for almost an hour, then returned?"

"Thank you, you've been very helpful. Remember not to share our conversation with anyone. I'll be in touch later." Sam came around the side of the desk and put the receiver back in its cradle.

"Are you going to tell me what that was all about?"

"Let's go outside."

Sam took his cell out of his pocket and punched in Casey's number. On the sixth ring it went to voice mail. He tried again—same thing.

"Casey was here. The nurse told me that Norma came in around two and another lady came in around three. But, the second lady was only there for about five minutes. They left together. The first lady came back about an hour later, but the second lady never came back. I dropped Casey off just before three and told her I'd be back in a couple hours to pick her up."

"Do you think Norma is involved?"

"I do. I hope she bought that little song and dance I performed for her in Bella's room. Casey's a tough broad, but my gut says she's in trouble. She'd never leave here without calling me to let me know where she was going."

"What are you going to do?"

"Just stay with me. I might need your help." Sam walked back to the information desk. "Please call the security office and see if Officer Warren is still here."

The volunteer didn't hesitate. She handed Sam the phone. Officer Warren identified himself.

"Hi, Mark, it's Sam Summers. I'm in the lobby. I need to see you stat. I believe we have a problem."

"Thanks," Sam turned to Greg. "He'll be right up." Sam paced back and forth in front of the desk.

It wasn't long before the big, burly white haired man in a security uniform with a Falmouth Hospital patch on the right chest pocket emerged from a door behind the information desk. "Sam, twice in one day. What's up?"

"We've got a situation. Can you readily access your security cameras?"

"I can. Let's go back to my office, you can explain on the way."

Sam motioned for Greg to follow. They followed Officer Warren back through the door behind the desk.

"A direct line to security?" Sam asked.

"Exactly. If we have problems in the lobby, we haven't got time to use the regular elevators and stairways, so we have our own little tunnel system." He shook his head. "And, we've had to use it on a number of occasions. Okay, let's get to your situation."

"I believe a lady named Casey Quinby is in trouble somewhere in your hospital. I don't have time to go into particulars, but I know something is wrong."

"By all means, Sam, I'll do anything you need me to do."

"Let me try to call her again." Sam punched in Casey's number. "In the meantime could you pull up images of the east wing, second floor nurses station." This time the call only rang twice before it went to voice mail. "Greg, try her number on your phone."

"Went to voice mail."

"What timeframe are you looking at?" asked Warren.

"Let's start at two-thirty."

Officer Warren pulled up the video images.

"Stop," yelled Sam. "Can I move them around?"

"Go ahead."

He sat down and started to examine the images. He moved back a couple frames and saw Norma and Casey leave Bella's room together. The time stamp in the right corner read five minutes past three. He printed the still, then resumed the video. He glued his eyes to the screen and hit the fast-forward button. "Stop," he yelled again. This time giving himself the command. The nurse on duty told him Norma left for about an hour then returned by herself. He advanced the screens to four o'clock, then moved the images one at a time until he came to the one showing Norma returning to Bella's room at four-ten. He made a copy.

He leaned back in the officer's chair. "Mark, this is half of what I'm looking for. See the girl with the blonde pony-tail? She's missing and I'm afraid she's tucked away somewhere in your hospital."

"Let me sit down for a minute." Officer Warren went back to the original video that showed Norma and Casey leaving Bella's room.

Instead of stopping, he watched them go to the elevator. "There—the other one pushed the down button, so that means they must have gotten off on the first floor. Let me open the footage from the first floor for the time frame in question." He typed in some commands then hit enter. The image of the elevator came up. He backed up the video to a little before three, then ran it to three-ten. "Sam, we do have a problem. They didn't get off on the first floor. That means they went to the basement and we don't have cameras down there."

"Greg, keep calling her number." Sam's breathing got heavy. "Tim, the woman that's upstairs in Bella Deluca's room is dangerous. I don't want to spook her, but you need to have somebody walk by the room to make sure Bella is okay. Then have your guy stand where he can see if Sheridan attempts to leave before the Falmouth PD gets here. Earlier Casey told me Chief Mills was going to have a plain clothes officer watch Bella and anybody who might visit her, but I don't know who he is and I don't want to alert Sheridan that she's being watched."

"Let me get that in the works, then we'll head to the basement." Officer Warren called one of his guards and gave him his marching instructions.

"I'm going to call Chief Mills while you get your guy in place." Sam made the call. "Chief, it's Sam Summers. We have a situation at Falmouth Hospital. It involves Bella Deluca, Norma Sheridan and Casey. If I had the jurisdiction, I'd do it myself, but since I'm in your territory, I need you to send a couple officers over to take Norma into custody. Right now she's in Bella's room and Casey is missing."

Chief Mills told Sam he'd send a car with two officers right over.

"Officer Warren will have one of his men waiting to take them upstairs. I've got to go."

"The security guard I sent upstairs is in place. I'll have one of the other guys come to the front entrance immediately to meet the PD."

Within two minutes the guard was in the lobby receiving his orders from Officer Warren.

"Everybody is in place. Let's get down to the basement."

Sam looked at Greg. "Any luck with the calls yet?"

"Nothing, just voice mail."

"Keep calling."

"I'm on it."

They got into the elevator and headed down to the bowels of the institution. "What's down here?"

"The maintenance department uses about a third of the area for storage. The rest is divided into rooms. Housekeeping used to store supplies in one of them. The biggest one, not counting the maintenance area, was used as an employee break room until we built the new addition. The rest of the rooms were used by different departments for storage, but now they're not used at all."

The elevator door opened. "Greg, keep calling."

They turned left towards the maintenance department. "I don't see anyone around." Officer Warren took out his master key ring, unlocked the door and let us in.

Once inside, we split up. "Casey!" Sam yelled. "Casey, can you hear me?" he yelled louder. Nothing. "Casey!"

Greg did the same thing.

They all took a section—checking every nook and cranny—opening every broom and chemical closet. Nothing.

"Let's head the other way."

"That's where the empty storage rooms and the old employee break room are."

Greg was still on his cell continuously punching in Casey's number. Officer Warren and Sam walked on the right side of the hallway and Greg walked along the left side.

"Casey, can you hear me?" Sam was frantic. He'd been a cop long enough to know Casey was in trouble. "Casey!"

The out-of-use storage rooms were locked. They still had the old locks and the master key on Officer Warren's ring didn't work in them. "Sam, I've got the keys for these in my office. They haven't been open for over a year. The only one we have used is the old break room."

"Sam, be quiet." Greg's voice lowered. He dialed Casey's number again. "I think I heard something. He walked slowly, still dialing. Suddenly he stopped. "Listen," he said as he leaned his ear against the wall.

Sam followed Greg's lead. He moved to the door two feet down from where they were standing and without saying anything, he motioned for Greg to make another call. There is was again—faint, but there. Sam's adrenalin took over and without hesitation, he kicked the door in.

Casey's purse was on the floor in the middle of the room—a folding chair beside it. There was no conversation between the three men. They scattered to find a hiding place big enough to conceal a body. Sam ran for the back of the room. There was a hedge of two foot by three foot cardboard boxes stacked three high and six long. The boxes weren't against the wall. He ran around behind them. "Over here!" he hollered. "Call for the emergency team." He leaned over to check for a pulse. It was so weak he had a hard time finding it. "Casey, I'm here." He whispered. "Can you hear me?" She was lifeless. She'd been hit on the head—blood ran down the side of her face. He didn't want to move her for fear he'd cause more trauma to her body.

"They're on their way." Officer Warren signaled for Greg to stand watch at the door so they'd know which room they were in.

Sam was on his knees, rocking. "Please be okay." He heard the footsteps from the medical team as they ran down the hallway. As he started to get up, he noticed something on the floor about two feet away from where she lay. It was a syringe. He pulled a handkerchief from his back pocket and carefully picked it up, then moved aside to let the medics tend to her.

"What's that," asked Greg.

"I'm guessing whoever shared this room with Casey, used this on her."

"Let me see it."

Sam pulled his hand back.

342

"I don't want to touch it, just let me see it." It took Greg less than three seconds to examine it. "That's an insulin syringe."

"How do you know?"

"Because I'm a diabetic and I use ones just like that."

Sam walked back to the medical team who were in the process of moving Casey onto a stretcher. "This was on the floor beside her." He held it out to show them. "I was told it's an insulin syringe. It's not Casey's—she doesn't have diabetes." One of the medics handed Sam a pair of latex gloves.

"We're taking her upstairs for emergency treatment. You can stay in the ICU waiting room and I'll come out and let you know her condition. She's not in good shape, so I can't tell you everything's going to be okay."

Sam's eyes watched every move until she was out of sight.

"Tim, I need you to close off this floor. This room is now a crime scene. Don't let anybody except the Falmouth PD down here." Sam held up the syringe. "I need to get this into an evidence bag. The two officers holding Sheridan should have one."

"I've got to make a report." Mark called his office to have someone bring him down a clipboard and paper. "I'll meet you on the second floor."

"We'll go there first, make sure Bella's okay, then fill the Falmouth Officers in on what happened. I'll give Chief Mills another call. I wouldn't be surprised if he comes over himself. If we finish before you, we'll be in the ICU waiting room." Sam tried to remain calm.

Mark nodded.

"Sam, if it's okay, I'd like to go with you. I want to make sure Bella is all right too. And, I'm concerned about Casey."

"No problem, Greg, come on." Sam nodded and they ran to the elevator.

CHAPTER 80

"Chief Mills got the call from the two officers holding Norma Sheridan. He's on his way," said Monica. "Also, Detectives Morse and Garrison should be there momentarily."

"I'll look for them," said Sam.

Sam and Greg didn't say a word on the short ride to the second floor. The doors weren't fully opened when Sam sprinted out and down the hallway to Bella's room. One uniform was with her, but Sheridan and the other uniform weren't anywhere in sight.

"Where's your partner?" Sam asked.

"He's got Sheridan in the break room. When we cuffed her, she started to get mouthy and belligerent, so we took her out of here. A black and white is on the way to transport her to the station."

Bella was awake and aware of what was happening. Tears ran down her face. She looked at Greg.

"Hey, Cous," he said. "It's going to be alright." His voice cracked. "I'm here with you." Greg leaned over and gave Bella a kiss on the forehead, then gently took her hand.

She didn't resist. "Where's Casey?" she asked softly.

"She's being tended to."

Bella closed her eyes and drifted off to sleep.

Sam found an empty bench near the elevator to wait for Chief Mills. He wasn't there two minutes when the door opened and the Chief walked out. He motioned for Sam to stay seated, then sat down beside him. Sam filled him in on what had transpired.

"That's it in a nutshell." Sam stood. "I'm going up to ICU. They're working on Casey." He didn't say another word, just turned and instead of taking the elevator to the third floor, he bolted up the stairs.

CHAPTER 81

"She's going to make it. It was touch and go for a while, but we finally got her stabilized. Give them a few minutes to get her into a cubicle and the nurse will come get you."

Sam held out his hand, "Thank you."

The doctor nodded. "You're welcome. I'll talk to you later." He turned and headed back inside the ICU.

Minutes seemed like hours. Sam sat, thinking about Casey. He couldn't bear the thought of losing her. He checked his watch. He stood up and paced the floor like an expectant father. The nurse finally came to get him.

"She's very groggy. Don't be alarmed if she doesn't recognize you right away. Talk to her, hold her hand, sit with her—just be there for her."

"I will," was all that came out of his mouth. He followed the nurse to Casey's cubicle. The nurse left him standing at the end of the bed.

She was hooked up to monitors and intravenous lines from both sides of the bed. He walked around and sat in the chair beside her. "Casey, if you can hear me, I love you." A couple tears ran down his face. He brushed them away. He slid his hand under her hand and wrapped his fingers gently around hers. "Hang in there kid, we'll get through this thing together."

"Yes we will," She said in a faint whisper. "Yes, we will."

He leaned over, careful not to disturb the monitor cords, and gave her a kiss. "Yes, we will," he whispered back.

CHAPTER 82

A month passed before I returned to my office in the Village. I promised Sam I'd opt for light duty cases for a while. Of course I crossed my fingers behind my back. But then, he knew that. His stays in Hyannisport have gotten longer and longer—but I don't mind at all.

With Candy DeMarco and Norma Sheridan behind bars awaiting trial, I can breathe a little easier knowing I helped put them there. Their stories are fodder for a best-selling novel. They'd have plenty of time to write it since they were never going to see the light of day again. Their trials were scheduled for September and October.

Norma Sheridan's brother, Kenneth Brown, was fired from the Falmouth Police Department and is out on bail awaiting trial for aiding and abetting in a crime. He also turned state's evidence and will testify against both girls.

Bella completely recovered and returned to the Falmouth Library to refresh her romance with Dewey. We'd become good friends. She was my first case and I was her 'hero'. I was able to give her and her brother, George, closure in the death of their uncle. After they rekindled the brother-sister bond, they cleaned up the books, sold Uncle Rocco's market to a local fisherman and completed the last chapter in the life of Rocco Deluca.

I felt good.

I walked over to the windows in the front of my office. Some people crave the sand and beach scene— for me, it's the view of the District Court to the left, Superior Court to the right and the District Attorney's Office straight across the street.

I was content. I was ready to unleash my inner Sherlock again.

My mind was still in dream mode, when I turned to walk back to my desk. The sudden knock on the front door send me straight up off the floor. I spun around. The sun was so bright I couldn't make out if the person who had suddenly pulled me back into reality was a man or a woman. I took a deep breath, walked over, unlocked and opened the door to reveal a little old man carrying a Macy's shopping bag with something wrapped in a bright pink towel inside.

"Can I help you?"

He looked at me, then up at my shingle. "If you're Casey Quinby you can."

"That's me." I stepped aside. "Please come in."

Made in the USA
Charleston, SC
14 January 2017